# names
# on a map

## also by
## BENJAMIN ALIRE SÁENZ

### fiction

*In Perfect Light*
*Carry Me Like Water*
*Sammy and Juliana in Hollywood*
*The House of Forgetting*
*Flowers for the Broken*

### poetry

*Elegies in Blue*
*Dark and Perfect Angels*
*Calendar of Dust*
*Dreaming the End of War*

### childrens

*A Gift from Papá Diego*
*Grandma Fina and Her Wonderful Umbrellas*

# names
# on a map

### a novel

## BENJAMIN ALIRE SÁENZ

HARPER  PERENNIAL

NEW YORK • LONDON • TORONTO • SYDNEY

for Ruben García,
whose name is holy on my lips,

and (again) for Patricia,
who brought me out of exile

HARPER ● PERENNIAL

P.S.™ is a trademark of HarperCollins Publishers.

HarperCollins books may be purchased for educational, business, or sales
promotional use. For information please write: Special Markets Department,
HarperCollins Publishers, 10 East 53rd Street, New York, NY 10022.

FIRST EDITION

Designed by Joy O'Meara

Library of Congress Cataloging-in-Publication Data has been applied for.

ISBN: 978-0-06-128569-1

08 09 10 11 12 ID/RRD 10 9 8 7 6 5 4 3 2 1

I still want to believe we will cure the human heart.

—C. K. WILLIAMS

# part one

## THE DAY THE WAR CAME

Let me tell you, brothers, what fear is:
a beast you've got to kill before you kill.

—Elie Wiesel

# a family

## El Paso, Texas, Saturday, September 16, 1967

An unsettling calmness in the predawn breeze.

A hint of a storm.

The faint smell of rain.

A coolness in the air.

Summer has lasted and lasted. And lasted.

Four o'clock in the morning.

The house is dark. The members of the Espejo family are in bed. Some are asleep. Some are restless, awake, disturbed. Each of them alone, listening to their own interior breezes.

Octavio—husband, father, son—is asleep. He is lost in an unwelcome dream, a gust of wind kicking up the loose fragments of memory, grains of sand in the eye. He is struggling to see. He is struggling to understand what his father is saying to him, his father who has been dead for more than three years. He has had this dream before. His father is trying to tell him something, give him words of wisdom or a piece of advice or some essential bit of information he needs to survive. Maybe his father is speaking in Spanish. Maybe his father is speaking in English. It is impossible to tell. His father's lips are moving. But the words? Where are the words? His father is young and he, Octavio, is a boy—small—and he understands that they still live in Mexico. All his dreams take place in Mexico. Mexico before the fall. They do not yet live in exile. When he wakes, Octavio will not remember the dream.

Lourdes is awake. Sleep is not something she needs—it is something she endures. She is listening to her husband's mumblings. She is accustomed to his dreams. He has never been a calm sleeper. Whatever disturbs him by day will hunt him down as he sleeps. She shakes him gently, comforts him. "Shhhh, *amor*." His mumblings recede. She smiles. When he wakes, she will ask him about the dream. He will say he does not remember. *You do not want to remember,* that is what she will think, but she will say nothing and smile and ask him if he wants to know what he was mumbling. He will say it does not matter.

She looks at the time on the alarm clock and wonders if Rosario will make it through the day. "Maybe today I will die. Oh, today let me die." Rosario repeats her refrain every day. She recites the lines as if she is in a play and she waits for Lourdes to answer, a one-woman Greek chorus: "Today, I will die. Oh, today, I will die." And then they will pause, look into each other's eyes—and laugh. It has become a joke between them—a joke and a ritual. Lourdes does not want to think about what she will do when the old woman dies. She has become addicted to caring for her mother-in-law. But it is more than an addiction. So much more than that.

Rosario, too, is no longer asleep. Every morning she wakes to the darkness of the new day. It is a curse, an affliction she has suffered for years, this lying awake every morning with nothing to do, this measuring of the hours that her life has become, this searching the room with eyes that are failing, this knowledge that you now inhabit a body that is shriveling and a mind that is ever alert, but a mind that lives now only in the past. She tries to think of something else, something kinder than this thing that is her life. Is this a life? But, today, she can think of nothing kind. Kindness has exiled itself from her world.

She is remembering the day her husband died, a perfect morning, the garden bathed in honeysuckles. "I'm going to read the paper," he said as he stepped into the backyard. "And then I'm going to take a nap. And then, who knows, I might just die." He laughed and kissed her as if she were still a girl.

He did read the newspaper.

He did take a nap.

He did die.

It was she who found him. She sees herself trying to wake him. She sees the smile on his face. *Bastard, you left me here. I don't forgive you. Oh, today let me die.*

Xochil, the only daughter in the house, is twisting and turning in her bed. No rest or peace in her sleep. Like her father, what is left unresolved tracks her down like a wounded animal. She is arguing with herself. She wants this boy. She is yearning to let him love her. She utters his name—Jack—and just as the name slips out of her mouth, she becomes still and quiet.

When she wakes, she will think of this boy, picture his face, his lips, the look of want in his eyes, blue as the sea. She will picture his hands, larger than hers but trembling with the same want that is in her. She will shake her head. *No, no, no, no, no.* And then she will reach under the bed and take out the picture she keeps as a comfort.

She will stare at the picture. It is not an image of Jack, but a photograph of her and Gustavo and Charlie. They are safe, her brothers, the harbor to which she's tied her boat. She is smiling, Charlie is laughing, and Gustavo is gazing past the camera. She always wonders what Gustavo is looking at. His eyes are staring at a future. That is what she will think to herself. *The future. Let it be beautiful. Let it be as beautiful as you.*

Gustavo and Charlie are sleeping in the room down the hall.

Gustavo, half asleep, half awake, wonders which he prefers, the sleeping or the waking. He wonders, too, if today is the day the news will arrive. He has been waiting for the news for what seems an eternity. The waiting, the pacing in his mind, the paralysis, the endless litany of cigarettes, the impossibility of escape, the inability to come up with a solution. The waiting is a limbo, the one he swore he did not believe in. Day after day, he hides the apprehension.

He is tired. He opens his eyes, then closes them. He slowly falls back into a shallow sleep.

Charlie. A child at peace. Nothing disturbs him. He has a mother and a father and a grandmother and an older brother and an older sister. He loves and he is loved. All he needs now is a dog. He is clutching a picture of a blond Labrador puppy from a page he has torn out of an old *Life* magazine. This is the dog he wants. This is the dog he is going to ask his father to get for him. This is the thought he was holding just as he wandered off to sleep. This is the dog he is dreaming.

Four o'clock in the morning.

The windows are open, the breeze winding its way through the rooms and hallways.

This is the family.

This is the house.

This is the day.

This is the season.

Summer has lasted and lasted. And lasted.

Let the breezes come, let the leaves turn and fall, let the trees stand naked. The crops in the field are clamoring for picking.

# abe

Four o'clock in the morning. Me and my new-found buddies were just coming back from Juárez after a night of clubbing. Clubbing, a nice word for getting drunk in Juárez dives. The morning was cool and the breeze felt good on my face as the cab drove us to the airport. For some reason I had this thing for rolling down windows when I was in a car. Never liked closed-in places. Sometimes I thought the jungle in Nam was gonna choke me. Sometimes I thought I was gonna stop breathing. No, I mean I didn't like closed-in places. I needed lots of air.

Four o'clock in the fucking morning. God, I was tired. All that drinking. Well, yeah, there'd been some whoring, too. Okay, there was a little bit of everything. We were eighteen. We wanted one last party. Why the hell not? We were leaving behind the old world. The familiar, dull, tired world. The world we'd lived in all our lives. Not that we knew the world we were stepping into. The future was like the fucking desert sky. It just went on forever.

God, the world was more beautiful and bigger than we had ever dreamed. Big. God, we wanted big. We were tired of small, tired of standing still, tired of being little men in a little world.

I'll admit it, I was a scared. Okay. We all were. Not that we talked about it. But mostly we were happy. God, we were happy and proud as hell. Sure we were. Me and Ricardo and Jeff, we were going into the Marines. That was a big fucking deal. Finally, we had a destination. We weren't lost anymore. That's how I'd always felt. Lost. And now, all of that was gone. It was like a fucking dream come true.

All we'd ever known was the desert and El Paso and high school and good girls. Mostly good girls, anyway. So that last night, it was a way of saying good-bye to everything we knew. Maybe that was a little bit sad. But we didn't have the time for sadness. We were gonna be Marines. Halle-fuckin'-lujah.

So long El Paso, Texas.

Marines. God, we were happy.

We were in, baby! And on our way to San Diego, California. Hell, yes, it was the promised land. You bet your ass.

But then it didn't start off so good.

Of course not.

The fucking flight was canceled. Canceled. Sure it was. God, we were disappointed. I swear I almost cried. And then we all looked at one another. I mean, why just hang out at the airport for twelve hours? And hadn't we already said our good-byes to our friends, our families? Who wanted to do that again? So we took a cab to the Santa Fe Bridge and when the clock struck midnight, there we were, the three of us, lost in a crowd of Mexicans as the mayor yelled, "*¡Viva Mexico!*" from the balcony at city hall. I'd forgotten it was the sixteenth of September. Everyone in the whole world was yelling "*¡Viva Mexico!*" Yeah, well, we were yelling *Viva Mexico,* too. Ricardo said, "What the fuck, when in fucking Rome." Ricardo, he was something. Short but strong as hell. He looked just like the kind of guy you'd take with you if you were gonna fight a war. First time out in Nam, he got himself killed. Got blown to pieces. Jesus. Look, he died a Marine. He died for something he believed in. That counts for something. Jesus. But on the sixteenth of September in 1967, he was alive and me and him and Jeff, we were having ourselves a party. It didn't matter to us that we were in a foreign country. I mean, going over to Juárez was normal for us. And one of the perks of living on the border was that their party became our party. So hey! *¡Viva Mexico!*

I had me some tequila. Cuervo. Good shit. I've always loved the way tequila feels when it goes down. It's like pouring some sun down your throat.

I ran into some guy I knew from high school. He took one look at me and wanted to start a fight. Sure he did. He started giving me the business about how he'd twisted his fucking ankle the last time he played basketball and it was all because of me and he was in pain for a fucking month. Hell, that guy really carried a grudge. He kept shoving me, and digging his finger into my chest. But I didn't shove him back. Nope. I was maintaining. Absolutely in control. But he wasn't gonna stop—and just when I was about to pop him one, this other guy, Jack Evans, he steps in. You know, he was one of those true blue guys, Jack Evans. I mean, we all called him Jack Evans. We used both his names. I don't know why. A real straight arrow. Straighter than me, and back then, I was pretty straight. So we both backed off and Jack bought us a drink. I told him we were on our way to San Diego and that we were gonna be fucking Marines. God, I was happy. And Jack, I mean, the guy kept saying, "Really? Really?" And then he said, "I'm gonna be right behind you, buddy. And we're gonna make things right over there." I got the feeling he'd already signed up.

"Yeah," I said, "we're gonna make things right."

God, that guy, Jack Evans, he was even happier than me. Look,

I've always been a patriotic guy. You know, normal. But that Jack Evans, I swear he shit the American flag. So we sat there that night in Juárez over shots of tequila and drank to the Marines.

I don't remember very much else about that night. The booze, I guess. You know, looking back, I'm glad we got some shit out of our system.

I'm even glad about the whoring. I really don't go in for that. You know those girls, well, it didn't seem right. They were poor. Felt bad. Guess it didn't stop me that night. The booze, I guess. I was raised to be a pretty clean-cut kid. But, you know, we were an inch away from being Marines and it was a long time before I had another woman. The next woman I slept with, I married.

So there we were at four o'clock in the morning, the three of us headed back to the airport. Jeff and Ricardo, they slept in the backseat of the cab, but me, I was in the front seat, wide awake. The breeze on my face was better than a cup of coffee.

The airport was really empty. Not that we cared. We just went up to our gate and slept it off. Our plane left at 9:38 Mountain Standard Time.

We smoked all the way from El Paso to San Diego. Better to smoke than to talk.

Smoked our hearts out.

We were scared. A little bit. But, God, we were happy.

It's a funny thing, ever since that day in 1967, every time I happen to be awake at four o'clock in the morning, I think of that day, when me and my buddies—me and Ricardo and Jeff—that morning when we were crossing back into El Paso from Juárez.

You know, up until that day, I'd never been in a cab. And I'd never been on airplane.

I'd been eighteen for all of three months. I just couldn't wait any longer to be a part of something bigger.

It was one of the happiest days of my life.

# gustavo

My father first attempted to initiate me into the world of the hunt on a sunny and almost too perfect October morning. Fall days were like that in El Paso, sunny and almost too perfect.

I was ten and working out on the front yard. I was complaining to myself about my sorry lot in life. I had a lot of complaints when I was ten. My father came out of the house and announced that he was going to take me deer hunting. It was more like a proclamation from an elected official. I, an ordinary and undeserving citizen, was the recipient of an act of generosity. I understood two things about his announcement: (1) I didn't deserve the gift; and (2) it was my job was to be grateful. He sniffed the air like he knew it was just the right time of year. And I thought to myself, *my sorry lot in life just got sorrier.*

My father wasn't a particularly rugged man. He didn't fit the Mexican macho stereotype. He was more complicated than that. He was tall and thin and he looked as though he might have been an ascetic, like a mystic, like he was hungry, had been born that way, would always reside in a state of physical and emotional want.

He wasn't much of a talker. I always felt that he was a disappointed intellectual. He'd come from a prominent family in Mexico who'd lost their land, lost their standing, lost their souls, if not their hearts and minds. They'd fled to El Paso. I think he made a conscious decision to keep the bearing of a wealthy man. Or maybe it just came naturally to him. He was an armchair historian, formal, always reading, aloof, and he was a disciplinarian. Strict and austere, he was more comfortable with rules than with his children, though he communicated those rules quietly. He liked quiet as much as he liked order.

It was he who looked over the classes we took in high school and made the final adjustments. It was he who told us when we could ride our bikes and when we should work. It was he who decided when we could watch television and what shows to watch. And it was he who allowed me to listen to the radio in my room—so long as I was also reading a book. Books were essential in our house. And it was the only area of my life that my father allowed me total freedom. He never censored what I read, though I knew he was displeased by most of my choices—just as he was displeased by almost everything else I did. I think I displeased him deliberately. There are some sons who live their lives pleasing their fathers. I wasn't one of those sons.

Displeased. That was his word. That word displeases me.

If our house showed all the signs of my father's passion for books, it showed no signs of his obsession for hunting. No stuffed deer or elk heads, no bear rugs, no trophies, no traces of the natural world, not so much as a painting of a mountain. I think my father liked the idea of going out into the wilderness with a lot of other men and getting away from my mother for a few days—

though really my mother was much better company than any of my uncles or any of his friends.

So there it was, my father's announcement: "We're going hunting." He seemed proud, happy. Happy was not something my father wore on his face very often. And it wasn't an emotion he wore with grace.

I smiled back—or tried to.

I knew he owned some rifles that he kept at my uncle's house. My mother detested guns. Hated, loathed, all of those words. She was fierce and resolute about this issue. *Fierce.* There's a word. If my father had rules and rituals, so did my mother. I remember when I was a boy, maybe four or five, he brought a rifle home one afternoon. It was the first real rifle I'd ever seen.

"Who are you going to shoot?" my mother asked.

"I'm just going to clean it," he said.

"Well, if you need to clean something, you can start with the bathrooms."

My father got up, rifle in hand, and slammed the door on his way out. He never brought the thing back into the house. So that afternoon when he decided to place that same rifle in my hands, it didn't happen at 1910 Prospect. He took me to my uncle's house, my uncle who lived in the middle of a pecan orchard, and there, in the middle of a bumper crop of pecans and far away from my mother's disapproving gaze, he handed me that rifle. I examined the rifle carefully, running my hands across the steel and wood. It was clean and sparkling and it was, above all, heavy. I handled it awkwardly even though I was big for ten, my hands large, almost a man's. I almost fell, then caught myself. I forced myself to stand there as if it were the most natural thing in the world. A boy carrying a rifle.

"It's beautiful," he said.

I shrugged.

"Don't you think it's beautiful?"

At the age of ten, I thought birds and dogs and big trucks were beautiful. I thought baseball fields were beautiful. "No," I said, "I don't think it's so beautiful."

I must have looked at him accusingly. *I did look at him accusingly.* I looked at him that way deliberately. I had always treated him as if he were a kind of enemy.

His gaze was just as accusing as mine. "You don't understand the aesthetics of being a man."

I'd never heard the word *aesthetics*—a word that betrayed his intellectual bent. Even before I went home and looked up the word, I had a feeling I knew what he meant. I looked back at him. "I just don't think a rifle's beautiful," I said softly. More firmly than softly.

And he and I, we were broken. Right then. And inexplicably and illogically, I wanted us to be broken.

He kept his eyes on me for a lot longer than I could stand. Then he just looked away. After a while, he gently took the gun away from me. He leisurely strolled back toward my uncle's house. I thought I heard him whistling. That's how he controlled himself—by whistling.

The interesting thing about my father was that he rarely exploded at any of his children. When you disagreed with him, he didn't shout you down, didn't bother to debate or convince you. He didn't waste his time. He just dismissed you. He just made you invisible. Invisible could be very, very good. Invisible could be devastating.

We were fighting a complicated war.

He went on that hunting trip without me.

I stayed home with my mother. She was better company.

That didn't mean that a part of me wasn't sad. *Of course, I was sad—and it was a sadness that lay beyond tears.*

• • •

*My father believed in the beauty of the hunt. But he did not believe in me.*

*The hunt was pure. And I was not.*

I wrote down those four sentences when I was supposed to be listening to my high school history teacher talking about the causes of the Spanish Civil War. My notebooks, like my mind, were cluttered with painful confessions. I didn't believe in priests, but I did believe in notebooks. Another time I wrote: *I sometimes wish I had the consolation of faith.* The consolation of faith was the subtitle of one of my father's favorite books. And still another time, I wrote: *When my father looks at me, I'm sure he thinks something is missing in me.* And he's right. Something is missing in me. I always felt as if my heart existed only in pieces, a brittle, fractured stone, abnormal, incapable of accepting the established order that was supposed to give my life direction. Once, at the dinner table, my father was going on and on about his ideas of order: "Order is like a compass. It tells you which direction to go." In class the next day, I spilled out another confession: *I was born without a compass.*

Over the years, I wrote down a hundred sentences, maybe a thousand. Thoughts as disjointed as the way I lived my days. The things I wrote down never changed a thing. Didn't change me. Didn't change what was wrong between me and my father. Didn't keep all the bad things from happening. Nothing could have kept all the bad things from happening.

The night before my first communion, my father sat me down in the living room and tried to talk to me. We both felt awkward—as if being in each other's presence were an unnatural act. He put down the book he was reading, and then informed me it was time for my quiz.

"Quiz?"

"Concerning your catechism."

"Did you quiz Xochil?"

"Your sister doesn't need to be quizzed."

"Why just me?"

He didn't like it when I asked questions like that. "Because you don't listen."

"I do listen."

"It won't hurt to make sure."

I wanted to yell at him. *They already said I could make my first communion! I already made my first confession!* I think what I really wanted to do was strike out at him. Physically. As in hit him with my fists. I kept myself perfect and still. "Okay," I whispered.

He started with his questions—though they felt more like bullets. I answered them calmly, went through the seven sacraments and explained them as best I could. He corrected my pronunciation of Extreme Unction. I tried to look like I was grateful for being corrected. I explained the rosary without stumbling around too much. I recited the joyful and sorrowful mysteries, the Apostles' Creed, the Our Father, the Hail Holy Queen, and the Act of Contrition. He nodded his approval, his eyes shut as he listened to my answers to his oral exam. When I finished, he opened his eyes and whispered, "Excellent." But he seemed to be whispering to himself. He informed me I had arrived at the age of reason. He handed me an envelope—my gift, my reward. I reached out and took it, my hands on the verge of trembling. I knew it was a card—the kind you bought at the Rexall Drugstore for special occasions. I thought and hoped it would have money in it—but I knew better than to open it in front of him. He didn't approve of behavior that made you appear too anxious or too needy—especially if that behavior was in front of him.

I thanked him.

He nodded and went back to reading.

I took the card to my room and opened it. The card did have money in it, and I smiled as I held the crisp ten-dollar bill in my hand. But my father, in his most careful handwriting, also gave me these words:

*At the beginning of time, the universe had no form. God sent his angel to hover over the dark waters, and out of the chaos, he created order. Son, when we create order, that is when we are most like God. If you remember that, your life will be blessed.*

I was as familiar with the story of creation as I was with my father's obsession with order. His need for control was a sickness. And my sickness was a need to escape him.

Having, as my father put it, reached the age of reason, I think he expected me to understand what he was trying to say to me with those carefully chosen words. I didn't—which was probably why I saved the card. I mean, I didn't exactly save it for sentimental reasons. His handwriting may have had a certain elegance, and his logic might have been accessible—at least to adults if not to seven-year-olds—but there wasn't any affection behind the words. Not even a hint of it. Occasionally, I would take the card out. I would read it and read it and read it. I never tired of analyzing his words. Xochil would grab the card from my hands and say, "What do you think you're going to find there?"

"Him," I said.

"He's not there, Gustavo. Give it up."

I didn't know why I just couldn't let it go.

I finally came to the conclusion that since I didn't share his need for order, then my life would never be blessed.

These are more thoughts I discovered as I thumbed through my notebooks:

*I cannot bring myself to believe that God could make someone like me holy.*

*I am incapable of understanding how being an American will save me.*

*I do not believe a war accomplishes anything—except that it kills all the wrong people.*

Hunting. God. Country. War. In my mind, they were all members of the same family. Brothers and sisters. Cruel. Savage. Not that I was above being cruel or even savage. I never thought of myself as being a virtuous human being. But that didn't mean that there weren't things in the world that were even less virtuous than me.

I stopped attending Mass in the ninth grade. I stopped placing my hand over my heart, stopped pledging allegiance, long before I earned the right to call myself a man. And the hunt, well, I went hunting only once. I was about fifteen years old—and I went only because of the guilt I felt over the time I had refused to be a part of his world. I got tired of giving that regret a home. It occurred to me one day that I should do something, *anything,* make some kind of gesture so that I could tell myself that I had tried. That I had really tried.

But my father and I were beyond healing, and that excursion left me startled and more ill at ease with myself than I had ever been. But then again I had always been ill at ease with myself. That hunting trip just shoved that awareness down my throat.

The four days of that hunting trip are still as clear to me as the gin my father liked to drink. From the day we headed north to New Mexico from El Paso, it seemed the entire trip was fated for disaster. One of the trucks broke down and had to be left with a small-town mechanic who smelled more of stale beer than he did of oil and grease. One of my uncles remained in his tent the entire time, sick with a severe cold and a fever that lasted two days. I stayed with him until the fever broke. When he woke, he stared at me as if he were confronting a nightmare. He kept his eyes on me, a look of confusion and uncertainty on his face. And I thought I saw something else: He was startled, afraid. Of me. Finally, he asked me who I was.

"Gustavo," I said.

"Gustavo?"

"Octavio's son."

"Oh yes, Octavio's son."

"Yes," I said.

"You're my nephew."

"Yes."

"You have a twin sister."

"Yes."

"Xochil?"

"Yes, Xochil."

"She's very nice, your sister. And beautiful. You don't look like her."

"No."

"You don't look like you're one of us. You never have."

"Maybe I'm not."

"That's right," he said. "You're on the other side." And then he stared at me as if I were something he might consider shooting. Then he went back to sleep. *The other side.* It's a strange thing, what fever does to a man. Sometimes it even makes him see the world he lives in.

That first night, as we made camp, we were greeted with an unexpected cold front that descended on our hunting party, making us feel as if nature had decided to turn the tables—and we became the hunted.

My four uncles and my father, and their four friends, they'd all been soldiers once. And all of them had seen action. The older men had been in World War II. The youngest two—my father's friends—had fought in Korea. Somehow, I could sense the wounds they carried. The fact that they'd all been in a war should have been of some help out in the wilderness, but the cold left them all off balance, left them exposed, reminded them that they were no longer young men with lithe, supple bodies that bent to their wills. I suspect they all recalled the scars that never healed, the things they thought had long since vanished from the world they inhabited—ugly, violent memories they no longer had the stomach or the strength to confront.

I've learned a few things about ugly memories—they shoot through the heart like a bullet that maims and disfigures. A bullet that doesn't have the decency to kill.

They'd all been to war once. They all had memories.

When my father accepted the invitation, I think he assumed they were all eager to rekindle some of that old companionship they'd once known and loved and counted on. Their survival had depended on that old companionship. But there was no going back. I think they must've cursed themselves for their nostalgia.

We'd been told the herds of deer needed thinning, but the deer were scarce. Not so much as a sighting. My dad and my uncles and their friends grew humorless, began to argue with one another—I could smell their breaths—and as the hunt wore on, the arguments grew fiercer, louder. I became half afraid that if we found no game, they would begin to turn their rifles on one another.

Perhaps they weren't seeking that old companionship at all. Perhaps all they wanted was a kill. Any kill at all. What did it matter if it was a deer or a man.

On the evening before we were to leave, we had one last chance to make a success of our failure. There was a quiet watering hole, about three miles southwest of our camp. On the advice of one of my uncles we went upwind of that spot. Upwind, the deer would be unable to smell us. That was the thing with hunting—you needed to grab what little advantage nature handed you.

We climbed halfway up a hill and hid as best we could. Down below, we could see the watering hole without obstruction. The water shimmered, a piece of liquid silver in the light of a sinking sun.

The deer would come. All we had to do was wait for them to come and drink. Water was the principle of order by which these animals lived.

We waited.

Just as the sun was about to set, the deer began to gather. It was as if the herd of deer had learned our tactics, knowing that they would not be shot by night. They had acquired an intelligence of the way we operated. They knew that rifles were allowed to kill only bucks. They carried that knowledge in the way they moved, in the way they lived and organized their society. We expected only the females to approach the water. And that is exactly what happened next. But we were patient, knowing the bucks were hiding, waiting to come to the water. Dying for a taste.

We prayed silently that the bucks' thirst would be greater than their patience.

We waited. And we waited. We held a hope that at least one fearless buck would come to drink before darkness descended.

No one spoke.

We could scarcely hear our own breathing.

Then we saw him: a buck—magnificent specimen of nature—walking toward the beckoning water, large as our imaginations and far more graceful. Cautiously, thoughtfully, he looked around, sniffed the air, turned his head left and right, left and right, searching, his antlers glistening in the dying light. And then, satisfied he was safe, he bowed his head and began to drink.

We could see everything clearly through our scopes.

My uncle put his finger gingerly on the trigger of his rifle. We had drawn lots beforehand in order to determine whose kill it would be. The success or failure of our hunting endeavor rested in the resolve of this man—this man, my uncle, who had been gleeful as a boy at his own birthday party when he had selected the longest twig.

I studied him as he looked into his scope, his rifle steady. I could see the lines on his face, his youth gone. I could see his concentration, his will banishing any residual uncertainty. He trembled slightly—and then his trembling ceased.

Everything was still, quiet, perfect.

I could hear my own heart. I could hear it thumping, thumping. And then I heard the shot—deafening—as it echoed in the dusk. The buck looked up, took a step—then stumbled to the ground.

This—*this was why we had come.*

It *was* a beautiful thing.

I never went hunting again.

# xochil

That was the war that defined me and my brothers and my generation. At least that's how my mother put it. I rewrote my mother's observation in my head. I replaced the word *defined* with *scarred*. *Defined* implies something fixed, a sense of closure I have always lacked. And anyway, I've never been drawn to speak on behalf of an entire generation. I'll leave that job to someone else—someone who's in love with the word *defined*. I'll stick with *scarred*.

And something else: *scarred* lends itself to metaphors. I've always been in love with symbolic language.

Whatever else that country was or is or meant—for me, it became a symbol that very nearly swallowed me whole. How many wars does that word *Vietnam* conjure? How many? In one war, there are a thousand wars within that war—each one private, singular, inaccessible, a fragment, a piece of a larger whole, parallel yet forever separate. And all we ever do in life is struggle with our impoverished efforts to put our war into words. I don't believe most of us ever succeed in our translations. It's an art most of us never conquer. That's why we argue with one another. We're like countries—each of us clinging to our separate histories. We're fighting one another about our translations, about what really happened. Which is another kind of war.

I was born two minutes after Gustavo. I came to consciousness listening to his heartbeat, listening to his voice long before he knew how to shape and utter words. We shared a womb, a mother we very nearly worshipped, a father we came close to hating, a younger brother we adored. Our father never tired of reminding us that he was a child of exile. "We didn't belong to Mexico. And we didn't belong to the United States either. *You are,*" he said, "the first generation to belong." Belong to what? One man's belonging is another man's exile. I didn't make that up. I got that from my grandfather. He, too, was an expert on the word *exile*.

For the first eighteen years of our lives, Gustavo and I listened to my father and my mother, observed the nuances of their difficult and beautiful love, told each other secrets, argued about the books we read, listened to the cadences and rhythms of our words and silences.

And yet it was all those silences that had the last word.

Gustavo and I—twins—genetically and emotionally tied to each other. A knot we carried around inside us that shifted from our minds to our stomachs to our hearts. Sometimes we even forgot the knot was there.

We were born in El Paso in 1949 at Hotel Dieu, a Catholic hospital run by the Sisters of Charity of St. Vincent DePaul. My mother said we were as calm as a desert night when we came out of her womb. My father never referred to the day we were born, but he liked to tell people that his son and daughter were born in the middle of the American century. I don't know why, but he found some consolation in saying that. I think it had to do with a Mexican psychology of that word I just mentioned, that word *exile*. That was my theory anyway. He used to tell us that we were destined to live through the same history. Gustavo looked right at him and said, "I want to make history, not live through it."

"Only great men do that," my father said.

Gustavo ignored the insult. "So maybe I'll be great."

"Not with your grades," my father said. They used words like bullets. Such wasted ammunition. It made me angry, the way they treated each other. In the end I was angrier with my father. He was the adult. I held him to a higher standard. And anyway, my father was wrong. Gustavo and I did *not* live through the same history. *No one* lives through the same history. Not even a set of twins.

He was born a man.

I was born a woman.

The world asked him to a fight a war he did not want to fight.

The world asked me to fight a different kind of war.

I wish I knew what it was like to be Gustavo, to inhabit the small piece of the world he inherited. When he said, "I hate this war," I wondered if he was saying the same thing I was saying when I said, "I hate this war." I wondered if he was saying the same thing my mother was saying when she said, "I hate this war." Maybe we were all saying different things. And Gustavo was forced to say something I never even had to consider: "I do not want to fight in this war." And my father, he didn't even come close to repeating our words. All he could manage was "I hate what this war has done to my family." This is what I think he was really saying: "I hate what my family has done to this war." We're back to the issue of translation.

And my youngest brother—Charlie—the family saint? He mostly kept quiet. I wish I knew what his silence meant. Maybe his silence meant belonging. Mostly I think it meant love. That sounds insipid—even to me. But things can sound insipid and still be true.

We lived in the same house. That much was true enough. But mostly we lived in our own particular and peculiar bodies. Bodies we didn't choose. We hear, we see, we smell, we feel with our eyes and noses, ears and hands. We have minds. We have hearts. We have mouths and tongues. That is all we have. That is the only way we know anything—through the smallness of our own insignificant bodies. And so we remain separate, residents of our own small, separate countries.

In one war, a thousand wars.

I can only tell you about mine.

My war began earlier than Gustavo's.

Rape. That is more than a word. I knew what it was before I knew the word that went with it. That's when the war began for me. That's when the woman in me was born. It was a summer evening. Why is it that everything is always quiet and normal and calm before something bad happens? Why is it that one minute there's innocence and on the other side of that same minute there is violence? One minute you live in a wondrous solitude, and on the other side of that minute, you are swept up in an irredeemable crime.

A summer evening. An eleven-year-old girl is walking down an alley. She is going to meet a friend. She had been told to keep out of allies—but she had her own mind, never listened. Of course, she didn't. Her not listening is part of the plot of the story. And so, for a long time, she blamed herself. But it wasn't her fault.

That's how it was. I thought of a *girl*. Of a *her*. But it was me. I stopped blaming her. And *she* became *me* again.

I was going to meet Leandra. We were going to buy an ice cream cone. That's when it happened. The violent side of the innocent minute. I was daydreaming about something. Because that's what I did. Maybe I was thinking about a boy I liked or about a dress I wanted or about a movie I wanted to see, or maybe I was rewinding my tape and playing over an argument I'd had with Gustavo. I don't know what I was thinking and I don't how it happened.

I just remember an arm around me, pulling at me, a hand covering my mouth. I almost couldn't breathe. And I hardly had the words to describe what was happening, though the fear and pain I felt did not depend on words. I smelled that man for many months, the rancid sweat, the breath that smelled like a dying animal was buried inside him. And then I began to think *it was only fifteen minutes of my life*—or maybe less. Why should those few minutes rule my life? But it wasn't those minutes that mattered. It was the aftermath. The aftermath is always what matters.

The aftermath has been life.

My war began early.

I felt fragile and shaken for a long time. I made myself tough. Mentally, I mean. My mother once told me, "You're so strong. It's almost frightening."

"I'm not," I said. I was afraid she was right. I didn't want to be frightening.

But strong or not, I had dreams and he was always in them. I kept smelling him on my skin. Every day for weeks, I washed myself meticulously. And then the dreams stopped. Because they found the man—dead—six weeks after he touched me, though *touch* is a kind word for what he did to me. Touch—that's symbolic language.

Someone shot him. They found his body in that same alley. It was then that I learned his name. A veteran, an alcoholic, mentally disturbed, a man "utterly destroyed by war." That's what my mother said as she stared at his picture in the paper. He was beautiful in the newspaper, young and dressed in a uniform, an American flag in the background. My father said a man like that didn't deserve to be killed—not like that. A terrible thing. A war veteran. But I knew. There was a reason someone had killed him. I knew in my heart it was a woman. I hoped they'd never catch her.

Whatever he had caught in Korea—*him*, Eugenio Escandón— whatever he caught there, he transferred to other people. He transferred it to me. And to others, too, I think. He passed out wounds and scars like a general passing out medals.

A few weeks after they buried that bastard in the ground, I began dreaming that it was me who'd shot him. I was strong in that dream—and I wasn't afraid.

Maybe it was true, what my mother said, that he was a man *utterly destroyed by war.* So the world that had conspired to destroy him had finished the job. Someone had put him out of his misery, though his misery continued to live in the woman who killed him.

He was dead.

He couldn't hurt me anymore.

Once, my father asked me to throw the trash out. I refused. "That's a boy's job," I said.

"I thought you didn't believe in dividing the world into boys' jobs and girls' jobs."

"I don't throw trash out," I said.

"The alley's only a few steps away." His voice was stubborn, insistent.

"No," I said. I could out-stubborn anyone—a gift I discovered I possessed when I was five. Just then Gustavo walked into the house.

"Your sister won't throw out the trash."

Gustavo shrugged. "She thinks she's too good. You know, way too good for manual labor."

I didn't argue. "Yes," I said, "I'm way too good. I'll break a nail."

Gustavo and my father laughed. I didn't have nails. Gustavo threw the trash out.

Years later, Gustavo and I were running late to catch a bus. "Let's cut through the alley," he said.

"I hate alleys," I said.

"They're just unpaved roads," he said.

"Where people store their trash," I said.

"So?"

"It smells."

"So?"

I grabbed his hand and pulled at him. "Let's run," I said. "We're late."

We ran through the streets, Gustavo chasing me, then passing me, then me chasing after him, begging him to slow down. "You're the one who said let's run."

We missed the bus.

Gustavo tried to chase it down. He gave up and when he walked back to the bus stop and caught his breath, he lit a cigarette. "You're too good to run through alleys and you're too good to throw out the trash. What's with you anyway?"

"I'll never be too good for you, baby."

He shook his head. "Ha, ha, fucking ha. I don't get you."

"That's because I'm a girl."

"Yeah, well, we're probably going to miss the damned movie."

"We can go to a later one."

We waited in silence for more than half an hour. Even after we boarded the bus, he refused to speak to me. I didn't care. I was safe. I was sitting next to him. On a warm seat. On a bus. And I knew he would forgive me.

I have never set foot in an alley again. Not since that day. Not since I was eleven.

There are reasons I have a penchant for the word *scarred*.

# adam

## Da Nang, Vietnam, September 16, 1967

A soldier.

His name is Adam.

Eighteen months older than Gustavo. El Paso High, class of '66.

High school days are a long way from Da Nang, but sometimes, his mind wanders. Today, he is thinking of a girl named Xochil. She was more beautiful than any girl he'd ever touched or kissed. He remembers the day he spoke to her. He doesn't know, doesn't care why he remembers every detail, her eyes, her hands, her smell, her Catholic school uniform. The hint of perfume. He watches himself bump into her as her books spill onto the hall floor. He hears her voice: "I'm sorry, I'm sorry. I wasn't watching what I was doing." He sees her shrug and explain, "I'm looking for my brother."

He sees himself picking up all her books and handing them to her. "Your brother?"

"He goes to school here."

He watches her as she hugs her books. And then he sees the stupid look on his own face as he blurts out: "I enlisted. I'm going to be a Marine."

He sees her smile, sees her shrug. He wants to ask, Do you think you could ever love me?

She looks at him and asks, "You enlisted?"

He nods.

"What if you get hurt?"

"Hurt?"

"I don't want you to get hurt." He hears her say that, and then sees her smile, and then sees her walk away.

He wants to call her back, wants to ask: "Why don't you want me to get hurt?" He sees a sadness in his own eyes. He shakes his head and chastises himself for playing the insignificant scene over in his head. The scene never mattered. Not to her.

He listens to the rain.

He vaguely hears someone calling him. *Camera.* No one calls him Adam anymore. Sometimes he even forgets he ever had that name. Maybe a name is like an old pair of pants that no longer fits. Or like a year that's come and gone. Come and gone, like a breeze, like a storm, like a cloud. Nothing more than a memory.

The others are all awake. He hears them talking. There were ten of them yesterday. Now there are only seven. They are discussing what they should do next. A plan. There is always a plan. Their muffled voices make him think of his brothers—early risers all of them. Except for him. They would wake and talk. He remembers yelling at them. He remembers telling them to shut up. He is sorry for the yelling. They were boys, smaller than him, younger. He chastises himself for being a bad brother. He shuts out the memory. He doesn't want to think of home. And yet, that is all he thinks of.

He listens to the rain. Who ever said a fucking poncho kept you dry?

A cup of coffee. He would like a cup of coffee to go with the rain. A cup of coffee to go with the morning. And a newspaper. He loves newspapers—especially the photographs. Sometimes he does this, begins making a list of things he wants and doesn't have, the things he misses. But the list always stops after one or two items. It's too sad to continue the list. It's useless to be sad.

He didn't sleep long, three hours. No more than that. He remembers last night's explosion. Another fucking antipersonnel mine. They fucking shattered you as if you were a piece of glass. Bill had been hit. They'd rushed to him. A missing leg. Fuck. But he'd lived. Yeah. Fuck. He'd lived.

Arizona Territory. Wonders where the fuck it got its name. Fuck you, Route 4. Fuckin' road to An Hoa. Might as well pave the whole fuckin' area with grunts. Might as well make them all lie down and let the fuckin' convoy run their asses over.

*We're lucky. Down south they got to deal with fuckin' Charlie and he's fuckin' everywhere. In every village. Up here we get to fight a real army.*

Yeah, we're all lucky as shit.

Bill didn't fucking die. Didn't make a fuss. A lifer. Almost thirty. Knows what he's doing. Careful. The squad, all of them like the way he has about him. Keeps them together. More like a coach. Calls some of them "son." No one minds.

And we got Patsy, Patsy who dropped out of medical school, but knows everything there is to know about wounds, teaches us things. *Bill, he'll be all right.* If Patsy says he'll be all right, he'll be all right.

Blood. *You'll get used to it. Blood don't mean you'll die.*

Blood and rain. And mines and fucking bouncing Betties. *Theater in the round, baby.* That's what Salvi said. *We're just these fucking bit players and just when we turn north, they're all around us, watching us. Salvi.* Gone back to San Antonio. Didn't take his legs with him.

*And whoever told you that you were going on a fucking picnic?*

Two others wounded last night. Wounds didn't look too bad—not according to Patsy. "Not bad enough to go home."

"Nope."

"Well, fuck it then."

"Yeah," he said, "fuck it." Though sometimes he found himself repeating everything everybody else said.

They'd radioed for help.

The wounded were safe now.

Shit.

Two more days. Then back to Da Nang. A day at the beach. And a joint. *Pot makes it okay. Fuck no, nothing makes it okay. It makes it better. Well, fuck, yes, it makes it better.*

"This area was supposed to be fucking cleaned. Convoy's coming through tomorrow."

"Dammit, we cleared it."

"Well, I sure as fucking hope you clean your ass better than you cleared this area."

He thinks of his brothers. They're home. They're complaining about what a stupid place El Paso, Texas, is. *Can't even buy a rubber without the whole town knowing.*

He feels the rain on his skin. He will never again be dry.

He feels himself rising, standing. He takes a few steps, then takes a leak.

He puts on his helmet and smiles at his fellow soldiers. He keeps himself from shivering.

"What are you fucking smiling at?"

"I'm not dead."

They all laugh. And it has been raining for days.

# charlie

No one believed the war would come. Not my mother, who'd lost her only brother in Korea; not my father, who spent the last days of his youth burying the dead in the Italian countryside; not my sister, Xochil, who almost broke, shouting and cursing and throwing her perfect mind against its inevitability; not my brother, Gustavo, who became its reluctant, defiant lover. And not me, especially not me, Charlie Espejo. Charlie, the most un-Mexican member of the family, the youngest son, who had a disturbing lack of appreciation for tragedy.

We lived in El Paso—which was as close to nowhere as you could get. Take a step or two, then spit—and find your DNA in Juárez, Mexico. Isn't that nowhere? Isn't it? If you asked any gringo, he'd tell you. If you asked any artist, writer, business-man from Mexico City, he'd tell you. Juárez, Mexico, is nowhere. That's what they'd all say about El Paso too. So how could the war come to nowhere? How could it enter our house? How could it take over everything we had, the air we breathed, the fragmented, senseless thoughts that entered into our heads, the inadequate words that stumbled out of our quivering lips? I sometimes still wonder in awe and in dumb disbelief—like Adam and Eve discovering their own nakedness, not knowing where to hide, what to do. Isn't it strange, how you can live on a piece of ground that is very nearly invisible and still be destroyed by America's large and devastating dreams?

You can't hide from America even when you're not really a part of it.

I didn't know that, not in 1967.

There're a lot of things I didn't know in 1967.

I think all of us go over those last few days. It was less than a week. I think we keep those few days locked up in our heads. And, sometimes, we unlock our brains and search the contents— me and Xochil and my mom and dad and Gus. We all do that. I think all of us repeat to ourselves, *How could this have happened? How could this have happened?* All of us, we are like Adam and Eve being thrown out of the Garden. Stunned.

I remember everything about that Saturday—that Saturday when the war arrived at our house on Prospect Street. I remember the soft light of the sun, the shadows on the run-down Victorian houses, my mother's oleander bursting with red blossoms, the reflection of the light on Gus's eyes. Gus. God, I remember Gus, my older brother, who was harder than the bricks the houses were made of, harder than anything I've ever touched or loved and softer too—which makes no sense at all except that it happens to be true.

Gus. When I was a boy, he was the largest figure in my life. My brother, my brother, my heart.

Gus and me and my sister and Mom and Dad, we lived in Sunset Heights. Sunset Heights, the place of my grandfather's exile when he fled the revolution, the Mexican one, the one everyone on the border is addicted to talking about. Names like Washington and Jefferson and Franklin rarely passed our lips. Villa, Zapata, Madero, Porfirio Díaz—these are names we pronounced and argued about. "People were like confetti back then," my grandfather used to say. "Generals grabbed us in their fists and threw us up in the air like we were little pieces of paper. And, me, I landed here, in El Paso. I floated across the border with the help of a few pesos and a sad and steady wind." And then he'd wink at me, take a sip of brandy, shake his head, and laugh, his fists making like he was throwing confetti in the air. My grandfather made life seem as though it were a story that was supposed to be told as you sipped your favorite wine. The problem was that I believed him. I thought that we would all end up as happy and sweet as my grandfather. The man died smiling. He had just taken a shower and put on a freshly pressed shirt. He had just combed his hair. He had just walked into the backyard and sat down in the morning sun. And then he died. Yeah, I thought we would all be like him.

All these years later, I laugh to myself. And if you want to know the truth, it's a sad, almost broken kind of laugh. It's so obvious to me now that all we've ever done in our house is talk about war and how it has given and taken away everything we possess. So how was it possible that we were all so stunned when the war arrived? How was that possible? The house we lived in was invented by that word. Maybe that's what's wrong with the Espejo family—every road we took led us to this destination. All the signs were legible and we were literate (in two languages!). And yet we were profoundly ill prepared for the journey. Only the dead have a right to be that unconscious.

I remember everything about that afternoon.

When the war came.

*The war, the sad, damned war.*

## gustavo

He woke to the shrill sounds of birds at war. They liked to fight, birds did. He'd studied them since he was a boy and had been surprised to discover they could be so mean. *A thing can be beautiful and mean at the same time. For example, birds.* He'd written that in one of his notebooks.

He listened intently to the screeching birds, focusing, trying to picture the scene, the birds wrapped around each other, becoming almost one, then separating, then attacking each other again, twisting, pecking, then flying away only to come back for another round. It was the mockingbird, he thought, fighting off the other birds from coming close to the nest. They did that, when they were protecting a nest, got aggressive, attacked. He'd seen mockingbirds swoop down and peck at dogs—even people. He listened to the small battle, the chirps and squawks. Then it was silent again. He waited. Nothing. A surrender. Or a truce.

He sat up on his bed and shook his head like a wet dog trying to shake off water. He stretched out his arms and decided to take a run. He looked at the clock, almost six, didn't have to be at the body shop until eight. He smiled. Saturday, only had to work until noon. Maybe Xochil would take him so he wouldn't have to catch the bus. Not that he minded the bus.

He looked over at his little brother and almost smiled. He still looked like a boy—especially when he was asleep. Sometimes, he felt more like a father than an older brother. He liked that feeling—like he could take care of somebody, like there was someone who mattered more than the things he carried around in his head, someone who needed caring for. He remembered when Charlie was a baby, how he and Xochil liked to play with him. They begged their mother to let them change his diapers. It had all been a game. A serious one. Xochil and he had been let's-pretend parents.

He reached under his bed and felt for his tennis shoes. He grabbed them, then tossed one across the room at his brother. It hit him with a soft thud. Charlie opened his eyes. He smiled. God, he smiled at everything. At everyone. Always. "Hi," he said through his yawn.

"You planning on sleeping the day away?"

"You pretending to be Dad?"

"Don't compare me to that guy."

"He's not that bad."

"Go back to sleep."

"Is that why you woke me—to tell me to go back to sleep?"

"Yes."

They both laughed, and in a second, his little brother was asleep again. He could do that—wake up and have a conversation—then fall back asleep. Gustavo shook his head, then fished his shoe out of Charlie's blankets. He stood over him for a moment, just watching him. Did he only seem to be perfect? He had the urge to hug him, hold him, but he checked the urge. He remembered when Charlie had first moved into his room—he'd just turned two. Every morning he'd crawl into bed with him. "Gus," he'd say—and then he'd pat his chest. "Go get Mom," he'd tell him. "No," Charlie'd say. "Gus." Gus, Gus, Gus. He shook his head and finished changing into his running clothes.

On his way out of the house, he saw his father sitting on the front porch, drinking a cup of coffee.

Gustavo waved.

His father nodded.

He bounced down the steps, and as his feet hit the sidewalk, he heard his father's voice. "Working today?"

"Every Saturday till noon, Dad."

His father nodded, that look of disapproval washing over his face. Working at Benny's Body Shop, the way his father always said that when he talked to his uncles—like he had just eaten something bitter and the taste was attacking the lining of his mouth.

He ran down the street, trying to forget that look of disapproval. But other thoughts entered his head, random thoughts, most of them accusations, a whole litany of them, his father's words or looks, the way the officer had looked at him when he showed up for his physical as if everything about him made the soldier sick, *You proud of that hair, son?* His civics teacher's remarks on his essays, *You are either confused or un-American.* . . . Lydia's words to him on the last day of school, *You think you're God's gift to the universe.* . . . Monsignor La Pieta's warning, *Your youth is a very small weapon with which to fight the fires of hell.* . . . He heard each voice as he ran, each accusation, and each vowel made him run faster, faster, until finally his breathing made the voices disappear.

He looked up. Two birds were fighting on a telephone wire.

# abe

*Enlist.*

I had that word in my head for a long time. It was like a song I listened to every day. A tune in my head.

My father fought in World War II. He didn't talk very much about what went on in the war. Sometimes he'd mention something, but then it always seemed like he was sorry he'd brought up the subject. Not that he wasn't proud of what we'd done over there. That's how he always put it. "We."

My mom said he was just a boy when he went into the army.

My dad said my mom had it all wrong.

He spent the last year of the war in France, my dad. He said he didn't much like the French, but they were a step up from Hitler. My dad, hell, he earned the right to think whatever he wanted to think. And *freedom* was the most important word in his vocabulary. That's a beautiful thing. Not that he gave me much freedom. He gave me a lot of another important word in his vocabulary: *discipline*.

You know, he loved me. He loved me like a man is supposed to love his son. He gave me and my mom and my sisters and my little brother a good life. I guess I loved him right back. I guess you could say that enlisting was a kind of payback to him but also a kind of freedom.

Freedom was a chance to understand my father's words from the inside. Freedom was a uniform and the chance to prove that you were worthy of your country. "Not every man is worthy," he said. I wanted to be worthy.

A lot of people think that freedom is doing whatever the fuck you want to do. But that's not at all how I saw it back then. I was very serious. I knew what I was doing. I was focused.

I thought a lot about the war and about being a Marine and about things my father said. I thought a lot about my place in the world and my duties. *Duty*. That was another one of my father's words. The day came that I'd had enough about thinking about all these things. I remember the day.

It was a Friday and we didn't have school because of some kind of teacher training. Something like that. I was playing basketball with a group of guys—Jack Evans and Gustavo and Jorge and Conrad and Steve and Marcos. They were just guys I went to high school with. They weren't my friends. I didn't really hang around with them. But I knew them. They knew me. You know, high school friends—and we all lived in the same neighborhood. I don't know how we wound up playing ball together that day. I don't think we planned it. Maybe we were all just out looking for something. And, hell, we found one another.

So there we were playing basketball on a school-yard blacktop. Somewhere between the playing and the talking and the normal shoving that went along with playing ball, Jack Evans and Gustavo almost came to blows. It was over the war (but I think it also had something to do with Gustavo's sister, Xochil). You know, Jack was gung ho and Gustavo, hell, he just didn't get it. Just like we didn't get *him*. And Jack Evans, he was mad as hell, kept telling Gustavo he didn't know two cents about the price people had to pay for freedom. Gustavo had no respect for that word. No, sir. And he just looked at Jack and told him he didn't know what the fuck he was talking about. They looked like they really wanted to hurt each other. I mean, those guys used to be tight. But, the way I see it, their friendship was bound to explode. Those guys were different as day and night. Jack Evans was straight and steady and decent. Gustavo Espejo was nothing but a rebel who was always looking for trouble. Argued with teachers at school. You know, a friendship between those two guys just wasn't in the cards.

The only reason there wasn't blood on the basketball court that day was because of Conrad García. He patted Gustavo on the back and said, "C'mon, let's play ball." Just like that Gustavo took the ball, tossed it toward the net, and hit a swisher. Jack Evans laughed. Then we all laughed. And we just played ball.

But you know, I gotta say it, I really felt like pushing my fist down Gustavo's throat. A part of me really wanted to beat the holy fuck out of him. To begin with, I never liked the guy. Just didn't. You know, he was kind of a bookworm. I was never into books. Not my thing. It's like, what are you trying to prove, reading all those books? I don't mean to imply that Gustavo was some kind of uncool sissy. That's not what he was about. I mean, the guy had long hair and all of that and I never met a girl whose heart didn't beat a little faster when that guy was around. One of my sisters told me he was the most beautiful boy she'd ever seen. I told her boys weren't supposed to be fucking beautiful. And to keep away from him.

And another thing, the guy was into pot. You could just tell.

He and a group of fellow long-haired types took to wearing black arm bands to protest to the war. I guess they were sort of like hippies. Only they were all Mexicans, so I'm not sure if that was the right thing to call them. They called themselves Chicanos, that was it. But I more or less just kept away from them. Anyway, what the fuck did they know? Where did they get off disrespecting the guys in Nam and calling themselves Chicanos when they should have been calling themselves Americans? You know, Gustavo, he was one superior son of a bitch. So he read a lot. Big fucking deal. That didn't mean he knew more than the rest of us, didn't fucking mean he was better. His whole family was like that. I know that most Mexicans weren't into books. At least that's how I saw it. But that family, they were real different.

You know, back then, most Mexicans were pretty much poor. But the Espejos, they weren't poor. And they were a pretty formal family. I went to their house a couple of times with Jack Evans. And hell, there were books everywhere in the house. It was kind of strange. I mean, who had that many books? And his dad wasn't even a professor. I didn't get them. But God, Gustavo's twin sister, Xochil, she was a looker. Jesus Christ. She would have made a believer out of an atheist. But that Gustavo, well, I just didn't like him. And I sure as hell didn't like his attitude. He didn't give a damn about the guys fighting in Nam. He didn't. Him and his fucking long hair. You know, when he talked to Jack that way, I decided right then that I was going to enlist. Right then and there. That day. Fuck Gustavo Espejo and his fucking attitude. If the guy didn't get what this country was all about, well, hell, Mexico was just a spit away. He could take a hike across the bridge and never fucking come back. That's how I saw it. Where did he get off? Look, everyone has a right. But shit.

That afternoon, I went and talked to someone about enlisting. I was only seventeen. He said my parents had to sign. I told him I was about to turn eighteen in a few months. Hell, I knew my father would be proud of me if I enlisted. But I also knew he'd never sign for me. I knew he wanted me to finish high school. So, hell, I had to wait. Man, those last few months of school seemed like a goddamned lifetime.

Fuck Gustavo Espejo.

# adam

## Da Nang, Vietnam

You remember the day you enlisted.

You borrowed your mother's car. You made up some lie about a girl. You held the thought *Marine* in your head as you drove. You see yourself signing the paperwork, getting a physical, arching your feet that were always too flat.

You see the look on your mother's face when you finally decide to tell her. Marine, she whispers. She makes the word sound like a prayer.

You see yourself holding your orders.

You see yourself sitting on a plane and smoking all the way to San Diego.

You arrive at the airport, call the number from a phone booth. A voice yells at you and tells you where to wait. When the military jeep arrives, the driver looks as if he might spit on you. As you sit in the jeep, the driver keeps repeating that you better be fucking ready. *You sorry piece of shit. You don't look ready.*

You tell him you have your orders and you hand them to him. He takes the orders and then slaps you and smiles. *Who the shit asked for your orders? Who asked you?* You say nothing as he drives you to the base and he orders you to sit up and look straight ahead. As you drive, you forget and turn your head to look out the window. He reaches over and smacks you on the head. *I said look fucking straight ahead.* A little later, he smacks you again.

You become a statue. You do not move.

When you arrive at the base, he makes you stand on some yellow footprints that are all lined up in front of a building. You stand at attention with others like you. Your drill instructor looks you up and down until you understand you are nothing. You are taken in to get a haircut. You feel your hair falling away from you. You hear your mother's voice: *Such beautiful hair.*

You are marched back out and again you stand on the yellow footprints. You catch a glimpse of a man in the window of the building. Windows can be like mirrors and you are staring at the man. And you think he is the ugliest thing you have ever seen. Then you realize that you are looking at yourself.

The man is you.

# gustavo

You study your face in the mirror as you shave.

Such a strange thing, your face. You wonder what they see—your sister, your mother, your brother, your father, that girl who said she would carry your touch until she died. But what did that girl know anyway? You were a face she liked, a body she liked to touch. And what did it mean, anyway, to like a face as if it were nothing more than a nice picture hanging on a wall?

You look deep into your own eyes and wonder at the darkness, wonder if those are the eyes of a soldier. You look at your hands—hard and pitiless—and wonder if those are the hands of a solider. They are callused from work. They could hurt. You have always known that. And that rage in your heart? There is a fire there that could scorch, that will kill. You would make a fine soldier.

But you remind yourself that a solider does not kill for sport. He does not kill because there is something in his eyes or his hands or his heart. A soldier is made. He is trained. And he must believe in the fight. In the cause of the nation. You remember your uncle telling you that soldiers were like priests—they had to believe in their sacrifice. You wanted to tell your uncle that you did not believe in that religion. You will not make a sacrifice of yourself. You do not think it is beautiful to donate your blood to a thankless earth and a heartless country. That is what you told your civics teacher when she gave your class a lecture on patriotism. You remember the hate in her face, how your words hit her like an unexpected slap. *You know nothing! Nothing! You're a boy!* She held you in contempt. You wonder why her contempt mattered so much.

You try to picture yourself in the jungles of Vietnam. In a uniform. With a rifle in your hand. Or a machine gun. Or whatever weapon they hand you. You refuse this image of yourself.

You wonder what will come of your refusal. In the end, you will succumb. You will put on a uniform. You will let yourself be trained. You remember what your father told you once: *You do not have to believe to attend Mass. There are other reasons to go.* But your father had been silent about those other reasons.

You think it's strange, now, and you don't even know why, but you grew up with a feeling that something was going to go wrong with your life—and you know it's no one's fault and you don't blame anyone; no blame, no blame, not even your father. You do not know where the feelings come from. You will never find the source of that river.

Your mother reminds you that you are an angel, but you know your wings were broken from the day you were born, a premature Icarus. And anyway, your mother holds overly generous opinions regarding her children. She is especially generous in her opinions of you. But you have never made the mistake of taking her literally. And even she has always known that you resided in an exile that was beyond her reach. You were never like your brother, Charlie, never had his innocence, his optimism, his unforgivable ability to forgive *everyone for everything.* You laugh to yourself and you want to keep the envy from your heart. Envy is a poison you refuse. You will not sin against your brother. He belongs everywhere he goes. So at ease, as if the world were a suit he tried on one day and discovered it fit him perfectly. You do not know what that is like—and you will never know.

Charlie—the center of the world. You have always resided on the margins, always felt awkward, uneasy, out of place. When you were a small boy, you read books that had little games: *one of these things is not like the others.* You were one of those things. Not like the others.

You remember telling Xochil that some people weren't meant to be happy.

"Are you some people?"

"Yeah, I think I'm one of those people."

"You're full of cold coffee." She loved saying that to you. Cold coffee. She kissed you on the cheek and said, "Pursuit of happiness, baby." She held your face in the palms of her hands and said, "You know what your problem is? You're too Mexican and too tragic and too serious. You can't help it. But if you're going to be that way, you should at least enjoy it." She laughed, and then she poked your heart. She liked poking your heart. You picked up that habit too. All the good things about you, you got from her.

It wasn't true, anyway, what Xochil said, not any of it. Maybe the Mexican part—you always thought of yourself as Mexican. But you weren't tragic and you weren't serious. Not serious at all. Most things were nothing more than a game to you. It was Xochil who was serious. Serious, beautiful, brilliant, brilliant Xochil. When you were growing up, she was the most serious human being you'd ever known, that girl, that sister, minutes younger than you. The most serious person in the world. And the happiest. No—Charlie—Charlie was happier. He couldn't even get mad convincingly. You ask yourself, How can they be your blood, these perfect creatures?

All those years when you were in school, if something was going wrong, you'd think of Xochil and Charlie. Having them in your head made you feel like nothing bad could ever happen. You were immune from the harsh judgments of the world because they lived in you—in a part of you no one could ever touch. Your body was a map and their names were cities—and you took refuge there.

Xochil and Charlie, they were your religion, your gods, your heaven, your only road to paradise. And because of them you would whisper to yourself, *Gustavo Espejo, you're going to have a beautiful American life.* You would smile and look at yourself in the mirror. *A beautiful American life.* You have practiced keeping that smile far away from the people you meet on the street.

Practice makes perfect.

Your face became a book no one could read.

You finish shaving. *You know nothing! Nothing! You are just a boy!*

It is no good to think of your face.

It is no good to think of anything.

And suddenly these words appear in your head as if your head were a page waiting to be written on: *It is not the earth that is thankless—it is you.*

You wave your hand in front of your face.

You are erasing the words.

You will go to work. And work will be everything. That is what you tell yourself.

You do not believe your own lie.

## xochil. gustavo.

Xochil parked the car in front of Benny's Body Shop on Texas. "Got you here with ten minutes to spare."

"You're a terrible driver."

"I'm not."

"Okay, let me put it another way—*manejas pa la chingada*."

"You like to cuss in Spanish, don't you?"

"I like to cuss in English too."

"Well, English or Spanish, I'm a good driver."

"You're not. You're too careful."

"Too careful?"

"You drive like Mom."

"You know what?"

"What?"

"Mom would say you shouldn't be careless with other people's lives."

"Yes. That's what she'd say. But there is such a thing as being too careful."

"Not that you'd know." She always got the upper hand. With words, anyway. "And what would Mom say if you told her that she drove *pa la chingada*?"

"She'd slap the holy crap out me—maybe."

"Maybe?"

"She's not into violence."

"That's true. But she really hates verbal violence too."

"Verbal violence?"

"Cussing."

"But she can be cool."

"And you're just the kind of guy who'd take advantage of her coolness."

"I have scruples."

"No, you don't." She hit his arm with her elbow. "Want me to pick you up?"

"No, I'll walk."

"You sure?"

"I'm sure."

"It's far."

"Not so far."

"Gustavo time, huh?"

"Something like that."

"You're doing a lot of that Gustavo time lately. Is it a girl?"

"You need Xochil time. I need Gustavo time. It doesn't have anything to do with a girl."

"It's a girl."

"I've sworn off girls."

"That's hilarious."

"It's true." He took out a cigarette.

"Don't light that thing. Mom hates when you smoke in the car."

He rolled the cigarette around in his fingers. "So, what are you going to do today?"

"Are you changing the subject?"

"What subject?"

"Girls."

"Yes, I'm changing the subject."

She shook her head, bit her lip. "I'm going to apply for a job."

"A job? Aren't you going to school?"

"I just want something part-time. You know, bread, baby. Bucks. *Dinero.*"

"Yeah, sure, bread. What do you need it for? You're living at home. You have a scholarship. Dad's paying for your books and your fees. And what about hitting the books?"

"I *am* hitting the books. You think I can't handle school and a job? No problem. And I want money."

"I'll give you an allowance."

"Money I earn myself."

"Oh, so this is a Xochil thing."

"Exactly."

"Dad's not gonna like it."

"Dad doesn't like anything."

"He likes Jack Evans."

"Do we have to talk about Jack Evans?"

"I hate his fucking guts."

"Oh, I didn't know that."

"I don't like sarcasm."

"Okay. You know, maybe you should make a list of things you don't like and hand it in to me."

"Is this an assignment?"

"We're fighting."

"No, we're not."

"Yes, we are."

"No."

"Yes."

"Bet you're gonna see him today."

"There's a job opening in the jewelry department at the JCPenney downtown."

"Are you changing the subject?"

"Yes. I'm changing the subject."

"Fine. But what the hell do you know about jewelry?"

"What the hell do you know about car bodies?"

"Car bodies?" He laughed. "I learned."

"I'll learn too."

He looked at his watch. "Time to go." He opened the car door and blew her a kiss.

"I hate it when you laugh at me like that."

"I was just blowing you a kiss."

"You only do that when you're angry with me."

"Is that true?"

"Yes. I don't like sarcasm either."

"Well, Sis, sometimes we hate the same things." He shut the door, lit a cigarette, and walked toward the entrance of the garage.

*Sis,* Xochil grumbled. She turned on the ignition, then honked the horn. Gustavo looked back toward her, shrugging, *What?* She shot him a look, then drove away. *Sis my ass. He calls me that only when he's really pissed.*

# gustavo

He looked back at his sister as she drove away. He stood motionless for an instant. He imagined the look on her face, the way she squinted her eyes when she was angry, the way she tapped her teeth together and made a faint clattering sound, the way her fingers tightened.

*I should be more patient.* It was a recurring sentence in the confessions he'd scattered throughout his notebooks, a fist beating his chest, a reminder that he was not in control of himself despite all his efforts. He hated making her mad, hated that wiseass tone in his voice when he wanted to get that desired response from her. *Rewind the tape. Go back. Do it over.* That's the game she always played with him. She'd give him the scenario, play it all out, then say, *This is what I'd do different.* Then she'd tap her finger as if she were playing with a tape recorder, rewinding it. Then she'd give him the new, improved scene. *I'm always better the second time around.* He tried doing that, replaying the scene, then stopped himself. The second time around he would be the same. He couldn't help himself. Or maybe he didn't want to be any other way than the way he was. Which made no sense. It made no sense at all.

But did she always have to be right? Well, most of the time, she was right. About most things. *She was.* She connected dots between ideas, knew how to construct arguments, had been a champion debater in high school and in their house, could write logical essays, could control words, could even write poetry— though she never showed her poetry to anyone. Not even to him. Once, he'd caught her writing one—a poem—and had tried to make her read it to him. She'd gotten angry. *It's mine. Can't anything just be mine?* Okay. Okay, okay, okay.

Lately they'd been fighting more. He hated that. *You shouldn't fight with your sister. She's rare and beautiful.* That's was what his mother had told him. He'd written it down somewhere. Rare and beautiful. But she was stubborn and she could be mean when she wanted to be.

And maybe she was right most of the time, but did that mean he was always wrong?

He thought of the battle that had been raging outside his window when he woke. *A thing can be beautiful and mean at the same time. For example, birds.*

*For example, Xochil.*

# xochil

*I don't care what he says.*
*I don't care what he thinks.*
*I don't care. I don't—*

Once, at school, she had watched her brother play tetherball. She remembered thinking that she was the ball and he was the rope. What was a tetherball without the rope? It made her angry that she thought those things. And so later, she asked him, *Do you wish sometimes we weren't twins?* And just for a second, she could see the hurt on his face—just before he turned himself to stone, just before he hid behind those dark eyes.

But he could never hide. Not from her.

But the reverse was also true. She always felt he could see right through her—though he couldn't. There were so many things he didn't know, couldn't even fathom about her. And yet somehow he knew everything that mattered.

They *did keep* secrets from each other. They had to. It was one of the strategies of survival. They had to prove they were separate, individuals, independent. *Do you wish sometimes we weren't twins?* That hurt on his face. She couldn't stand that look. But she couldn't repent from the thought. And he'd felt the same way. She knew that. Just because he never said it didn't mean he never thought it.

Being a twin. That complicated everything. Every damn thing became a negotiation. *Every single damn thing.* It was as if she could never see herself without thinking of what he would think, what he would see. When she saw a boy she liked, she wound up wondering if Gustavo would approve. Half the time, Gustavo didn't even care or notice. Once she saw a boy on the street and whispered to her brother, "I think he's beautiful." He shrugged. "Really?" He seemed surprised and he watched the boy, trying to see what she saw. He shrugged again. "Should I talk to him?" He shrugged again. "Why not?" He wasn't interested in running her life. He wasn't. But his voice and his eyes were inside her. Was that his fault? She wanted to exorcise him, cast him out.

A twin could be a demon.

Jack Evans. Gustavo disapproved. No, that word was inexact, incorrect, wrong. *Disapprovel* was a parental word. *I can't stand his fucking guts.* That was more than disapproval.

But she half hated Jack too—and probably for the same reasons.

"He's just another predictable gringo." That's what Gustavo had said. But he'd been angry.

"But you've been friends forever."

"We were just kids who liked playing baseball. I don't play baseball anymore."

"But you still play basketball."

"And we're never on the same side."

"You're just mad at him."

"Yeah, well, like I said, *he's just another predictable gringo.* Ever heard him talk about Mexicans?"

"He doesn't mean those things."

"You know what he means? Do you? Look, you can be his friend if you want."

So Jack and Gustavo had stayed friends—for a little longer anyway. Everything normal. And then that day, when he'd kissed her—she'd kissed him back. And things between Jack and Gustavo started to go to hell. It didn't have anything to do with her. She knew that. They had their own friendship. She wasn't responsible for that. He's just another predictable gringo. She tried translating what that meant. It meant he fell in step, didn't color outside the lines. It meant he'd never smoke a joint. It meant he never disagreed with his teachers, always said yes sir when his father asked him to do something. It meant he'd never wear his hair long. It meant he was a straight arrow. That's what it meant. Gustavo didn't suffer people like Jack Evans. He didn't have it in him. And she wasn't so different from her brother. She didn't give people like him the time of day. Not most of the time. Why was Jack Evans the exception?

Didn't a part of her hate herself for what she felt for him?

Was she angry with Gustavo? Or was she angry with herself?

*God, Xochil, you always have to do this—have this discussion with yourself. Damn it! Damn it, damn it, damn it! Can't you just let yourself like a guy? Any guy? Can't you just do that?*

*Okay. Go back. Rewind the tape. Play it over. . . .*

*Gustavo walks away from the car, lights his cigarette. She gets out of the car, follows him. "Gustavo, I think I might love him."*

*He looks at her. "You're wrong about him."*

*She looks back at him. "Then let me be wrong."*

*She smiles at him.*

*He smiles back. "Okay then, be wrong."*

*"Okay."*

*"Okay."*

# abe

A week before I left for the Marine Corps Recruit Depot in San Diego, I ran into Conrad García. The guy was walking out of the Circle K, a pack of Marlboros in his hand. He wasn't with Gustavo. He and Gustavo, they were pretty tight, always hanging out. I didn't have anything against Conrad. Okay, so he was Mr. Pacifist. Yeah, yeah, I rolled my eyes at the guy. We all did. He was harmless.

He smiled at me and said, "I heard you're going into the Army." Everybody in Sunset Heights knew everything about everybody.

"Army?" I said. "C'mon, man, don't talk to me about the fucking army. I'm gonna be a Marine."

He nodded, then smiled. "Marine," he said. "Sorry. Look, just take care of yourself." He had this really soft look in his eyes. Look, I knew why everybody's mom and dad liked Conrad García. Even my dad, who said pacifists were cowards looking for an intellectual excuse, even my dad liked Conrad.

"I enlisted," I said.

He nodded. He shook my hand. The guy was a gentleman, I'll give him that.

I looked right at him. "You don't like soldiers, do you?" I don't know why the fuck I asked him that. I mean, I didn't really want to get into it with him. Why was I picking shit with a pacifist?

"Soldiers are just people," he said.

"Yeah, sure. And you like people, so soldiers are cool."

"Look," he said, "I just wish I lived in a world where we didn't need soldiers." That's what he said.

"Well, that's not the world we live in, buddy," I said.

"Yeah," he said.

"So, Conrad, are you gonna enlist?" I knew I was being an asshole.

He looked straight at me. "No." That no was hard as a brick.

"What if they take you anyway?"

"They won't."

"You hate us all, don't you?"

He lit a cigarette. "No," he said, "I don't. But the possibility exists that it's you. Maybe it's you, Abe. Maybe you hate me."

He was right. I did fucking hate him. But it didn't feel good. Shit, sometimes, nothing feels good. He offered me a cigarette. I took it.

We sort of walked together for a while. We didn't say anything. And then he asked me. "Are you afraid?"

"Nah," I said, "I'm not afraid."

"I don't mean about going to war, I mean, aren't you afraid of what war will turn you into?"

"It'll turn me into a man."

"Life will do that on its own."

I don't think I really understood what the hell he was asking me. The thing about Conrad was that he was born old. I mean it. I don't think he was ever young. Always thinking. Not like the rest of us.

"War does things to a man," he said. "My uncle. He was never the same after Korea."

I nodded. We just kept walking. "Thanks for the cigarette," I said finally. I wanted to say something else. But I didn't know what.

"Sure," he said. Then he looked at me. "You really want to go to Nam?"

"Yeah," I said.

He nodded. He lit another cigarette. That guy could smoke. "Come back alive, will you?"

We sort of smiled at each other. That Conrad, you know, he could make anyone smile.

After that, I went walking around. You know, just running some things through my head. I got to thinking that Conrad was wrong about being a pacifist. You know, sometimes you had to stand up to evil. You just had to do it. You can't go around letting people beat the crap out of you and stand around and do nothing. I was no expert on what was going on in Vietnam. But I knew there was a fight and I knew whose side I was on. Maybe that was my politics. Pretty basic, I know, but that's the way I felt.

Politics? Fuck, what was that? Eighteen-year-old men don't know shit about politics. Guys like Gustavo and Conrad, they got themselves politics when they were sixteen. But it was just a game for them. You know, head games. But for me, it wasn't a game. This was real. My country was fighting a war. Look, I was no Jack Evans. I didn't have his purity. But if you don't belong to your country, where do you belong? Jack and I, we were on the same side. Gustavo and Conrad, I don't think either one of them understood what it meant to love a country. Any country. To me, that was the saddest thing in the whole fucking world.

# gustavo

To take a car, bent and mangled in an accident—then make it appear as if that accident had never happened. *That* was an art. He liked the idea of his job, sometimes even imagined the accident, the sound, the crunching, the look of terror on the driver, and, afterward, having survived with minor injuries, the look of disgust—*shit!*—the impatience of waiting for the tow truck. Sure, he liked his job, the pounding, the sanding, the smoothing, the shine of the new paint. Sometimes you had to be rough, mean, pound like hell. Sometimes you had to be gentle. After the pounding, there was the thin layer of putty. Not too much— just enough. And when the putty dried, the sanding until it was smooth as ice cream. That's what Mr. Ortega liked to say. "Like ice cream at Dairy Queen." Sometimes, when he ran his hand on the smooth surface, he didn't think of ice cream. He thought of girls. He thought of their bodies.

At first, Mr. Ortega had told him he was too slow. "I don't

like lazy," he said. But after a few weeks, Mr. Ortega had been impressed. "A good worker." A compliment. Work. That's what made you a man. From an old world, Mr. Ortega. He knew his business, the sort of man who was overly proud of what he did. Compensating for what he didn't have, for his bad English, for the poverty he had been born into. A good man, fair, honest, but a complainer. And rigid like his own father—though they had come from different Mexicos. Certainly they had taken different sides in their views on the revolution.

They liked each other well enough, the two of them. Not that he and Mr. Ortega were natural friends. "Listen, Gustavo, cut your hair." He would smile when he said it, but it was a command not a question.

"Girls like long hair."

"But not good girls. Not the kind you marry."

"Who wants to marry?"

"When you find the right one—then you'll cut your hair."

"Maybe."

"No. No maybes. Girls don't like it when your hair is prettier than theirs."

They laughed, smiled at each other, enjoyed the banter—but underneath, there was the knowledge that they could be enemies, turn on each other. Though for now there was a laugh, a smile, both of them shaking their heads, both of them knowing that there was no true understanding.

Things got worse when the discussion turned to music. Mr. Ortega listened stubbornly to a Mexican station, hour after hour, day after day—nothing but rancheras and mariachis and trios singing ballads from the thirties and forties. Sometimes, when he'd leave on an errand, Gustavo would find an FM station, and he would nod and sing along with the Stones and the Doors and the Beatles, but Mr. Ortega would return, changing the station and grumbling, "It's shit!"

"No," Gustavo would answer, "it's just the Beatles."

"They're not even American."

"Neither are rancheras."

"The Beatles are shit," Mr. Ortega would repeat—then turn up the volume on his rancheras.

Work was what they had in common.

One day, Gustavo had shown up wearing a black armband. Mr. Ortega had pointed at his arm and asked, "What's that?"

"It's a protest."

"What are you protesting?"

"The war."

"You don't know anything."

Gustavo looked away.

"If you wear that thing tomorrow, you're fired."

"Okay," Gustavo said. Nothing on his face.

"Your father? He lets you wear that?"

"My father doesn't own me."

"You disrespect your father?"

"Maybe my father disrespects me."

"Maybe I should fire you."

"When I don't do my job, fire me."

That's where they left it.


"That's good. Nice touch. Very good hands."

Gustavo looked up from his work and grinned at Mr. Ortega. "I got good hair and I got good hands."

Mr. Ortega laughed. "Mrs. Rubio will be pleased. To please her, that's not easy."

Gustavo nodded.

"Time to close."

"Yeah."

"Yeah?"

"Yes, sir."

"That's better. Respect. Remember." Mr. Ortega shook his head. Sometimes, he just wanted to talk. About anything. Gustavo watched him as he took out his wallet and fished out a picture. "My oldest," he said.

Gustavo stared at the picture of the dark-skinned man. The uniform made him look even younger than he was—like he should still be in high school. "How old is he?"

"Nineteen next month."

Gustavo could see the pride in Mr. Ortega's face. He wanted to say something, but didn't know what. "He looks like you," he said finally, though there wasn't much of a resemblance.

"No. He looks like his mother."

Gustavo shrugged. "Does he like the army?"

"He doesn't complain. He's a man now."

"Where's he stationed?"

"Vietnam. He's serving his country."

"That's good."

Mr. Ortega smiled. "He cut his hair."

Gustavo let himself laugh. "The army's like a good woman."

Mr. Ortega laughed too.

Gustavo handed the picture back to him.

"His mother worries," he said.

"And you? You worry?"

"Worries are for women."

"You never worry?"

"I worry about food on the table, and money to pay for it."

Gustavo nodded.

"And you, Gustavo? Have you gotten your letter?"

"Not yet."

"It will come. Your armband won't protect you." Mr. Ortega smiled and ran his hand against the side of his hair and made a buzzing sound.

# adam

## Da Nang, Vietnam, September 16, 1967

Him. The soldier. The grunt. *You know why they call you fucking grunts? Cuz when you fucking put on those backpacks, you grunt like you're taking a fucking dump. That's fucking why.* The soldier, he is photographing a bird as it lands in a small clearing. He snaps a photo of a medic stepping out into the clearing. The soldier, Adam, is happy with his photograph. He believes he has captured that look of apprehension that soldiers wear when they enter a new environment, the searching eyes, at once confident and tentative. At once frightened and frightening.

They could kill.

Those eyes are in his camera now, on his film. Happy. Happy with his photograph. He half wonders why he isn't covering the war instead of fighting it or why he decided against going to college. He wanted to be a photographer. That dream still lives somewhere inside him. He will be turning twenty in a few months. He tells himself there will be time. When the war is over or when his tour of duty ends. There will be time.

But for now he makes use of his good eye—the same eye that sees a good photograph senses the enemy. He is good on patrol. He has a useful gift. The gift will keep him alive. He smiles at the nickname the men in his platoon have given him: Camera. He likes the name.

Today, it is quiet. Only the sound of the rain. But the weather is the enemy too. That is what he told his mother when he wrote to her last. He doesn't talk about the battles. Battles, shit. Nothing but skirmishes. Snipers. Sometimes some artillery from the north. *They're picking us off a couple at a time. Nickel and diming us to fucking death.* But that is not what he tells his mother. He makes no mention of the skirmishes, of search and destroy missions, of security patrols and perimeter defense and all the things that make up the life of a grunt on the ground. He tells her other things, tells her about the cities where the members of his squad are from. Explains things to her about platoons and companies and battalions and regiments and divisions, tries to describe the landscape and the taste of the bad food. Tries to describe the weather. *Guy down here says it's like the Florida Everglades. Not exactly. But something like it. I wouldn't know. I've never been to Florida.* Even as he wrote that, he laughed, remembering what Whit had said. *Florida Everglades my ass. Don't look nothin' like it.* Didn't matter. He was just making small talk with his mother.

Today, there is a pause in the rain, the sun making an appearance after a long absence. And the air does not feel so suffocating. The jungle rot in his right leg seems to be healing, and he feels almost whole. He has time to reread one of the two letters that he carries with him always. He takes the letters out from where he keeps them wrapped in aluminum foil. A trick he invented. Keeping them dry is a game he plays.

"Why you readin' those fuckin' things again? They ain't gonna change."

Camera sneers at his friend. "Fuck you, Whit."

"Fuck you in the ass."

"Fuck you in the mouth."

They laugh. "Wish I had me a beer."

"Well, you got cigarettes."

"And I wish I had me just one day with Sasha."

"One day and one night. Yeah, yeah."

"The things we could do."

"Well, all you got's a fist."

"I'll take a fist any day to your fucking letters."

"So why don't you just let me fuckin' read 'em in peace."

"No amount a readin' gonna change what they say."

"Shut up and give me a cigarette."

This is the way it goes, their talk. Whit knows everything about the letters Camera carries—just as Camera knows everything about the letters Whit gets from his girlfriend. The war has given them to each other, these young men, one a black man who grew up in a house a spit away from the University of Chicago, the other, a white boy transplanted from Jasper, Indiana, to El Paso, Texas, whose father was once a member of the Ku Klux Klan before he settled down and married a good Catholic girl. No reason they should be friends. Except they're in a war. And they took to each other. For no reason.

---

Dear Adam,

I know it's been almost two months since I wrote to you. I've been trying to write you this letter for weeks and weeks. Every time I pick up a pen and try to put something into words, I break out crying. You know, I've been a big baby all my life.

You know that. I mean, you were the boy who used to make me cry in first grade. In second and third and fourth grade too. You remember. So, I guess I haven't changed all that much. Well, I'm engaged now, guess I told you that in my last letter. I told you then that if you had asked, things might have been different. But neither one of us was ready. And really, you didn't have a thing for me—at least not like I had for you. And Alan, well, he had two kids and his wife's been dead for two years and he was lonely. I was lonely too. Some people are like that, I guess, they got this loneliness inside them. You were never like that. But I don't want to analyze you too much. Mom says I should go to school and get a degree and get paid for analyzing people. Maybe I'll do that.

I'm just clearing my throat here, I think. I don't know how to say what I'm going to say. Your mom, she said it was okay if I told you. I mean, they didn't have the heart, but everyone agreed that you have a right to know. So here it is. Jeff was killed in a skirmish in Vietnam on May 28. In his last letter, he said he was near a place called Dac To. I don't know, but I guess that's where he got killed. Unless his company got moved out somewhere else. His brother's crazy mad. Wants to know everything about Jeff's death and the military isn't too keen about giving him too much information. And he went down to Fort Bliss and almost got himself arrested. And the whole family's kind of a mess right now. But that family never was very stable. Not like yours. I got to tell you that your mom is true blue.

Anyway, I know how much Jeff meant to you. I mean, we all grew up together, me and you and Jeff and Sandy and Stacy. And when Sandy was killed in that awful accident in high school, her shit boyfriend drunk as a mean skunk, well, you remember how we all cried and held on to each other and went to Juárez and got drunk.

And you had to keep Jeff from falling apart because he'd always had a thing for her. You were a good friend to him, Adam. And Stacy, well, I won't talk about her. I won't. I don't forgive her and that no-good coward of a man she married. I won't talk about that.

I guess there's only me and you left, so we have to take care, don't we?

I pray for you every day, Adam. And I know you're going to make it. I know you're going to come home and we'll throw a party. And I'll keep writing. And I'll keep praying.

Always, always, always,
Evelyn

# charlie

Charlie knelt over his map of the city, ironing it with his hands. He looked at his watch, noted the time—eleven o'clock—then turned his attention back to the map. His father was meeting with Dr. Chesbrough this morning. Dr. Chesbrough's office was on the corner of Mesa and Baltimore. He pointed to the place on the map. *There. He's right there.* His mother was at the grocery store. She always shopped for groceries at the same place: the Safeway store on the corner of Kirby and Mesa. He studied the map. *So she's right there.* Gus, he was working at Benny's Body Shop on Texas Street, four blocks up from Campbell Street. He scrutinized the map. *So he's right here.* And Xochil, she had come home after she left Gus off at work and said she was going shopping downtown with Margie. They had left together on foot at 9:30. He had heard Xochil say she was going to the Popular. The Popular was on San Antonio Street. *Right there. She and Margie are right there.*

*And me, I'm right here.* He pointed to the X that stood for their house. *And Grandma's asleep. And she's right over there.* He pointed to his grandmother's bedroom.

Putting everybody's name on a map made him happy. If their names were there, they were safe.

*Someday you're going to make a wonderful and neurotic father.* That's what Xochil said.

Gus was always warning him about his obsession. *You can't map the world.* They had a running argument about his thing for maps and mapping. *A way of making you believe that you can own and control the fucking earth.* That's what he said. *But they have mapped the world, Gus.* That was always his standard response. *They have, Gus, they've mapped the whole world. And they've named all the countries and all the cities and we're there, too, Gus. We're right there on the map.* Sometimes he would point to the globe that he kept in his half of the room. Sometimes he would get out his world atlas, the one he'd bought with his own money, the one he kept under his bed. He would take it out, place it in his lap, and repeat. *Look, See. They've mapped the whole world.* Gus remained unimpressed. *That's only a representation. It's not real.* Sometimes Gus had a hard head.

When he turned eight, his father had given him the globe as a birthday gift. He studied it for hours and hours. "Look, Gus, we're right here!" his finger pointing to the corner of Texas where it met New Mexico and Mexico.

"No," Gus said, "We're right here. In this room." He pointed to himself and then to Charlie and then reached down and patted the floor. "We're right here, Charlie."

"Well, you know what I mean."

"Well, you probably know what I mean too." Gus half-smiled to himself and returned to reading his book.

*"And why do you always need to know where everything is on the map?"*

He never had an answer for Gus's question.

His argument with his brother ran through his head as he studied a map of Mexico. He was looking for Dolores, the village where the Mexican Revolution began, the birthplace, that's what his father called it. He tried to picture the scene, the people of the village rising early as they heard the church bells calling them to gather. He pictured the priest, Father Miguel Hidalgo. He pictured the people all around him in the church. He pictured them grabbing the banner of Our Lady of Guadalupe and yelling, *"¡Viva Mexico!"* He pictured the stern priest telling the crowd that it was time to fight. He pictured the entire population of the village, all of them shouting, *"¡Viva Mexico!"* That's how it began, the war for independence. He counted the years in his head: *1810 to 1910, that's 100 years. And this is 1967, so that's 57 more years, so that's 157 years ago. One hundred fifty-seven years ago, Father Hidalgo yelled "¡Viva Mexico!" The grito everyone talks about.*

In the *M* volume of the *Encyclopaedia Britannica*, he looked up Mexico. He shook his head as he read that Father Miguel Hidalgo was hunted down and shot a year after the fight for independence started. He saw that the war lasted for eleven years. He added up all the statistics. It was estimated that 450,000 civilians lost their lives during the war for independence from Spain. He shut the encyclopedia and put it back on the shelf. He wondered how many bullets had been fired to kill 450,000 people. How many bullets? What kind of thought was that?

He walked up to his globe and found that Dolores was missing. It must have been too small, too unimportant. He was glad Gus wasn't in the room. *Villages don't count on maps. See what I mean, Charlie?* That's what he would say.

He found the village near Guanajuato in his atlas. He went back to the globe and put his finger on the globe. *Here. Here it is. ¡Viva Mexico! Viva, viva, viva.* He felt as if the shout lived somewhere inside him and someday that shout would come out. He pictured the villagers following Father Hidalgo through the streets, happy and smiling.

Maybe he would ask his father if he would take him to Dolores someday. So he could see the birthplace. But he knew what his father would say. He would say, *Once you have left a place, you can never go back.* He'd said that a hundred times. Why couldn't you go back? Why not? There were so many rules. Everyone had them. Gus had them: *you can't map the world.* Xochil had them: *never go into an alley by yourself.* His father had them: *you can never go back.* His mother had them too. Only she kept her rules to herself. And him? What rules did he have?

He looked at his globe and spun it around. *¡Viva Mexico!*

When the globe stopped spinning, Charlie walked toward his grandmother's room, knocked softly, then turned the knob and entered. She turned toward him. He smiled and waved. "Hi," he whispered.

*"Hijito de mi vida,"* she said, her voice weak. But it had been weak for so long that it seemed normal. She patted the bed, motioning for him to sit, her old, old hands soft and bony.

"We're alone," he said.

"Are you afraid?"

"No," he said.

"Good." She laughed softly. "You are going to be the most beautiful man the world has ever known."

He laughed. "Sure, Grandma."

"Don't be disrespectful."

"Gus is going to be the most beautiful man."

"Let me tell you something. Gustavo is nearly divine. But you are an angel."

"I don't want to be an angel."

She laughed. *"Amor, te adoro."* She placed her hand on his

cheek. "I want to tell you a story. When I left Mexico, it was early in the morning. Have you heard this story?"

"No. Dad doesn't like to talk about that. He says Mexico didn't want us."

"Your father is bad at forgiving."

"He can't help it."

She smiled at him. "You're not like him."

"I can't help that either."

"Oh, *amor,* you are such an innocent." She patted his check and let her hand drop. "I woke him up and took him in my arms. He was three, your father. A smart boy. Beautiful. But not as beautiful as you. We traveled for a few days. I don't remember how many. It was dangerous. But your grandfather had men and money. He never had to shoot anyone. He bought them off. Do you know what that means?"

"It means he bribed them. Gus calls it a *mordida.*"

"I'm glad you have Gustavo to tell you these things."

He smiled at her.

"When we came to this country, your grandfather hated it. He pretended everything was fine."

"Gus is like that."

"Yes, I know. There have been a lot of good pretenders in this family."

"That's sad."

"Yes, *mi vida.* Very sad."

"Did you hate it here too?"

"No. I pretended. I pretended to hate it. I was a pretender too. But I didn't. I felt free, Charlie. I did. I didn't have to run a house. I didn't have to have servants. I could cook in my own kitchen. I learned English. I learned how to drive a car. It was a miracle for me. I never knew I was in prison until I came here."

"Mexico was a prison?"

"I think it was."

"Grandpa didn't think that."

"No. He didn't. He loved Mexico." She shook her head. "No. What he loved was his idea of Mexico. And someone took that idea away from him."

"And so you had to leave?"

"Yes. We had to leave. And I was free here, free of Mexico."

He pictured Father Hidalgo and the villagers. He pictured them shouting, proclaiming their freedom. He bit his lip. "But Mom said this country was cruel to people. She said they put the poor Mexicans in a camp and didn't want them and called them names when all they were trying to do was to save themselves from the guns of the revolution."

"Your mother's right."

"Why didn't they put you and Grandpa and Dad in a camp?"

"Oh, *amor*, because we had money. Because we had position."

"It's not fair."

"No, *amor*, it's not fair. *All countries are cruel.* You must always remember that."

He thought about his globe and all his maps. "Isn't there any place we can go?"

"Someday we will do away with countries. We'll be better off without them, *amor*." She closed her eyes. He knew she was tired. He waited for a while, then started toward the door. She opened her eyes. "Kiss me," she whispered.

He walked back toward her, smiled, then kissed her. He didn't mind the smell. *"Te adoro, Abuelita,"* he whispered. She liked to hear him speak Spanish. She opened her eyes and nodded. "Play for me," she whispered. She placed her hand on her lips, blew him another kiss, then drifted back to sleep. His mother was always telling him not to tire her out. But he'd done it again. Always asking her too many questions.

He walked back to his room and stared at his globe. He wondered what his globe would look like if there were no countries.

*If you didn't have countries, then maybe you wouldn't need maps.* He took out his diary. And that's what he wrote. And then he wrote: *My grandmother is dying. I can hear it in her voice.* And then he wrote: *Dolores, Mexico, is not on my globe.*

He walked back toward his grandmother's room and opened the door. She was mumbling in her sleep. "I'll play now," he whispered. He walked back down the hall and sat at the piano.

He knew which piece to play.

## lourdes

*Eggs/milk/coffee/bacon/cheese/*
*bread/tortillas/lettuce/tomatoes/*
*flour/sugar/oatmeal/baking powder/*
*ground beef/chicken/fideo/tomato sauce/onions*

On most days she didn't mind the lists, the shopping, the errands, the getting out of the house, the time to be alone, the sitting in the car before and after, listening to a song or two on the radio. But today her husband had said something as he walked out the door. "Try not to spend so much."

"It's food," she said.

"Just try," he said.

He got that way, sometimes, that man, Octavio, her husband, that man whom she knew and did not know. Yes, he got that way. Got worried. About money. Not that they were poor. Not that they were rich. But he worried. Sometimes he mentioned the word *retirement*. She hated that word, had uttered it out loud as she washed the dishes, wondered about where that word came from. Charlie had asked her about it once as it slipped out of her mouth. *Look it up.* Charlie had run to the dictionary: *withdrawn from the business of public life.* She'd nodded. *Yes, it means that your father doesn't have to work anymore.* She remembered the curiosity in Charlie's eyes and his editorial comment. *But it also means this: seclusion, privacy.* He'd smiled. *I think Dad's already retired.*

"Oh, Charlie," she whispered. "Oh Charlie, Charlie, Charlie." She shook her head. "Oh, shit! To hell with retirement." Octavio was only fifty-four. Not old. But ever since he'd introduced that word into their house, he got that look in his eyes. She hated that look. The accusation. The wife who did nothing but spend. The wife who understood nothing of work and money. *In six years, I'll be turning sixty.* And in six months she would be turning forty-five. There was time. For her. Nursing school. The thought entered her head. No, didn't enter, had never left. Becoming an actress, that had left. Becoming a professor of letters, that had left. Becoming a nurse, that had never left. She'd be working in a hospital by now. Octavio's objections would not have stopped her. But there was the fact of her mother-in-law. Her mother-in-law. A fact. A hard and beautiful fact. Most days she didn't mind the sacrifice. Except when he said things: *Try not to spend . . .*

She walked to the frozen food section, selected a gallon of ice cream and a frozen apple pie. Octavio hated frozen food, hated, hated it. She stormed over to the vegetables and looked over the avocados. They were expensive, *try not to . . .* She put four of them in the basket. Bread/milk/eggs/bacon—dammit I hate this, all of this!

"Lourdes, you're scowling."

She put the avocados in the basket. "Avocados. They're expensive."

"You were scowling about avocados?"

"No."

Sylvia smiled at her. "Were your ears ringing?"

"Why?"

"My mother was taking you to task last night."

"About what?"

"Gustavo."

"Gustavo?"

"She holds you responsible."

"Because he doesn't go to Mass?"

"You'll burn in hell."

"I'm sure I will. But for that?" She laughed. "And to make matters worse, I let him wear his hair long."

"Yes, exactly. And you allow him to wear that black armband."

"Black armband. Who does he think he is? What does he think he's doing?"

"And where's his mother?"

"His mother? Well, I wash that armband, sometimes, you know?"

Sylvia laughed.

"Don't laugh."

"I'll tell my mother it's clean."

"I use Tide."

"I'll tell her."

"Why doesn't Octavio get the blame?"

"He's not responsible."

"Why not?"

"Women raise children."

"And men, what do they raise?"

"Crops."

"Right. So women get the blame."

"And if Gustavo becomes a doctor?"

"Octavio will get the credit."

"Right. I see. I don't like your mother's logic."

"She hates herself. Or just other women. She says Gustavo probably has lice."

They laughed.

"It's not funny."

"No, Lourdes, it's not funny. But what am I going to do with her? Shoot her?" She shrugged. "Let's have coffee."

"The ice cream will melt."

"Screw the ice cream."

Lourdes shrugged. "Well—"

"Come gather round people—"

"Are you singing?"

"I love to sing."

"I hate Bob Dylan."

"No you don't."

"Yes I do."

"Nobody hates Bob Dylan."

"He can't sing."

"I love that song."

"The song is fine. Just don't sing."

"Okay. I won't sing. We'll have coffee and I'll tell you all about my husband. How if he hadn't died of a heart attack, I was going to leave him."

Lourdes looked at her but said nothing. She always made announcements like that, brought up serious topics by introducing them as jokes. She hated that habit.

"What's that look on your face?"

"Why?"

"Why? Why was I going to leave him? I thought you didn't like him."

"That's not the point. I wasn't the one who was married to him."

"The *why*'s still on your face."

"You didn't answer the question."

"Because I'm thirty-seven years old."

"And?"

"Because I married him when I was seventeen."

"And?"

"Because he was a beautiful gringo and God knows I like gringos. Because he seemed sad and I thought I could fix what was wrong with him."

"We're getting closer."

"You asked what men raised? In my house, the man raised his fists." Her lip was trembling. "And you know why else I was going to leave him? Because our oldest son enlisted to please him. And shit, Lourdes, he's gone AWOL."

It was strange and beautiful, all that pain in her voice. Lourdes nodded softly. "Let me put the ice cream back." *And the apple pie too.* She smiled. She could see Sylvia was fighting back her tears. "Let's have some coffee."

Sylvia nodded. "You can't let Gustavo go. Lourdes, if they call him, *you can't let him.*"

She placed her hand on Sylvia's shoulder. "Let's have coffee."

"He'll go to jail when they find him."

She grabbed Sylvia gently by the arm. "Come on. Let's get out of here."

"You think he's a coward?"

"Men who go AWOL, they have to be brave. I've always thought that."

Sylvia looked at Lourdes, tears running down her face. "You really believe that?"

"Yes. I really believe that."

## adam

You were eighteen.

You didn't know what you were supposed to do with your life. Except that you wanted your life to matter. You saw your father waste away into nothing. You saw him live his days as if they never mattered. You tell yourself you will not throw your life away as if it were nothing more than a wadded up piece of paper.

Your life will matter. That is why you enlisted.

You did not enlist because they were going to take you anyway.

You did not enlist because you were a true believer.

You did not enlist because you were patriotic.

You did not enlist because you were political. What the hell was that, anyway?

You wanted to go. To fight. To be in a war. A war that could be yours. You did not join because you wanted to save America.

You did not even join because you were going to win the war. It was the fight that mattered.

You wanted to be a man. You were eighteen.

This was the test. You knew you could pass the test.

Politics was nothing. Men who made laws were nothing to you. Just as you were nothing to them.

You wanted a gun and a uniform. And a chance.

So you go and get trained. And the men who train you tear you down. Tear you down until you are nothing. And slowly, slowly, build you back up again. And then you understand that you belong to something bigger than yourself.

You are stronger, more beautiful than you have ever been.

# octavio

Better early than late. That's what Octavio told himself as he sat in the car, windows rolled down, the sky as clear and blue as he'd ever seen. The blueness didn't fool him. He could smell the rain. He could almost taste it on his tongue. Tonight, it would come, he knew it, lightning and thunder, a real storm. He knew about rain.

He lit a cigarette and took out his file, thumbed through it, though he knew it by heart. Thorough. He didn't like overlooking anything, didn't like surprises. If his life was a city, then there was not one piece of litter on the streets. Everything mapped out perfectly.

He put down the file, took a puff from his cigarette, then let out the smoke slowly. He tried to remember why and how he'd gotten into this business of insurance. How had curiosity ended up as a twenty-five-year career? Good money, good job, respectable colleagues, respectable clients, good hours, good money, just right for a man like him, a family man, a man who liked to read, who liked quiet, who liked his words on a page but not his tongue, a man who was good at paper work, a conservative man who could be trusted. A fine thing to be trusted. An insurance man, yes, but a special kind of insurance with special clients, and getting more lucrative every year. Insurance for doctors. *Liability*. The word that fed his family. Who had thought of that? Insurance for clients who always paid up. Brilliant.

There would be a bonus at the end of the year. There had always been a bonus.

His list of clients had grown longer. He didn't mind the Saturday morning appointments, the meetings after-hours. He liked doctors, mostly; well, at least respected them. Some of them drank. Some of them were kind. Some of them weren't fit to be around other people. He knew that. He could see it. But, mostly, they were like anybody else. And Dr. Hallbecker, he was one of his oldest clients, had referred him to others, a good man, liked to talk.

The business part of their appointment would last twenty minutes. But their meeting would last more than an hour—maybe longer. He would listen patiently, the list of complaints about those goddamned lawyers and the patients who refused to take his advice and his bad second marriage and if he'd known he would have stuck with the first one but at least this one was beautiful and knew enough to keep her mouth shut in public and wasn't marriage like an interminable war and *Octavio, I'm glad as hell I wasn't born Catholic, no offense, but that divorce thing . . .* Or maybe today he'd talk about his stint in Korea. *I was just a young medic. Cut my teeth there. . . .* He always had a story about Korea. He didn't mind the stories about the war.

Dr. Chesbrough. A good man. A pain in the ass. Unhappy. But a good doctor. But spoiled too. Liked to be deferred to. Doctors. They were all spoiled and they all complained about money, and they all had too much of it.

But he had a good job, didn't he?

But didn't he hate it? God, it was true. He hated it. Bored him. Twenty-five years. Jesus Christ on a cross. Twenty-five years. What had happened to his life? What had happened to the young man who'd wanted to become an attorney? What had he told himself? What had kept him from packing his bags and leaving for law school, his acceptance letter now lost somewhere among his old letters in the basement?

You couldn't put your heart in a basement.

And whose fault was it anyway? And what the hell. It was a good life. He had nothing to complain about. He provided. His children had never wanted for a thing. Didn't that count? Didn't that matter? Everyone had to swallow a piece of their heart. Everyone had to chew on a stone sometime and pretend it was bread.

He looked at his watch.

He saw Dr. Chesbrough's car pull into the parking lot.

He stepped out of his car with his briefcase. He took a deep breath. You couldn't tell by looking at the sky, but it would come, the rain. He was certain of it.

He was good with doctors. And good, too, at predicting rain.

# gustavo

Y our book. You forgot."

Gustavo turned around and stared at the familiar face. For a second, just one second, the face seemed young. And then it disappeared, that young face, replaced by the face he saw six days a week.

Mr. Ortega waved a book in the air and repeated, "It's yours, yes?"

Gustavo nodded, walked toward him. "Yes. It's mine."

Mr. Ortega studied the book, then studied Gustavo's eyes. "What does it say?"

"It's just a book."

"¿San Agustín?" That question in his eyes.

Gustavo nodded.

"It's good. You read the saints."

Gustavo shrugged. "Yeah, they all had long hair."

"Wise guy."

"Yeah. That's what I am."

"Gringos, they're wise guys. Don't be like the gringos."

"I can't help it."

Mr. Ortega shook his head. *"Agringados todos."*

Gustavo hated that accusation. Of becoming just like the gringos. He didn't get him. He was just like his father—that whole generation—they wanted their sons to stay Mexican. Yet they wanted them to love America, absorb its history, its customs, fight in its wars, fit in, belong, speak English perfectly. And when you fit in and were as American as you could possibly be, they turned around and hated you for it. He smiled. "I'll never be a gringo. I'm a Chicano."

"Chicano? That's bullshit. Don't start with that shit."

"Okay," he said. "But if I'm not a gringo and I'm not a Mexican, what the hell am I? I'm a Chicano, that's what."

Mr. Ortega handed him his book, a sign he didn't want to have this discussion. "What does it say, this book?"

He knew the real question. *Why are you reading it?*

"There's things in it," he said. "Things about Chicanos."

He laughed. "Wise guy."

"Yeah. *Agringado.*"

"I've seen you reading it when you eat your lunch."

"I like to read."

"That's good. Where did you buy the book?"

"I borrowed it from my father."

"Your father, he reads?"

"Yes."

"It's his book?"

"Yes."

"You shouldn't leave your father's books lying around in a garage. Have respect."

Gustavo nodded. "Yes, sir."

"You like the book?"

"Yes. It's fine. I like all kinds of books." He nodded, smiled at Mr. Ortega. "I like Shakespeare. He had long hair too."

Mr. Ortega laughed. "I don't understand you. You listen to shit rock music and read the saints. You're crazy. Go home. Bother somebody else." He took out a folded check from his front pocket. "Here. You forgot your check. Don't get drunk. And don't smoke that marijuana shit."

Gustavo laughed. "Yes, sir."

*. . . There is one war after another, havoc everywhere, tremendous slaughterings of men.*

*All this for peace. Yet, when the wars are waged, there are new calamities brewing. To begin with, there never has been, nor is there today, any absence of hostile foreign powers to provoke war. . . . Massacres, frequent and sweeping hardships too dire to endure are but a part of the ravages of war. I am utterly unable to describe them as they are, and as they ought to be described; and even if I should try to begin, where could I end?*

Gustavo put down the book. He wondered what his father thought about the writings of St. Augustine. Every time he read a book he always wondered what someone else would think—maybe because he knew he had a strange way of looking at things. *You translate Augustine differently than Dad and that's a fact.* That's what Xochil had said. She was probably right. And anyway it was useless to read Augustine. Everything was useless. Some days, he knew exactly what he believed and didn't need Augustine or anybody else to give him fucking permission. Other days, he didn't know anything, didn't know what he felt, what he thought, what he should do. Were wars wrong? How the hell did he know? Was it right that his country was in Vietnam? Was it? How the hell did he know? *No one died and left you God.* Xochil loved saying that to him. *Are you a pacifist?* Conrad had professed to be that, a pacifist, had talked endlessly to him about how he'd arrived at his position. *But don't you just want to hit somebody sometimes?* Conrad had just looked at him. Well, screw it, he wasn't a pacifist and wouldn't pretend to be one. So why was he reading Augustine's *City of God*? Why was he looking for what he had to say about a just war? *A country who wages war has to be moral and legitimate. . . .* Conrad's voice in his head—Conrad, who was so sure, Conrad, who was a good Catholic, Conrad, who was gentle and smart and good and decent. He would never hurt anybody. He was like Charlie. They didn't even know how to make a fist. They knew something about the city of God, how to build it. Well, at least they dreamed it.

He shut the book. He'd go home and put it back on his father's shelf.

## abe

I kept running my hand over my buzz.

Look, the truth is that I missed my hair. But I was also free of it. *You'll look at the world differently, son.* That's what my father said. And already it was happening. I was fucking free. But it was weird.

The drill instructor took an instant dislike to me. I didn't take it personally. He took an instant dislike to all of us. It was part of the whole deal. And the other thing was that I lost my first name. My name wasn't Abe anymore. My name was Williams. Williams and "maggot." I shared that name with everyone else.

We lost our names along with our hair.

I was tired as hell.

Apart from the fact that hangovers made you feel like crap, they also made you dog tired. My hangover was written all over my face and my DI made the most of the opportunity. My DI, he never lost a chance to make you feel like scum.

"All that booze make you a man, maggot?"

"No, sir."

"You smell like shit."

"Yes, sir."

"You're lower than whale shit."

"Yes, sir."

"You know why you're lower than whale shit, maggot?"

"No, sir."

"Why don't you know, maggot?"

"I don't know, sir."

"You don't know? You don't know? I'll tell you why, maggot. Whale shit, it sits at the bottom of the ocean."

"Yes, sir."

"And you're even lower than that. And that's low, maggot."

"Yes, sir."

"That's low, maggot. Do you hear me?"

"Yes, sir."

"Repeat after me, maggot."

"Yes, sir."

"I am lower than whale shit."

"I am lower than while shit, sir."

I thought I'd yes-sir my way into hell. After all the yes-sirring, I was on the ground. I'd never done so many fucking push-ups and squat thrusts in my goddamned life. I thought my lungs were gonna fucking bust. I swear.

I tried to imagine my father as a young Marine. I tried to imagine everyone I'd ever known as a Marine. Even Gustavo. Hell, the guy didn't know it, but he had all the makings of a great Marine. Him and his anger and all those smarts. A great fucking Marine. Our DI would have kicked his ass into shape. But you had to want this. Otherwise, you were fucking dead, and Gustavo, something inside him was all wrong. He wasn't put together like me or Jack Evans. He would never let himself give in to the idea. *Marine* was not a word in his fucking dictionary. I just didn't get that. Maybe I got Conrad a little more. I mean, he wasn't angry about anything. I don't know. There was something about Conrad that kind of followed me around. Nah, Conrad and Gustavo and Marine—those things just didn't go.

So there I was that night, thinking about all these things that I didn't want to think about and guys I didn't even like. Why wasn't I thinking about my dad? Why wasn't I thinking about my mom? Shit.

When I got woken up the next day, it felt like I'd slept for a couple minutes. It was dark and I stumbled out of bed, confused. That first night was the last time I stayed up thinking. After that, my body was so tired that all it wanted to do was sleep.

For the rest of my time at basic training, I would be hungry for sleep.

# lourdes

*He'd just blown up at me. I went to my room. And I was*
*thinking: Thank God he didn't hit me this time. Thank God*
*he didn't hit me? That's what my life had become? That was*
*my life? And then I heard a strange sound in the living room.*
*I don't know. I was hiding in my room. That's what I was do-*
*ing. But something made me go out into the living room. And*
*there he was, in convulsions, clutching at his chest.*

*He was dead by the time the ambulance came.*

Lourdes sat in the car and listened to Sylvia's voice in her head.
Her life had been one thing and now it was another. *That's what*
*my life had become?* Become? Was it as passive as all that? Were
we as stationary as trees in the wind? Did we just let life take us
along as if human beings were no more sentient than the water
a river swept to the sea? She wondered if Sylvia would have really left her husband. She was talking a good line now. What

had prevented her from leaving him? When was she going to begin living her life instead of hiding in her room? And her? *Her*—Lourdes Espejo—what prevented her from—from what? From doing what?

She thought of Rosario, whose life had become a waiting to die. Like Sylvia, she did nothing but wait. Just like a million women in the world, waiting for something to happen, something, anything. Is that what her marriage had become? A waiting? Sylvia had done nothing to change her life. Were it not for her husband's bad heart, she would still be waiting. So was life reduced to the something in between the waiting?

What did it mean then, to live? To live one's life?

Gustavo and Xochil, they were impatient with their inheritance. The lives they had been given—they weren't enough for them. Greedy children, they wanted more. More than to walk on familiar streets. More than to buy and sell and die. They did not want their lives merely *to become.* She thought of Gustavo, remembered his refusal to go hunting. She remembered the day he faced his father and said, "I won't go to Mass. I don't believe." A boy holding firm, trying to have integrity and dignity without even knowing the words. A boy whose mind and heart flew in the face of all their conventions and habits and rituals—conventions and habits and rituals that they all loved more than they loved the children they gave life to. Gustavo. Trying to live his life. And Xochil too. Such brave and beautiful children.

She found herself angry at Octavio. She chastised herself. Then chastised herself again—for chastising herself. Why shouldn't she be angry? Why shouldn't she be? Such a careful man, her husband.

But so careless with his children. She forgave him everything—but not that.

# charlie. gustavo.

Gustavo sat on the front steps, tired and lazy as the desert breeze. "Sometimes I think I'm just gonna fuckin' die." He scanned the street, his black eyes calm, steady, almost inanimate, a camera taking a photograph. Except that he wasn't taking in the scene, not really, not the scene directly in front of his black, steady eyes: the old brick Victorians that littered the neighborhood, the trees that looked as old and weathered as the generation that planted them, the adolescent boys who rode up and down the sidewalks wishing their hand-me-down bikes would miraculously turn into motorcycles haloed with chrome, wishing a girl was hanging on to them, wishing they could will themselves into becoming men instead of the bony, inarticulate boys they were. But Gustavo took in nothing of the sincere, pedestrian dramas unfolding before him. Perhaps he was looking past the scene, a sage, a seer, a shaman. Perhaps, like most young men, he was afflicted with blindness, incapable of comprehending the beauty of the facts before him. It was as if his immutable gaze dispensed with the physical world.

Charlie looked over at his older brother and smiled to himself—Gustavo was practicing being hard again. He was so afraid of being soft, as if soft was something bad, unacceptable, repugnant. And so he was always trying to make himself into something unbreakable. But he was more flesh than stone, and nothing he said or did could ever change that.

Sometimes, when he spoke, his words always had an edge, like a knife, like he meant each word to hurt, to stab, to cut. Like he didn't care who the violence touched or wounded or scarred, like he was letting loose the thoughtless, sharpened knife that he kept inside and he didn't care who it would wound or hurt or slice, as if blood was nothing, not his own blood, not anybody's blood, nothing. Blood. He could be mean and ugly like that when he spoke. But when he was still and quiet, his face and eyes were kind, as kind and good as anything, as kind and soft as an orange poppy in bloom, as kind and tender as the leaves of a mesquite, as kind and sweet as his sister's voice when she sang to her sleeping grandmother. A kind face, absolutely—unless he was angry, and in those moments he was frightening, his expression turning as wild as his hair, a gale blowing through him, a moment of chaos so pure that it was not only startling but very nearly beautiful, like lightning reflecting off the surface of the desert.

Gustavo unlaced his boots, pushed them down the steps and watched them fall. "Just fuckin' gonna die."

"Of what, Gus?" Only Charlie was allowed to call him Gus.

"Of fuckin' afternoons like this."

Charlie laughed. He wanted to reach over and hug his older brother. He hated that urge, that reflex or whatever it was, hated, hated it. That kind of thing wasn't allowed, a rule, strict; he knew the rules, wrote them down in his head and his heart, all of them. Boys were exempt from the rules, and he'd loved those years of exemption, but they were gone now—not a boy anymore—of age now. He knew that a part of him would always be uncomfortable in this place, this residence, this harsh address. He did not want to live there. But there was nothing he could do about it. He remembered he had overheard his uncle telling his father, "*Ése chico,* he'll always be a little tender, *manzito.*" He knew the remark was not intended as a compliment. *Manzito. Tame.* A toothless animal. Still, he knew there were other rules that would help him survive. He could still hug Xochil. That was good. Sweet as raindrops on the tongue. Sweet as Mexican candy. Almost like going to communion.

"Fuckin' die of afternoons like this," Gustavo repeated.

"What's wrong with afternoons like this?"

"There's nothing."

"Nothing?"

"You'll never get it, Charlie. All you know how to be is content."

Content. The way he said it. An insult. Charlie opened his mouth, then shut it.

"Charlie, you can sit on the front porch all frickin' day long and never get tired. You look out and daydream or read a book or even read the *pinche* clouds. I've watched you sit still for hours. You're like a fuckin' statue. Like one of those angels in church. Even Xochil says you are."

"Leave Xochil out of this. Look, I'm not made of stone."

"What's wrong with statues?"

"They're not people."

"Well, sometimes you're so still you *are* more like a stone. More like a stone than a human being. Hate to break it to you, Charlie."

"Not true, Gus." Charlie pinched his arms, the best argument he could think of to refute his brother's awful claims. "See. Look. I'm not."

"All right—maybe you're not a statue. Maybe you're just a frickin' angel."

He pinched himself again. "Angels don't have skin. Look. *Look.*"

Gustavo held back a smile, but the grin was there, in his eyes. "All right, but I never met a guy could read so many damned frickin' books. You're so fuckin' content it makes me want to spit."

"You read more books than me, Gus."

"No."

"Yes."

"No."

"Yes. And what's so bad about staying calm? Isn't that what you're saying—I'm too calm? What's so bad about that?"

"Shit, bro, look around you. We're fucked. And you're sittin' there like a goddamned cow eatin' alfalfa."

"Knock it off. You're making me mad. You always do that."

"Do what?"

"Make me mad—that's what you do. And put me down."

Gustavo reached across and slapped his brother lightly several times. "I'm not putting you down, bro, I'm just trying to describe you. Trying to get at what you're like, bro."

"Bro, bro, bro, what's that?"

"It means brother. It means we're cool."

"Cool? You don't know shit, Gus."

"I'm not a fucking idiot, Joe."

"Don't call me Joe—I hate that."

Gustavo let loose a smile. Straightest, whitest teeth in all of Sunset Heights. "I'm just telling you that you don't know shit about being bored—that's all I'm saying. Look, some people don't have it in them. Some people are just, well, you know, they're just kind of peaceful. You know, just, you know, peaceful. That would be you." He pressed his finger into Charlie's heart. He took a cigarette out of his shirt pocket and looked at it as if it were something astonishing, something he'd never seen, not ever. He tapped his cigarette on his wrist, took a matchbook from his shirt pocket, tore out a match, struck it. Jesus, it was good, his cigarette. He sucked the smoke into his lungs, held it for a long second, then let it out into the clear, September day, his smoke the only blemish in the pure and spotless sky. Charlie watched the cigarette smoke float into the clear blue of the afternoon. He could sit on this porch forever and watch his brother smoke and talk. And talk. And talk. And smoke and talk. About anything. All day. All night. His voice. Sometimes deep. Sometimes higher, softer, a tenor about to break into song.

"What year is it?"

It was a game they played. Something Gustavo made up. For the longest time, it was something between Gustavo and Xochil. And that was okay, because they were twins and twins had something between them. That was another rule, a rule everyone knew about. The twin rule was the most unbreakable rule of all. But as he grew older, they let him in. First, they let him watch. And then one day they let him play. The game. Charlie clapped his hands and smiled. "It's 1967."

"And what's the most important thing that's happened in 1967?"

They both looked at each other and laughed.

"Dad bought a car!"

Gustavo stuck out his right thumb. "Yup. Dad bought a car. A brand-new Chevy Impala—blue as the *pinche* sky."

Charlie broke out singing, *"See the U.S.A. in your Chevrolet . . . "*

Gustavo shook his head. Sometimes, his little brother, sometimes—hell, he couldn't help but smile. "Okay, that was important. But it wasn't the most important thing. Nope, not by a long shot." He winced, then blew the smoke out of his nose. He looked old right then, older than eighteen. Like he'd been a man for a long time. Xochil, she had that look too, that look that reminded people that she was strong and untouchable, that warned people not to come too close because she knew something that could break you.

But Charlie wasn't afraid. Not of Xochil. Not of Gus. They'd never hurt him. He nodded. "Okay, I got it. Mom yelled at Dad in front of his poker-playing pals."

"That was a moment, wasn't it? One for the record books, I'd say. Xochil really got off on the look on Dad's face. That was good—tough stuff. Bitchin' as all fucking get out—but it wasn't the most important."

"Okay. I got it. You graduated from high school."

Gustavo stuck the cigarette in his mouth and locked his hands in the back of his head. He mumbled through the cigarette. "Think, Charlie. How important could that be, *ése?*"

He smiled at the word *ése*. He liked that word. His father hated it, said it wasn't a word worthy of them. "Well, *ése*," he said, trying to keep from laughing. "Dad said it was a miracle from God."

"Dad always thinks the worst things about everything. He's the original pessimist." He raised his arms and stretched.

"He's proud of you."

"He's not proud of me, Charlie. He's not proud of anyone."

"Yes, he is, Gus. You know he is."

"Look, Charlie, I'm not gonna fight with you, not on this one. He's proud, okay, proud. Yeah, fuckin' sure. It's a diploma, Charlie. Any idiot can graduate from high school. It just means I can read and I can write and that I can put up with teachers who don't get paid enough to love me. The thing is, Charlie, that I'm not great at adding up numbers—which is fuckin' okay because I haven't got a dollar in my worthless Mexican pockets. Shit."

"But don't you have money now that you're working?"

"Sure. I'm a fucking millionaire."

"You might be. Someday. It could happen."

"Nope."

"Sure it could."

"Not to me, Charlie. Now, Xochil, she's something. She's really something. And she knows a few things. And she's smart. Einstein smart. And she's got something inside of her that's bluer than Dad's Impala and bluer than any sky you'll ever see if you live to be a hundred. Yeah, she's something. Not me. Listen to me, Charlie, are you listening? Graduating from El Paso High wasn't the most important fucking thing that happened in 1967."

Charlie nodded. He was breaking the rules of the game. It wasn't supposed to get serious. Not ever. He thought a moment. "Oh, I got it! I got it!"

"What?"

"Music, Gus!"

"Now, you're talking. Now you're fuckin' talking. That's the most important thing."

Charlie smiled. He was back on track. That's the way the game went—Gus was always in charge and he made up the rules as he went along. The game depended on his mood. The game depended on what was on his mind. All Charlie had to do was keep guessing until he hit the right spot in his brother's head.

"And, my favorite song is?"

"Let me see. Wait, wait—"

"Name three. Can you name three?" Gustavo took a final drag from his cigarette and tossed the butt down the steps, aiming for his boots.

"Okay, okay, I got it. Let's see, 'Respect,' that's one."

"Aretha!" He said her name like he was friends with her. "That's good, that's good, keep going."

" 'Somebody to Love.' "

"Jefferson Airplane—that's fuckin' excellent."

"And anything by Johnny Rivers."

"Johnny Rivers, bro? C'mon, hey, that's passé, baby."

"Okay. I got it. The Doors."

"Yesss! The Doors."

" 'Light My Fire.' "

Gustavo laughed. "I'm fuckin' impressed."

"Sure you are."

"Fuckin' impressed. I mean it. And what else?"

"You said three."

"You're on a roll, baby."

" 'Purple Haze.' "

"Yessssss! My man Jimi! *I am fucking impressed.* I mean I am, Charlie."

Charlie smiled and looked down at the cement steps. "And mine, Gus?"

"Let's see. You always like those candy ass songs."

"Knock it off. I can like anything I want."

"Yeah, that's right, free country, oh yes. Free, free, free. They're fightin' in Nam so you can listen to anything you fuckin' want."

"Don't mess with me like that, Gus."

"Me? Mess with you? Not me, Charlie. Let's see, now, you like Simon and Garfunkel."

"You're making fun."

"I'm not. They're cool. You know, in that gringo kind of way that's way urban white cool. New York cool. But you know, they don't know shit about Chicanos."

"No one knows shit about Chicanos. Not even the Doors."

Gustavo winced. "What do you know, anyway?"

"I know. I fucking know, Gus."

"Hey, hey, nice mouth."

"You say *fuck* all the time."

"How old are you?"

"Fourteen."

"Fourteen, bro?"

"Well, okay, I'll be fourteen in three months."

"So that makes you what, thirteen? I bet you don't even get it up yet."

"Knock it off, Gus—"

"You're blushing. Just like a gringo."

"Knock it off. I mean it, Gus. And you know what? Mom says you sometimes act like you're ten."

"Yeah, Mom, well, you know, she's Mom."

Charlie nodded. "Yeah. But she's great."

"Yeah, she is great. But you think everyone's great."

"No, I don't."

"Yes, you do. Look, bro, that's a good thing. You're a good little guy. I think you should keep it that way."

Good little guy. He hated that.

"Yup, you like Simon and Garfunkel—and you like the Monkees, too."

"Everyone likes the Monkees."

"Everyone who's thirteen. They suck, bro. They really suck."

"Well, I like Peter, Paul, and Mary—and I like that song 'Society's Child.'"

"Peter Paul and Mary, huh?" He seemed to be studying the sky. Not that he was really studying anything. " 'Society's Child,' huh? Yeah? That's good. That's way cool, Charlie. Maybe there's some hope for you. But you know, that song's way too old for a little guy like you."

*Little guy.* Charlie hated that.

## lourdes. octavio.

Lourdes Espejo looked out the living room window, awed by her two sons on the front porch—talking, laughing, sometimes even touching. They were beautiful. Together and separately—beautiful in ways that only boys could be and only mothers could appreciate. And beautiful in such singular and different ways. It was obvious to her that most young women who had the good or bad fortune of encountering her oldest son would halfway fall in love with him. Seduction was part of his genetic makeup, the graceful, casual way he inhabited his own body—so graceful that you didn't even call it grace. But there was also something dangerous about him—*and even that* was a part of his beauty, part of what made you look at him. Young women liked to flirt with danger, especially young women who didn't understand how easily a life could be ruined.

Her younger son was arresting, lovely, fragile. His face, a magnet. She saw the way people stared at him, as if they could hardly believe such a creature existed. A woman at a shop asked her once, "Is he real?" She'd nodded and smiled, but she herself had asked herself the same question. Despite his almost feminine features, he was stronger than most suspected, and she wished all men possessed his kind of poise—the kind of man who was incapable of making you afraid, the kind of man who would rather absorb pain than inflict it. He simply didn't comprehend cruelty. She asked him once why he had lent his notes out to the girl down the street. *"She's taking advantage of you."*

*He smiled and shook his head. "No, she's not."*

*"But they're your notes."*

*"It doesn't matter, Mom."*

*"She's just using you. She doesn't even like you."*

*"I don't think I like her very much, either."*

*"Then why are you helping her?"*

*"Because I want to."*

*"But she'll get a good grade using your notes."*

*"Why does that matter?"*

*"You're helping her cheat."*

*"How would it help if she flunked?"*

*"Then maybe she'd study."*

*"No. She'd just flunk. She's poor. Her dad's a drunk. What does she have? She'd flunk, Mom. I don't want that."*

She smiled at the memory. No one could talk him out of anything once he decided on a course of action. Because he was kind, you hardly noticed his stubbornness. She had stopped being afraid for him.

It was Gustavo she was afraid for. He was easily wounded, despite the mask he wore. Like his father, he did not possess the necessary tools to handle pain when it came his way. He would get hurt. That hurt would disfigure him. She was sure of that. What then? What would become of all that beauty?

She clutched at the curtain as she saw Gustavo laugh at something Charlie said. She had always been surprised by the great affection they shared. She couldn't help but smile as she watched them. Playing—that's what they were doing, what they did. Because they were boys.

"Are you spying on them again?"

She stood motionless for an instant, then answered her accuser without bothering to turn around. "I like to watch my sons."

"Why is it you never watch Xochil that way?"

"Xochil isn't a foreign thing."

"Maybe that's because she's just like you."

She turned around and faced her husband. "Is she?"

"Yes. Even the way she laughs."

"I'm not so sure. I think it's Gustavo who's more like me."

"He's not like you at all. Gustavo's not like anyone." He nodded to himself.

He was filing something away. It was like he had pockets inside him where he kept things so he could take them out at just the right moment. Lourdes half cursed herself for noticing every small detail about her husband. It wasn't always a good thing to know someone so well. Surprises were hard to come by.

"You like to watch them too much, Lourdes."

She turned around and watched them again, Charlie frowning at some callous remark his brother had uttered. Her older son was careless with his words. And Charlie was so literal about everything. "Better to watch your sons than to watch television."

"Depends on what you're watching. Television can be enlightening."

"Watching your sons can be even more enlightening. They're good together. That's a beautiful thing."

Octavio nodded. "Well, maybe not so beautiful. I don't want Gustavo infecting Charlie."

"Infecting?"

"That's the word."

"He's not a disease."

"He has ideas."

"Which only means he has a mind."

"Not much of one, I don't think."

"He has a very fine mind, *amor*. Better than most."

"Is that why he hangs posters of revolutionaries and prostitutes on his bedroom walls?"

"César Chávez is fighting for good pay, *amor*. Good pay for workers. I don't see anything revolutionary in that. Imagine, workers getting paid for what they do." She let the curtain drop from her grasp. "And Jane Fonda is an actress, *amor*, not a prostitute."

"All actresses are prostitutes."

"And Mexicans eat nothing but beans."

"Are you picking a fight with me?"

"Today, *amor*, I'm up for a fight if you are."

Octavio shook his head. He wasn't at his best—not today. "You spend your days looking for ways to excuse his behavior."

"I spend my days caring for your mother, *amor*, and taking care of this house." She knew how to silence him, an easy enough art.

He took out a cigarette and lit it. "It doesn't do any good to defend him."

"From what? From whom?" She turned around and faced him. "What exactly has Gustavo done to make you dislike him?"

"I don't dislike him."

"Maybe that's the wrong word. Maybe the word is stronger than dislike."

"You always get that look on your face when you're accusing me of something."

"What look?"

"Damn it to hell, Lourdes, I don't dislike my own son."

"Cursing, *amor*? Is that for emphasis? I can do that too. I can roll around in the mud with the best of them. Is that what you want?"

"I want you to discipline your son."

"Because you can't?"

"Because you find everything he does acceptable." He got up from his chair, walked up to where he kept his liquor, and poured himself a healthy bourbon. He turned to his wife. "Would you like something?"

"A Tía Maria and a new husband."

"I can take care of the Tía Maria. The new husband is up to you." He was surprised by the sound of his own laughter.

She joined in, why not, yes, sure, why not? He could be charming—even now.

He poured her the dark coffee liqueur in one of her favorite crystal glasses. He walked across the room and handed his wife her drink. He peered out the window. "He wears armbands. They're black. Like his eyes. He says he hates war—but then hangs up posters of Che Guevara? Did he think our revolution was bloodless?"

"Ours? Which one was ours, Octavio?"

"We're American, Lourdes."

"Well, yes, since we have to choose." A look of impatience moved over her face, then disappeared. "Well, anyway, what difference does it make which revolution? American, Mexican, French, Russian, they're all marinated in blood."

"Marinated?"

"That's the word." She kept her smile far away from her lips. She studied Octavio's face, the look of disapproval that was so intimate and familiar. "We turn men into meat, isn't that so? Aren't wars like favorite dishes?"

"I'd forgotten you'd once wanted to be an actress."

"Changing the subject insults us both."

He offered her a puzzled smile. He thought a moment, focusing his attention back to her absurd expression. "Marinated," he repeated.

She could almost touch his disdain. Wars to a man like her husband were honorable and noble and she was impatient with his romantic notions of soldiers and warriors and the sacrifice of their blood. "Marinated," she said again.

"You think revolutions shouldn't be fought because people die?"

"People don't die in revolutions, they get killed."

"Killed. Yes. Fine, Lourdes. But revolutions are necessary. We both know that, *corazón*."

"Which revolutions are necessary? Which ones? Fidel Castro's? Russia's?"

"Not all revolutions are of equal—"

"Now we get to it."

"Are we fighting about the merits of the revolutions of the world?" He shook his head. He would not argue, did not want to argue with her about this subject when there could be no agreement. "All I'm trying to say, *corazón*, is that Gustavo doesn't know a damn thing about war."

"Che Guevara isn't a person, *amor*—not to him. He's an idea. War? Revolutions? He hasn't a clue. I think we should keep it that way, don't you, *corazón*?"

"Are you mocking me?"

She pointed her face at him. "Because I called you *corazón*?" She smiled.

"Men learn to work, and part of their work is to learn about war. It's what we're born to."

"It's women who are born to work, Octavio. And the last time I looked, it was women, not war, who turned boys into men."

He laughed, then breathed in the smell of the bourbon. He

took a sip, then held it on his tongue. "By the time I got to Italy, the war was almost over. All I did was pick up bodies."

"And that made you a man?"

"I never said it did."

"You're contradicting yourself, Octavio."

"Am I?"

"And so you're telling me picking up bodies didn't make you hate the war?"

"It made me hate the Germans. It made me hate Mussolini."

Lourdes put the crystal glass to her lips. It was cold. Not even winter yet. "He says he won't go."

"Go?"

"To Vietnam."

"You encouraged him?"

"He says he won't die for something he doesn't believe in."

"You practically put the words in his mouth, Lourdes."

"The only thing I put in his mouth is the food he eats." She took a sip from her liqueur. "I listened, Octavio. It's not a crime for a mother to listen to her son."

*"You should take that armband off—before your father gets home."*

*Gustavo listened as the water from the tap cracked the ice in his glass. "I'm not afraid of him."*

*"That's not the point."*

*"What is the point, Lourdes?"*

*"I'm not Lourdes, I'm your mother."*

*He tapped his cheek as if to slap himself. "Sorry." He drank down the water, part of it cold, part of it still tepid, then sat at the kitchen table. "What good's the quiet, Mom?"*

*"The quiet's good for reading."*

*"This family's overread."*

*"Overread?"*

*"We read too much. Doesn't seem to help us get along, does it?"*

He smiled, laughed, shook his head. "Mom, you can't spend your life playing referee."

"I have spent my life playing referee."

"Then you have to stop."

"You don't agree on the war. Just leave it."

"We don't agree on anything. And leaving it doesn't do any good. I feel like all my words are stuck in my throat. I can't breathe."

She knew what that was like. "You can say the words, mi amor."

"Just not to him, is that it, Mom?"

"That's right."

"Why does it have to be that way?"

She placed her hand on the black armband, searched for the knot, then began to untie it. "Where did you get this?"

"I have some friends. We get together."

"Starting a revolution, are you?"

"Not much of one." He laughed.

"He won't listen. Here, I'll wash this for you."

"Great. Okay, Mom, wash it." He felt her unloosen the knot and watched her as she held the black cloth in her hand. "What happens if I don't go?"

She searched his black eyes and wondered where they came from. Some other continent. Some unreachable place. Eyes with a different history, a different future. Yes, she hoped a different future. But didn't they come from her, those eyes, from a part of her she'd buried?

"What happens if I don't go, Mom? What will happen to me?"

He waited for her to nod.

She looked away.

"Mom, I don't know if I can go. If I can't die for something I don't believe in, why should I kill for it?"

What will you do? She did not ask him the question. She stood over him and kissed the top of his head. He smelled clean. Still new in this decaying world. Still a boy. "What should I make for dinner?"

"Arroz con pollo."

*"Your father's favorite dish."*

*"Mine too."*

*"Peace at last."*


"You know he'll have to go—if his country calls."

"I hate that expression. His country barely knows him."

"You're being unreasonable."

"You have so much faith in the rules and reasons of nations. Where did you get that, Octavio? Where did you learn to believe everything a country told you to believe?"

"We owe allegiance—"

"To what, Octavio?"

"This country has been good to us."

"I have been good to you, too, *amor*."

"You're talking like a—"

"Don't say Communist. I go to Mass every Sunday."

"I wasn't going to say Communist."

"What were you going to say?"

"Like an ingrate."

"Like an ingrate?" Even she was surprised by the bitter taste in her mouth as she laughed. *"I'm talking like a mother, Octavio. A mother who doesn't want anything to happen to her son."*

"Nothing will happen."

"You don't know that."

"Nothing will happen. He'll go. He'll fight. He'll come back."

"But he'll be different."

"Yes. In some ways he'll be harder. In some ways he'll be softer."

"Except he'll hide the softness."

"He already does that."

She looked at her husband. "I'm surprised you notice."

"Lourdes, he's my son."

"Yes. Your son." She turned her head toward the window again. "The world never changes, does it?"

"It's a small conflict, Lourdes."

"It isn't so small for the men who die, Octavio. And for what?"

"For ideas, Lourdes."

"I'd rather die for bread."

He shook his head. They were silent for a moment. It was a lie, what she'd said. Even she knew that. "This country is an idea, *amor*, is that so bad?"

"Well, it's a good deal more than that, isn't it?" She cleared her throat. "It's so easy to say that, Octavio. But whose idea is it? Mine? Yours? Whose? Tell me. It's one thing to put up a poster—it's quite another to pick up arms." She wanted to scream, lecture, say everything she'd ever felt about the dirty business of war and manhood and everything else that had been scarring and scratching at her heart—but she stopped herself. That's what she was best at—stopping herself. She turned around and combed her husband's hair with her fingers, a tender habit she'd developed over the many years they'd been together. She took a deep breath and let it out slowly, almost as if she were smoking a cigarette. "I promise you I'll never make you die for my ideas, *amor*. Promise me you'll never make me die for yours."

"What are you talking about, Lourdes?"

"If they take Gustavo—"

"If they take Gustavo, it will be his own damned fault."

"What are you saying?"

"He knows the rules—but no, he wanted to wait before he went to college. First thing he does after he graduates is get a job at Benny's Body Shop."

"He likes his job."

"Likes his job? I didn't raise him to be a common laborer."

"Whatever happened to our respect for the working man?"

"It's got nothing to do with respect. That's not the kind of work I want for my son. What is he doing with that good mind you claim he has?"

"He's eighteen. He has time to find himself."

"Oh yes, that's what they all say now—they need to find themselves. What in the hell does that mean exactly? It sounds like an excuse. Look at Xochil, she started attending college two weeks ago. But Gustavo, he's left himself open—"

"So, if he goes to war, it's *his* fault? He's a boy, Octavio. He wears the armor of a man—but he's a boy. And by what logic do we blame him for our world, for our ideas, *amor? We are the adults. And damn us to hell for what we do to our children. I did not birth a son to put a rifle in his hand. And what will happen to Xochil if she loses him? Did you ever think of that?*"

He smiled at her, as if the smile might ease the rage in her voice. "You're still that fierce girl I married."

"I'm afraid that fierce girl has acquired a politics."

"Well, what's a lioness without teeth?"

They stared at each other, their smiles breaking into laughter. They knew exactly how to keep the truce.

He pulled her close to him. "If he goes, he'll come back. He'll marry. He'll have children. That's the way the world is."

"Yes," she whispered, "that's the way the world is." She pressed herself into him, the clean smell of the soap he used filling her, and for a moment, she remembered the first time she had ever washed his shirts, how she had been lost in that sweet and lovely and perfect task.

"Nothing will happen, Lourdes."

She pulled away from him.

The crystal glass had warmed in her hand.

She'd been of no comfort to Gustavo when he came to her. What will happen to me? She looked out the window and stared at them, her sons, her Gustavo, her Carlos. Still talking. Still laughing. It was September. But it could've been summer. Yes, yes, yes, it was still summer. What could happen on such a perfect afternoon?

She took a drink.

*If I can't die for something I don't believe in ...*

The taste of sweet liqueur.

*Why should I kill for it? Why?*

Nothing bad would happen.

# adam

Da Nang, Vietnam, September 16, 1967

---

Dear Adam,

   I hope and pray this letter finds you safe. Your last letter
made me a little sad. I know you signed up for this war and
I know you believe in what you're doing. I know you're a real
patriotic guy and I've always tried to respect that. And you were
always pretty clear about what you thought about my attitude.
I've always believed that we're all entitled to our differences. Not
everyone has to be the same. Everyone has a right to believe
what they want. But I have to tell you that you had no right to
call Jim all those names. You filled up an entire paragraph with
curse words. What gives you the right? Just because you're like
a brother to me and just because you're fighting a war doesn't
give you the right. Let me tell you that my Jim doesn't call you

names, now does he? I know there are other guys who are starting to call you guys over in Vietnam all kinds of things but you
won't ever hear those names from me. Or from Jim, either, for
that matter. He's a peaceful man. Gentle in ways most people
don't understand. Why is it a man can't be gentle? Tell me,
Adam, why is that?

And my Jim, he was willing to go to jail, but I talked him
out of it. My parents don't forgive me. My old man called me
a fucking bitch and a disgrace and a traitor and a goddamned
ingrate. And other things too. Well, you know him, so you can
picture all of it without too much trouble. And, hell, let's not put
all of what's wrong with us on our disagreement about this thing
in Vietnam. Me and my parents have been fighting our own war
since I was eight. Me marrying a "peacenik" was the last straw, I
guess, but my Jim isn't a cartoon character. He's flesh and bone
and he's my heart. And you, too, Adam, you're a piece of my
heart and that's the truth. And I just can't let that go.

Me and Jim, we're applying for Canadian citizenship. We're
never coming back. Does that mean we can't be friends? I've
always believed you were good and decent and I still do. You
were the first boy that ever kissed me. The first boy that ever
looked at me. You probably don't even remember what you said
to me that day. We were in the eighth grade and my dad had
taken a belt to me and I was smarting—but mostly hurting on
the inside. And you said, "You don't deserve that. Not a pretty
girl like you."

Words can heal. I guess you know that, don't you? Your
words that day, they made a real difference to me. And I never
thanked you. I don't know if you want me to keep on writing to
you, but until you tell me not to, these letters are going to keep
coming. Evelyn said to leave you alone. She can be mean and
stubborn and as rough as hands that pick cotton. The last thing
she said to me was that she was glad I was moving to Canada
so she wouldn't ever have to look at me again. She said I was a

pothead and that all I was good for was licking coward's asses. There wasn't any use in arguing with her.

I guess we're all taking sides. Is that the way it is with us? Are we still friends?

Love,
Stacy

P.S. I hope you're still taking pictures. You got a gift. Everyone says so.

---

"You're readin' that fuckin' letter again?"

"You writin' a book?"

"If I knew how to write a fuckin' book, you think I'd be here right now?"

"Which one you readin'? The one from Evelyn or the one from Stacy?"

"Stacy."

"I knew it."

"If you know so goddamned much then why are you asking?"

"You know what I think?"

"Shit. Here it comes. Here it fuckin' comes."

"I think you fuckin' hate the fact that Stacy signed that letter, love. You hate that. I mean you really fuckin' hate that. Makes it hard for you to fuckin' hate her. Besides, mostly you hate her cause she fuckin' married someone else."

"You been giving this some thought, have you?"

"Sometimes, I think about things."

"Well, think about something else. And fuck you. And that guy she married probably doesn't even have a dick."

"You prove me right with every fuckin' word."

"You don't shit from the rain."

"*This rain is shit*, I'll tell you that. I used to like the fuckin' rain. Piss on it. Piss on all of it. When I get back home, I'm moving to fuckin' Tucson, Arizona. The real fuckin' Arizona, not this piece a shit Route 4 named by some whitebread jive-ass general who thought he had a fuckin' sense of humor. You know, if I never see another fuckin' tree, well, that be all right by me."

"I thought you said you were moving to New Mexico."

"Arizona, New Mexico—it's all the fucking same."

"You're talking out your ass."

"What the fuck do you know?"

"You think all deserts are the same. You're full of shit. I'm from fucking El Paso, Texas, asshole. I know something about fucking deserts."

"Yeah, well, fuck El Paso. I want a piece of some real desert."

"Like Tucson."

"Yeah, like fuckin' Tucson?"

Camera grinned and lit a cigarette. "All my old man did the last two years of his life was fuckin' cough. I swore I'd never smoke. And here I am smoking my ass off."

Whit looked over at him and shook his head. "You wanna be a good boy? That what you want? No room here for good boys." He laughed, his gold tooth glistening in the light.

"That tooth's gonna get you killed."

"It's a goddamned lucky tooth. Damn lucky. Got it put in on my sixteenth birthday."

"Yeah, yeah, I've heard it. That fuckin' lucky tooth got you drafted, Goldie."

"Last guy that called me Goldie has two assholes. And don't blame my tooth for something your fuckin' Uncle Sam did."

"Don't talk shit about my uncle."

They laughed, fell silent, each of them smoking in the damp air, both of them looking up, knowing the rain would start again, but happy it was gone—even for an hour.

"They say you can see a hundred miles ahead a you in the Arizona desert. That's for me. Ain't no war in Arizona. No one sneaks up on you in the desert."

"Shut up about the desert, will you? Just fuck the desert."

"Yeah, well, fuck that fuckin' letter. You know, I don't like that letter. Don't know why you're always fuckin' readin' it. It just pisses you off. And then you piss me off. So, you know, first chance I get, I'm gonna steal that away from you and stuff it down Charlie's throat."

Camera looked up at the sky. The clouds were closing in again.

Whit grinned. "Better smoke you another cigarette. It's fuckin' gonna pour again. Man, I'm gonna dream of Tucson tonight."

"Yeah, well, I'm gonna fuckin' dream about a girl named Xochil."

# octavio

You remember too many things about the country your father fled—though you never knew that country. It was night when they shook you awake—such a strange and gentle waking. You remember the rooms of the house, large and full of things that caught your eye, the chandeliers, the figurines made of porcelain, the Talavera plates and urns you were not allowed to touch. You remember your new house in the new country with the new language, smaller, that house, but you liked it. You felt closer to your mother and your father and your four brothers and for the first time you felt as if you were part of a family instead of just another possession in a large house.

In Mexico, everyone was always preoccupied, busy, the house full of men discussing things, arguing, and you still remember the looks of worry and anger, your mother always rushing you out of rooms and telling you, "Octavio, do not ask questions. There are no answers." But why were they so angry? You kept asking, always asking. But no one heard your questions. In Mexico, there was never any time for you. You did not exist. There was only the talk of politics and presidents and talk of traitors and business and the running of the house, and the whispers of men who spoke in rooms you were not allowed to enter—everything more important than any of the people who resided in that house. That is what you remember—but you wonder why. You were too small, a child, old enough to talk but not old enough to think.

But it is not Mexico you remember.

You cannot remember what you never knew. You remember only the fragments that were lodged in your father's memory. He gave you those fragments. That is your inheritance—the legacy he left you.

Mexico was nothing more than a ghost that wounded your father's heart, that haunted your father's memory, that followed all of your father's footsteps. Not even the new country—the country of amnesia—could erase his memory.

You were three when you left. You remember your mother dressing you, putting a coat on you, telling you it would be cold. You remember asking her why she was crying. Mothers cry is all she said. You remember the hushed voices, your father with a gun, your uncles with rifles. You remember horses and two wagons. You remember your mother embracing the women who had cared for you all your life. You remember her sorrow as she held your face between her palms.

Your brothers were older and you watched them as they stood on the sidelines, quiet and anxious, worry written on their faces. You asked them what was wrong, and they shrugged and told you to be quiet. You remember crying and one of them giving you a piece of candy and telling you that you were all going to a new place, telling you that you would have fun there, all of you, fun. You did not believe him. You remember that. But you did not ask any more questions. Your mother was right—there were no answers. There was only the sorrow that hung in the air. There was only silence. And lies. Yes, there were lies. That is all there was.

On the road, no one except your brothers spoke to you. No one. Because you were too small. Because you were of no consequence. You were passed from one person to another. You existed as a comfort. That is how you remember it. They were calmer when they held you. And then they let you go. Passed you to someone else.

You remember the sound of bullets, the sound of men dying. Deer die with more dignity than men—that is what you thought the first time you ever went hunting. You hate the way men die. And yet you know that is the duty of men. That is what you have always believed. That is what you told yourself many years later when you were in Italy, the dead all around you. Men. Dead. Dismembered. Arms, legs, hands, torsos. Blood and fields of men. You dreamed that harvest for years.

You remember asking your mother if it was a war when you heard the sound of guns. You remember your mother's trembling smile. *"No, hijo de mi corazón, nomas es un batalla. No es gran cosa."*

You smiled back at her though you did not understand the word *batalla*.

You remember that your uncle was shot. That is the first time you ever saw blood. You did not cry. Your father smiled at you, kissed you, whispered your name, Octavio, *mi rey*.

You remember a train ride.

You remember the first time you heard your father speak in a foreign tongue. "English," he said—and you repeated it. *English*.

You remember too many things about your father, stories always on his lips, though you did not understand any of them—

stories of men whose names became as familiar to you as your fingers—Villa and Emiliano Zapata, Porfirio Díaz, Carranza, Huerta, Obregón, Francisco Madero—names that were thrown around like rocks breaking through windowpanes every time your uncles gathered around your living room, a shattering rage in the sound of their voices, Mexico ruined because of those bastards. Except Díaz. *¡Que viva el Porfiriato!*

You remember coming home from school one day and telling your father you were reading a book about Abraham Lincoln and your father looked at you and nodded and you understood, understood because you were fifteen and old enough, understood that your father did not care about the civil war of his adopted country, and then he smiled at you and said, "Villa is dead. He was assassinated." And then he laughed and you knew that your father was happy though you did not know where that happiness came from. "He's joined Zapata in hell, that bastard." And you dreamed about Zapata and Villa in hell. And you dreamed about their assassins and they were in hell too.

*Assassins.* It was a word you were raised with: *¡asesinos!* A familiar word. You held their images in your head, knew what they looked like because you had seen all the pictures, and you half thought that they were handsome and strong, and had wondered if you would ever look like that. And you felt you were betraying your father and so for a long time you refused to look at pictures of the revolution.

Mexico was a song that broke your father in half, the only song he ever learned by heart. And he stopped loving you. There was room for only a lost Mexico and your mother. That is what you remember. Like Mexico, you, too, became a ghost.

Many years later, you remember your own son hanging up a poster of Zapata in his room. You remember the river of anger that ran through you, a river made of flames. You remember tearing it down, shredding it to pieces, your son watching you, a look of stunned surprise on his face. You remember the words that came out of your mouth: "You are spitting on the grave of your grandfather."

You remember your son looking away.

You remember thinking that you were a ghost again.

## abe

You wake in the morning and you think, *No, no, God, please, no, sleep, God, sleep.* You feel your body ache as it has never ached, your legs, your arms, your chest, your stomach. There is no muscle in your body that does not hurt.

For an instant you do no know where you are.

But after that long second of being lost, you know exactly where you are, the men all around you, shaking off their sleep, their movements like the sound of worker bees. Like them, you rise in silence and a part of you thinks you have become a monk. You do not want to speak. The words of a maggot are useless. You make your rack, make sure the sun reflects off your shoes. As you stand at attention in front of your row of metal bunk beds, you hear the voice of your DI staring all of you down, Very good, ladies. You know he is pleased. As pleased as he will ever be. Mostly you are maggots, but sometimes you are ladies.

You stand there, as still as you can, almost lifeless. You yearn for the smell of your mother's coffee, the sound of your sister's voice, singing as she combs her hair, the sound of your younger brother's impatient questions, *Why can't dogs talk?*

You make the thoughts disappear.

These thoughts will not help you.

Focus. Discipline. That is what will help you.

You will force your mind tell your body to do what it must do. You will not screw up. Not today. Not ever. You will never make your platoon pay for something you did not do.

You start looking out for the ones who will make you all pay. You hate them.

But you know you are all in this together.

All day, you are kept busy. You run an obstacle course and fall. You hear the word *maggot,* and you pick yourself up and finish. You fall. Your DI places his boot on your back as he makes you do push-ups. You do not stop. You finish. You will not let anyone see you quit. Not today. Not ever. And then you hear the words "Get up, maggot. Someone's gonna crush you, maggot. Are you getting this?"

"Yes, sir."

"You are dog shit. You are chicken shit. You are buffalo shit. You are pigeon shit. You are the smell of a garbage truck. Are you getting this, maggot?"

And then, for the moment, you are released. You fall in line. You file into a classroom. You listen to military history and the history of the Marines. You are learning. This is like school, you tell yourself, but it is not like any school you have ever attended.

You eat. You do not taste the food. But you've never been hungrier.

And then, finally, when the long day ends, you take a shower alongside your fellow recruits. You smile to yourself. Maggots. Ladies.

Someday you will all be Marines.

When you fall into bed, you start to utter a prayer, but do not finish. You sleep. Too tired, you will not dream. You will not dream again for months.

Your dreams will begin again when you go to war.

# xochil

Xochil Espejo, Xochil Espejo, Xochil Espejo."

She placed her hand over his mouth. "Stop saying my name."

"Why?"

"Expand your vocabulary." She looked at him, laughed, kissed him.

He pulled her close, closer, never averting his eyes, never blinking. He felt her breath, as clean and new and warm as anything he'd ever been close to. He ran his fingers though her long black hair, and the thought entered his head that her hazel eyes were a kind of sky. "I don't care about words, Xochil. I care about you." She opened her mouth, but before any word came out, he put his finger on her lips as if to gently silence her. "Who told you girls were supposed to kiss guys?"

She pushed him away. "Who told you that boys always had to be in charge?"

"My dad."

"He actually told you that?"

"Well, no, not exactly. I mean, I just kinda watch him. Your dad's the same way. Don't tell me you don't see."

"I'll tell you what I see, Jack Evans. Dads couldn't explain the difference between 7Up and dishwater. Don't you know that? You think my dad's in charge at our house?"

"Well, your mom, isn't she taking care of your grandmother?"

"Your point?"

"She's your dad's mom, right?"

"Oh, I get it. You think my mom does that on my dad's orders?"

"Well—"

"You're a very special gringo, you know that?"

"Don't call me a gringo."

"That's what you are." She laughed. "If it was a bad thing, do you think I'd be kissing you?" She laughed again. "And if you want to know the real score, it's not as if my dad ordered her to take care of his mother. Families aren't like the army. My mom and my grandmother, they have something."

"Like what?"

"Something most people don't have. And my dad, he's just on the sidelines. A lot of guys, they're like coaches—they sit around, get fat, get paid for doing nothing. It's the players that count."

"Coaches count. And your dad's not fat."

"Don't be so literal."

"Coaches count, Xochil."

"Uh-huh. Sure." She shook her head. "My grandmother, she's really sick right now, you know? I hate that. She'll be gone. And my dad doesn't know what the hell to do. But, my mom, she's the real soldier. She worries and figures out what needs to be done, takes her out to get some air, bathes her, takes her to see her doctors, sings to her, asks her all the right questions. She's the one who knows what hurts and why. And at night, I can hear my grandmother whisper my mother's name. And if she's in pain or has a bad dream, do you think she calls for my dad? *That's her son, Jack.* Do you think she calls out his name in the night? Hell no. She screams out for my mother."

She pretended not to notice the way he watched her.

"I hope you don't grow up to be like your father."

"That's a mean thing to say."

*"He doesn't like Mexicans, Jack."* She hadn't meant to bring up the subject. Not today. But she'd said it—and there it was. That subject. Staring at both of them.

He looked at her, almost waiting for her to take her words back. The steel in her eyes. He could almost taste that steel—bitter and cool on his tongue. But he had some steel of his own. "It's not that he doesn't like Mexicans. It's just that, well, he's a little uncomfortable. He's used to people being more American."

"More American. Great."

"He's not a bad guy, Xochil. You gotta give him a chance."

"Like he gave Gustavo a chance? Gustavo used to be your friend." She watched him, waited for him to say something.

*Used to be.* He wanted to tell her that they'd argued, that they'd almost gone at each other the last time they'd run into each other. *If I ever catch you touching my sister again, I swear I'll cut your fucking balls off.*

"Jack?"

"I'm listening."

"Are you?"

"Yes."

"Listen, Gustavo can't even go over to your house because your father goes fucking ballistic over his hair."

"Pretty mouth."

"Don't pretty mouth me, Jack Evans. I'm not June Cleaver. I don't intend to live a conventional life vacuuming carpets in sensible flat shoes and collecting double S&H Green Stamps on Wednesdays at the local Safeway so I can get something new for my kitchen."

"Right. That's why you put on a uniform every day for the last four years at an all-girl's Catholic school—because you're not going to live a conventional life."

"That was my father's decision. If you think I'll be a good Catholic girl the rest of my life you got a *tuerca* loose in your pretty head."

"Pretty head?"

"To go with my pretty mouth."

"What's a *tuerca*?"

"Screw loose, gringo. Learn Spanish."

"I will."

"Don't say things you don't mean. Maybe you and your dad should move to Iowa."

"Iowa? Don't be crazy."

"The people there—well—they're more American."

"Stop it, Xochil."

"I won't stop it. You're dad's a bigot."

"He's not. He just doesn't like long hair."

"Gustavo's the most beautiful man in the world."

"That's nice, that you worship your brother like that."

Xochil looked at him, locking her jaw and wincing. After a few moments, she smiled at him, an idea lighting up her eyes. "In our English classes, Sister Marie used to give us a word for the day—so we could expand our vocabularies. She said to expand one's vocabulary was to expand one's mind."

"Is that right?"

"Yes, that's right. And one day she gave us the word *condescending*."

"Okay. Look, don't fight with me."

"I'm not fighting."

"I don't like that word."

"You're eighteen years old. You should get to know words you don't like."

"I try to avoid words."

"So do alley cats and pigs."

"Don't, Xochil."

"Jack, listen to me. *We are the words we use.*"

"That's a crock of shit. Touch—that's what's important."

"Now, that's a crock of shit. You don't believe in touch. You believe in foreplay."

"What?"

"Foreplay. It's a word."

"Can we drop this word thing?"

Xochil shook her head. "Your English isn't much better than your Spanish if you ask me. You know what? I gotta split."

He ran after her, panic in his voice. "Don't go. Don't. Don't be like this, Xochil."

"Like what?" Sometimes she was still making her mind up about him. She could be like her hazel eyes—some days dark and muddy, some days almost green as a leaf.

"I've enlisted." He hadn't meant to tell her—not like this. He looked at her. She looked right back at him. He couldn't read her, not today. "I'm probably going off to Nam. And I love you, and—"

"What?"

"I said I've enlisted."

"Why?"

"To fight, Xochil."

"Fight who?"

"The Communists."

"Why?"

"For my country."

"Okay."

"Okay?"

"What do you want me to say?"

"You should be proud of me."

"Okay."

"I'm doing this for you."

"For me?"

"For all of us."

"All of us, Jack? Did you take a poll? Did you go door to door?"

"Stop it, Xochil. You sound just like your brother."

"Do I?"

"Just stop."

"So you want to be a man, is that it?"

*"I am a man."*

"What makes you a man? A high school diploma? The fact that you shave? The fact that you have hair on your balls? You want to be a man? Then don't put this on other people. Don't put this on me. Just don't do that to me, Jack. You're just a boy with a limited vocabulary who thinks going off to war will—hell, who knows why. Who knows? *You don't even know."*

"We're fighting against the Communists, Xochil."

"Explain Communism, Jack. *Explain it to me."*

Her and Gustavo. They thought the same. "Shit. I don't have to explain anything."

"Can you explain who the Viet Cong are? Can you tell me why they're fighting?"

"How the hell do you know anything?"

"Ever hear of newspapers? Magazines? The news?"

"Fuck the news."

"You don't know *condescending*, you don't know *Communism*, and you don't know how to speak Spanish. You don't know *anything*, not about love, not about war, not about anything—*and you're not even a very good kisser."*

Jack grabbed her arm and squeezed it.

She glared at him.

He let her arm drop.

"I have a vocabulary word for the day too," he whispered. "*Superior*. You think you're fucking superior."

"Maybe I do," she whispered back. She looked into his blue eyes, then smiled, and she half wondered to herself what her own smile meant. She reached for him, placed her hand behind his neck, and bent his head toward her. She placed a kiss on his forehead. "Don't go," she said, "don't be a soldier."

"Don't be a little girl. The world *needs* soldiers, Xochil."

"The world needs food. It needs clothes and jobs. What it gets is soldiers."

"Soldiers get us food and clothes. And they get us freedom so we can have schools, and they—"

"Well, shit, Jack, then why the hell do we need teachers or social workers?"

"You live in the clouds."

"Wish I did, baby. And what's my other choice—your father's world? I hate your father."

"I love him, Xochil."

"You can't love two people who hate each other."

"My father doesn't hate you."

"He hates my brother. And if he knew me he'd hate me too."

"You don't know what you're saying, Xochil. You're just a girl."

"Jack Evans, I'm more woman than you deserve." A part of her wanted to tell him about that summer evening, about the word *rape*, about how that evening had reshaped her words, her mind, her body, how it had made her old and callused her heart and parts of her that were too young to be callused. But she knew she wouldn't tell him, not ever, not him or anyone. And she knew, too, that she was condemned to be older than everyone around her, and perhaps angrier. Always. And just then the thought occurred to her that as much as she hated her curse, she was half in love with it. But a part of her still envied his innocence. He was wrong, of course. She wasn't a girl. But he, he *was* a boy—in every way. But he was right about the word *superior*. Sometimes she wore that word like a nun wore a habit. She kissed him again. "Go and fight your war, Jack Evans."

"When I come back I'm going to marry you."

"I won't be at that wedding, Jack."

"We have to believe in each other."

"What you mean is that I have to believe in you. What you mean is that I should just shut up about all the things I believe in. *Jack, I don't believe in boys who believe in war.*"

"You don't know what you're saying."

She shook her head and turned away. *I know exactly what I'm saying.*

"Where are you going?"

"Home," she said. "I'm going home." She felt her feet walking away, but it didn't seem like she was touching the ground at all. It was like she was torn, or the earth was torn, or maybe she and the earth, they were both torn. She looked up at the afternoon sky. Blue as Jack Evans's eyes. Such a perfect Saturday afternoon. And the grass in the park was green with all the August rains, and even though it was already September, it was still summer. She felt the hot tears on her face.

"I'm leaving in two weeks," he shouted.

"Go," she whispered, "just go."

And then suddenly, without wanting to, he ran after her, grabbed her, held her. "Why can't you just accept that we're different?"

"War isn't like accepting the heat in the middle of summer. War isn't like accepting the fact that it's cold in December or accepting that trees lose their leaves."

He stared at her. "Where did you get that? Where did you get that from?"

"Not everyone thinks like your father." She pushed away from him.

"Normal people—they think like my father."

"Normal? That's not something I ever wanted to be." She smiled, though really all she wanted to do was cry. "My mom, Jack, she has this funny idea that men like to fight because they lack imagination."

"You're mother's wrong."

"She's got a thumb that's smarter than you are, Jack."

*"She's wrong, Xochil."*

"Oh, she's a girl too."

"Let me get this straight—my father's wrong, but your mother, your mother, she's right. Is that it?"

"Yes," she whispered, "that's right." She squeezed his hand, then let it drop.

"You're acting crazy, Xochil."

"I'm acting crazy. Yes. Crazy. You sign up for a war to kill people you don't even know for reasons you don't even know—"

"I know the reasons."

"I don't think you do, Jack."

"Don't you know about the domino theory?"

"You believe that?"

"They're all godless, Xochil."

"You don't know that."

"Xochil, this is your country."

Just the way he said that. Just the way he looked at her, as if she were beneath contempt. Just for that instant. There was nothing to say to him. No, that wasn't true. There were too many things to say to him. And it was all too much work. Useless work, because he would never understand the things she carried, would never respect her because the things he held in his head and in his heart would keep him from appreciating anything about her. He was in love with her looks. She was something beautiful that he wanted. That's what it must have been all along. Looking into his pleading eyes, she knew that he wasn't pleading for her to understand him, but to change. To change herself. To destroy herself. To make herself into whatever image of "American" or "woman" that he believed with all his heart she should become.

She would never reach him. Just like her mother had never reached her father.

"Yes, you're right. I'm acting crazy." She whispered it, but something in the way she said those words paralyzed him. And so, they stood there, both of them, standing, staring, searching, trying to find a road they could both walk. Side by side. But that road did not exist.

She didn't know how long they stayed frozen like that, looking at each other.

She didn't remember who walked away first.

She found herself moving toward home. "You think I'll love you as a soldier?" She knew he didn't hear her.

Such a perfect Saturday afternoon. And he'd ruined everything. And why had she thought that this boy was so special? *You're not you're not special nothing special at all I hate you I hate you and your blue eyes and your hair the color of straw hate you and hate the way you say my name hate you till there's no more air in the sky.*

# lourdes

You watch and watch your children. Your life is lost in the watching.

You have done this watching from the instant they took their first breaths, all of them hungry for air. Watching them is your passion, your addiction, the habit you wear every day. You are a nun, a sentry. You have never wavered from your vocation.

There are days you hate your husband because he does not share your addiction. He loves so differently. He wants only to control. His control is a fiction. His children cannot be controlled. You are right about this. You *are* right about this. But what is your watching, anyway? That, too, is control.

You tell yourself you will stop. Your watching will change nothing. They are rivers, wild and raging, and they will follow their own courses. But you cannot stop.

Your body is a diary of their lives.

You have become nothing more than a camera that photographs your children as they grow. You see what they were. You see what they have become. You keep their images inside you. You see how your daughter has become a woman, and you know that already she has paid a price. There is a sadness in her face that makes her more beautiful than you ever thought possible. And you know you cannot take away the pain. You cannot heal her. Something happened to her. She will not speak of it. But there is a knowledge of something in her eyes. And you did not protect her from this thing. You see her, your daughter. She is and is not a mystery.

You remember the first time you held your son. You remember the terrible pain of his birth, the dark eyes that stared into your face as if he were born studying everything around him, and how you felt he was already old. The most beautiful thing you'd ever seen. All your life, you have loved him more than you have loved anything else. You have loved him more than your husband, more than your daughter, more than your youngest son, who is an angel. And you wonder why you have committed this sin of choosing one above the others. There are days when you hate yourself for this sin. You know you would do anything to protect him. But you also know there is nothing you can do to protect him.

You have watched this son of yours fight a war with your husband all his life. When you first stumbled upon the war, you told yourself you would remain neutral. But you already knew, even as you made that promise, already knew you had taken sides. And there are moments when a piece of you wants to hurt the man she loves. Because he has never learned to love his son.

He cannot hide from you, this son of yours. But he does hide.

They all hide, all of them. From one another. From you. And yet there is no place to hide.

You remember what your father-in-law told you before he

died: "Lourdes, stories are all lies. We want them, cling to them, write them as if they have a nice beginning and a middle and an end, as if they are novels with neat morals, but it is all a lie. Your husband—my son—he does not know this. He will never know this. But, Lourdes, believe me when I tell you we have only pieces. We have theories and ideas and moments and memories and the lies other people tell us. That is all we have. We tie our ideas and our memories and the lies we tell ourselves, and all of the scenes we remember—the scenes we were in, and all the other lies we have been told and have believed, we tie all those things together like beads in a rosary. And it becomes our prayer. But it is a lie, Lourdes. There is only chaos." You remember you wrote those words down so you would never forget. And you have kept those words somewhere on a piece of paper and someday you will give them to your children. You remember Enrique. Your father-in-law. How he laughed when he gave you those words and you remember thinking that he had embraced the chaos. He, who had lost what he loved most. He had let it all go. All of it. That is when he died.

But you? You are not ready to let go of what you love. Sometimes you think you will break. From all the things you know. From all the things you feel. From all the wars you see. From all the things you have heard. *And sometimes it is all chaos.* The heart cannot live there.

And your heart, your tired heart, you feel it is turning to stone. To keep your heart flesh—your life has been reduced to that.

# rosario

You lived in Paris for a year. You were sixteen when a handsome man invited you and your mother to see the Eiffel Tower. At first you did not love him, though you always loved his face.

You remember.

Already your father had married your three sisters off to wealthy men. But you were promised to the church. You would become a nun. Your family would be blessed. It was your duty to obey. Your father had made a promise. A sacrifice. A virgin for God. His gift.

Enrique saved you from a life you did not want. You remember that day when he came to ask for your hand.

"She belongs to God." That is what your father said.

"She is not a horse to be traded."

"She will be a blessing to this family."

"You cannot bribe God with a daughter."

You remember the rage in your father's eyes.

You remember being taken to the monastery. "You will take your vows." You remember your father's stubborn voice. "When you are ready, we will come and witness the sacred event and you will dedicate your life to praying for the sins of the world." You will never forget those words. You will never forget the look on your mother's face as they left you there, in that beautiful monastery, so stark and lovely and sad. You remember thinking *there are worse prisons in this world.*

You refused the tears. Because you were hard. You had always been hard. And you wonder now what Enrique saw in you, you who had been so proud and arrogant.

Enrique came for you the next day. The nuns did not stop him. "I have bought them a new chapel."

"You paid for me?"

"No. I did what your father did. I bribed them."

You remember his smile. You remember his kiss. And you thought maybe he would own you. But your father owned you too. Enrique would be a better owner. And so you married him.

He bribed your father too. He was a master of that art.

A month after Madero had been assassinated, you arrived in El Paso, the Ides of March, a cold day, the sky like a blue piece of ice. You will carry that day into paradise.

You remember leaving, traveling, arriving. You remember Enrique, who could be hard and cruel, Enrique, who was angry, Enrique, who loved you and never stopped loving you.

You are happy to die in this house in a country that was never yours.

What do you have now, anyway? You have Lourdes and a son who does not deserve her. You have her children. They are the only country you needed.

Everything is in order. Your piano for your Charlie. Your jewelry? What good was it? You remember your attorney informing you that your jewels could buy a mansion and the furniture to fill it. That is how he put it. That is the day Lourdes told you, "Come and live with us."

You offered her your jewelry, all of it. She would have none of it. Enrique loved her too. She was incapable of being bribed. And so you leave your jewels for her daughter. You know Enrique would not approve. You know Octavio will not approve. You do not care. You are tired of being approved of.

You are leaving this earth.

The jewels will belong to Xochil. She will do with them as she likes. She will belong to whomever she wishes to belong.

You listen to your Carlos play the piano. Just as you asked. He is playing the piece of music you played for Enrique. The day he died, you played. You never touched the piano again.

You hear your father's voice.

You belong to God. And you think, *Yes, now you can belong to God.*

# lourdes. rosario.

Maria del Rosario Espejo Zaragosa. Her name, a piece of Catholic theology, a fragment of Mexican history. Her dying more like a slow fading, a quiet disappearance. She is sleeping fitfully, half mumbling to herself.

Lourdes walks into the room, sits on the bed, combs her hair with her fingers. "Shhhh." But her mumbles continue and Lourdes translates her mumbles. Complaints—complaints that she still finds herself inhabiting a body. "I know, I know," Lourdes whispers. "You're tired."

The room is dark, small, the faint smell of Rosario's decaying body clinging to the air. The walls are cluttered with old photographs, images of better days, days when Rosario had been younger, healthy, mobile, days when her husband had been alive, taken care of her, loved and adored her, read her words from poets who kept lovely ideas in their heads. The room haunted by photographs. You can almost hear the dead revising her biography.

Lourdes draws the curtains and lets in the westering sun. She scans the walls, searching, her eyes falling on the same familiar spot, a photograph of Rosario holding Xochil and Gustavo, newly born. She keeps her eyes on the three of them for a second too long, grief replacing the ephemeral moment of joy. Was that what it was? Joy? That word had disappeared from the world too long ago now. But that was the only word that described the day Xochil and Gustavo had come out of her, screaming and kicking and stronger than anything she had ever seen. *My God from me they came from me and oh that day had been so perfect* and she had never been more alive *oh yes it had been joy* though she had not deserved anything so pure as that. Now she feels as if her Xochil is changing in ways that are sad and complicated and her Gustavo, too, and there is nothing to be done about it. Nothing at all, nothing to be done about the things that happened as you grew, as you aged and your heart turned as sour as your breath. And there is nothing to be done about Rosario's passing. Watch. That's what you can do. But, God, how she'd learned to love this woman. All that loving—and for what? All loving ever did was take your heart and squeeze it until you bent over in pain.

Who was the liar who said love was kind?

Who was the liar who said love was a comfort?

Lourdes sat on the old leather chair next to the bed and took her mother-in-law's hand. *Oh, I don't regret. I don't regret this love, amor.*

The old woman quiets down, then opens her eyes. She smiles, the late afternoon sun on her face. "Lourdes," she whispers.

"Shhh, Shhh, I'm here."

"Lourdes," she whispers, a smile moving over her face. She opens her lips as if to say something else—then turns her head away.

Her eyes open wide like pieces of stained glass reflecting the harsh and dying sun.

## September 16, 1967

Today. Twenty soldiers dead.

They had names like William and Robert and Jerry, names like Abe and Ernest. Names like Lawrence and Laifelt and Donnie and Harlan. They were named after fathers and uncles and grandfathers. Named after generals.

They came from Alabama, Wisconsin, and California; Washington, Michigan, and Pennsylvania; Missouri, New York, Oklahoma, and Colorado; New Jersey, Arkansas, Ohio, and Canada.

They grew up in towns with names like Rifle, El Toro, Dover, Albany, Holly, Pittsburgh, Portland, New York, Kylertown, Birmingham, Milwaukee, Frederick, Philadelphia, De Soto, Kettleman City, Tacoma, Soldotna, Barnesville.

They were Marines.

They were in the army.

One was in the navy.

They died in places with names like Quang Tri, Quang Nam,

Dinh Tuong. Places with names like Thua Thien, Bihn Dihn, Gia Dinh.

Two of the soldiers were nineteen.

Two were twenty.

Five were twenty-one.

Two were twenty-two.

Two were twenty-three.

Four were twenty-five.

Two of the men were thirty.

One of them was eighteen. A man barely an hour.

Some were drafted.

Some enlisted.

*You'll get used to it. Blood don't mean you'll die.*

## a family

Mr. Rede is late in delivering the mail. On Saturdays, he likes to start early, get back home at a decent hour. But today, he feels as if his life is running in slow motion. He is tired, not feeling well, and his arm keeps going numb. He feels as if he is carrying the weight of a dead body. He looks at his watch. It is five o'clock, and he finds himself standing in front of the Espejo house. 1910 Prospect. Gustavo and Charlie are sitting on the steps. They are talking and laughing. He has known them all their lives. He thinks it is a strange thing to watch the children in the neighborhood grow up. He thinks it is an even stranger thing to be an old man.

Lourdes Espejo smiles to herself as tears run down her face. She notices the time. She almost laughs. She remembers the Lorca poem she used to read to Rosario, about the death of Mejía, the bullfighter. She repeats the last lines of the poem to herself. . .

*¡Ay que terribles cinco de la tarde!*
*¡Eran las cinco en todos los relojes!*
*¡Eran las cinco en sombra de la tarde!*

She looks at Rosario's face, half expecting her to nod and say what she always says at the end of the poem. *Lorca, how could they have killed him? Such a beautiful man. How could they have killed him? Franco will pay for this in hell.* Lourdes breaks down and cries and tells herself, *Finish! Finish with these tears!* At five o'clock in the afternoon, *a las cinco en punto de la tarde,* her mother-in-law is dead. She looks back at the difficult road she has traveled. But there is no one there. The travelers are gone.

Xochil is walking home. Her heart is climbing up her throat. She wants to vomit. She wants to renounce her body. What is this surge of feeling in this strange and savage heart? And what of her mind? Her mind—that too is beautiful and strange and savage. And this boy, this pretend man? He wants only her loyalty? She will not give him what he does not deserve, what he has not earned, what he has no right to ask. *She will not.* She stops and sits on the sidewalk. She breathes in and out, and in and out— then she continues down the street. She wants to tell her mother. She will not tell her. *I will not, will not tell her.*

Gustavo and Charlie are quiet, their game over, though there are a hundred songs running through Charlie's mind. He is happy. He has spent the afternoon with Gus. It has been a perfect day— that is what he is thinking. Gustavo sees Mr. Rede. His heart skips a beat. Perhaps today. He thinks about that notice every day. When he sands down the body of a car, when he smokes a cigarette, when he wakes in the middle of a dream. A part of him hopes the notice will come. Everything will be official. Another part of him hopes he will get another day's reprieve. But there is no peace in that kind of waiting. He hears himself having a conversation with Mr. Rede as he pretends not to notice or care about the contents of the envelopes.

In Vietnam, it is already September 17. It is seven o'clock in the morning. Camera is sleeping fitfully. He is dreaming he is in a car. He is driving to Canada. He is going to find Stacy. As he drives, the highway turns into a jungle and then he understands he is driving a jeep and there is no more road but he keeps driving through the jungle and suddenly Salvi is sitting next to him. He notices Salvi is dripping blood like a candle dripping wax, his legs missing. He looks up and sees Salvi's legs dangling from a tree. Whit shakes him awake. *It's a dream, man. That's all it is. It's just a fucking dream.*

Octavio is sitting in his leather chair. He is reading an article in *Time* about the war. . . . *Something has happened to the psyche of the American people over the summer. Call it ambivalence, call it confusion, call it impatience, but certainly it is a disease that is quickly overtaking the populace like a bad epidemic. There is, at the root of this sickness, a growing consensus that U.S. involvement in Southeast Asia is aimless, undisciplined, and lacks a cohesive plan. Such directionless is not sitting well with the American people. Added to that, the Vietnam conflict is becoming too costly both in terms of human lives and budgetary resources. Though opposition to the war is growing, there is still no organized . . .* He puts the magazine down. He does not have the stomach for this today. He looks up, and suddenly he sees that young man. Trembling. That young man in Italy—at the end of the war—that look on his face, no pride left, no fear, nothing, just a vacant look, as vacant as the landscape, dreamless, a look that almost begged, *Go ahead and kill me.* He sees the man, not a man, a boy, not seventeen, a ragged uniform, trembling. He sees his captain offer the man a cigarette, and the solider boy taking the cigarette, lighting it, taking the smoke into his lungs, tears falling down his face as he falls to his knees and weeps. He sees his captain lift the boy to his feet. He hears his captain whispering, "It's okay, son, it's over now."

It is five o'clock in the afternoon.

# xochil

The sight of the two of them almost made her smile, her brothers, more beautiful than the shadows on the sands of the desert that appeared like embers, burning and haloed; her brothers, more beautiful than lightning in a night sky, more beautiful even than a boy named Jack Evans. They *are* more beautiful. Funny that she wasn't in a hurry to reach them. Hurry had left her and she felt she had become incapable of moving. She saw Mr. Rede walk up the steps to their house. She saw Mr. Rede and Gustavo exchanging small words of greeting, could almost hear what they were saying: *Fine, fine, Mr. Rede, my parents? They're doing real good.* Mr. Rede, he liked asking questions—some of them more innocent than others. She closed her eyes, opened them, closed them, opened them—the gesture almost mechanical. As she reached the front of her house, Mr. Rede stopped in front of her and smiled. "You're almost a woman now, Xochil."

She nodded. "Yes. Almost."

"I have a son, you know."

She nodded. "Yes, I know."

"You should come over and see him. He's shy."

Yes, she thought, shy and nice to look at and cruel and full of himself and carrying too many secrets. She had long ago decided to keep away from him. "I'm shy too," she said, though they both knew it was something of a lie.

He nodded. She nodded back.

They had the same conversation every time they ran into each other. That's what happened when you had the same mailman for fifteen years, a mailman who lived in the same neighborhood and knew everything about everybody, including what bills they owed and from what catalog they ordered their clothes from. She knew what he would say next. She smiled to herself and waited for him to say the words.

"I've known you and Gustavo since you were three."

"Yes," she said, taking away his next line. "I could talk—and Gustavo couldn't. Took him a long time to say Mama."

She noticed he was offended, yes that, offended in that small and pedestrian kind of way, offended by the fact she'd ruined the ritual that he'd established. She'd transgressed against the order of his universe. "Well," he said, trying to be graceful, "he certainly knows how to talk now, doesn't he?"

"Yes," she said. "Sometimes he even talks to the people he lives with." She smiled at him, and it seemed to her that he was a small and pathetic figure of a man. But she thought mean things when she was sad or angry or hurt. She was sorry for the thought. She didn't want to think anything bad about Mr. Rede. He was a kind old man and he had always been good to her and she hated herself for being so mean. She felt a strange pain in her gut and she knew she was going to start crying again—shit, crying, no. No, no, no and just when she thought the red was beginning to disappear from the corners of her eyes, the tears were coming back. No, not again, what was that, these tears, and why did she just want to say, *Jack, Jack, Jack?*

He handed her an envelope. "Something for your *cuate,*" he said.

She looked up at him. *Cuate.* What a strange equivalent for twin. But she liked the slang word in Spanish. It sounded almost like *cuete.* Firecracker. Also a word for drunk. She laughed to herself.

"Are you okay?"

"Fine," she said. She stared at the envelope in her hand.

He smiled. "I guess that letter just got stuck in my hand. Give it to him, will you?"

Xochil stared at the letter, then shoved it back into his hand. "Not my job," she said quietly. She turned up the sidewalk and headed toward the house. *I'm mean, I'm mean. Today, I'm just plain mean.*

She didn't hear what he said as she walked *away.* All she could hear was Charlie's voice, his laughter, but it was far and it felt as though she were losing her hearing or perhaps her mind, no, not her mind, not that, just her control, and that made her heart skip a beat, she was good at that, control, and it made her afraid when she lost it, control, a word, a thing, a gene, a way of living she'd inherited from her mother and she half wondered why she'd been named Xochil instead of Lourdes, and then the thought occurred to her that her mother had attempted to free her from the old religion and it was odd that she should be thinking such a strange thing when really she wanted to be empty, hollow, heartless, empty of love, empty of hate, empty of words, empty of tears, just empty. A car with no gas. A church with no believers. No, no, no, no, no. All she wanted to feel was Jack's hands, his hands, God, anywhere, feel them anywhere on her body, her face, her waist, anywhere, and then the tears were hotter than anything she'd ever felt—like a brand on a calf, like a cigarette being put out on her skin, and she noticed the look on Gustavo's face as she walked past him and into the house.

She heard his voice as she shut the door: "Xochil?"

# gustavo. charlie.

Mr. Rede walked back up the walkway to the Espejo house. He squinted his eyes and shook his head. "Something wrong with your sister?"

"She's a girl." Gustavo smiled, his teeth almost glowing.

Mr. Rede smiled back. "Must be losing my touch. Last week I delivered Mrs. Navarro's social security check to Mrs. Casillas. Not good—they don't get along. Haven't heard the end of it. If I do it again, Mrs. Navarro swears she'll have my job." He shook his head. "Here's one more for you, got it mixed up with another batch." He glanced at the letter as he handed it over.

Gustavo took it casually and tossed it alongside the rest of the mail.

Mr. Rede stared at the pile and almost winced—as if treating the U.S. mail so matter-of-factly translated into disrespect for his profession. "It looks important," he said.

Gustavo looked up at Mr. Rede from the place where he was

sitting on the steps. He was looking tired, but his eyes were full of questions. "We're the Espejos," Gustavo said, something firm in his voice, something playful too. "We don't get important mail in this house."

"It's from the government."

"We don't know anyone in the government."

"It's addressed to you, Gustavo."

Gustavo was impervious to Mr. Rede's probing. "I probably forgot to pay my taxes. Or maybe it's from the president. Maybe he wants to ask my advice about something."

Mr. Rede shook his head. "Young people. I don't know. You and your sister, sometimes I think—well, what are you going to do? You should have more respect."

Gustavo nodded. "Yes, sir, I think you're right." That's what he always told his father, I think you're right, sir, *I think you may be right, sir, I think you may be* . . .

Mr. Rede kept himself from frowning. "Well, you have yourself a nice afternoon young man."

Gustavo gestured with his chin and watched Mr. Rede walk toward the next house. "He's getting old."

"He's all right." Charlie looked over at his brother. "He's nice."

"Everyone's nice."

"Knock it off, Gus."

"Don't you just want to hit someone sometimes, Charlie?"

"Just you."

They smiled at each other.

"Mr. Rede thinks you're disrespectful."

"I am disrespectful."

"Not really."

"Yes, really."

Charlie stretched his chin to take a look at Gustavo's letter—the one that was from the government. "Are you going to open it?"

"Later," he said. He took the letter, then hopped down the stairs. He pulled on his leather boots. "Think I'll take a walk." He lit a cigarette and flashed his brother the peace sign.

Charlie watched him as he walked down the street. It seemed like his brother was always moving away just when he thought he was getting close to him. Moving away and *never never never* coming back. He wanted to run after him, *Come home come home,* an illogical panic sweeping over him like a sudden gust moving over a still desert. He wondered where and why all these things came from, these fears he had inside him as if someone had scattered weeds everywhere inside his body and they grew big sometimes and grabbed and clawed at him, grabbing and choking him until he felt like he would suffocate. He took a deep breath and then another. *He's only walking down the street.*

# xochil

Where's Mom?"

"She's tending to your grandmother."

Xochil nodded.

Her father studied her for an instant. "You were with that boy." It was neither a question nor an accusation. Her father liked *that* boy.

"Yes."

"Next time invite him to come over. There's no need to meet in alleys."

"Parks," she said. "I don't like alleys."

"Yes, I remember. Okay, parks. You have a home."

She nodded.

"He's a good boy."

Her father loved good boys. "Yes. He likes guns."

"What?"

"I said he likes guns."

"That's a strange thing to say."

"He's a strange boy."

"You don't like him?"

"Sure. Everyone likes him."

"Well, he seems easy enough to like."

"If you like guns."

"What is this thing about guns?"

"I don't like them."

"Well, he's a boy, not a gun." He laughed to himself. "Just like your mother."

She wanted to laugh. Her conversations with her father were often like this. Not conversations at all. "Next time I'll ask him to come over."

He nodded and turned back to his book.

She was glad he didn't notice that she'd been crying. It wasn't always bad that he didn't notice things.

She went looking for her mother.

Her mother noticed everything.

# abe

Shit birds. That's what they call the guys who can't cut it. I see a couple of them. I watch them, study them. I don't really feel anything for them. I don't. I can't. Already, I see two shit birds. Barely hanging on. Maybe they'll last a week. Maybe. Maybe ten days. And then they'll start them over at day one. They'll start them over and over until they're strong. Whatever it fucking takes. That's how it is.

Today, a guy named Gonzalez, DI stepped all over him. Gonzalez, he has to learn. Likes to talk. Likes to joke around. Made fun of the DI in the shower, said he was born with very little between his fucking legs and he's been pissed off ever since. That was Gonzalez's explanation. Gonzalez's explanation for everything boiled down to sex. He was Freud from the fucking barrio. We laughed. We all laughed. It was our little moment.

But Gonzalez didn't know when to quit. He laughed. In front of the DI. That was his fucking sin. He fell over laughing. The son of a bitch made us all laugh. "You think that's fucking funny, maggots? You're nothing but stink on shit. All of you."

We all paid. Goddamn it, we paid for the rest of the day. And we hated Gonzalez for it.

After this, we knew to keep our laughter to ourselves.

And Gonzalez learned to keep his laughter a fucking secret.

This is fucking serious, baby.

This is not a fucking joke. To be a warrior is no laughing matter. There is a fucking war going on. *You think that's fucking funny, maggot? Maybe a bullet up your ass will make you laugh, too, huh, maggot?*

The DIs, they go to school and learn their lines. They teach us ours.

They will tear us down, minute by minute, hour by hour, pull up by pull up, push-up by push-up, squat thrust by squat thrust. Our minds and bodies will be transformed. I won't be me anymore. I'll be a part of a team. The team will be what matters.

The team will be the only country you love. You will fight for them. If they live, you live.

I understood all this. From the start, I understood everything. I fucking knew I was going to learn to fight. And I was going to live. This was my war. Mine.

It all made perfect sense.

He took the envelope, studied it, scrutinized it, almost willed the contents of the letter to change. But he'd already gotten the first half of the news, the one that had ordered him to report for a physical. He'd told no one, had taken the letter the day it had arrived and hidden it in one of the books he'd been carrying. He'd reported for his physical, had taken the bus, had answered the questions on the forms, had thought about lying—*Yes, he had thoughts of suicide; yes, he was a homosexual; yes, he was a member of subversive groups*—but he'd told the truth, answered everything correctly, though he was not convinced he was a loyal American. There was only a few of them that morning, maybe fifteen, and there had been seven doctors. "You're lucky," the doctor said, not so busy this morning. His hands were warm. "A fine, strong boy. Damn strong, almost perfect." The doctor himself was a former member of the draft board. "I fought in the Pacific theater," he said, already half bored with his own story, as if the war he'd fought in was nothing more than an epic tragedy with millions of people watching in their seats. Or perhaps he wasn't bored at all. Perhaps it hurt so much that he had to maintain a distance. The blood had been too real. The price had been too high. The pain had been too much to bear, and all of it was still there, the battles, all of them bottled and corked like an old wine and he could still smell the rotting bodies, the fields of burned flesh, the bruise on his back where a dismembered leg had hit him, knocking him to the ground after the bomb hit, the head, helmet still on, eyes still open, George, no just George's head, George who had been smoking a cigarette and laughing not ten minutes before and then the doctor's eyes suddenly returning to the room, that quiet controlled, friendly smile on his face. "You're more perfect than I ever was."

Gustavo looked into the old doctor's eyes. "You could have been killed."

"It's a roll of the dice, son. Some are meant to die and some aren't."

"Lucky you," he said.

"Now son, don't take that tone." He studied Gustavo's face for an instant. "You got the look of someone who's going to live a long time."

Gustavo nodded. *Right, so now he's fucking Nostradamus.*

The old doctor patted him on the shoulder. "Strong as an ox," he said. "You'll do just fine. Good eyes, I can see that. Good reflexes. Be a good soldier, I think. And a good shot."

Yeah, sure, good shot. What was the difference between a ten point buck and a Viet Cong guerilla? What a thing to be thinking. *Sick, sick, you're fucking sick, Gustavo. Sick.*

"Yup, a good shot."

"What's it like, to kill a man?"

The doctor shook his head. "We have to do what we have to do. And if we think about it too damned much, it'll make us crazy. The world doesn't need more crazy. Are you listening, son? Are you listening?"

His voice was kind. He was old and seemed decent, not like the others who half hated you and looked at you and your long hair like maybe they'd just as soon kill you as kill the Viet Cong. Yes, the old doctor had been kind. But—*if we think about it too damned much*—

So the fucking letter had arrived. The notice. Hell, maybe he could sleep now. Maybe the dream would go away now, the one where someone was chasing him, someone with a gun or a rifle, someone he thought might be a soldier but he was never sure, never saw the man who was chasing him and he'd wake up in the middle of the night drenched in sweat and he'd be trembling, his lips quivering and he would walk quietly to the kitchen and try to quench a thirst that would follow him into the day. *Well, Gustavo, no more fucking waiting.* He walked toward downtown. He lit a cigarette. When he got to San Jacinto Plaza, he opened the letter. There was a date and time to report. Two weeks. That was all he had. "Two fucking weeks."

An old man sat next to him and stared. He pointed his chin at him and asked him for a cigarette.

Gustavo handed him what was left of his pack.

The old man took it, not an ounce of gratitude written on his face. He carefully took a cigarette out of the pack, then looked at Gustavo. *"Los cigarros matan."*

Yeah, yeah, Gustavo thought, cigarettes kill. There're a lot of things in this sad damned world that could kill a guy. Maybe cigarettes were the least of it. He nodded, stuffed the letter in his back pocket, and walked across the street. He walked into the Kress and bought himself a pack of Marlboros. He remembered the Saturdays his mother had brought them with her as she did her shopping. She would stop at Kress and buy them popcorn. He remembered how he and Xochil would feed Charlie the soft kernels, how Charlie would hold each morsel, then lick it, then chew it slowly. He remembered how he'd kiss them when he finished and yell, "More! More!" And then he would kiss them again. A born kisser.

He opened the pack of cigarettes. He lit one. He decided he'd go to Juárez. Anywhere but home.

# lourdes. rosario. xochil.

There would be enough time to do. To do the duties that the house demanded, to do the dishes, the pedestrian chores that made up her life. There would be time to sweep up the mess, the litter that the dead left behind. There would be time to do—and the doing would swallow her—if she let it. To hell with it. To hell with it all. She would take this moment, small and insignificant as it was, and make it hers. She would stop the clock. She would sit and hold her daughter in her arms as if she were still a child instead of the woman she'd become. She could feel Xochil's tears on her cotton dress, her heart pounding, her breathing very nearly desperate as she sobbed. Her Xochil was lost, though she was unsure if her confusion had anything to do with death. Perhaps it had more to do with that boy whose name she was always forgetting. Young women were more frightened by boys than they were of death, not even realizing that boys *were* a kind of death. She didn't remember anymore, not really, what it had been like to be a young woman in love. Octavio had grown old on her so quickly. Long before it was necessary.

How could a woman who didn't remember falling in love help a daughter? Perhaps it wasn't necessary to help her. Love never needed any help from mothers or fathers. She realized at that moment that she had found it easier to understand her mother-in-law than to understand her own daughter. It was all a function of age. Was that it? There was no other explanation. Daughters. They were sometimes as familiar and intimate as honeysuckles in bloom, but mostly daughters were mysteries. They lived in rooms you had long since abandoned and could not, did not, ever want to reenter.

Finally, she felt Xochil's tears subside. She rubbed her back softly, just as she had done when she was a baby.

"Are you thinking about her?"

"Yes," Lourdes whispered. "She loved you."

"Yes. But really it was you she loved."

She laughed. "I was only a daughter-in-law."

"You're wrong. It was you she loved most of all."

"She loved your father."

"I don't think so. Not really. He was only the car that drove you to her. But you were the destination."

"Where do you get these ideas, these things you say? You're just a girl."

"I have eyes, Mama."

"So do I. And I see that not all your tears are for you grandmother."

"I don't want to talk about this in front of my grandmother."

"Oh, I think she'd like to hear."

"I don't want to talk about him."

"He won't leave until you do."

"Leave?"

"He'll live inside you until you talk, until you throw him out."

Xochil shook her head and broke away from her mother's

arms. She sat on the bed and stared at her grandmother. "I've never seen a dead woman before."

"She's the first of many, *amor*."

"Don't say that."

"Don't run from it, Xochil."

Xochil nodded, then placed her hand on her Grandmother's chest, almost as if she were making sure her grandmother's heart had stopped beating. "Do you remember?"

"Remember?"

"What she was like when you met her?"

*"You're absolutely sure you love my son?"*

*"Why else would I marry him?"*

*"Women marry men for as many reasons as there are leaves on a tree."* Rosario turned toward Lourdes, her hair perfect and pulled back, her skin still flawless, her gray eyes direct and unforgiving. She was a severe beauty, as severe as the desert. Lourdes wondered if she had always been that way. *"You're poor."*

*Lourdes almost smiled at the accusation. "We're all poor. What's the use in pretending?"*

*"In Mexico, we had—"*

*Lourdes cut Rosario off before she could finish. "Mexico is all in the past."*

*"Mexico still owns us."*

*"Mexico exiled us."*

*"No, it was Villa who did that."*

*"Villa's just a man. He'll die soon enough."*

*She looked as if her pain was more physical than emotional. "Everything's gone now." She looked away from Lourdes, then reached for her cup of coffee. She sipped on it, then looked back at Lourdes. "I never could make a good cup of coffee. Maybe you'll do better than me."*

*Lourdes shrugged. She'd been making coffee for her parents since she was ten. Not an art that challenged her.*

*"You think you're better because you were born in this country."*

*"No. I don't."*

*"I don't believe you."*

*"All right then. I think I'm better."*

*"You're not."*

*"You see. It doesn't matter what I answer."*

*"I knew your mother in Mexico. You were born late to her. A consolation. Was she disappointed—"*

*"Never speak of my mother."*

Rosario nodded. *"I apologize."* She put down her cup of coffee. *"I heard you had planned to go away. To study letters. Or was it theater? Isn't that what I was told?"*

*"I have no idea what you were told."*

*"Have some respect. You're not talking to some peasant."*

*"Neither are you."*

Rosario looked directly into her. *"I can see that."* She paused. *"Is it true?"*

*"It's not a crime to love poetry and books."*

*"My son wants children. You'll have to learn to read your books as you nurse."*

"When did she learn to love you?"

"It started, I think, on the day you and Gustavo were born." Lourdes laughed softly. "I'd almost forgotten how she'd hated me. Not hate, really, now that I think about it. She was just afraid."

"Afraid?"

"That things would turn out badly for her son."

Xochil nodded. "We're all afraid, aren't we?"

Lourdes studied her daughter's face. "You're sad today."

"Yes."

"It isn't just your grandmother."

"There's a lot to cry about, Mama."

Lourdes found herself whispering, "Tears are like clothes—hang them out in the sun for a few minutes and they dry."

That made Xochil smile. Her mother was always saying things like that. "Mom, tears aren't anything like clothes."

"Maybe not." She walked across the small room and opened the window, letting the cool breeze hit her face. She took a breath. "Bring me the roses from the vase in the dining room. I'll call the doctor."

"What for?"

"He'll pronounce her dead."

"Pronounce her dead," Xoxhil repeated. "And the roses?"

"I'm told it takes away the smell of death."

"I don't mind the smell."

Lourdes nodded. "I don't either."

"Should I tell Dad—"

Lourdes paused, then shook her head. "I'll tell him. I just need— I'll tell him."

Xochil nodded, then left the room.

Lourdes looked toward the door, then sat on her mother-in-law's bed. She squeezed the old woman's lifeless hands and decided she would stay for a while longer. There would be time enough to tell her husband, time enough to call the doctor and the priest, time enough to call the mortuary, time enough to call the relatives. There would be time enough for everything.

The dead had learned how to wait.

## adam

## Da Nang, Viet Nam

When you were growing up, Vietnam was not a country that existed on your map. Your world was small then. You did not even know the capital of North Dakota. You remember driving across Texas once with your family. You remember your mother's submission in the face of your father's anger. You pretended to study the map that was on your lap.

There is too much remembering now.

The rain is coming down again. Not a downpour. Not a drizzle. *Wet, for sure, for fucking sure.* Sometimes, you can't even smoke a cigarette.

You huddle together, you and two other members of your fire squad. You have each other and a poncho and a helmet. But you are *always, always* wet. And you are *always, always* cold. You cannot sleep. You wish you were like Whit, who can sleep standing up.

There is nothing to do but listen to the rain and think.

And when you think you think only of home.

You remember the day you left El Paso. You had your orders, your papers, your few possessions, in a backpack: a few pictures of your brothers, your mom, a picture of all your friends, a picture of Glen, who was killed when you were eight. You do not know why you keep the picture of Glen—but you keep it. To remind yourself that you were the one who lived? That you are a survivor? Is that why?

Your few possessions and a plane ticket to San Diego. Eighty-four dollars and sixty-two cents. A hangover. That is what you had when you left home.

You are looking over your room. You are glad to leave. But now you would be glad to return.

You see yourself standing on the steps of St. Patrick's Cathedral, posing for a picture with your brothers. Smile, smile, smile, fucking smile. And you do. You are walking into the church and you are kneeling down to pray, though you do not know what to pray for. You are not scared. You want to go. You want to learn about that word *man*. And that word *war* too. You want to know.

But your mother is sad and you hate that. She says she is proud. But you wonder about her tears, what they mean.

You pray for your mother. You pray for the soul of your father, who was a bastard. You do not miss him, but you light a candle for his eternal soul, though a part of you hopes he is burning in the pits of hell. You light another candle, one for your mother. You tell God to take away her tears.

Outside, you take a picture with your friends.

You take a taxi to the airport. Alone. That is the way you wanted it.

You remember laughing and joking with the group outside your house, all of them who had come to say good-bye—but you remember none of the jokes. But you still see yourself. With them. And you think you might have been happy.

You remember the way your mother smelled. Good-bye, good-bye. You see yourself waving. You feel kisses on your cheek, the embrace of Sam, your high school friend who taught you about weed and the art of looking at a girl so she would look back.

Sometimes you want to be in that church again, lighting a candle.

Sometimes you want to be sitting in your mother's old beat-up Ford, windows down, at the Oasis Drive-in. You can see the straw in your mouth. You can taste the root beer. The sun is out and there is nothing in the world except you and the root beer you are drinking.

You remember what Whit tells you: "I'm gettin' short. Two months, fourteen days. I'm getting' short, buddy. I'm going back to fuckin' Chi-town and I'm gonna get me a shirt that doesn't smell like buffalo shit and a bottle of Jack and I'm gonna fuck for five days straight and then I'm gonna sleep and then I'm fuckin' gonna move to Tucson, Arizona. And I'm gonna stop off in El Paso fucking Texas and give your momma a big kiss."

You see Whit giving your mother a kiss on the cheek. And you smile at the thought. Mom. Home. Shit. You have been here only five months. Eight more months. You have your short-timer's calendar. But you are not yet a short-timer. "Not by a few months, baby." You smile. Whit. He says things that make you laugh. You wonder what you will do when he leaves.

Someone else will make you laugh.

You picture the streets of El Paso and you list some of the names of the streets: *Oregon, Santa Fe, Campbell, Kansas.* You try to hold the map of the city that you love in your head. A map. The city that you love. You did not know you loved your home. But now you know. The members of your squad and your platoon. They say El Paso and laugh. *What the fuck is there?* Heaven.

That's what you want to say. Heaven is there. Heaven and four brothers. And your mom.

And a girl. A girl. You forgot to tell that girl you loved her. Or maybe you only fell in love with her sometime after you left. Xochil.

# gustavo

Gustavo walked south on Santa Fe Street. He kept thinking about the doctor who'd examined him. He'd had a way about him. He knew how to touch people as if they mattered and his breath had smelled of mint. The doctor, he was clean and relaxed and he seemed almost kind—except that he'd made him feel like some kind of prized animal who'd been readied *strong as an ox . . . good reflexes, good teeth . . . be a good soldier . . . good eyes . . . be a good shot.* His friend Joaquin said they were just part of a fucking war machine. But Joaquin was dead now, playing Russian roulette with his friends, all of them stoned out of their minds, their bodies and brains swimming in booze and heroin and pot, and no goddamned war machine had made him play that game except himself and the substances he'd given himself over to. Joaquin, shit. Dead. He'd loved the high. The high had been the only god he'd come to love. *Shit, Joaquin, shit.* He looked up and tried to focus on the sky. His brother, his brother could do things like that. His brother could focus. His brother could hold the entire sky in his head. His brother could study a cloud and watch it hover in the sky for as long as the cloud was there. If he could just hold the color of the sky in his head for a few seconds, just for a few seconds, if he could be like his younger brother for just a moment, then maybe whatever was trembling inside him would leave his body and he could be free.

He stopped walking, stood still for a moment, then took a deep breath. He closed his eyes. When he opened them, maybe he would find himself somewhere else: in a park when he was eight, on a seesaw with Xochil, or walking down Stanton Street holding his mother's hand when he was four, or holding his newborn baby brother and smelling him, the cleanest smell he'd ever held in his lungs. He opened his eyes. *Still here, still here.* The problem with living was that you were always here.

He found himself standing at the doorway to an alley between two abandoned brick buildings. He squinted into the light of the setting sun cutting between the two buildings. He thought he saw a figure leaning against one of the buildings. It was a man, he could see him, a man who seemed old and bent, crooked and made more of bone than flesh. He moved toward the man, who seemed to be catching his breath, as if he had been running. The sun lit up his face as if he were a candle burning inside a glass, like the ones in church, as if he were something sacred—and Gustavo couldn't help but stand and stare as the man stood motionless in the bright and fading light. Sometimes things appeared to him as still photographs, unmoving, inanimate.

And then everything was moving again.

He suddenly felt caught in this stranger's black eyes, alive, frightening, and he was surprised and startled by the moment, by the man. He wanted to look away but couldn't, so he focused on the man's face, dark, indigenous, glistening, sweat pouring out of him, and he could hear his heavy breathing. And then the sun disappeared behind a building, the stream of light gone.

"I'm fucking tired." he said, his voice as unsteady as his legs.

"Were you running?"

The man nodded.

"Is someone after you?"

"The fucking cops. Who the fuck else?"

Gustavo nodded. "Who the fuck else?" he repeated.

"I'm fucking thirsty and I'm fucking hungry and I'm fucking tired." He was rough, an unpaved alley, a piece of broken glass that didn't know how to do anything except cut whoever handled him.

Gustavo nodded. He took two dollars out of his pocket and handed them to him.

The man's hands trembled as he clutched the bills and stuffed them in his dirty jeans. "What the fuck is this gonna buy me?"

Not that Gustavo had expected gratitude. He winced, gritting his teeth, almost as if he were filtering his possible responses through his mouth before answering. "Buy a bowl of menudo at the Hollywood Café. You'll even get change." That's when he noticed that the man wasn't old. Not old at all. Maybe thirty. Maybe younger than that. Yes, younger. But old, too.

"I'm not hungry for fucking food."

"What then?"

The man took his trembling right hand and made a motion as if to inject something into his arm.

Gustavo nodded. "Nothing I can do about that one, bro."

"Fuck you then."

"Man, listen to me. You'll die if you keep doing that shit."

"Motherfucker. What the fuck do you know? Heroin's not half as mean as God. You know, the one you pray to in the fucking Catholic Church."

"Not gonna argue with that one."

"You got a pair of balls don't you?"

Gustavo shrugged. "Sure."

The man laughed. "You don't know shit about having balls."

"Maybe I do. Maybe I don't."

"Maybe, maybe. Fuck you. I'm telling you that you don't know one damn thing about having balls. You know what having balls is?"

Gustavo shook his head. "You fucking win. I don't know shit."

"I killed someone," he whispered. "All I do is remember. I remember and remember and remember. That's all I fucking do, is remember. If you were me, you'd want to fucking die. And then you'd know balls, motherfucker."

Gustavo shrugged. "Maybe." He took out his pack of cigarettes, lit two of them at the same time, then handed one to the man.

"Maybe, maybe." The man laughed, then took the cigarette and sucked on it like it might save his life. He almost smiled.

"What's your name?" Gustavo had no idea why he'd asked.

The man stared at the air as if he were confused by Gustavo's question. He took another drag from the cigarette, then another, then another. "Angel—that's my fucking name."

Gustavo nodded. "You should get some help, Angel."

"Is that why you stopped—to give me fucking advice? I got my mother for that."

"Maybe your mother's not wrong."

"You don't know shit about my mother. She's a goddamned whore who still works the fuckin' streets."

The light was disappearing and Gustavo cursed himself for stopping in an alley to talk to a screwed-up junkie who was pissed off at the world. He took out a five-dollar bill from his wallet. "It's the best I can do."

The man took the bill, then sat himself on the ground. "Go fuck yourself," he said.

"Well, if I could do that, then maybe I really would have balls." Gustavo tossed him the pack of cigarettes and turned away.

"One of these fucking days, you're gonna know what it's like to fight a fucking war every day of your good-for-nothing life. You're gonna wish you'd never been fucking born."

Gustavo shrugged.

"You think I'm nothing."

"You don't know shit about what I'm thinking."

"You fuckin' do. I can see that."

"I don't think you can see anything, bro."

"I'm not from your *pinche* barrio. I'm not your fucking bro." His hands trembled as he reached for the pack of cigarettes Gustavo had tossed at him. He lit another cigarette. "Look at me! I killed someone. Got that, motherfucker. *Fucking look at me, goddamn it!*"

"I'm looking," Gustavo said, a calmness in his voice—though now all he wanted was to leave, be on his way, turn his eyes from this poor, beat-up man who wasn't even a man anymore, this sad, sad man who made him feel bad, bad about living, bad about breathing, bad about the fact that he was clean and had a house and a normal life—even if that normal life was something he'd never thought very much about or even valued because it had been too ordered and too clean and too safe, but seeing this man made him want to be in that place. Safe.

"The world fucking threw me away."

"Maybe you did that on your own, bro."

"You don't shit from piss. You don't know."

"You're right on that count, *ése*."

"Don't call me *ése*, you fucking sellout. Bet you call yourself a Chicano. Bet you think you can take the world by its balls and make it plead for fucking mercy. Guys like you are fucking cheap as bubblegum. I used to be just like you. Take a good look motherfucker—I'm the future. Got that, Chicano, I'm the fucking future they didn't tell you about."

Gustavo grimaced. He was losing patience, but something, else too; he was afraid damn it, damn it he hated that. He knew that feeling, familiar, that thing inside him that made him tremble and feel sick, like the first time he'd had to hit a dog with the baseball bat he was carrying because the dog was attacking him and already had him on the ground or the time he made another guy bleed with his bare fists, a guy who swore he'd kill him, that ache in his chest, that swelling in his throat that made it hard to breathe, that awful kind of fear, that untamable animal that lived inside him and twisted him like a rag—and this man named Angel was making him feel small and grotesque and helpless and mean, and he hated this man, he did, and he found himself making a fist. He wished to God he hadn't given away his pack of cigarettes. "It's getting late," he said. Then turned away.

"Motherfucker, come back here! *Culero, hijo de la chingada, mamón,* Chicano, my fucking ass. Motherfucker . . ." As Gustavo walked away, the man's voice grew more distant until he couldn't hear his words cutting into him.

As he neared the Santa Fe Bridge, he shook his head and grimaced.

*Angel. Yeah. Sure.*

# part two

The endless corridors of memory, the doors
that open into an empty room
where all the summers have come to rot.
—OCTAVIO PAZ

## adam

Da Nang, Viet Nam, September 17, 1967, 5:00 a.m.

You were having yourself one bad motherfuckin' dream."

"Guess I was."

"You kept calling for Salvi."

"Don't remember."

"Wish I could do that."

"What?"

"Keep myself from remembering my fucking dreams."

"Don't matter."

"Fuck. Mine follow me all day long. Don't know which is worse, this fuckin' war or the one I take to sleep with me. Fuckin' A, man, I hate to fuckin' sleep anymore."

Whit was hungry for talk. His voice was good, loud, but soft too, that deep voice that was always on the edge of laughter. He'd always liked the sound of it. Let him talk.

"Camera? You listening?"

"Man, I hear you. But you know what, you're a lying sack of

shit. You can sleep standing up. So don't give me that shit about not wanting to sleep, when I fucking know that's all you want to do."

"You want to give me a fucking lecture or you wanna hear my fucking dream?"

"I'm listening. I'm always fucking listening."

"Don't give me that shit."

"We gonna argue or are you gonna tell me about your goddamned badass dreams?"

"See, there's this one dream. I see all these soldiers. And they're us. Well, they look like us. Me, you, Salvi, Ellis, that asshole Pete, they looked like all of us. And the whole place looks like a fuckin' cemetery. And there's a thousand dead soldiers sitting side by side. I mean, a fuckin' thousand soldiers, and their heads are all together, like they're listening to one another talk. They're dead but it's as if they're alive. And the whole goddamned earth feels like its all torn up. And when I wake up, all I keep thinking is that all those dead soldiers, hell they're still dreaming. And you know what they're dreaming? They're dreaming war. They're dreaming fuckin' war. And they'll dream it for fuckin' ever. Tell you what, it scared the holy shit out of me."

## lourdes. octavio.

She's gone, *amor*."

Octavio looked up from the book he was reading. Always a blank stare before focusing in on his interloper. That was the problem with Octavio, everything was an interruption.

Except today.

Today the blank expression was replaced by another kind of look—sad, startled, almost afraid, the veneer of his control gone, and in its place a dark and sober expression that resembled the stare of a beggar on the street, hunger everywhere on his face, desperate. He started to say something, then stumbled, unable to find the words. He shut the book. He stood and looked at Lourdes, her eyes red, her hair half combed. "I'm sorry." He was almost surprised by his own words, by their softness, by his own pathetic hurt. *I'm sorry.* The two words seemed large and heavy, larger than Lourdes, larger than any words he'd ever heard or spoken. For an instant he felt as paralyzed and silent as a corpse being shoveled over with dirt. And then his wife's face reappeared again.

"What are you sorry about, *amor*?"

He focused on her face. "I have a list—of the things I'm sorry about." He was whispering, a dryness in his throat, and she knew he was working at beating the tears back, as if he could turn his eyes into a dam made of steel and concrete.

"A list, *amor*? Throw it away."

"I can't."

"You don't need it."

"Because you know what's on the list?"

"I've always known."

He placed his hand on her cheek. "I'm sorry," he repeated. "That look on your face—" He shrugged. Just like a boy would shrug. At once graceful and awkward. They stared at each other, their eyes searching in the same way they'd searched in that time when they were young, curious, hungry—and full of want.

"Are you—will you, I mean—"

"I'll be fine, but you—"

"Me? I'm fine. I'm—"

"You're lost, *amor*."

"Lost?"

"Yes."

"I don't know what to do. I don't know how, I mean, I don't—" He shrugged again, but now his shrug made him look like an old man. "There are things, Lourdes—" He stopped. "I sell insurance. That's what I'm good at. But I wasn't good at being a son. Too formal. Too distant. I'm like that. I wasn't any different with her than I am with my children."

"You don't have to do this, Octavio."

"It's true."

She could hardly bear to hear the grief in his voice, the regret, the rebukes, the recriminations that bordered on self-hate. She sometimes hated his distance, his coolness, his aloof demeanor, his emotional complacency. But she was more pained by those rare moments when he took his fists out and turned them on himself. She kissed him softly. "We can't help how we love."

"Is that true, Lourdes?"

"Yes. I think that's true."

"You forgave her."

"Of course I did."

"Where did you learn to do that?"

"It wasn't so difficult."

"She wasn't good to you—"

"Shh, Octavio."

"She said—"

"Shhh, Octavio. It doesn't matter what she said. Things don't always end the way they begin."

"She loved you because *you made her love you.*"

"Love is work, *amor.* It's not something that just happens."

"I never learned how to do that kind of work."

"Octavio—"

"Don't, Lourdes, please." He took her face and held it between the palms of his hands. "I'll call the doctor. Then I'll call the funeral home. Then I'll call Rosa and Sofia. They'll call the others. Then—" He stopped in mid-sentence. "I'm good at chores."

"There's nothing wrong with that, *amor.*"

He nodded and almost smiled. "She was a good woman."

"Yes."

"Why can't I love?"

There was nothing she could do to stop him from punishing himself. She sat for a while, silent, watching him. She did not know how long she sat there.

She did not even notice when she left the room. Later, she was surprised to find herself in the kitchen.

# xochil

Just after she died, I tried to crawl under her bed. It's an odd confession to make but that's what I tried to do. It was as if my body were reaching back to the past. History delivers us to the present but there are fingerprints all over us and they are there forever, irremovable, fossilized on your body. Waiting for future archaeologists to come along and dig us up.

Crawl under her bed. That's what Gustavo and I used to do when we were small. We'd visit her and Tata Enrique and we'd play a game of hide and seek. We were always the hiders. She was always the seeker. We would search everywhere for a place to hide and after running up and down the house and entering the basement and every closet, we'd always wind up hiding under her bed.

Sometimes we waited there for what seemed like hours. There was something frightening about that wait. What if she never came? What if she never found us? Would we be lost forever?

But there was something beautiful about the waiting too, because I was with Gustavo. And Gustavo always knew when I was afraid. He was at his best when he sensed I needed him. That's when he and I would tell each other secrets. Sometimes Gustavo would even sing to me. He had a beautiful voice, deep and soft and kind and every note he hit was perfect.

He could make you cry when he sang.

Gustavo would stop singing when we heard Grandma Rosie coming. She would have a broom with her when she came into the room. And she would say out loud, "I think I'll sweep under the bed." And Gustavo and I would laugh and yell, "No, no, we're here! We're here!" We'd laugh and come out from under the bed and she would embrace us like we were sponges and she was squeezing all the water out of us, kissing and kissing us, saying, "Oh, I've been looking for you. I've been looking for you everywhere." Sometimes, I was so happy that I would cry and Gustavo would comfort me, saying, "Don't cry, don't cry."

I tried to crawl under the bed. That's exactly what I tried to do.

Maybe Gustavo would come and sing.

Maybe my grandmother would rise up, a broom in her hand.

But it was all so futile. Everything was gone, the hiding and finding, the songs, the broom.

I sat there with Grandma Rosie and I began whispering her name, Maria del Rosario Espejo Zaragosa. I remembered the story about how her father had dragged her to a convent. I wanted to tell her about Jack, the boy I loved and hated. Jack, the boy my body wanted and my mind rejected.

Instead, I reached for a book of poems by Lorca. Why speak to your grandmother about a boy named Jack when you could read her a poem by a poet she loved.

I knew which poem to read, a poem she had read to me many times, a poem we had talked about and analyzed, a poem I never fully understood despite all our talking and analysis. I picked up her worn book and read it softly, whispering, whispering, until I got to the last two stanzas. I read those last two stanzas in the same way she'd taught me. I pronounced each word just so, breathed in each syllable—then breathed it out. I wanted to hear her voice in mine. . . .

> *Tú sólo y yo quedamos.*
> *Prepara tu esqueleto para el aire.*
> *Yo sólo y tú quedamos. . .*

I remember thinking she was smiling as I read to her. But, of course, the dead don't smile—they're done with smiling and laughing and crying and all of the rest of those tiring and emotional expressions of want and need and pleasure. But I needed to think of her in that way in that moment—her smiling at me as I finished reading that poem. That poem by that beautiful and tragic Spanish poet who never lived to be old, that Spanish poet whom the world killed, that poet she learned to love because of my mother.

Right then I found a moment that was quiet and still and very nearly perfect.

That moment belonged to us. To Rosario and Xochil.

# charlie

The warmth of the concrete on our front porch.

Me and my brother talking about music.

A letter from the draft board.

Gustavo's absence.

Mr. Rede (who, as it happened, died of a massive heart attack that same evening).

My Grandma Rosie whispering my mother's name and finally letting go of her tired body. (That particular scene I made up in my head, but I swear to God it happened.)

My mother's dignified grief.

My father's reserve, an unwelcome confusion just beneath the surface of his calm. The feel of his unshaved face against my cheek as he kissed me, the last time I was ever to receive that gift.

Gustavo's absence.

My mother's moment of madness. (The undignified side of

her grief. Later she told me that grief was a kind of insanity. "Like love," she said.)

My sister, Xochil, rocking my mother in her arms as I squeezed my father's hand.

The smell of my aunt Sofia's perfume.

The fact that it rained.

The smell of my Grandma Rosie's room when they took her body away.

My sister Xochil's tears.

Gustavo's absence.

The fact that it thundered.

All my father's relatives arriving at our house, tears in their eyes, memories dripping out of them as if they were broken faucets, old and tired, dripping out water, one drop at a time, water, sweet water and everyone so thirsty, all my relatives clutching me as they arrived, whispering things into my ear, though really they were talking to themselves.

I remember things by keeping a list.

The problem with trying to recover the past is that a list is like a deck of cards. In time, the cards get reshuffled, and the order of things loses its shape. All that's left are scenes. I take out each scene—almost out of context. I don't know why, but the thought has come to me more than once that holding on to these scenes makes me feel poor. Poverty comes in many forms. Sometimes it comes in the form of the lists you keep. This makes sense to no one—except to me.

I could see past my mom's poise as she and my father spoke quietly in the living room, almost whispering. They were in the middle of something. Private and painful, too, I think, and I got the sense that they were both grateful for my interruption. I hugged my father awkwardly and wanted to say something, but nothing came out, and just when I thought he was going to break down and sob, he kissed me. And then he pushed me away.

Gently. He was always afraid to hurt me, though he didn't suffer from that particular fear when it came to Gus.

I remember sitting down on the couch and watching my mother, who was completely focused on my father, studying him like an artist studying a model's pose, or a photographer waiting for just the right moment to click the camera, or a psychiatrist trying to decide if his patient was stable enough to be left alone.

My father picked up the phone and dialed. I didn't really pay any attention to who he was talking to, but the tone of his voice was quiet and somber and controlled and his voice was as distant as it had ever been. Everything seemed dull and muffled, the light, the voices, even the aromas of the house. I swear I could almost touch my mother's grief, though she was trying desperately to hide it. She was good at hiding her pain. In that way, she was a lot like my father. Except that my mother hid her pain because she was busy taking care of other people. My father hid his pain because he was trying to pretend it wasn't there. Even at that moment, even at thirteen, I was addicted to analyzing my parents.

But I swear above the din of my own cluttered thoughts, my mother's sorrow soared. Her sorrow, a bird in flight who had lost his sense of direction.

We sat there, my mother and her pain and me, and we watched my father make phone calls. I don't think either one of us was really listening. We were just waiting. That's what people did after someone died. Maybe not really waiting, just taking a breath. Maybe that was it. Without even realizing it, my eyes were glued to my father's movements. It was like I was watching some kind of ballet in slow motion. Distant as he was, my father was very graceful in those few moments.

I don't even remember my mother leaving the room.

# lourdes

She was once your enemy.

Now you see them taking her away, dead and frail, more bones than flesh, more skeleton than woman. Once, her voice took aim at you, hurling stones of disapproval. A shallow beauty, that is what she called you. *With a shallow brain to match. No money, no history to your name.* She thought worse of you than that. And you remember, too, how that voice grew soft, forgiving, tender. Once, in November, you sat in the backyard, watching the snow of leaves as they were torn from their trees in the wind. You sat and watched, the both of you. She kissed your hands and called them lovely. She became your closest friend, an ally, a blanket of sympathy. You fought and loved, resented and embraced for more than twenty years. Twenty years of loss and grief. You held her bent and breaking frame as she pushed against your breast the day her husband died.

Now there is nothing but her memory. What is a memory compared to a life?

You see them taking her away. It is only her body. That is what you tell yourself. Why should you look to a lifeless body? Let them take it. Let them take the fleshless bones. Let them take the heart that's ceased to beat.

You see the men dressed in black suits who have learned to comport themselves formally, respectfully, solemnly. Men who speak in whispers and know the dead but do not know the living. Why are they allowed to carry her body away? Why should they have that honor, these mercenaries, these men who did not know, did not love her? *Why?*

You feel yourself running toward the hearse where they are placing her. *No, she will be cold.* You see yourself attacking them, calling them names. You hear yourself yelling, *Rosario! Rosario!* Your shouts become demands, *Give her back! Give her back to me, you bastards! Give her back! Bastards! Bastards! Give her back!* You feel your fist on the funeral director's chest. You pound and pound, but he is a locked door that will not open. You feel your daughter's hand, grabbing your fist, stilling your storm to an unsettling quiet. You hear her voice, "Mama, shhhhh, Mama, shhhhh." You feel yourself sobbing, the cruelty of grief slapping at your bare and exposed heart, your heart, the heart you thought was callused only to discover that it was still a soft and tender bone. You feel the pitiless ache of Rosario's death, Rosario, Rosario, your sobbing, your sobbing, the succumbing, your surrender to your daughter, to the strength of her arms. You are falling into her breast and you are in awe of her voice, "Shhhhh, Shhhhhh." She combs and combs your hair. "Shhhhh. Shhhhhh."

Her voice is a sea, blue, warm. You want to bathe there, swim there, drown.

I go back there. To basic training. I don't know why. I don't like to think about those days. Maybe it's easier for my memory to visit that place than it is to visit the war. But look, the war, I don't have to visit it. The fucking war visits me.

Someone asked me once what the difference was between boot camp and war. I fucking shook my head. What a question. "Look," I said, "no one died in boot camp. Not a fucking soul."

Sometimes, I remember the rank smell of a bunch of sweaty guys smelling up a room. It's a helluva perfume. God, sometimes that smell attacks me, beats the crap out of me.

Sometimes I just see faces.

Some of the faces want to talk.

Some of the faces just look at you. Wordless and blank.

Some of us were already a little mean when we got to San Diego. Some of us were aching to let that meanness out. That's not a bad thing. Not for men who are about to be sent to war. At a dinner table you're supposed to be nice. But war isn't a fucking banquet. War has its own etiquette, its own rules, its own rituals.

I learned to live with hate. That's not a bad thing either. My DI, he taught me something about living with rage. I swear that guy was born in hell. Hell or Mississippi. This guy, Rogers, who bunked right next to me, he swore he'd rather be in hell than in Mississippi. He said he hightailed it out of that fucking state when he was fifteen, two dollars in his pocket. Rogers, he told me his life story in ten minutes. I swear. But after those ten minutes, all he ever said to me was "Hey." Sometimes he asked for a cigarette.

I remember Gonzalez. I studied the look on his face. He got meaner and meaner. I remember thinking it was too bad we were all gonna get split up after we left basic. I'd have liked to have that guy right next to me in a fucking battle.

The DI, he owned us. No, that's not quite right. The Marines. That's who owned us. And we wanted to be fucking owned.

We did what we were told.

We didn't ask questions.

We didn't offer editorial remarks.

Hell, they even told us to write letters. Look, I wasn't into letters, but there was a story that went around about a guy who didn't write home. This guy's mom, well, she's a mom. She's worried about her baby. And she knows someone who knows a senator. The senator makes a phone call to some general and wants to know why the goddamned Marines aren't letting their sons write home. Well, let's just fucking say that when the word came down that some sorry-ass-would-be Marine wasn't writing home to his mother, well let's just fucking say, this guy and his whole platoon didn't have a very good day.

Yeah, I wrote home.

I hated the writing. But it made me think. I'd think about what I was going to say to my family. But what the hell was there to say? Mom, I'm in hell. But I'm in fucking heaven too. You got that?

# charlie

The doctor and the sober, middle-aged men from the funeral home arrived almost simultaneously. They dressed alike, the doctor and the mortuary men, black suits, black ties, black shoes perfectly laced and shined.

My father did all the talking. He greeted them at the door, shook hands, offered them coffee. He led Dr. Muñoz into my grandmother's room, the funeral director and his two assistants staying behind in the living room. My mother left them there, holding cups of coffee. Dr. Muñoz—like my grandmother—was among the last who still carried the memory of Mexico inside him, every sign of that burden in the way he walked. A memory could bend and break you. If you let it.

He examined her, though the examination came to nothing. She was dead and he had been summoned to confirm that simple and inevitable fact. We all stayed in the room watching—me, Xochil, my mother, and my father. Where was Gus?

The sober men from the funeral home who were waiting in the living room came in and took Grandma Rosie away. Their car was waiting out front, a black car that was as shiny as their shoes, a car designed especially for transporting bodies—with or without a casket. My mother lunged at them as they were loading her body in the car. She was like a hungry cat leaping at a lame bird. I stood and watched, unable to move. In an instant, Xochil was there, holding my mom like a child. She knew exactly what to do. Where did she learn that?

She walked my mother back inside.

And then the house was deadly quiet.

Xochil disappeared. I knew she would emerge from her room with an unwounded air about her. She was like that. It's not that she pretended she wasn't hurt, it's just that she carried her hurt with a kind of grace. You almost didn't notice it was there. Unless you looked. And I was always looking.

My mother, calmer now, went to the kitchen, my father followed her. Not knowing what else to do, I chased after them. My father whispered something into my mother's ear. She placed her hand on his cheek. "I went mad," she said. And then she laughed and in her laugh I thought I saw the girl she used to be. The one my father married. And I was crazy happy for the laughter.

And me?

I was lost.

Everybody had gone to their own separate corners. My mother in the kitchen, Xochil in her room, and my father back to the telephone. I imagine he was calling relatives and friends, and anybody else he felt he needed to notify. He was taking care of business. Business was what he was good at.

I walked into the backyard and thought that maybe now would be a good time to pick up smoking. It would have given me something to do. I don't know how long I loitered there, sniffing the air like a dog that had nothing else to do. Finally, I walked back into the house. I found my mother in the kitchen, writing in her journal. I remember turning on the light because the sun had gone down and there was nothing but dark in the room. Mom wasn't writing, though she had a pen in her hand. She had written a sentence on a blank page of her journal. She was sitting there, staring at her words. She looked at me, giving up her struggle with words. She seemed dazed, stunned, and it seemed as though she didn't recognize me. That scared me. I had never seen her disoriented, not ever. She had always had a way about her, never afraid and always sure of where she was and where she was going. It was like she had a map inside her. She must have read something in my face. "Don't be afraid," she said, "it's just me." And just like that, she was back, my mother.

"Are you sad?" I asked.

"Come here," she said.

I sat next to her at the kitchen table. She looked into my eyes. "What do you remember about her?"

"She was always sick."

"Yes."

"What was it?"

"Arthritis. The kind that bends your bones as if they were pieces of plastic."

I nodded. "It hurt her."

"Yes."

"That's why she always looked sad."

"Yes."

"I liked her laugh."

"Me, too, *amor*." And then she kissed me. A sad kiss. Kisses could be sad. "Will you tell your father we need ice and more coffee? Your uncles and aunts will be coming."

I kissed her back. She smelled faintly of jasmine. She always did. Only the people who were close to her ever noticed she wore perfume. "Mom? Are you okay?"

"Yes," she said.

"Are you sure?"

"Grief takes you away. But it always brings you back."

I believed her. Later I would come to think that when grief took you away, it never brought you back to the same place. There was no such thing as a return. But that was later.

At that moment, I believed her. I believed her completely. With all my boy heart.

I remember, too, how sad Xochil was that afternoon. I kept returning to her face, her tears, unbearable, sad. Sad, sad, sad. And not just because she loved and adored and worshipped my grandmother. It came to me that she'd come home crying that afternoon and she hadn't known anything about Grandma Rosie. I knew it had something to do with her and Jack Evans. I never really liked that Jack Evans. No, that's not true. I'm already revising what I felt. Well, we do that, don't we? No, I liked him. He was fine. He was this clean-cut all-American boy who believed everything they told him about being a man, about being an American, about girls and what they were like and what they should be. He was a decent and sincere guy who never learned how to question anything. That's what I liked about him. He thought the world was better than it was. He didn't think the world needed changing. In a way, he was an innocent. But Xochil wasn't capable of considering those qualities a virtue. Her mind was tough and sharp and she was determined to live her life using that weapon. She questioned everything—including herself. Like my father, Jack Evans was the kind of man who would spend his entire life living by the rules he inherited. Xochil would live her life raging against those same rules.

Jack and Xochil weren't a good match. They both knew it. Or at least Xochil knew it. But knowing something doesn't mean you have power over it.

And the problem with being eighteen is that the body begins

to want. And I think something in Xochil's body ached for something in Jack's body. Their bodies trumped their minds. I was a witness. I was there when they fell in love. I saw it happen. Right there on our front porch. The porch. That's where everything happened.

*"You're staring at me."* She combed her hair with her fingers.

*"I'm not. I'm just looking."*

*"Take a picture, Jack Evans."*

*"I don't have a camera."*

*"Too bad."* She rocked herself more deliberately on the old rocking chair. *"Gustavo's not here."*

*"How do you know I came to see Gustavo?"*

*"Well, you're friends aren't you?"*

*"Yeah, we're friends, but—"*

*"But what?"*

*"Maybe I came to see you."*

*"Maybe you're full of shit."*

*"Maybe I am. But maybe you like me."*

*She looked away.*

*"I know you like me. I can feel it. Last week, when we were playing basketball in the park, you were watching me."*

*"What you felt was the wind."*

*"The wind?"*

*"It was windy that day."*

*He smiled. "Sure."*

*"I was watching my brother. He's a good player. Better than you."*

*"Yes. But not by much."*

*"You're a conceited boy."*

*"Will you go to the prom with me?"*

*"No."*

*"You don't want to think about it?"*

*"Some things aren't worth thinking about."*

That's when he walked right up to her, bent down, and kissed her. And she kissed him right back. Nobody knew. It was all very private at first. Then everybody knew—though nobody talked about it. It was probably love. It's hard to say. They were young. And I was even younger. I didn't understand everything I saw. Just because you witness something doesn't mean you understand it.

## adam

## Da Nang, Vietnam

You are tired of remembering. But the rain will not let you sleep and you do not want to think of how cold you are, how wet you are, how you are beginning to believe that your country and your God have abandoned you. You do not want to curse the rain because the rain is not human, has no ears to hear you.

You do not want to curse the war because it is as useless to curse the war as it is to curse the monsoons.

You think of Conrad García, who was the purest man you ever met. You remember how tall he was and thin and how everybody thought he looked like St. Francis.

You remember hating him. You remember how you taunted him, calling him "the priest."

You remember how his friend Gustavo threatened to send you to heaven sooner than you'd expected.

You remember striking the first blow.

You watched as Gustavo hit the ground. As you were about

to kick him to make sure he'd never threaten you again, you feel Gustavo grabbing your leg and twisting it. You see yourself fall to the ground gracelessly, him on top of you about to put his fist through your face.

You hear Conrad's voice interrupting the intimacy of the fight between you and Gustavo. "Why are you doing this?" He repeats his question. "Why are you doing this?" He demands an answer. He looks into your face. Then looks at Gustavo. "Why do you do these things to each other?"

Neither you nor Gustavo have an answer.

You want to strike out at Conrad, tell him to shut up. You want to tell him that you and Gustavo are just living. You want to tell him that men want to live. That is your answer. This is what you want to say to him.

You wonder why you still feel the shame—and feel it even now.

You understand a guy like Gustavo. He is just like you. But you wonder about men like Conrad, wonder what they are made of, wonder why they have no appetite or patience for the way things are. "Men hurt each other, Conrad, don't you know that?"

You do not hear yourself whispering to the ghosts of your past. You do not hear the rain punishing the land, the wind ripping at the leaves of every tree.

# xochil

Those sober, sober men in neatly pressed black suits, all of them with name tags and all of them wearing sunglasses, they were taking away my grandmother's body. An escort service for the dead.

I found myself on the porch, a spectator.

And then it happened. Like everything else, it happened in an instant. My mother raced out the door. I don't remember what she was screaming, such a strange and foreign thing, to hear those sounds emanating from my mother, she who was always in control of her emotions. She'd never yelled, not once, not at me, not at Gustavo, not at my father. But in an instant of grief, she was transformed, became a frightening animal that could have killed. The funeral director was no match for her. I thought she'd tear him apart. I never knew she had that kind of rage inside her.

But I was so like her. An animal watching, waiting to leap. And that's just what I did.

It wasn't as if I thought about what I was doing. It was a reflex. Instinct. I don't know. I suppose I just wasn't any good at being a spectator. I found myself running after her, grabbing her, holding her, pushing her head against me as I rocked and rocked her. I wasn't going to let her go until I calmed her back to sanity.

It was the most natural thing in the world.

Up to that moment, I had talked myself into believing that rape had transformed me into a woman. *But rape did not make me a woman.* Holding my mother as she sobbed, feeling her grief pour out of her. *That* is what made me a woman.

# gustavo

There was a long line of people passing the toll booth. He thought of the line of men who had appeared behind him when he'd gone to get his physical, all of them young, quiet, as if speech had been drained out of them and they had been rendered inarticulate, all of them with strained looks on their faces, looks of apprehension that made them appear suddenly older, more passive. But the looks here on the bridge were nothing like that. Not like that at all. The faces were relaxed, happy, people chattering in English and Spanish, fishing out the two cents to get across from pockets and purses; there was an eager energy in the movements of everyone around him.

He paid his two pennies at the window and walked across the bridge, ignoring the beggars with twisted arms or legs, ignoring the Tahurumaran women holding children in one arm and holding out the other for the spare change any stranger would bother to place there, almost as if it wasn't a hand at all, but a slot, a machine that no longer felt anything, not even the warm coins that were placed there. He ignored the children selling Chiclets and piñatas and images of a bloodied God on a cross, even ignored the darkening sky, clouds beginning to move in. Maybe a storm. Storms came—even after perfect breezeless days. On another day, he would've smelled the approaching rain, might have smiled at the prospect of a downpour, sweet rain. Sweet, sweet rain.

He continued walking down Avenida Juárez, the litter of the parade lining the crowded street and even more crowded sidewalk. He smiled, remembering what day it was, *el diez y seis*. It was then he noticed how the streets were overflowing with vendors selling tacos, burritos, children's toys, *aguas frescas, elotes*, along with the usual cigarette vendors. He stopped, bought two packs of Marlboros. Ten cents a pack. American cigarettes, untaxed. He gave the man a quarter and waved the change away. *"¡Que viva Mexico!"* the man said, not quite shouting it. Happy, the vendor, content with his job and the day, the faint smell of beer on his breath. Gustavo shoved a pack in his shirt pocket and opened the other, tearing open the foil. He took out a cigarette. He lit it, looked around at the crowded street, kept walking. As he passed a taxi, the man gestured to him. "You want girl?" The cab drivers, they didn't really know English. They memorized lines, *You want girl? Boy? Sex? You want something better than sex?* That meant drugs. They could get you anything, the cab drivers. They could take you places.

He grinned, almost embarrassed, shook his head, and kept walking. He'd been to la Calle Mariscal, had almost gotten up the nerve to get himself laid. He'd changed his mind. "Why pay for it?" he'd told himself. But he'd been scared. He didn't know of what. Maybe of himself. Maybe of the prostitutes. He hadn't been scared with the other girls he'd been with. But that was different. He'd known the girls, had studied them, kissed them—and they had studied him. These women, well, they were women. And they reminded him that he was only a boy instead of the man he wanted to be. And anyway, the whole scene had seemed cheap to him. Cheap and sad as hell.

He laughed nervously to himself, walked another half block, and made his way into the Kentucky Club. He pushed past the crowd that stood around the entryway and found an empty stool at the back of the bar. He finished his cigarette. Then lit another. He sucked in the smoke, the goodness of it, the way it almost hurt when he took the nicotine into his desperate lungs, the way his whole body came alive with whatever the hell was in them.

After a few drags, he felt calmer, and that ugly thing that Angel had brought out in him began to burrow itself back into that place inside him where it slept. He wished to God that angry animal would go to sleep forever. But that animal would wake up again. He knew it would. Someday, it would wake up growling. Happy. Go hunting. Kill.

He tried to think of something good. He thought of Conrad. *I just told them that I would never carry a gun. I told them I would never kill another human being. That's what I told them.* Conrad. He hoped to God—even if he didn't believe in God—he hoped to God that the cruel and pitiless and brutal world of men in the military would leave him alone, leave Conrad pure—him and Charlie. He raised his beer to them, to Conrad and Charlie, to them who lived so close to that word *peace*. Yeah, sure, to them.

He ordered another. Nothing felt so bad after a few Tecates.

# xochil. lourdes.

Tell me why my children love these steps."

Xochil turned her head at the sound of her mother's voice. "Because they lead to heaven." She patted the cement floor of the porch and motioned for her to come and sit. When she felt her mother next to her, Xochil placed her head on her shoulder. They sat there for a moment, quiet, still.

Xochil listened to the sound of the house full of people, the voices, almost like a song. She closed her eyes and took in her mother's smell. "You can see everything from here," she whispered, "the sky, the neighborhood, everything."

"You can't see Paris."

"I don't care about Paris."

"Your grandmother loved Paris. It's where she met your grandfather."

"I loved hearing her tell that story, that thing in her voice."

She looked straight into her mother's face. "But I still don't care about Paris."

"But you care about a boy named Jack."

"I don't want to talk about him."

"Why not?"

"I don't want him in my head."

"Maybe it's too late for that."

"I'm eighteen years old. It's not too late for anything."

"You're a wise girl, aren't you? You talk like you're thirty."

"I'm probably older than that."

"Yes, I think you are. You scare me sometimes."

"I want people to take me seriously."

"The whole world takes you seriously, Xochil."

"Everyone but Jack."

"Oh, he takes you seriously."

"Mom, you don't know that."

"I've seen him look at you."

"It's a guy thing. His looking at me is just a reflex."

"What is that supposed to mean?"

"It means the guy has a body, Mom. It doesn't mean he has a brain."

"I see."

"You're smiling. You're laughing at me."

"Not really."

"Yes, really."

"Well, maybe." She took her daughter's hand and squeezed it. "I scared you today, didn't I? I scared everyone. I think I even scared myself."

"Don't be sorry."

"I've never—grief—grief, Xochil, it can steal your mind if you let your guard down."

"I thought you were beautiful."

"And frightening."

"Yes." Xochil smiled. "Terrifying."

"Mad as the empress Carlotta."

"Stop it, Mom." They burst out laughing, tears running down their faces. When they finally stopped, they listened to the laughter coming from inside the house.

"It's a nice comfort," Lourdes whispered, "that they're all here, talking and laughing."

Xochil nodded. "Everyone's talking and laughing and crying—everyone but Dad."

"Don't be mean. It's been a very painful day for him."

"I don't understand my father."

"Why do you have to understand him?"

"Then maybe I'd love him more."

"Do you understand Jack Evans?"

"No."

"And you love him anyway."

"I never said I loved him."

Lourdes smiled. She left it alone. Her daughter would have to solve the puzzle of boys and men and what she felt for them on her own. She didn't need protecting. Certainly, she didn't need to be protected from Jack Evans, who wasn't mean, wasn't dangerous, and wasn't remotely her daughter's equal. They sat there for a moment, saying nothing. "Such a beautiful night," she whispered. "Nights always remind me of Gustavo."

"It's his eyes."

"Where is he, Xochil? Where has he gone?"

"He disappears sometimes, Mom."

"Today is not a good day for disappearing."

"You worry too much about him."

"Your father says nothing will happen to him. He says he'll go to Vietnam and nothing will happen to him."

"Are you angry?"

"What else should I be?" She closed her eyes and looked up. "Maybe you're right," she whispered. "I worry too much."

"He knows how to take care of himself. He always has."

"He's always had you to watch out for him."

"I do less watching than you think."

She didn't believe a word her daughter said. "He's careless, Xochil. That's the way he is."

"No, Mama, he's not careless. He just has to go his own way. Even being a twin, it's like a prison for him."

"For you too."

"Yes. Sometimes. But it's different for him, I think."

"He adores you."

"It's not that. It's that there's something in him, something that makes him uneasy. He's like part of a flock of birds going south. Only he wants to go in another direction."

"That bird will die alone, *amor*."

"Maybe it's the flock who'll die, Mama. Maybe he doesn't want to die with them."

"I wish it were that easy, Xochil. He's not a bird, he's a boy."

"He's a man now, Mama."

"Well, countries are bigger than boys. Bigger than men too." She looked up at the sky. "It's going to storm."

"Good. We could use the rain."

All during boot camp, sleep became an obsession.

This is the truth: we weren't minds; we were bodies.

And so our bodies were worked and worked and worked. Training is training. Like our DI said, "You are not here to take a vacation, maggots. You're maggots and maggots never sleep. They're always crawling around. If they stop crawling, they die. I'm here to make sure you don't die. You hear me, maggots?"

Hell, we did our share of crawling, that's for fucking sure.

In a way, it was like Lent. You gave up everything you knew and loved. You gave up your family. You gave up women. You gave up trying to be an individual. The only thing you had was your body and you were being trained to make it survive. If your body survived, then your mind survived. If your mind survived, you knew you were still alive. That was the name of the game—to stay alive.

But, God, I was tired.

All the time, tired.

It always felt like I'd slept for ten minutes. That was exactly what it was like. I would hit the rack and ten minutes later, some asshole is waking me up with a fucking bugle. Man, you don't know how bad I wanted to shove that bugle up someone's ass.

All I wanted to do was sleep. I was in love with the idea of it. Sleep was almost as good as a woman. Some days, I wanted to hop that fence and go get myself laid. And some days, I swear I wanted to hop that fence, rent me a hotel, and just sleep. Screw sex. Just let me fucking sleep. You know, I dreamed only a couple of times during basic training, and both of those dreams were about sleep. I dreamed I was sleeping. It was like having a wet dream. It was fucking unbelievable.

It's strange, but I never thought much about sleep till then. Sleep was something you did when you were tired. End of story. Yeah, but that changed. Shit, I mean to tell you I wasn't in bad physical shape when I went in—but, hell, I never knew what my fucking body could take. Course, it was mostly in the mind. I think I always had this thing, when things got tough, I could just make myself take it.

You know, no one got to sleep in our unit, until their fucking little piece of the world shimmered like piss in the sun. And when your little piece of the world was actually cleaner than your butt when you were a baby, you'd hear the voice of God telling you to fucking hit the ground and do push-ups. And you would do them until you thought your arms and chest were gonna explode. They did that to us only a couple of times at the beginning. Mostly, they never fucked with our rest. Well, almost never.

You know, all you tell yourself is that you're gonna go to fucking war, and this is just practice. If you're not ready for the big game, you're gonna leave your ass in some rice paddy and never see the fucking sun again.

By the end of the second day, I'd already learned how to take a man's hate—how to breathe it in. How to let it sit inside me for a while. It's like processing food. I'd sit and chew on it. And I knew I'd find a way to shove it back down his lungs. See, that's how I prepared myself.

When I think about it, no matter what else pops into my mind, I have to say it: I took to that life. Almost like fucking love at first sight. The second night, I was shining my boots like I'd been born doing it. And it wasn't about the boots. It had nothing to do with the fucking boots. It was like I was home.

War doesn't fucking begin the first day they drop you off in a battle zone. War doesn't even fucking begin when you get to boot camp. Oh no, baby, it begins way before that.

# charlie

Countries are bigger than boys.

I heard them as they talked, my sister and my mother. At thirteen, it was a hobby, listening in on other people's conversations as if it were an entry into the world of the living. That's how I used to feel—like everyone around me was more alive than me. Especially Xochil and Gustavo. If ever two people were alive, it was them. They were a wind. I sometimes felt like a tree, and they were blowing right through me. All I could do was bend in the face of their force.

I don't know when it began, but I became something of a spy, a ghost that haunted the house. I think I liked being invisible—it was better than being the beautiful, virtuous boy—the role my mother and father and even Gus and Xochil had decided I would play. Families are like that. They choose roles for you and sometimes they even give you lines to speak. I was obedient enough to play the role. It was the only way I knew how to love them back.

I sat under my mother's oleander that night.

The oleander was as old as I was—older—and had grown so tall that it was more like a tree. I liked sitting under it, right there in that small space between the wall of the house and its thick branches and poisonous leaves. I fit there. And since it was on the front corner of the house, I could hear everything that was being said on the porch. I used to sit there and read books—especially when the weather was good.

That night, I didn't go there to spy—I went there to disappear. My aunt Sofia had hugged me and whispered, "*¡Que cosa!* Beautiful! Astonishing! *¡Que cosa tan linda!*" And I didn't know what was happening, but I knew I had to get away, couldn't breathe, just couldn't breathe, and I was trembling.

I made it out the back door before anyone could see I was crying, and I was glad the house was full and no one noticed. It wasn't Aunt Sofia, that wasn't why I was crying. I was crying because it hurt me to see that look of grief on my mother's face. I was crying because I'd loved Grandma Rosie, because she'd taught me how to tie my shoes and how to iron a shirt and how to read the stars in the sky and how to read Spanish and how to pronounce it so that Mexicans wouldn't laugh, and she'd taught me the names of things—flowers, trees, bushes, the saints that lined the walls of the church. I was crying because I would never hear her voice again and I had never known a world without her in it. I was crying because I somehow knew that the letter Gus had received was going to take him away, force him to fight a war he and Xochil hated. I had heard them talking endlessly about that war—though they refused to speak to me about it. That's why I was crying. Because I was a boy and didn't want to be one.

I don't know how long I sat there sobbing, but it was the first time in my life that I understood that emotional pain wasn't emotional at all—it was something physical, was something that made the muscles and the organs ache, was something that could break your body if that pain came along at the wrong time. And then I began to understand the people who wandered around downtown without homes or family and the weight of the things they must've carried.

I sat there for a long time.

I think I got tired of being alone, and that's when I found myself listening to the voices of my sister and my mother, who were speaking to each other on the front porch. I listened and fell in love with the listening, and I forgot the hurt I felt. All I wanted to do was make myself into a tape recorder so I could replay the tape and listen to the sound of their voices in my head until I was an old man.

Your mother is dead.

Now you are an orphan. Your father, who was always a stranger, who was kind, who loved his wife, who was gentle, whose heart ached always for Mexico, your father who laughed and cried and whose manner was always foreign, your father who tried to make you softer than you could ever be, your father died in her arms, your mother's arms, your mother who is dead.

Is it possible to be a son when your parents are gone? You are a sky with no sun. The blue is gone. You are a river that holds no water. You are a tree without its leaves.

You grieve but you do not know how to grieve.

You do not live in your heart.

You live in your head.

You are fifty-four years old. You have provided for three children, a wife, and for your mother, who is dead. You are a man. You have no need for fathers or mothers.

You remember what your father said when he was forced to leave Mexico, forced to leave the only piece of earth he'd ever love. *Todos somos huérfanos en este maldito mundo.* Orphans all of us in this cruel and breaking earth. But orphans with mothers and fathers. And now that office has been torn away from you, that office of son. Such a lonely office. Now there is only the office of father. Only the office of husband. Those offices, far more lonely and austere than the office of son.

You think of her, your mother. She was the world when you were small. She was the water you bathed in. She was the smell of the food you ate. She was the only song you knew. She was a tree, she was the shade, she was the breeze.

You loved her. And yet it was your wife who cared for her. You loved her. And yet it was your wife who touched her. You loved her. And yet it was your wife who spoke to her, sang to her, bathed her. You loved her. Yet, as a man, you never touched her.

You loved her. But your love was silent. You tell yourself that she knew the truth of that love and that is all that matters. And then you know: Your wife's heart is made of tender flesh. Yours is made of something much harder. You wonder why. The wondering will change nothing. Yet the wondering continues. Perhaps all of this is part of God's plan. To some, He gives hearts of flesh. To some, He gives hearts of stone. You have received the lesser gift. Your life is the lesser life. It is your cross to bear. *And you must bear it. You must stand it.*

You see the look on your wife's face. That sorrow, that look that laid bare her great and generous love. Why is that look not on your own face? Why? You remember your mother teaching you how to read a book. You remember the smell of her skin as you slept on her shoulder at Sunday Mass. You remember the songs she sang and then you catch yourself singing one of the songs—*hay unos ojos que se me miran*—and you feel the strange tears on your face.

And you wonder.

Did you grieve for your father? Did you grieve for the man who carried you in his arms into this new country, this country that is yours but never his? Did you thank him for his laughter, which fell over his house like holy water? You remember that the largest part of you was always angry at this man. You do not want to remember. And then you remember his anger too, and you do not want to remember, you do not want to remember, you do not want to remember. But you see his face. His face the day before he died. You hear his words: You're too hard on your son. A son can be an enemy ¿que no sabes? Listen, a son is a beautiful thing. But you, you are blind. You have always been blind.

The accusation was a slap. You still feel that slap. But you were blind too, my father.

You want to resurrect him, to remind him of things he forgot, to tell him he forgave himself too easily, to tell him he was a good husband but a bad father, to tell him he was wrong. Resurrect him? Only to tell him he was wrong? Was he wrong? What was he wrong about? You are no longer so sure. Of anything.

The slap. On your face. You feel it still.

The strange tears on your face. Salty as the sea.

How can this be? Your heart is made of stone.

*To thee do we cry poor banished children of Eve.*

# gustavo

The smell of the bar, the light that shone on the dark wood, the reflection of light in the bottles that lined the wall. So many bottles and shapes, so many smells that became one smell. It wasn't clear to him why he felt calm just sitting there. Calmness was not something that came easily to him. What came easily to him was the appearance of calmness. But that's never how he felt. Here, in this bar, he fit here—or, at least, he didn't have to fit. That was what he liked about bars. The rules were different. Different from his father's.

He caught a look at himself in the large mirror behind the bar. He seemed older to himself than eighteen, older, tired, nothing resembling a boy. And right then, he liked the way he felt, a man not needing a mother or a father or a brother or a sister, not needing anything except to be sitting there. It was strange, that need *not* to belong, that need to be untethered to the spinning earth, and strange, too, to have that ache, that desperate need to be a man, and he wondered where that came from, that need, that ache, as if knowing the source might cure the disease. But there was no cure, no inoculation. The only cure was to fall in love with the disease.

He wondered if all men felt that need. Of course they did. Of course. Maybe all men were born with that need and lived their whole lives trying to discover a way to become that large, violent, brutal, unfathomable thing. He thought of his father and how he liked the silent, stoic life of the mind but also loved the hunt. Did he love the drama of it, the ritual, or was it something else? The visceral beauty of it? The smell of it? The power of it? The act of becoming God? The act of becoming the giver and taker of life? He thought of how his father had tried to recruit him into that world of his and how he'd failed. *I don't think it's beautiful.* He'd lied. Of course, it was beautiful. So beautiful that it could have devoured him whole.

He thought of Jack Evans, who'd signed up to go fight in a war he didn't know anything about. And hadn't he done it because that was his way of being a man? His way of showing the world that he wasn't afraid, wasn't afraid of being swallowed whole? *Come and fucking get me.* Wasn't that part of the reason? Jack could prove to his father and to his uncles, to his mother and to his aunts, prove to his country that he was brave and that he would do his part, make of himself a sacrifice, lay his youth down for beautiful things and beautiful ideas and beautiful words, even though he didn't understand any of the things, any of the ideas, any of the words—but if he died, laid down his life, then at least those he left behind would never doubt his manhood, his virtue, his beauty, despite the fact that there was nothing beautiful in the war he had decided to fight. Nothing beautiful in this war or any war, nothing beautiful at all. And he wondered why the words they exchanged had been so unintelligent. They had acted like inarticulate boys. Was it better then? Better to be boys than to be men?

• • •

"Shit, Gustavo, you're just looking at me like, shit, man, like I don't know what."

"You're crazy, Jack. What's wrong with you?"

"What's wrong with me, Gustavo? What's wrong with me? Nothing's fucking wrong with me. We're fighting a war."

"Is that what we're doing? I thought it was a conflict. Isn't that what your father said, that it was a conflict?"

"Conflict, War. What fucking difference does it make? We're in this thing and—"

"We?"

"It's our fucking duty."

"Why? Just tell me fucking why."

"You know why."

"No, I don't."

"You're playing games."

"Which of us is playing?"

"Gustavo, people are dying so you can fuckin' wear an armband and wear your hair as a long as a girl's."

"Is that right? Is that fuckin' right? That's why people are dying? Really? A whole fucking war just so Gustavo Espejo can live his life the way he wants? And you're such a good fuckin' soul and love me so fucking much that you'll pick up a gun and kill some poor bastard who was raised in a village whose name you and I can't even pronounce just so I can have a few fuckin' rights? Wow, fuckin' wow. Tell me something, Jack, because I just don't fuckin' get it. I just don't get how this thing we're doing in Vietnam is going to make the world a better place. Explain it to me because I'm a fuckin' idiot."

"Or maybe just a goddamned Communist."

"Fuck you. I don't even know two fucking dimes' worth about Communism. You think I've read Mao? Marx? Engels? You don't even know who they fucking are, do you? I do. Big fucking deal. Just because I know who they are doesn't mean I know what they wrote. You think I've read the fucking the Communist Manifesto? You think I want to fucking start a revolution? Me, Gustavo Espejo? You're full of shit, buddy. I'll tell you one thing, the only person I know who knows anything bout Communism is my sister, Xochil. You know her, don't you? The girl you like so much. But not me, bro. I wouldn't know a Communist from a cockroach."

"They're the same thing as far as I can tell."

"Is that right?"

"Yes, that's fucking right."

"You're not a soldier, Jack. You're just a fucking parrot. You just repeat the things everybody around you says, what your father says, what your mother says, what your uncles say. Repeating words isn't the same thing as thinking."

"I'm smart enough to know whose side I'm on."

"Well, you're one up on me there, bro."

"Don't call me bro, you motherfucker. You're a fucking stranger, Gustavo. I just can't respect a man who doesn't love his own country. Or maybe you're just an ordinary, average coward. I don't fucking respect that either."

"Respect. That's funny. That's real funny. I'm gonna tell you two things, Jack. The first thing is calling a man a name isn't an goddamned argument. Any high school kid who took Mr. Holland's senior English class could tell you that. You can call me a Communist and you can call me a coward, and you can call me an asshole, a spick, a prick, a smelly long-haired Mexican, a pot-smoking grifo, you can call me anything you fucking want—but it's just name calling, Jack. That's all it is. And the thing is, Jack, just because you join the army—"

"I joined the fuckin' Marines."

"Wow. The Marines. Fucking wow. Just because you joined the fuckin' Marines doesn't make you brave. It doesn't make you better. It doesn't make you smarter. It doesn't even make you more American."

"Fuck you, Gus!"

*"Don't ever call me Gus. My name's Gustavo, Jack. And if I ever catch you touching my sister, I swear I'll cut your balls off."*

*"Sounds like a threat. Some pacifist you fuckin' are."*

*"Pacifist, Jack? Pacifists are angels, baby. All I know is that if I'm gonna kill a man, I need a good reason to do it."*

*"I know what I'm doing."*

*"Sure you do, Jack."*

He wondered why they hadn't gone at each other. Maybe it was because of Xochil or maybe it was because they'd been friends since seventh grade—though now it seemed that their old friendship was dead and buried and neither one of them was moved by any kind of nostalgia for their boyhoods. Maybe, despite their words and their anger, neither one of them had the stomach for a fight. Just because they were no longer friends didn't mean they wanted to be enemies.

It was Gustavo who had finally walked away. *Walk just walk,* he heard that voice in his head and turned away even when he heard Jack yelling, *Come back here you goddamned motherfucker. Let's just fucking settle this right now.* Jack's rage didn't seem real to him, far and hollow, and he wondered why he felt as if his whole body had gone to sleep, and anyway, he thought, if Jack wanted to take a swing at him, well, he was more than welcome to come after him.

*So, Jack, baby, you think I'm a Communist and you think I'm a coward. You sure as shit like to throw words around.* He sipped on his Tecate, then lit another cigarette, then scanned the room with his eyes. He concentrated on a gringo couple who was sitting in one of the booths. They seemed to be having a war of their own, their loud, angry whispers not quite lost in the noise. But there at the bar, there was nothing but a row of stools occupied by men who seemed to have settled in for the evening, most of them much older than himself, all of them with a look of exhaustion from their own tired lives, the not-enough-money days and too-much-sad-damned-work days and wives and children and whatever hell their lives brought them, leaving them exhausted or just plain beaten down, rocks pulverized to dust.

He wondered why his father and his uncles had never found themselves in bars. It was, he thought, as good a place as any to find yourself. Or lose yourself. Or both. Perhaps they found themselves in other ways. He wondered where Charlie would find his place in the world—though he doubted Charlie would suffer about such things. He would be more original than the rest of them. He would escape the violence, would find a way of escaping being a cheap copy of the men who'd come before him. *But not me, Charlie. I'm like every other guy in the goddamned world—just like the rest of them.* He often whispered things to his younger brother. It made it appear as if he weren't talking to himself.

He shook his head. Too serious. Xochil always said that. *Hiding your good mind in a bar.* That's what his mother would say. But if he'd have had as decent a mind as his mother thought, then what the fuck was he doing sitting in a Juárez bar with nothing to keep him company but a beer, a pack of cigarettes, and the voices of a bunch of guys who were mostly talking about how the world was beating the shit out of them. *Yeah, Mom, hiding my good mind.* He took a drag from his cigarette and laughed. Well, everyone had to find a place to take a vacation—especially people who didn't have the money to take one. Everyone had to find their own Kentucky Club, a place where you didn't have to be responsible for a damned thing. A place where you could feel alive, free, and it didn't matter a damn that it wasn't true. It was true enough for those few moments. A bar. A cigarette. A beer. It didn't surprise him at all that some men spent hours in a bar just sitting there. Drinking. Talking. Retreating from whatever it was that kept them down, escaping from their homes that offered them—offered them what?

He finished his beer, and took out the letter, read it, brief, clear, inelegant, as if it were a machine that was sending you to war and not a country. Nuance, irony, subtlety held no sway. His mother would have hated the lack of attention to aesthetics. But Octavio would have approved. *What did you expect, a work of literature?*

He folded the notice so it was as small as a pack of cigarettes. He stuffed it in his shirt pocket.

Two weeks to report. Maybe he would sit here at the Kentucky Club for two weeks. Maybe he would sit here for the rest of his life. *Yeah, yeah, sure.* He ordered another beer. He pictured Charlie pointing to a place on the globe with his long, steady finger: *Look, Vietnam. It's right here, Gus. Right here. Look.*

## adam

**Da Nang, Vietnam, Saturday, September 17, 1967, 7:00 a.m.**

They're coming for us."

"I thought we had another couple days of this."

"Change of plan."

"Because Bill was hit."

"That would be my guess."

"So it's back to the base?"

"The bird's comin', that's all I fucking know."

"Well, thank God—that's all I fucking gotta say."

"You're always thanking God for things. Thank God for what?"

"I'm fucking drenched down to the bone. And I need to get dry. That's what I need."

"You're a good Catholic boy, you fucking know that?"

"Well, maybe Catholic, but maybe not so fucking good. How many saints you know picked up a rifle?"

"Maybe more than you think, cracker."

"Cracker?" Camera laughed. "Thank God for fucking crackers."

"Back where I come from, that's not what we thank God for."

"Guess not."

"We thank God for the beauty of a woman's legs."

"Maybe I should switch religions."

"You got that right. So what you gonna do when they take us back to the base?"

"Take a fucking shower. Sleep."

"Shower, shit, man, me too, I'm fucking gonna take me a good long hot fuckin' shower. Maybe we'll get us a fine evening at the beach. Toke up. Dream of Chi-town. And you can fuckin' dream of El Paso."

"Toke up, toke up—that's all you think of."

"Never seen you turn it down—and you're not even fuckin' payin' for it."

"Never turn down what's free."

Whit laughed. "Fuck you. And I bet you're gonna write a letter."

"Bet you are too."

"Who you gonna write to?"

"My mom."

"Good fuckin' choice. You lay off writin' to those women who badger your ass. Especially that Evelyn."

"Shut the fuck up."

"Just write to your mother. Tell her a black-assed Methodist who don't like to pray sends regards."

"Regards?"

"Ain't that what white people say?"

They heard the sound of the helicopter. They laughed. It was raining again.

He could have gone over to Conrad's. *Oh God, he called I forgot to tell*— Yes, he might be at Conrad's. Conrad, who loved Eugene McCarthy and politics and philosophy and the Rolling Stones and Joan Baez, Conrad who could talk for hours, Conrad who was always trying to convert someone to a different way of thinking, who should have been born a Buddhist or a Quaker instead of a Catholic. Yes, Gustavo could be there. Be there. She hoped. She pictured them talking, her brother listening intently, Conrad waving his arms as he spoke with those gigantic hands and the way he enunciated his words as if he were always in front of a large audience, his thick lips constantly in motion, and his eyes looking straight at you, his dark, droopy, beautiful eyes—and why wasn't she interested in Conrad instead of Jack? Yes, that's where he was, Conrad's—or he could be at Josie's. *God, no, not Josie's.* If he was there, they wouldn't be talking—especially if they went riding around in her new Mustang, the date car, the bribe car, God, she was desperate and she tried not to picture them together, but, no, he wouldn't be at Josie's, Gustavo didn't like her, not really—even though she was always throwing herself at him and even though she was pretty and smarter than most people gave her credit for. Gustavo never liked girls who were too needy, no, he wasn't at Josie's, absolutely not. Maybe he was just taking some Gustavo time—or maybe he went over to Jorge's, God she hoped not, all they ever did was light up a joint, and listen to Procul Harum and Frank Zappa over and over until you thought your head would come flying off. *God, if he came home stoned tonight, Dad would—*

"Hi."

She smiled at Charlie and waved him in.

"Everyone's gone home."

"I know."

Charlie looked around his sister's room. She knew what he was thinking, too neat, everything in its place. She watched him. She knew he was studying her desk, the only messy thing in the room, the pile of books, the papers, a piece of white paper in the typewriter with words on it.

She smiled at him. "You always do that."

"Do what?"

"Search my room."

"I'm not searching."

"Your eyes, they search."

"You working on a paper for school?"

"See what I mean."

"I can't help it."

"I know."

"Dad's angry."

"He's going to kill Gustavo when he gets in."

"He's not."

Xochil sat up on her bed, patted it, and motioned for Charlie to sit down. She reached over and kissed him softly on the top of his head. "You know, it's sweet that you think the best of other people, Charlie. But I swear, Dad's going to kill him."

Charlie rubbed his head. "How come you like to kiss me there?"

"Where?"

"On the top of my head."

"Because you're so short."

"I'm going to grow."

"And then what? Are you going to beat me up?"

"Don't be crazy."

"Do you want me to stop kissing you?"

"Not ever." He looked around the room. Nervous. "I'm worried about Gus."

"You always worry about him. You're like Mom. You worry about everything."

"No, I don't."

"So tell me why you play that map game? The one where you keep track of where everyone is on your map?"

"It's just a game."

"It's a sign."

"Of what?"

"Of being a worrier. Hate to break it you."

"Maybe it just means—"

"You're a worrier."

"So what? Wish I had a cigarette."

"What?"

*"Wish I had a cigarette."*

"What would you do with it?"

"Don't be a wiseass. I'd smoke the thing."

"You're too young."

"Yeah, okay. When did Gus start?"

"I can't remember."

"Bet he was my age."

"Maybe. He's not a good role model, you know?"

# gustavo

I wasn't drunk. Not exactly drunk. For sure I wasn't sober. I was in between two states of mind. I had always lived there.

I could see the thunder in the distance. I loved the thunder and the sky and the smell in the air. And it was funny because that's what I felt right then. Love. For the world I lived in. It was strong and beautiful and overwhelming and it didn't matter a damn that the world was so imperfect and mean and a fucking mess. I was in love, if only for a second.

And then the second was gone.

I just kept walking.

I wasn't in a hurry.

When I reached the top of the arch of the Santa Fe Bridge, I looked toward Sunset Heights. Nineteen Ten Prospect, the only house I had ever known.

I stood there. Still. I closed my eyes. Well, okay, I was a little drunk. I took a breath. And then another. And there, with my eyes closed, standing in between two countries, all I could see were small fragments of the things that had happened in that house: Xochil staring down Octavio. Xochil coming into our bedroom late at night when she couldn't sleep, whispering *Gustavo? Charlie?* And me and Charlie waking up immediately to the sound of her voice, and then all of us taking our places in that room, me on my bed, Charlie giving his bed over to Xochil, and him lying on the floor in between us, listening to us, mostly listening, and I knew how much he loved us, how much he loved us both, and I wondered if I had that kind of love inside me, and I wished I were like her, like Xochil, who would come into our room to talk and talk. *Okay, okay, what are you most afraid of?* And the answers flying around the room like paper airplanes. *Mom dying dad dying me dying you dying me being buried alive you being shot by a gun. Shot by a gun? Where do you get these things? What gun? Buried alive? Too many Vincent Price movies, baby? Mom—she'll never ever die. Dad, he's dead already. Not funny. That's not funny.* And then I felt an ache as I picture Charlie falling asleep between me and Xochil. Why did that hurt?

And then the rain. The thunder. The lightning.

I don't know why, but I just had to go back and look for Angel. I think a part of me didn't believe I'd met him. *I just didn't believe it.* And the more beer I drank, the more I began to believe I'd made him up. Completely invented him. Isn't it strange, how we don't believe the things that happen to us? If we don't believe our own lives, what can we believe?

I didn't mind walking in the torrents of rain. It was like taking a shower, and I fought the urge to find a place that would protect me. I didn't feel like being protected, didn't deserve it. I just wanted to let the rain pelt me. Let the rain beat the holy shit out of me. I just didn't care. And just like that, the rain stopped, though there was thunder and lightning all around the city and I knew the rain would come and go all night.

I was drenched and cold and trembling.

But I kept walking toward that alley. Where I'd found Angel. I don't know what I was expecting to find. I half thought he'd be gone. But he was there, sitting under the dim light of a blinking lamppost. His eyes wide open, looking up toward the heavens, a needle at his side.

So this is how the world ended for people like Angel.

He looked almost like a painting in a museum: *Angel looking toward heaven.* Only he wasn't a painting. And he wasn't sitting in a museum.

*I'm the fucking future.*

I'm making this up. I'm making this up. I'm making this up.

I ran. That's what I did. I just ran. I stopped running only when I crossed the bridge over the freeway into Sunset Heights.

That's when it started raining again.

## xochil. charlie.

Would it be so bad, if I were like Gus?"

"No, it wouldn't be so bad. But you're not him, Charlie. You're you. Be yourself."

"It's boring to be me."

"No."

"Yes."

"No."

"Yes."

"You're beautiful."

"Sure." He took a breath. "Where is he?"

"I don't know. But Dad's going to kill him."

"You better not let him."

"Mom will stop him before— Shhh—" She put her finger to her lips. "That's him," she whispered.

They froze. Listening, dogs with their ears up, alert, ready.

"It's him. He's home."

"They're arguing."

"No. Dad's lecturing."

"That's a bad sign. Dad never lectures. That's a really, really bad sign. You think we should go out there?"

"No."

"Why not?"

"It's just not a good idea, Charlie. It will only make things worse."

"Worse?"

"Trust me. Shhh, shhhh, listen—"

## octavio. gustavo. lourdes.

Your grandmother dead—and you stumbling home drunk at midnight?"

Gustavo stood in the middle of the living room, his head down, his lips quivering. He felt his head pounding, couldn't think, felt as if he'd just been hit on the head with the sharp edge of a broken stone and he half expected to feel blood running down his face—did feel it—just rainwater running down his wet hair and God, he couldn't keep himself from trembling. He wanted to say something. He felt the word *sorry* swelling up on his tongue. But it seemed such a thoughtless and shallow thing to say, and his tongue felt numb and thick, the news of his grandmother's death leaving him stunned and even more wordless than he had ever been—and how could his father break the news to him like that, in the form of a lecture, as if she had meant nothing at all to him and suddenly he remembered how she would hold him and smell him and tell him he had the odor of a cloud about to burst with rain, rain!

"Where were you?"

Gustavo refused to look up at his father.

"Where were you?"

"Juárez."

"Looking for a woman."

"I was just drinking."

"Where?"

Gustavo hated this, hated his father's need to know details as if they mattered, as if the details were part of an equation that was crucial to the understanding of life and all its deeper questions or something profound like that, hated his father when he became an interrogator, and he wanted to scream at him, *The fucking Kentucky Club, downing beers and smoking cigarettes and thinking about a junkie named Angel who told me he was the fucking future, what else do you want to know Dad? The number of bottles lining the bar? The stunned look on the man when his wife poured a beer on his head and told him she knew he was screwing someone else? Do you want to know everything I heard tonight, Dad, the hundred tragedies that don't matter a damn to anyone but—*

"Gustavo? Answer me."

He pushed his wet hair off his face. "The Kentucky Club," he mumbled.

"Everyone was here tonight, your uncles and aunts, your cousins. And you?"

Gustavo said nothing.

"Look at me."

Gustavo shook his head.

"I said *look at me.*"

"Here. Put this on. You'll catch a cold." He stared at his mother as she held out the clean, warm T-shirt. He wondered at the softness of her voice, but it was also firm and in control, and he wished he were her because she wasn't lost and he *was*, God, lost, and how had he gotten lost in just one afternoon?

"Lourdes, we're not finished here."

"You can finish your lecture after he changes into something warm."

"Lourdes—" he stopped himself, took control of his voice. "Let's not argue."

"Good." She shoved the shirt into Gustavo's hands. "Go change," she said. "And dry your hair. And put on a dry pair of jeans."

Gustavo stared at his mother, her eyes, tired but alive, her hands holding a towel, offering it to him. He moved his face away from her, taking the gift, then looked at his father. He was tired too, only his eyes were hard with relentless anger. He had seen and known those eyes all his life. He looked down at the floor.

"There's no excuse for this."

*I didn't know she was dead.* It was the truth and he clutched at the thought—*I didn't know.* His father knew that. *He knew that.*

"I'm sorry," he said. He felt the hot tears on his face, hated that they were there, didn't even know *why* they were there and he hated himself for his graceless and pitiful inability to control his own body as if he were a boy pissing in his pants, hated himself for his self-pitying tears and for the limp way he was standing, ashamed, half drunk, but not drunk enough, sober enough to know everything, sober enough to feel the pain and he kept thinking of his grandmother and the way she'd always looked at him, and if he'd known she was going to die today he would've kissed her one last time and smelled her old skin and combed her hair with his fingers the way he'd always done when he was a boy and God he hated this crying in front of his father. *In front of his father.* He felt his whole body shaking, trembling as if he were going to come apart from the inside, getting ready to explode, self-immolate—and then he felt his mother's arms around him, her push leading him gently into his room.

"Cry all you want," she whispered, then slowly unbuttoned his shirt and dried him off, dried his wet hair and his wet back and his wet chest just like he was a baby, and she held him in her arms and all he did was sob and her voice kept whispering *Cry, cry, cry all you want.*

## lourdes. octavio.

He didn't know she was dead."

He let her almost-whispered statement hang in the air.

*"He didn't know she was dead."*

He stared at his wife's lips for an instant. "He would've known if he had stayed home."

"But he didn't."

"He didn't ask permission to go out."

"Does he need our permission?"

"He lives in our house."

"Our house?"

"Maybe he should just leave."

"Maybe he will."

"He's not old enough to drink."

"He's certainly old enough to pick up a gun."

"Don't, just don't, Lourdes. You sound just like them, adopting their arguments—what next? You're not a child. You're not eighteen. Soon you'll be borrowing Xochil's clothes."

"The way you say that—their arguments—as if your children are enemies."

*"He's not old enough to drink.* The Kentucky Club. What is he doing in the Kentucky Club?"

"Running away, I think."

"Running away? From what?"

"From us."

"He comes home, dragging the smell of a bar along with him, and you think that's acceptable?"

"I have very little patience for drunks. I have even less patience of cruelty."

"Disciplining a son is cruelty?"

"Your mother adored that boy. And *he* adored *her.* In the past two years, did you ever bother to get off that chair, walk into your mother's room, and watch your oldest son as—Octavio, you should have seen them—all of your children. They loved that woman. You should be proud. You should be happy. He walks into the house and you spit out the news of her death like so much saliva."

"I don't spit."

*"He didn't know she was dead."*

*"He was drunk."*

*"Drunk or not, there's no defense—"*

*"I'm sorry I wasn't more tender with—"*

*"Don't take that tone. He's a boy."*

*"It's damn time he becomes a man."*

*"It's damn time you become a father."*

"Lower your voice."

"Lower yours." She took a breath.

"And what's that supposed to mean—damn time I became a father?"

"It means you should be kinder to your son. More tender—as you put it."

"So you want me to excuse his behavior?"

"Apparently that job belongs to me. Just as it's always been my job to excuse yours. But not tonight, *amor*. Not even tonight." She walked toward the cabinet and studied her husband's collection of liqueurs. She took out a crystal glass, examined it. She took a breath, then another. "I can't figure out what I want."

"Drambuie. You like Drambuie."

"I'll have a brandy." She watched herself pour the thick gold liquid into the snifter. She took out another glass, then poured a second drink. "I want peace in this house."

He took the drink from her and nodded.

She touched her glass against his.

"I can't tell what you're thinking."

"I can't figure out what I want."

"Sometimes it doesn't matter what we want."

"When does it matter?"

"What?"

"When does it start to matter?"

He let the brandy numb his tongue.

"Gustavo was crying."

"You think I don't care."

"He was sobbing. Is your heart so hard?"

"I'm sorry."

"Sorry?"

"He doesn't want me to love him."

"What?"

"Can't you see that? He doesn't want me. He doesn't want his father."

# gustavo

I was sitting on my bed. Numb as a stone—except that stones don't cry.

Xochil and Charlie must have heard my sobs.

My mom dried me off and held me, then let me alone. The last time she'd done that I was five. She was good enough to know when to leave the room.

I still felt the cold rain on my skin, and I was shivering and sobbing—and then there they were, Xochil and Charlie.

I have fragments of that night floating around in my brain, forever floating there. They're like these soft pieces of light—that's how I remember it—they were like leaves raining down on me, but the leaves were made of light.

I don't think I was crying just because my grandmother was dead. I was crying because I was afraid of going off to fight in Vietnam. What if I got used to killing? What if killing would become something normal to a heart like mine, a heart that could lose its discipline so easily, a heart that could explode? I was afraid of going into the army. I was afraid that the men in the military would be as disapproving as my father, as if that disapproval could turn me into a man. I was afraid of everything, and I didn't know what to do and the beer had done something to my ability to hide the things I felt, and I was so addicted to the hiding. My mom was wrong about me trying to hide my good mind. I wasn't trying to hide my mind—I was trying to hide my heart.

And I didn't even know if my heart was good or bad. I just knew it was the source of all pain.

I remember sobbing and Charlie taking my hand and holding it, just holding it, and I squeezed his hand back as if it were the only hand in the world. And Xochil pressed me against her chest, and I cried into her. I tried to let them comfort me, but so much of me was inconsolable and in some ways I've remained that way—numb and inconsolable.

I remember Charlie's voice, the smallest and kindest voice in the world, and he kept whispering, "It's okay, Gus, nothing can ever hurt you." It didn't matter that it wasn't true because I knew what he meant: *right now, we're here, me and Xochil,* and that meant I was safe.

I wondered about the savage mystery of the human heart. Everything that ever hurt me ran across my mind like mean, careless children stomping across a park—Leandra, the first girl I ever made love to, who moved away to San Antonio and told me I'd ruined her; the time a swarm of bees attacked me and wouldn't stop biting me, my whole body swelling up until I thought I would burst like a balloon; the time Charlie almost died when he was four and had to be hospitalized and me and Xochil refused to leave his room and how Xochil clung to me and kept telling me, *Don't let him die don't let him die make it stop Gustavo make it stop,* and me unable to do anything but hold her; the first time Dad looked at me with that look of disgust in his eyes; the first time I got into a fight with Alberto Pedregon and understood that I had a frightening violence in me; the look on my grandfather's face when he died, how he seemed to be looking at me with a combination of fear and relief; the afternoon Grandma Rosie held my face between her soft and ancient hands and told me she wanted to die and that I should pray for that, for her death; the day I got the notice to report for my physical exam. Everything was there, every ache, every hurt, every memory.

And then, I don't know, I just stopped crying.

I could see Angel's eyes, open, lifeless, full of torment, full of a punishing, relentless despair, but still clinging to that last molecule of hope, a wanting, a waiting for a moment of grace that would never come.

## xochil. gustavo. charlie.

Are you better now, Gus?"

"What's the greatest book ever written?"

Xochil and Charlie looked at each other, smiled, then broke out laughing. He was playing the game. He was talking and he was alive and he wasn't broken. He was back from wherever his pain had taken him. "Wait, wait," Xochil laughed. She sounded like she had a cold. Because she'd been crying. "I need my spot." She threw herself on Charlie's bed, and threw a pillow on the floor. For Charlie. That was his spot, on the rug between the two twin beds. Sometimes, they would all lie in the room, none of them talking, all of them reading, and then someone would say something, and they would talk. Mostly Charlie listened. Sometimes they argued about the meaning of the books they'd read, or about something they'd heard, or about their friends, or about the news reports, or about, well, sometimes they just argued. Xochil always won.

Charlie turned off the light, then threw himself on the floor and folded the pillow. That's what they did, talked in the darkness.

"You smell clean," Xochil said.

Charlie laughed. "You always say that when you lie on my bed—but you never tell me the smell. What's the smell?"

"Freshly mowed grass."

"I smell like freshly mowed grass?"

"Yeah. A little more subtle than that—but like that, yes."

Gustavo laughed. "Sometimes he smells really bad."

"He is in the room, Gus."

They laughed. And nothing bad had ever happened. There was only the game. "The greatest book," Gustavo repeated.

"The Bible."

"Doesn't count."

"Doesn't count?" Charlie tried to imagine the look on his sister's face in the darkness of the room. "Why not? Because you're an atheist?"

"No, that's not why—and I'm not an atheist."

"Yes, you are."

"Maybe I am. Maybe I'm just an agnostic. And anyway, we're talking novels, Xochil."

"Novels? You said books."

"Implied."

"Not implied, but okay, novels. Greatest novel? *Great Expectations*."

"Hell, no."

Charlie laughed. "He doesn't like English novels, Xochil."

"I forgot."

"He is in the room, Carlitos."

God, they laughed. Sweet. Good. Laughter. Like rain.

"Screw the English."

"*Ulysses*."

"Haven't read it."

"It's the greatest novel ever written."

"Haven't read it, either. You threw it against the wall, remember?"

"*Moby-Dick.*" Charlie knew he was wrong even before he opened his mouth.

"No."

"It's a great book."

"Yeah, groovy." He only said *groovy* when he was mocking someone.

"*Walden.*"

"Novels, Xochil."

"It's a great book."

"Yes, it is," Gustavo said softly. "Charlie's right—not a novel."

"*War and Peace.*"

"Nope."

"Why?"

"It's fine. It's a fine book—but, well, too Russian."

"Too Russian. That's stupid, Gustavo."

"Not the greatest book."

"*The Grapes of Wrath,*" Charlie yelled.

"Yes," Xochil yelled.

"Wrong."

"It's a great book."

"Yes, it's a great book. Wrong."

"Wrong? You're crazy, Gustavo."

Charlie loved the outrage in her voice.

"Wrong," Gustavo repeated.

"How could it be the wrong book? And it's a proletarian novel."

"Steinbeck disowned it."

"He did not."

"He did too."

"No, he didn't."

"Yes, he did."

"Doesn't matter—it's a great novel."

"A great, great book. But not the greatest."

"Yeah. And since you're God, you get to decide. *Ulysses*, no. *War and Peace*, no. *Grapes of Wrath*, no."

"Whoever starts the game gets to be God. You know the rules."

"Sure. I know the rules. You know, Gustavo, that's the thing about you. You hate all the rules—unless you're the guy making them. There's a word for that. You know?"

"A word?"

*"Duplicitous."*

"Duplicitous," Gustavo laughed. "Look, Miss Dictionary, I know the word. And I have to say, it's not an accurate description of my person."

Charlie laughed softly to himself. He wanted the game to go on forever, just so he could lie there and catch their voices as they floated above him. And then suddenly, without even knowing why, the answer came to him. *"Johnny Got His Gun!"*

"What?"

*"Johnny Got His Gun."*

"How'd you guess that, little guy?"

"Don't call me that. I hate that, Gus. And don't get mad."

"I'm not mad."

"Yes, you are."

"How'd you guess it?"

"Dad confiscated it a couple of weeks ago. He shoved the book across the table at Mom and said, 'Do you see what your son is reading? He was a Communist.' And then Mom said, 'What are you talking about? Who was a Communist?' And then Dad said, 'Dalton Trumbo.' And then Mom said, 'Octavio, finish your coffee.'"

Xochil laughed. "Charlie, when you grow up, you can be a court reporter."

"Don't make fun. I'm just telling you what happened."

They all broke out laughing again.

"*Johnny Got His Gun*," Xochil repeated. "I've never read it."

"You've never read it?" Gustavo couldn't quite bring himself to believe her, she who devoured books, she who dreamed them, she who spoke about them as if they were lovers.

"Never."

"Read us a section."

"Mom has it."

"She does?"

"She's reading it."

"Charlie, you're a spy."

"I like to know what's going on."

"Of course you do. We're cities on a map. And you're the family cartographer."

"Maybe I am."

"Does she like it?"

"I don't know, Gus, I don't read minds."

"I bet you memorized a section."

"How do you know?"

"You memorize sections of all the books you love. You've done that since you were thirteen. Remember? That's when you read *Fahrenheit 451*."

"Really, Gus?"

"I just thought it was cool how people became a book."

"And you've tried to memorize books ever since."

"Without success."

"Except you always memorize at least one passage."

"Yeah, well, it's a habit."

"Tell us, Gus. Recite the section. Recite it."

"It's too sad and it's too serious and it's too tragic."

"Just like you, Gustavo."

"Right."

"Don't fight it."

"Tell us, Gus. Let us hear it."

He hated the pleading in his brother's voice. "Okay," he whispered. "But it's not pretty."

"Just get on with it."

"Yeah, Gus."

The room was quiet for a moment, as if Gustavo was gathering the words, like raking a pile of leaves in a yard. He cleared his throat and then began, his voice just above a whisper: *"Put the guns into our hands and we will use them. Give us slogans and we will turn them into realties. Sing the battle hymns and we will take them up where you left off. Not one not ten not ten thousand not a million not ten millions not a hundred million but a billion two billions of us all the people of the world we will have the slogans and we will have the hymns and we will have the guns and we will use them and we will live. Make no mistake we will live. We will be alive and we will walk and talk and eat and sing and laugh and feel and love and bear our children in tranquility in security in decency in peace. You plan the wars you masters of men plan the wars and point the way and we will point the gun."*

The room was quiet for a long time. All three of them lying in the stillness, Gustavo's whispers echoing in the room.

" 'And we will point the gun,' " Xochil repeated. "That's the saddest thing I've ever heard."

## Da Nang, Vietnam, September 18, 1967

Dear Mom,

It's not raining today and it looks like it might be clear most of the day. I think I'll go to the beach. A day at the beach—how about that, Mom? I slept in. Guess I was just really tired from our mission. Being out there really makes me tired, have to be alert, you know? When I finish writing this letter, I'm going to take a long hot shower—another one! When we got back to the base, that's the first thing I did, took a shower. Now, I'm going to take another one. You're going to have one clean Marine of a son, Mom, I'll tell you that.

Did I tell you that I'm growing a mustache? How about that? What do you think? When it grows in, I'll send you a picture.

Maybe later in the afternoon, I'll go over to the PX and buy some cigarettes. They're cheap, so that's good, something I can afford. Not that I have anything to spend my money on, not really. And listen, Mom, I know you said I shouldn't be sending you my hard-earned money, but listen, Mom, I want to help you out. I know it's been hard since Dad died, and I know you have a pretty decent job typing letters and filing and all that for those lawyers, but still, Bobby and Tom and Mike, they need stuff. I know how that goes. I don't want them to do without. I can't make them rich, but, you know, every bit helps. Just tell them to keep up their studies. I know I'm one to talk, but I did finish high school, at least I did that, and I plan on going on to college after my tour here, tell them that. Especially Bobby. I know he's chomping at the bit to join up—but he's just fifteen and he's the smart one. Everyone knows that. Tell him that maybe he can get a job this summer and start saving some money to go to college. Tell him to get some use out of the brain God gave him. Then later, he can tend to this Marine thing or his army thing or whatever hell branch he damn well chooses. By that time, this war will be long over, and he can give Uncle Sam his due in a nice office in Germany or Belgium.

Did you know that they have a big base in Belgium? It's called SHAPE, the Supreme Headquarters of the Allied Powers in Europe. Did you know that? Belgium. They say it rains there all the time. That's what I hear. Just like the monsoon season here in Nam. I'll tell you what, Mom, I sure am getting to hate the rain. Remember, when I was a kid, how I used to like to go and play out in the rain, and Dad would tell me I didn't have any sense in me. Not an ounce of sense. Well, I'm still playing in the rain. Only now it's pretty serious playing.

Look, Mom, tell Bobby and Tom and Mike to be good to each other. Tell them that their big brother's doing just fine and that when I come home, I expect them to buy me the biggest root beer in the state of Texas.

God, I miss root beer.

I know you're praying for me. Keep those candles going over at St. Patrick's.

Love,
Adam

---

He sealed the envelope.

He didn't tell her about their wounded.

He didn't tell her about his dreams.

He didn't tell her that he sometimes smoked weed when he went to the beach at night.

He didn't tell her that he'd been so cold that when he was under the hot shower he'd almost cried. Hell, he had cried. What the hell was wrong with him?

He didn't tell her that already he'd heard talk that they were going out on patrol again and that the next patrol sounded a lot more serious. Accompanying convoys was always more serious. And word was, this was supposed to be something big, this convoy. If a grunt like him knew that, then the enemy knew it too. At least that's how he figured it. They would attract a lot of attention.

No, he didn't tell her.

In her last letter, she had asked about Whit and Salvi. He hadn't had the heart to tell her that Salvi was back stateside—getting used to life without legs. It was a mistake to tell his mother about his friends. When something happened to them, what was he supposed to tell her? He wouldn't mention his friends anymore. It was better that way.

You had to be careful what you said to your mom.

# lourdes

She didn't know how long she'd been sitting there. In the dark. Only the light of a candle burning in the room. On Rosario's bed, sitting, trembling. And trembling not because she was cold but because her anger completely owned her now.

She tried to calm herself by watching the flame of the flickering candle.

She stared at the letter she'd found in her son's shirt pocket. She wanted to rip the letter to pieces and swore she could do the same to the men who sent it. Rip them, rip them all to pieces.

She rocked and rocked herself and found something, at last, to comfort her—the fact that her son had thought about these things, had thought and thought about them. Perhaps he'd found no solutions, but he had refused to think of the war as something graceful and noble and inevitable. He had refused to be like so many young men, ardent and enthusiastic for war as if war— any war—was some kind of game that would transform them into virtuous and valiant creatures, ardent, yes, so many boys so desperate for glory because they did not know how to look into themselves and discover their own beauty and value and so they looked for their virtues in places where it could never be found, places that twisted and callused their hearts.

Another woman would convince him to go and do his duty, convince him it was right to serve his country. Another mother would beg him to don the uniform and tell him with a straight face how handsome he looked. Another woman would pull him to the side and say to him: *What does it matter if you believe or don't believe? Go. It will not be long before you come back to us.* Another woman would swallow her heart and her mind and her tongue and stand by and watch her son be taken, watch him come back in a casket, accept a flag with the words *from a grateful nation.*

## octavio. lourdes.

Octavio found her sitting in his mother's room. "You're sitting in the dark."

"The candles all burned out." She slipped Gustavo's letter under the pillow. "I don't mind the dark."

"I went to bed. I was waiting." He turned on the small lamp next to the bed.

"The room still smells of her."

He nodded.

"It's so quiet."

"I'm sorry I was harsh with Gustavo."

"Are you?"

"Yes."

She nodded. "There's time to make it right."

"Yes, *amor*, there's time."

"Imagine, Octavio. Imagine her voice gone from this world forever. Never to be duplicated. A whole sound gone. Extinct. A song never to be heard again. What if all the birds died, Octavio, what we would do without their songs?"

"Lourdes, the birds are still singing."

"For how long?"

He sat next to her on the bed and wiped her tears. He gently pulled her toward him and felt her sobs echoing against his chest.

"I don't deserve you," he whispered.

"I know," she said, her sobs becoming a soft laugh. She pulled away from him and stared at his smile. Why was his familiar smile so strange, so foreign?

"Let's get some rest."

"God, I've never, never been this tired."

He kissed her eyes.

"Octavio?"

"Yes."

"I'm not careless with words."

"No, I don't think you are. No one should be careless with words."

"But sometimes we are. And you, *amor*, you're more careless than I am."

"How can you say that?"

"Because you are."

"What are you trying to tell me?"

"You said I was an ingrate."

"That's not what I said. I said you were talking like an ingrate."

"I was not talking like an ingrate. I am not an ingrate."

"You make too much of what I said. You're misinterpreting. I wasn't assaulting your character, *amor*. I meant only that this country has been good to us—and that we should be more conscious of—"

"I am not an unconscious human being. And I know what you

meant. I am not an ingrate, Octavio. I want you to understand that."

"All right then, you're not an ingrate."

"Don't humor, me."

"I want to humor you."

"I want you to understand."

"I do. I do understand."

"You don't."

*"Amor—"*

*"I am not an ingrate."*

"Let's go to bed. You're tired. We're both tired."

"I mean it, Octavio. I would rather be called a Communist than be called an ingrate. Do you understand?"

# gustavo

You wake. But there is too much of yesterday in the new day, and your head is throbbing. It is the pain of knowing that your grandmother's voice is gone, the pain of knowing that forever is permanent, unfathomable; it is the pain of knowing that a letter from the government has changed the course of your life; it is the pain of facing the sham of having spent hours and hours in a bar with nothing to keep you company but a pack of cigarettes and bottles and bottles of beer.

The light of the day is in the room.

Your sister is gone. She is back in her room or she is awake and doing the things that people do, the people who are alive. She has always been alive. For that sister whom you love, the world is an altar where she places her offerings—her laughter, her rage, her intelligence, her tears. And your brother, he, too, is gone. He, too, has risen. He, too, is alive—alive with all that generosity and gratitude. You smile. You see him when he was four as he turned to you and said, "Look at the bird, Gus!" He took your hand and made you bend so he could whisper in your ear, "Is it okay, Gus, to thank Jesus for the birds?"

You envy them. The pain of that envy is worse than the throbbing in your head.

Only you remain in your bed. Only you remain in your room. *What will happen now?* You hold that question. You repeat it. Then repeat it again and again.

You wonder about your grandmother and you suddenly whisper to yourself, She's lucky. She's dead now. She's earned her rest. But you have not earned yours. You are eighteen years old. You have not known pain or suffering. You have had sex with only four girls—and one of them you loved. You loved, *you loved that girl.* And you remember how you lost her and how you hated the pain that resided in your heart. That is the only loss you know. That is your only loss? So what do you know? You see the way your father always looks at you—that accusation in his eyes. *What do you know?* And for once, you know that your father is right. You have not known losses and woes and the tiredness that comes with disappointments. Your grandfather lost everything, his land, his riches, his country. Your father inherited exile. You have seen the quiet losses your mother wears on her face without complaint. And you? You are eighteen years old. The world lies before you. The new and large and vast and beautiful world—it lies before you. You ache for it. You yearn to make it yours, this large and vast and beautiful world.

But the world is made of bullets.

The world is made of a draft card.

The world is made of people who are urging you to fight as if a war were nothing more than a football game and you, on the team, carrying the football down the field. *Run! Run! Score! For God! For Country!*

It is morning. You wake. The world is new. It is not the

world you hoped for. And your heart is lonely and bare and desolate. Your heart is a piece of fallow land—an empty field where nothing will ever grow. Not one stalk of corn. Nothing. Not ever.

And the taste of stale beer is buried in your throat.

## abe

I liked Sundays when I was growing up. Not that we really did the church thing. But we did the family thing and I liked that. It was real nice. My mom, my dad, my sisters, my little brother, we'd all hang out. My mom and dad would listen to the radio and read the newspaper and talk. My dad would make waffles, the only time he ever did anything in the kitchen.

My mother was Catholic and my father was a Lutheran. They must have fought about how to raise us. I know my father promised to raise us Catholic because they were married in a Catholic church. But I got the feeling my father didn't mean it. He wanted to marry my mother, but he wasn't much interested in marrying her religion. Yeah, I think they fought about it. In the end, I think they both gave up the church thing. They chose each other over religion.

So none of us were religious. Whatever that meant.

It's not that I didn't believe in God. He was there. I didn't fucking doubt that. But the thing is, he was over there and I was over here, and we pretty much left each other alone. We sort of got along that way. And me and God, well we sort of came to an understanding after a while. I used to watch all those people in my neighborhood go to Mass every Sunday, all dressed up, everyone either walking to Holy Family Church or driving to St. Patrick's Cathedral. Sunset Heights was like that, full of Catholics and families with lots of kids. It seemed like a nice way to grow up. But everything always seems nice from the outside. And it wasn't as if we weren't a good family.

Still, somehow, the other families seemed more, well, you know, more like real families, going to Mass and then coming back home and sitting down to a Sunday afternoon dinner, then everyone sitting around the television and watching *The Ed Sullivan Show* in the evenings. Well, we had all of that in my house, too. Except the Mass. We even prayed before we ate. You know, the Bless us O Lord thing.

I missed my family on Sundays. Missed them like hell. And at basic training, you know I got into this thing of doing busy work, while about half the guys went to do their church thing. You know, Sunday mornings, we'd clean our guns one more fucking time, shine our shoes another fucking time, do all that fucking busy work they had us doing. Your boots could never be too shiny. Your gun could never be too clean. In the Marines, when you train, if you're awake, then you're doing something. No such thing as doing nothing.

You know what a vacation was? It was having the time to smoke a fucking cigarette. It was having the time to listen to some jackass tell a joke you'd already heard.

You know, one Sunday, those of us who didn't go to church, we were doing our busy work and these two guys went at it. We had to break 'em up. All I had to say was that I wasn't gonna fucking run PT just because those two hotheaded assholes with no fucking discipline hated each other. That's what I told them too. Motherfuckers. Told them they had to work this shit out another way, and that was it. Told them it was a fucking waste of energy to make enemies out of each other when there was a real enemy out there.

Shit, we were lucky there weren't any DIs around.

I mean, some of these bastards, they just didn't think.

That's the thing. War is a thinking man's game.

And Vietnam? Well, if I ever got the chance to wind up there, I was gonna be a fucking player. I wasn't gonna go just to be fucking cannon fodder. Not this guy. Not this half Catholic, half Lutheran, non-churchgoing Marine guy. Hell no. There was just enough religion in me to make me a fucking man.

*Conrad García has a conscience.* I found that thought written in one of my notebooks when I was in the seventh grade. I don't remember writing it, but there it was—in my handwriting.

Conrad García. To borrow from my brother Charlie's obsession, if my body was a map, then Conrad García was a holy city. A religious capital. He was Rome. He was Mecca. He was Jerusalem.

I met Conrad in the first grade at Holy Family School in 1955. He was holding his mother's hand. That was my first memory of him. He looked up at his mother, squeezed her hand, smiled, nodded, and whispered something to her. She walked away. Slowly. Xochil and I were standing there, just waiting. For school or life to begin. He waved at us tentatively. We waved back.

At recess, some of the boys decided they were going to kill a horny toad they had cornered against the building. Even at the age of six, Conrad never approved of mob mentality. Group think, that's what he called it. Somehow, he managed to become a part of the mob, take possession of the horny toad, hold it in his cupped hands, then run across the playground and set it free.

He watched it run away. I remember running after him. I remember his smile.

One of the boys threatened him and called him a *joto*. Sissy. Queer. He shrugged. The words didn't seem to have an effect on him. The rest of us ran from that word, protested, yelled back, fought, argued, anything but that. Conrad stared at the word, then let it fall to the ground like a dead leaf.

He didn't win any friends that day. Well, except for one guy. Me. I decided I liked him—not that liking someone is a decision. That's not exactly how it works. I think he made me feel ashamed of myself for going along with the group think of the rabble— because something in me knew the rabble was wrong. And the rabble was mean. I don't think I cared about that horny toad one way or another. But there was something disturbing about the way a group of boys behaved on a playground when adults weren't around. Conrad's presence changed the equilibrium of things from the very first day of school. He brought something out in me—and I was happy to discover that I had a conscience too. It wasn't as well developed as Conrad's, but it was there and it made me feel better about myself. I always needed to feel better about myself.

When we were in the sixth grade, a group of guys was throwing rocks at a stray cat. One of the rocks hit the cat in the leg and hurt it. The cat, unable to move, tried to be brave and futilely clawed at the air and made a screeching sound. The cat had nothing left to rely on except instinct and strategy. Sensing that he was about to meet his end, the only thing left for him to do was to try and scare off its attackers. But my classmates, good Catholic boys all of them, smelled blood. They were poised to stone the cat to death. And they would have stoned him too—except that

Conrad García happened to be around, hovering, like some kind of guardian angel.

His response was swift and immediate. He ran to the wounded cat, picked it up amid the rock throwing, and held the cat in his arms. A rock caught him in the shoulder, another in the thigh. The cat scratched him. That was his only reward. But he remained unfazed. Conrad never built his life around a system of rewards. Everyone walked away, cursing Conrad, though I think some of the boys wouldn't have minded throwing a few rocks at Conrad instead of the cat. Conrad was a bigger target. Easier to hit. But they weren't brave enough to face the consequences.

Conrad had ruined their fun. They hated him.

He sat down on the ground until he calmed the cat. I walked up to him and shook my head. "What are you going to do with that cat, Conrad?"

"Take it home."

"It probably has fleas. Or something. Maybe rabies."

"Is that a reason to kill it?"

I smiled at him. "Guess not."

When we were walking home that day, he was holding the cat in his arms. And he started to cry. It was then I realized that Conrad paid a price for having a conscience.

"Don't cry," I said. I didn't know what else to say.

"Why, Gustavo? Why do we always have to be so mean?"

I had no answer.

That Sunday morning when I woke, disoriented, the taste of stale beer and cigarettes was still in my tongue, my throat, the pores of my skin. The whole world had changed.

The house was empty.

It was Sunday.

Everyone had gone to the twelve o'clock Mass at Holy Family. I felt lost and hung over and sad and depressed and numb and I didn't feel that much better after I showered. I walked into my grandmother's room and stared at all the pictures she had hanging on her walls. There was one picture in particular, one I'd always liked—it was taken at Charlie's first communion party. In the picture he is standing between me and Xochil and he is staring at the camera, the happiest kid in the world. And Xochil, already she has the look of a woman—though she was only twelve. I'm looking down and grinning and I'm sure Xochil must have said something to me and I was trying not to laugh.

I took the picture off the wall. I felt entitled to it. I put it under my bed, stared at my hands, and saw that they were trembling. It was then that I thought of Conrad. I picked up the phone and called him. "My grandmother died," I said. And then I blurted out, "And I got my draft notice." I was surprised at my confession. But I wanted to talk to someone—and I trusted him. Not that I didn't trust Xochil and Charlie and my mother. But it seemed easier to talk to Conrad—because the knowledge that I'd received my draft notice wouldn't wound him.

"You want to come over?"

"Sure," I said. He lived a couple of streets down. "I'll be right there." I hung up the phone and left a note.

We went for a walk. Conrad talked better when he walked. Xochil was like that too. It's because they couldn't sit still. I couldn't either—that's why I smoked. But walking was better for you than smoking, so, of course, I elected to smoke.

It was a clear and soft day, that's what I remember. The storms from the night before had cooled off our part of the world and the air smelled clean. I can still picture Conrad talking to me as we walked. I can still hear his words. "Will you go?"

"I don't know."

"You might know."

"What do you mean I might know?" I lit a cigarette.

"Sometimes we just keep things from ourselves."

"That's not possible."

"Sure it is. People keep secrets from themselves all the time."

"So you think I know what I'm going to do?"

"Yes. You just haven't let yourself know it yet."

"This isn't helping."

"Sorry." He reached for his own cigarette, held it, "You know what I think?" He lit his cigarette.

"I always want to know what you think."

He smiled. "Sure you do." He took a deep drag, blew out the smoke through his nose, then turned his head, popping it. He did that, popped something in his neck or his shoulders.

"You don't," I said.

"I don't what?"

"Keep secrets from yourself. You always know what you think."

"Not always."

"You know exactly what you think about killing. You know exactly what you think about the war."

"So do you."

"I'm not a conscientious objector."

"There is more than one way to object to the war."

"But you're doing it the direct way."

"I got turned down, Gustavo."

"What? When did you hear?"

"I met with my lawyer on Friday evening."

"And they just turned you down?"

"Yes."

"But you had letters from teachers and people who've known you all your life and a letter from Sister Angelina—and even a letter from Father Sullivan."

"Doesn't matter."

"Of course it matters."

"Not to our draft board, it didn't."

"But why?"

"They didn't say why."

*"They have to tell you why."*

"No they don't."

"Why not?"

"Those are the rules."

"Fuck the rules."

Conrad laughed. "Well, actually, it's the other way around—the rules fuck us."

"And what did your lawyer say?"

"She said she talked to one of the members of the draft board. Off the record, he told her there was no such thing as a conscientious objector. And she told him that he was being ridiculous and reminded him that Congress had made a provision for conscientious objectors and that there were certain religions that didn't allow for military service—the Quakers and Jehovah's Witnesses being but two examples."

"And what did he say to that?"

"He said I was neither a Quaker nor a Jehovah's Witness, and that Catholic boys did their duty just like everyone else and that on top of that Congress was wrong to have provided such a legal provision. And she told him that it was arrogant for a local draft board to behave as if they were above the law. And he reminded her that they were speaking off the record and that the draft board had made their decision and that their decision was final and then he reiterated to her that the draft board, unlike the Supreme Court, didn't have to state their reasons for their decisions."

"So it's final?"

"No. We're appealing to the State Draft Board in Austin."

"So you might still win."

"And I might still go to jail."

"And you'll go, won't you, you'll go to jail?"

"If I have to. I don't have a choice."

"Yes, you do."

"I don't. Gustavo, if there was no such provision in the law for conscientious objectors—"

"Which apparently there isn't, according to local custom."

Conrad smiled. "Well, we live in Texas."

"Yeah. Texas. Fucking great."

"But even if there wasn't a provision, I still wouldn't go. I wouldn't go, because I can't go. I can't go, because I don't believe in taking a human life. I don't believe my life is worth more than another's. I don't know how that sounds to other people. I know how it sounds to me. I have to live what I believe."

"If they turn you down on appeal, go to Canada."

"No."

"Why not?"

"This is the road I've decided to go down, Gustavo. I've thought and thought and thought about it." He flicked his cigarette. "If I was going to go to Canada, then I should have gone by now."

"Conrad, if you go to jail—it's not right. You're not a criminal."

"Some people wouldn't agree with you."

"Fuck those people."

"I got news for you, Gustavo. Those people run the world."

"Oh, so that's why it's so shitty."

Conrad laughed. "I like you, Gustavo."

The words slid out of him so easily. Why was it so hard to say *I like you too?* What was so hard about saying something as true as that?

"And you, Gustavo, what are you going to do?"

"I'm not as pure as you."

Conrad laughed. "Yeah, well, I'm not as pure as you think."

"I hope you win, Conrad."

"It's not about winning. It's about living your life."

We didn't say anything after that. We just smoked a couple more cigarettes and walked around. I thought about that cat he had saved. I thought about the time those guys were beating on him. I'd never asked him how and why that happened. But it was too late to ask. Sometimes, if you wait too long to ask a question, then you don't deserve an answer.

We bought a Coke at the Sunset Grocery Store. We'd done that all our lives, me and Conrad, bought Cokes at the Sunset Grocery Store. We finished our Cokes sitting down on the curb, watching the cars drive by—people waving. We waved back. Before he headed his way and me, mine, he told me he was sorry to hear about my grandmother. I nodded and I don't really remember what I said. I thought for just a second that I was going to cry and I thought, *What is this? Enough of this crying shit. What is this?* As I walked away, he yelled my name. I looked back at him and he said, "I don't think you'll go."

"Why not?" I yelled back.

"Because you can't," he said.

"How do you know?"

"Because you're a good Catholic boy. Like me."

"Yeah sure," I yelled.

He smiled. "You won't go."

And I smiled back and yelled, "Well, what if I do go, will you still love me?" It was supposed to be a joke.

And then he yelled back, "I'll always love you. Don't care if you go or not." It was just like him to say something like that. It was just like him to say something to break your heart—just when you thought it was already broken and couldn't be broken again.

When I was walking home, I wondered how a guy like Conrad survived in the world. A good Catholic boy? What did that mean, to be Catholic? Did it mean it was okay to kill strange desert lizards and homeless alley cats? Did it mean you didn't have to be literal about the sixth commandment? Maybe not killing was just supposed to be a metaphor.

Xochil loved metaphors.

Maybe I was too literal about things. God, I didn't know anything anymore. I did know one thing—the Catholic Church didn't deserve Conrad García. *I'll always love you.* My heart was breaking and my hands were trembling. I thought of the cat again. And then it hit me. I was just like that cat. The stones were coming at me from every direction. I was crippled. Unable to move, all I could do was claw and hiss, and hope it would be enough to scare off my attackers.

Shit. No one was afraid of Gustavo Espejo.

# lourdes

*Resurrection spits on my grief.*

Lourdes half smiled at the words she'd written in her journal. She didn't remember writing the words—but there they were, condemning her. She shrugged—but wasn't it true? Resurrection did spit on her grief. She wanted to hold on to her sorrow for a moment longer. Before she let it go. She was entitled to it, had earned it, and she refused to let a beautiful theology rob her of the only piece of Rosario she had left.

She shut her journal—then opened it again, and placed Gustavo's draft notice as a marker to her last entry.

She would have to find some time to speak to him. But what exactly was she going to tell him?

Ever since that day in the kitchen, when she'd taken off his black armband, she'd been thinking of the things she should have said to him. "I'll wash it for you," that's what she'd said. What a thing to say. What an inane and banal thing to say. Before that day, it had all seemed almost like a game, so innocent, his black armbands, his long discussions with Conrad and Xochil and his other friends, his strong feelings against the war—and then suddenly the innocence had gone out of everything.

She had shrunk from the task of being a mother. She had run. She would have to say something to him, something that mattered. She thought of Octavio, thought of what Octavio would say, Octavo, who believed in the rightness and the goodness of the cause of his adopted nation. Octavio, who believed that war was essentially a noble thing, Octavio, who somehow inexplicably believed that wars cleansed the world like a good rain and it was our duty to sacrifice our treasures and our sons and saw the whole matter as resembling the story of Abraham willing to sacrifice his son at the altar of God.

What if her son went to war? What if her son was killed, God and Country receiving the body he'd offered to them? What of that? She pictured her husband receiving the news of the death of their son, killed in action. She tried to picture the look on his face. With all the sincerity in his heart—and without a hint of irony—he would be proud and praise Gustavo's bravery, Gustavo, his son who had made the supreme sacrifice. He would think it was all too beautiful, what he gave. That's what Octavio would think. That's exactly what he would think.

She hated Octavio's sincerity because she could not fight it. How could she fight him, her husband, she who did not believe in the cause—she who had raised a son who also did not believe in the cause?

Resurrection was not the only thing that spit on her grief.

She poured herself a cup of coffee and checked the roast in the oven.

What could she tell Gustavo that he did not already know?

# xochil

I've always tried to imagine what Conrad and Gustavo were talking about that Sunday morning. The war, I think—an easy guess. They *always* talked about the war. When they weren't talking about the war, they were talking about the causes of poverty. They were odd and strange and lovely in that way. But that Sunday morning, I am certain they talked about the war.

They were discussing their options. That's how it was. Gustavo telling Conrad he'd been drafted, Conrad talking about how his application for C.O. status was going. Conrad trying to convince him to apply for C.O. status. Gustavo resisting: "It's too late for that." And Gustavo would've been right. It was too late for that.

I see them walking. Conrad loved to walk. Just like me. So I see them walking the streets of Sunset Heights, Conrad moving his hands, Gustavo smoking, Gustavo forcing a cigarette on Conrad, who takes it and smokes it. After that, my imagination fails me.

At first, I didn't understand why Gustavo didn't follow Conrad's lead. But he had one thing in common with his friend—he was incapable of being dishonest. Conrad could never kill. He didn't have it in him. He had the moral fiber, the sensibility, and the discipline of a systematic philosopher ingrained in him. He was also brave. People didn't think of Conrad as being brave, but he was. He was unbearably, heartbreakingly brave.

But it was more complicated for Gustavo. Once, we were walking under the bridge toward the Sunset Grocery Store. Three guys were beating up on someone. When we got closer, we could see that it was Conrad. Conrad wasn't fighting back. Of course he wasn't. He was just taking it. I think that made them madder. I think they were trying to force him to fight back. It was a mean game for them. And then they started kicking the crap out of him. Gustavo didn't even think. In an instant, he was on them. I saw what he could do, what he had inside him. He was strong and his rage made him terrifying. He was brutal in a fight, agile, had all the right instincts. They ran—all three of them. But he caught up with one of them and dragged him back to where Conrad was lying on the ground. At that point, I'd placed Conrad's head on my lap and was trying to ask him where it hurt. But Gustavo had this guy by the collar and was barking commands at him. "Say you're sorry, you bastard." The guy was trembling, but Gustavo didn't seem to notice—and he certainly didn't show any signs of mercy. "Say you're sorry or I'll break you're fucking jaw."

"I'm sorry," he whispered.

"What's your name?"

The guy started to cry. "Jorge," he whispered. "Jorge Gandara."

Gustavo shoved him away—like he was flicking an ant off his arm.

And then another side of him appeared. He got down on his knees and took Conrad's hand and squeezed it. *Are you okay? Are you okay?* He kept rocking him and rocking him. I thought he was going to cry—but he didn't.

We wrapped ourselves around Conrad, became his crutches, and slowly took him home, not far, not far at all. Gustavo insisted on going to the hospital with him. Two broken ribs, stitches across his brow.

Gustavo refused to leave the hospital.

Gustavo was good. Not pure. But good. Complicated. "That was brave, what you did." I told him that at the hospital.

"I only did it because of Conrad."

"You might have done the same thing if it was someone else. You might have done it if it was a perfect stranger."

"Don't give me so much credit."

He was too hard on himself. That was his problem, of course. He expected excellence from himself. And he could never live up to his own standards. He knew himself too well. He knew he had something violent and mean and ugly inside him. He was terrified of that side of himself—hated that side of himself, couldn't bear it. My brother, he couldn't take the road that Conrad took. It would have been a lie.

That Sunday, when we were driving back from Mass, I told my mom, "Teach me the secret to your mashed potatoes." I was in the back of the car, but I could tell my father was smiling.

My mom turned around. "Where did that come from?"

"I want to learn. And I wanted to make Dad smile."

That's when my dad laughed. And for no reason, we all broke out laughing. For no reason—except that we needed to laugh.

When we went into the house, we didn't change into our casual clothes. After Sunday afternoon dinner, the relatives would return for another round of rituals. My father read Gustavo's note—he'd left it on his chair. He didn't register any particular emotion, but I don't think he was angry. He liked Conrad, considered him to be a responsible and reliable young man. Somehow, my father could see past Conrad's politics, a politics he deplored.

When Monsignor La Pieta arrived, he and my father went into the living room. He was our guest for dinner that Sunday as he had been on countless occasions. But today, there was also business to conduct—helping my parents arrange for my grandmother's funeral. Monsignor La Pieta and my grandmother had become intimate friends over the years. Like her, he had left Mexico sometime during the revolution and it was obvious her death pained him. I liked seeing that shadow of pain wash over the old monsignor's face—it made him seem less severe. It made him seem more like a human being instead of a dispenser of sacraments and sermons.

My mother and I went to the kitchen. She'd left a roast in the oven, and she began teaching me how to make her mashed potatoes. There were secrets to making everything—even mashed potatoes.

Charlie was on the front steps waiting for Gustavo. If my younger brother's life had a title, it would be just that: *Waiting for Gustavo.*

Just as I was peeling the potatoes, I heard Gustavo and Charlie. They were laughing about something. They came into the kitchen.

"What are you smiling at?"

"I came to watch you cook."

"You think that's funny?"

"No. But it's like a lunar eclipse. When it's happening, you just don't want to miss it."

My mother laughed.

I tried not to.

"Are we having biscuits?"

Charlie, he was Mr. Biscuit. He loved them, loved popping the rolled carton of precut, prefabricated biscuits and placing them carefully on a cookie sheet and putting them in the oven. It was a ritual with him. It made him feel American, I think.

It was a quiet Sunday, that's what I remember, a Sunday filled with our ordinary familial traditions. Quiet and nice and normal. Gustavo helped my mother set the table—an event that happened as often as I helped cook. And when we sat down to eat, not once throughout the entire meal did Monsignor La Pieta give Gustavo a hard time about his lack of attention to his religious duties. It was hard for him, I know, but my father must have said something to him during their conversation. The only reason the old priest would've held back was as a favor to my father. He had always believed that Gustavo was on his way to being one of Satan's minions.

Gustavo sat across from me. We tossed knowing looks at each other, waiting for a grenade to go off. Charlie listened intently to my parents' memories of my grandmother as they spoke with the monsignor. My mother was serene and composed and radiant and it dawned on me that she was in the prime of her life—and that she would never be more beautiful. My father had always looked like a lean boxer, and at that moment, he looked weathered. If he had been a piece of furniture, someone might have dusted him off. Even so, he, too, had his own kind of loveliness.

Sometime during dessert, my father smiled at Gustavo and asked, "How's Conrad?"

"He's fine. He goes to the eight o'clock Mass." It was Gustavo's way of making a joke.

My father nodded. "He's a good Catholic boy."

Monsignor La Pieta said nothing.

Late that afternoon, before he left, the monsignor took Gustavo aside and said something to him. Gustavo nodded as he listened. It wasn't a lecture—something else was happening. When the old priest finished talking, he embraced my brother and held him. I have always believed that my father had something to do with the tender scene I witnessed that afternoon. It was my father's way of apologizing to his son. Through a proxy, of course. The world had always used proxies to do its business. Wasn't that what the war in Vietnam was all about?

Gustavo and Charlie and I washed the dishes. Charlie started the game. He'd never started the game. "The best movie ever made in the history of the world." He almost whispered it as he dried a dish and began a stack. I smiled.

Gustavo smiled too. "*Bonnie and Clyde*," he said.

Charlie shook his head.

"*The Great Dictator?*"

On the Sunday after my grandmother died, there were no shots fired in our house. There was only peace.

# gustavo

He unfolded the letter and stared at Xochil's typewritten note:

Gustavo—

I know you get mad at me because I never let you see my work. Well, it's mine. And you understand that everyone has to have something that's just theirs. That's hard in this house. But I wanted to give you these lines from a poem I'm working on. I hope you like them—and if you don't, then just shut up about it:

I want to wake and scream, and scream
again—clear all the litter in my lungs.
I want to look up at the blue
and in that quiet, quiet place,

I want to listen to my heart as it breaks.
I want to kneel down and wail like a wolf
forced to chew off his leg to free himself
from the trap.
I want to listen
to your words. I want to listen
and listen to your voice and put
your words in a cup—and drink them,
drink them down. I want.

That's all I have for now. Well, I have more, but it's not finished. It's a poem for you. But it's for me too.

I just wanted you to see it.

I'm off to school early even though I didn't lift a book all
weekend. I have an eight o'clock class, and I thought I might as
well go. It will help me not to think about all the other things I
have in my head.

You know what Mom told me last night? She said sometimes you just have to pretend that everything's all right, even if
it's not. "You can't live in chaos. You can't live in your head. You
have to live in the world." Living in the world, there's a thought.
We're fighting a losing battle in this house. My theory about
this family is that we are all addicted to living in our heads. So
the plan for today is not to live in my head. "Don't live in chaos."
That's the plan. Dad's blessed rage for order isn't all bad, is it?
Okay, okay, so maybe it's just another kind of insanity.

Xochil

He smiled to himself. He liked the idea of screaming. He
liked the idea of the wolf that would do anything to free himself
from the trap. He liked the idea of drinking down each other's
words—which is exactly what he and Xochil had always done.
Mostly, he liked all that wanting.

And as for living in the chaos—he wasn't sure about that.

He looked over at Charlie's bed. He was gone. Like Xochil, he'd gone to school. As usual, they were both way ahead of him.

He would go to work. He would take a car and make it look like it had never been in an accident. Today, he would pretend. He wished to the God he didn't believe in that the chaos was only in his head.

His mother and father were discussing the details of his grandmother's funeral when he walked into the kitchen. His father looked up at him and nodded—then he looked back down at the list he had written on his yellow pad. He looked across at his mother. "You pick the casket."

His mother nodded. "I'll take Sofia with me. I'll let her pick the dress."

He stared at his father's nodding head and wondered about the price of caskets, about fussing over what the dead would wear, about who should carry the body to the grave, and who should say a few words at the funeral and all the other minute details that seemed to matter so much. Their parents spoke of these things as if it were all so normal. He poured himself a cup of coffee, then sat at the table. "Why can't you be buried without clothes?" He hadn't actually meant to say anything. His question just spilled out of him.

"Because it's an open casket? You want the entire world to see your grandmother naked?"

Gustavo shrugged. "Guess not." He was sorry for having said anything. He was always saying the wrong things around his father.

He noticed the look his mother shot his father.

"Are you going to work?" The question was an offering.

Gustavo nodded.

"Tell Mr. Ortega you'll need to take off Wednesday afternoon, and Thursday. You might as well ask him for Friday too."

Gustavo nodded. "He won't mind."

His father nodded back at him.

His mother reached over and combed his hair out of his eyes. "You know, sometimes, when you nod, you look just like Octavio."

Gustavo looked across at his father and smiled. "I think she just tried to give me a compliment."

Octavio grinned, tentative at first, then broke out into a smile.

Lourdes softly tapped Gustavo on the shoulder. "You'll be late for work."

# gustavo

You have come to work.

Like a million people in the world, men and women and children, like them, you come to your place of employment. You do your work for the few dollars they pay you. This is how the world works. It does not stop because you have lost a grandmother. It does not stop because your world is in turmoil. It does not stop because there is a riot in your heart. It does not stop because you have been drafted and are left in a wasteland of indecision. It does not matter that in your head you are somewhere else. It does not matter that you are not really here in this garage that smells of putty and paint.

You are not here. You are not really here.

You think that your mother and Xochil are right. You cannot live in chaos. But there is a trick to pretending. You used to be good at that.

You see your arms and hands and fingers working on the

fender of the car. You see your hands banging out a dent with a rubber hammer. But nothing feels real. And you think for a second that living is not real. It is a fiction. And death, that is not real, either. That is an even greater fiction. And order? That is the greatest fiction of all. Chaos is the only thing in the world that is real. You wonder why you think these things. Maybe you think them because you wish them to be true. If everything is a fiction, then nothing can matter. And if nothing can matter, then your life and what you decide to do with it does not matter either. If there is only chaos, then you can give up.

But you think about the wolf in your sister's poem. The wolf does not give up.

Mr. Ortega comes over to speak to you. You tell him that your grandmother has died. Even then, your words feel hollow and empty. He nods his head when you tell him. He is hungry to hear the story, so you tell him as much as you know. You pretend you were there, though you were not. You know the story because your sister has told you everything that you missed. So you tell him what you know. He listens carefully and when he speaks, his words to you are soft and kind and he tells you that you do not need to work today and that you should take a week off. You must pay the dead with your time.

You want to tell him that you are mourning for many things and that a week is nothing, but instead you nod and tell him that it is good to work. You tell him it is good for your grief. You tell him that you will take some days later in the week.

And then, you don't know why, but you tell him that you have received your letter.

He nods. "You will look handsome in a uniform. Like my son." He is proud of you. He is happy that you have become one of them.

You nod back at him. You try to picture yourself in that uniform. Even now, you wonder if you will go to war. If you go, they will all approve. Your father will approve. All the men in the city where you live will approve. They will all love you. You want to be loved. You do not want to be despised or hated. You do not want that.

You have been having a ceaseless argument with yourself for many months now. You have talked ceaselessly about these things with your friends. You have worn a black armband as a protest to this war, but in your quietest moments, you are not sure of what you think. You are not sure as to what the right thing is. There are moments when you tell yourself that you will go. That is what you must do. You will go and get your orders. You will go to boot camp. You will spend thirteen weeks preparing for war. Then you will go and fight. You will go with men who are perfect strangers and they will become your brothers. Isn't that what the Bible says—that all men are your brothers? You will turn your back on them, these, your brothers?

You work.

All day. You work.

You work as you have never worked. You think of your sister's words, of how it is impossible to live in the chaos. You think of your sister's poem again, and you think of her wolf and you see her wolf chewing off its own leg. And you wonder what good a wolf is without one of its legs. How long will that wolf survive?

What good is a wounded wolf who limps on three legs?

What good is a man without a country?

What good is a man *with* a country?

Every time you ask yourself a question, you have no answer. But then another question rises up in your head. This is chaos—questions floating in your mind, questions that have no answers.

Mr. Ortega stops you and says, "You are working like a crazy man."

You nod and you hear yourself tell him that men work instead of cry.

He nods and you hear him say, "You will make a fine soldier."

You hate him for his words, but you hide your hate. And you see yourself smiling at him. And he thinks you are grateful for the compliment.

At the end of the day, you are drenched in sweat.

Mr. Ortega hands you a clean towel for you to dry yourself off. And you think of your mother handing you a towel two nights ago. And you think of how you became a child that night. But you think it is time for you to become a man.

It is time.

You take the towel from Mr. Ortega. He has been very kind to you today. And you are oddly moved by his kindness. Everyone in the world is capable of such kindness. And maybe everyone is both kind and cruel—and you—like everyone else in the world—you, you will hover between kindness and cruelty all the days of your life.

And you think that perhaps it would make no difference at all whether you went to war or not. It will not matter in the end. That is what you think. And so you are making yourself suffer for nothing.

This is what you tell yourself: It does not matter what you decide. Escape is not possible. In the end, you will always be a child of war.

## lourdes. gustavo.

His mother was sitting in the car in front of Benny's Body Shop when he walked out into the street. She honked the horn and waved at him. He walked up to the car, opened the door, and slid onto the seat. "Hi."

"Hi," she said.

"I was going to catch the bus."

"I know. I was running some errands and thought—" she stopped.

"Thought what?"

"I thought we should have a talk."

"A talk?"

"Yes."

"About what?"

She took the letter out of her purse. "About this." She handed him the folded up letter.

He took it, stared at it, then shoved it in his pants pocket. "Does Dad know?"

"No."

"Are you going to tell him?"

"I don't think that's my job, do you?"

"I guess not."

"Gustavo, are you going to tell him?"

"I don't know."

"I think you should."

"He won't think it's a bad thing that I got drafted."

"How do you know?"

"Just a wild guess."

"Don't be a wise guy."

"Mom, this is the guy who handed me a gun when I was ten. This is guy who said, 'Isn't it beautiful?' This is the guy who, when I told him that I didn't think a rifle was beautiful, told me I didn't understand anything about the aesthetics of being a man."

"He told you that? What a strange thing to say."

"I had to look up the word, *aesthetics*. I spent months trying to figure out what the hell he was trying to say to me. He always talked to me like I was an adult. You know, I don't know what I would have done without Xochil. She always translated my father to me. Just like you always had to translate me to him."

"That's an interesting way of looking at it."

"That's Xochil. She has a lot of theories about things. Look, I'm sorry about me and Dad."

"It's not all your fault."

"Well, it's half my fault, isn't it, Mom?" He took out his pack of cigarettes, then fingered the pack nervously. "I don't know if I can talk about this—"

"You tried to talk about it once before. Only I didn't let you."

"It's okay."

"No, it's not okay. I didn't want to talk about it because it was too hard. And it is too hard. But, Gustavo, we can't just pretend."

"Xochil told me that you said that sometimes we have to pretend that everything's normal because we can't live in the chaos."

"Well, sometimes I'm full of it."

"Don't say that."

"Why not?"

"You're not full of it, Mom."

"Don't idealize your mother. I'm just a human being."

"You idealize your children all the time."

"No I don't."

"All the time. Especially me."

"That's not true."

"Can we get out of this car so I can smoke?"

She started the engine. "Why don't we take a drive?"

"What are we doing in a cemetery?"

"I wanted to see your grandmother's plot. It should be right next to your grandfather's." She opened the car door and stepped out. Gustavo followed her as she wandered through the rows of gravestones, her eyes searching. She turned and nodded at Gustavo. "You can smoke if you want. I don't think the dead will mind."

"You're in a strange mood."

"Am I?"

"You know, Xochil's a lot like you."

"Maybe she is." She pointed to a gravestone. "Over there."

They walked toward the spot, then stood in front of Enrique Espejo's grave. "Your grandfather had a good life. You want to know something about your grandfather? He ran. He ran away from the revolution. He had to decide. And he decided to leave. He decided to come here. He left Mexico. He wasn't thrown out. He made a choice. Was that a bad thing, Gustavo?"

"I don't know."

"I don't either."

They stood for a long time saying nothing. "*Amor*, you can't be afraid of deciding."

"You think that's what I'm afraid of?"

"No. I think you know what you should do. But I also think you're afraid of hurting the people you love."

"You've always given me too much credit, Mom."

"All of this, *amor*, it's not your fault. Not any of it. Don't punish yourself like that."

"Okay."

She nodded back at him. "I'll take okay. Okay will do just fine." She stared down at her father-in-law's gravestone. "And one more thing. I don't want you in living in a cemetery."

"People don't live in cemeteries, Mom."

She placed her hand on his shoulder. "You catch on fast."

## adam. the dead.

Da Nang, Vietnam, September 19, 1967

He wasn't supposed to die. He was just wounded. Patsy said so. *"Blood don't mean you'll die." That's what he said. Fucking Patsy. What did he know?*

*Motherfuckers.*

*You had a bad feeling about this. You had that same feeling the day they hit Salvi. You hate these feelings. You hate them.*

*You try to think of your mother lighting candles in a church.*

*But motherfuckers, did they have to hit Bill?*

"Don't be thinking shit. I know you're thinking shit. Don't be doin' that."

He looked up at Whit. "You don't know what I'm fucking thinking."

"Look, it fucking happens. That's what we came here for."

"Don't give me that shit. He was a fucking good man."

"Yup and we all fucking liked him. And so fucking what?"

"He has kids."

"Look. He was a lifer. This was it for him. Being a fucking Marine. That's what he loved."

"Yeah, well, it sucks."

"He was thirty, man."

"What the fuck's that supposed to mean? Fucking thirty ain't old."

"Some guys get shot up at nineteen. Thirty's fucking old if you ask me. Look, he got shot up, bad. That fucking bouncing Betty got him good. Did you want him to hang around like Salvi?"

"Don't talk shit about Salvi. He's home. He's alive."

"I'm not so fucking sure."

"What the fuck's that supposed to mean?"

"Salvi, I don't fucking think— Look, never mind what I fucking think. Look, tonight, you and me, we go to the beach. I scored me some good shit. And, ooooh, baby, it ain't raining today. You can see a piece of sky. Shit, it almost looks like Tucson. C'mon, almost looks like fucking Tucson. C'mon. I'll buy you a beer. Buy you two—then we can head to the beach."

"I'm on duty this evening."

"Yeah, well, you're not on duty right now."

"Yeah, sure. A beer. A walk on the fucking beach."

"Enjoy, baby. We're heading back out in three days."

"I'm gonna be fucking ready this time. Camera's gonna be fucking ready." He remembered the day they got hit, the whole damned world spinning around, and the rain had been nothing more than a mist, and how calm he was, calm as he'd ever been, and he'd seen them, at least three of them. He'd seen them go down. It had seemed just like it was supposed to be. If there'd been more, he'd have gunned them down too. Every fucking one of them. But, God, after the shooting, there was only the sound of Salvi screaming.

"Camera, hey, hey, fucking stay with me." Whit snapped his fingers in front of his face. "Stay with me, buddy. Don't fucking go away like that."

# lourdes

Gustavo smoked a cigarette before we left the cemetery.

I let him drive the car. He loved to drive. I'd always hated cars.

We didn't say a word. He was thinking. As Xochil would have it, he was translating our conversation.

I had so many questions to ask him. And yet, what good were all my questions? I'd said too much already. He already knew what I thought—even before our conversation. Just as he knew what his father thought, what his sister thought—even what Charlie thought. He knew what he felt about the war. He knew the consequences of fighting in a war he did not believe in just as he knew the consequences of leaving the country. Or perhaps he could only guess at those consequences.

I could have made it easier on everyone if I had just decided to drag him all the way to Mexico City and lock him in my cousin's house. It would not have been so hard for me to leave the country along with my son. Maybe Octavio was right after all—*I was an ingrate.* But if I had to make a choice between a country and my son, then I would choose my son. Gustavo was right about that too. I did idealize my children. I thought they were all beautiful enough to save. All of them. Especially Gustavo.

I prayed he'd leave. I wanted to beg him. But I did none of those things—and would not do it.

There were no maps for him. There were no directions.

I knew that if he chose to enter the military, it would be for all the wrong reasons. Was that a crime? Was that a sin? Hundreds, thousands of young men were doing just that. Why should my son be any different? And yet he knew he had a choice. And that was the difference between him and a thousand other boys his age. He could imagine something beyond the piece of paper that a government had sent to him.

He had a choice to make. The choice would have to be his. And yet, I knew and he knew that it wasn't that simple. Everything seemed so complicated because it was so complicated. We were not afforded the elegance of simplicity.

I think he told himself he was confused. But I don't think he was confused at all. I think he knew all along what he was going to do.

He just didn't know how painful it would be. That pain. That ache. I was prepared for that. But he was eighteen. He was only eighteen.

It was the right thing to do, to let him drive home from the cemetery.

# xochil. jack. gustavo.

She didn't smile as she saw him walking toward her house on the sidewalk, didn't wave at him, didn't say *Hi Jack*, didn't betray any signs that she was glad to see him. But she was more than glad. She was happy. Why was she happy? But her eyes remained hard, steady, impenetrable stones as he slowly trudged up the sidewalk toward her, she sitting on the steps of the front porch wearing a dress the color of a gray cloud about to let loose thunder, lightning, hail. And he, he was carrying flowers and a frightened smile, flowers for her parents, she thought, for her family, maybe for her too, carrying flowers because he'd somehow found out that her grandmother had died. Pretty flowers to go with his pretty face and his pretty eyes and she wanted to shake her head and go somewhere, anywhere, but she stayed still, immutable. And then there he was, standing at the foot of the stairs, offering flowers, staring at her, waiting for her to say something, but she refused to move her lips.

For a moment, there was nothing but waiting.

Finally, the part of her that was her mother's daughter felt pity for him. "That's my sidewalk you're standing on," she said softly.

"It's a nice sidewalk."

"I don't want to see you."

"I thought I should come."

"Why?"

"I thought it was the right thing to do."

"You're always so sure about what's right."

"Not always." He held out the flowers. "I brought these for your family. I'm sorry. I am. Really."

"It's not your fault. She was old."

"You loved her."

"Love doesn't keep anybody from dying."

"Guess not." He blew out a breath—like it was cold outside and he wanted to see the fog of it in front of him. "Don't be angry with me, Xochil."

She got up, walked down the stairs, took the flowers. "I don't think *anger's* the word." She smelled the flowers. "They don't smell like anything." She almost smiled. "You can come in."

Jack followed her up the stairs. When they entered the living room, Charlie and Gustavo were talking to each other, telling stories about their uncles, though they were speaking barely above a whisper and Charlie was doing most of the talking. Octavio was in his chair, reading a book, Prescott's *History of the Conquest of Mexico*, a book he admired and loathed, a book his mother had given to him. Lourdes was placing a basket full of bread on the dining room table.

All the eyes in the room turned toward Jack and Xochil.

"Jack brought flowers," Xochil said. "They're nice. Not like him."

Gustavo laughed at her joke.

Octavio shook his head. "Be polite."

She smiled at her father. "It was just a joke."

Octavio shook his head again.

Lourdes smiled at him. "That's very sweet of you, Jack."

"I'm sorry," he said, awkward, uncomfortable. He offered Lourdes the flowers. "For your loss," he whispered.

Lourdes took the flowers from him and looked around the room, looking for a place to put them, flowers everywhere in the living room, the dining room—even in the bedrooms. She found a space on the coffee table. She walked toward Jack and hugged him, her movements graceful and sure. "Very sweet," she repeated, trying to help him feel less awkward. She was always moved by the expressions of shy and awkward boys.

Octavio put down his book. "Yes, that's a thoughtful gesture." Jack nodded.

Gustavo rolled his eyes, then caught himself. "Sweet." *That was a word. A Lourdes word.* "Gesture." *There was another word. An Octavio word.*

Xochil looked over at him. *Yeah, a Lourdes word, an Octavio word.*

Charlie knew they were thinking the same thing. Only he didn't know what that same thing was.

Lourdes looked at the table full of food: "Would you like a piece of cake?"

"Yes, he would."

Jack turned toward Gustavo, who smiled at him. Jack shrugged. "Sure. I mean, yes, ma'am, thank you."

"Here, let me get it for you." Gustavo walked toward the table and cut a healthy piece of the cake his aunt had brought over. "Really good cake," he said, "My aunt Utilia brought it over." He carefully placed the piece on a small plate and handed it to Jack—then served a piece for himself. "Why don't we eat this on the porch?"

• • •

Jack finished his cake, the silence between him and Gustavo making the chocolate cake in his stomach feel like lead. "Good cake," he said.

"Excellent. Now, I think you should get the fuck out of here. You brought the flowers, you had some cake. We're all fucking grateful as hell that you came."

"Your sister told me the same thing."

"I bet she was a lot nicer about it, though."

"Yeah. A lot nicer."

"Well, she's nicer. And she's smarter—except when it comes to you."

"Look— I— Well, you know it's the decent thing to do, you know, when someone dies. To visit them, I mean. I mean, I can't pretend I don't know you."

"Why not? I mean, *you don't know me,* do you?"

"Well, we're friends."

"Are we, Jack?"

"Friendships don't just stop. I mean, it's not that simple."

"Maybe it is that simple."

"Listen, Gustavo, well, see, we were friends. *Were* should count for something."

"I don't know what *were* counts for. Anyway, Jack, I'm not in the mood for bullshit. You're here for Xochil not for me."

"Gustavo— Look— I, well, look— I said some pretty hard things."

Gustavo took out a pack of cigarettes from his shirt pocket. He held the pack out toward Jack, offering him one. Jack took one, then handed the pack back to Gustavo. They lit up, smoking their cigarettes in silence. "The thing is, Jack. We meant the things we said, didn't we?"

Jack nodded. "Yeah, guess so. But, you know, I don't hate you Gustavo."

"Maybe I don't hate you either, but look, you know, sometimes people talk about living in different worlds. I used to wonder what people meant by that. Mrs. Blake said when people said things like that it was just a way of speaking, just a metaphor. 'Don't be literal about things,' that's what she used to say. She said we all lived in the same world. She was wrong. She was fucking wrong as they come. Jack, me and you, we don't live in the same world."

"That doesn't mean we should kill each other."

"You apply that rule to me—why not apply it to someone in North Vietnam?" Gustavo smiled, nothing soft or kind in that smile. "And, anyway, who said anything about killing, Jack? I'm not the one who's going to war."

"You'll go. You'll go to Nam same as me."

"Think so?"

"You'll go because they'll make you go."

"Yeah?"

"Yeah."

"Let me fucking tell you something. No one can make you do anything that you really don't want to do, Jack."

"You think you matter as much as this country?"

"Nope. That's for fucking sure." He smiled, his smile growing harder. He took a drag off his cigarette. "You come here to start another fight? I'll finish it this time. I swear to God, I'll finish it."

"Didn't know you believed in God."

"It's just an expression."

"Yeah." Jack shrugged. "I mean, I wish—" he stopped, not even really knowing what he wished, just wanting to say something to make everything better.

Gustavo, he understood Jack in that instant—but not enough to make him like the guy. "I wish too," he said, "I fucking wish too." He blew out a smoke ring, then winced. "You love her?"

"You wouldn't be asking if you didn't already know."

"I wish you didn't."

"Well, if it helps any, I think I wish I didn't love her either. But the thing is, I do."

"She loves you too, I think."

"Maybe."

"Yeah, maybe. Anyway, I meant what I said. If you hurt her, I'll hurt you back. I swear I fucking will. You won't get a chance to be a Marine. You won't get a chance to point your fucking rifle at some Communist in Vietnam—not if you hurt her." He looked up and saw Xochil hovering above where they were sitting. He smiled at her. "How long have you been standing there?"

"Long enough." Her eyes moved from her brother to Jack back to her brother. "And will you stop calling the people in Vietnam Communists? Can you do that, Gustavo? Vietnam is full of a lot of poor people who work hard and want a little say over their lives. Kind of reminds you of the Mexican Revolution, doesn't it?"

Gustavo shrugged. "Sure. Without Pancho Villa." He put out his cigarette in one of his mother's flowerpots, *Bad for the plants,* her voice always popping up in his head. He got up from where he was sitting and walked past his sister. She grabbed his arm, then kissed him on the cheek. "And stop threatening Jack, crazy boy," she whispered.

"I can take it."

"Didn't know you smoked, Jack."

"Just picked it up recently."

She shook her head, then slapped Gustavo gently on the cheek. "Crazy boy," she repeated.

"Yeah, yeah, crazy boy. The world is full of them. Full of crazy girls too." He turned and gave Jack a look—then walked back inside the house.

"I've been thinking."

"People do that. Some of them."

"You're not going to make this easy on me, are you?"

"I'm not that kind of girl."

"Look, I'm crazy about you, Xochil."

"Maybe you're just plain crazy."

"Maybe I am. I can't even sleep."

"And that's my fault?"

"It's not a matter of fault."

"Well, I hear war's a good cure for insomnia."

"I don't think that's funny."

"I don't say things to be funny. Not ever."

"Stop it, Xochil. I love you. I love you so much it hurts. Can't you see that?"

She hated the desperate sound in his voice. "I'm glad it hurts, Jack. And, something else, maybe you can tell me what that means."

"I love you means I love you."

"I get that part. But *I love you* means you want something from me."

"I don't want anything."

"Liar."

"It's true. I don't want anything."

"Bastard. Liar."

"Okay."

"So what do you want?"

"You. I want you, Xochil."

"All you want is me. You want me whole? Or do you want

me in pieces?" She took a deep breath. "Sometimes, I wished I smoked. You know, Jack, a girl isn't a car—you can't own her, you can't paint her any color you want, you can't just sit in her seat anytime you want, drive her anywhere you damn well please."

"I know that, Xochil."

"No you don't. You think you can just say crap like I love you and then I'm supposed to belong to you. You love me. You want me. You get me. My body, my arms, my legs, my heart, my tits, every other part of me. And me? What do I get, Jack?"

"You get me. That's what you get."

"What? A penis?"

"Don't talk like that."

"I want more."

"I don't understand that."

"I know you don't. How many times do you want me to say this? A Marine isn't my idea of a hero. Do you get that? Doesn't that matter to a boy like you?"

"Stop calling me a boy, goddamn it!"

*"You are a boy."*

"Then make me a man."

"What?"

"You heard me."


"He's a nice boy."

Xochil eyed her mother, then walked up to her father and took the book out of his hands. He looked at up her, not quite stunned, that same blank look on his face. Xochil dropped her father's book on the floor. "You should look at people when you talk to them. And yes, he's a nice boy. He's joined the Marines."

Octavio nodded. "A man has to do his duty."

Xochil shook her head. "There are so many things I want to say to you Dad." She picked up the book and handed it back to him. "But I don't think I'll say anything at all." She kissed him on the cheek, a habit she'd acquired when she was a little girl. "Yes, Dad, he's a nice boy. He's joined the Marines."

## xochil. gustavo.

Y ou're going out with him again, aren't you?"

"That's not a question, Gustavo, that's an accusation."

"Can't it be both a question and an accusation?"

"Guess so, smart-ass. Anyway he's leaving, so what difference does it make if I see him or not?"

"If it doesn't make any difference then why bother?"

She was wearing that look, the one that said his voice was nothing more than a noise in the room that annoyed her.

"Do you love him?"

"I might."

"Why?"

"I don't know why."

"I don't get it."

"I can't explain it."

"You with your giant fucking mind, you can't explain it?"

"No."

"What you mean is that you don't want to explain it."

"Okay, *I don't want to explain it.*"

"You're being intellectually lazy."

"What?"

"Isn't that what you're always telling me about everything? Isn't it?"

"This is different."

*"Because it's you and not me?"*

"Don't yell at me. I hate that, Gustavo."

"Me and him, we're not friends. Not anymore."

"I know."

"Don't love him. Please don't love him, Xochil."

"Whatever I feel for Jack Evans, Gustavo, it will pass." She put her hand on his cheek. "You. What I feel for you will never pass."

"You make it sound as if I'm a possessive brother. I'm not. It's just that he's not for you. That's all I'm saying. You deserve better."

"You've always said that about every boy."

"Not true."

"Joey Fernandez."

"He was an asshole."

"He's going to Berkeley."

"Oh, and that means he's not an asshole?"

She slapped him gently on the side of the head. "Felix Ungermeyer."

"No comment. I mean, just the name."

"He's sweet."

"You're starting to talk like Lourdes." He laughed. "Sweet, huh? That just means you agree with me."

She shook her head. "Okay, then what about Enrique Moreno? He wants to be an attorney. And he's going to Harvard."

"That's no reason to dislike him."

"Too skinny."

"Everyone is too something."

"Well, everyone *is* too fucking something."

"What will I do without you?"

"What are you talking about?"

"When are you leaving?"

"What?"

"Charlie said you got a letter. I remember. Mr. Rede tried to give it to me, but I wouldn't take it."

"You were crying."

"Yes, that's what I was doing. I was mad."

"At Jack."

"Because he was being an asshole."

"Because he's not good enough for you."

"I know, Gustavo. I know what's going on." She was whispering. "Charlie said that you were pretending that it was nothing. But it wasn't nothing. I saw the letter—the one they sent asking you to report for a physical. I saw it. I know you went to the base for your physical. Two plus two plus two equals six. You got drafted."

"Everybody knows everything around here."

"You're not going, are you?"

"I'm not Conrad."

"You'll go?"

"I don't know."

"You don't believe in the war."

"So?" He tried to smile. "I'll go to Canada."

"Sure."

"I will."

"Liar. You're not a very good liar."

"I'm an excellent liar."

"Excellent," she repeated. "You know something, you're my favorite book, Gustavo. I know everything that's written inside you. I know every word."

"Ditto, chick."

"I hate *chick*."

"*Vata.*"

"That's better. *Vato.*" She laughed. *I want to laugh forever. Let it be this way forever.* "Take me with you. Wherever you go—take me."

"I can't."

"Take me."

"Army doesn't take girls."

"You'll go then?"

"I don't know."

"It you leave—if you go somewhere—I'll go too."

"You mean, like, over the rainbow?"

"Why are boys so mean?"

"Because we have to be."

"No. That's a lie you all tell yourselves."

"Maybe it's a lie we inherited."

"Walk away from the lie, Gustavo."

"I'm trying, Xochil. I'm trying like hell. Listen, *I got drafted, Xochil. Don't you know what that fucking means?*"

She could sense the tears and the rage he was holding back. She pictured him coming in from the rain, her father's condemning look. She leaned into him and sobbed into his shoulders. *I hate this world. I hate it, I hate it, I hate it.*

"Mom got a phone call. Mr. Rede died," he whispered.

She nodded, digging herself deeper into his shoulder. *I hate, I hate this world.*

We used to say we got up at o'dark thirty.

When the sun rose, we'd already been up for hours. At least it felt that way.

I didn't have a watch. None of us did. They took away our hair, then they took away our grins and attitudes, then they took away our watches.

I figured we got up at four or four thirty in the fucking morning.

We'd eat. I'm not gonna talk about the fucking food. It wasn't Mom's cooking—but, you know, I never complained. There was a guy there, half Italian, half Mexican. Always talked about his mom's cooking. I guess I was lucky, I didn't drag any memories of good food into the Marines. My mom wasn't exactly a gourmet chef. You know, a lot of Jell-O salads, casseroles with cream of mushroom soup, macaroni and cheese, SPAM, stuff like that. Hell, when I was eighteen, I didn't have any nostalgia about home cooking. Bring on the fucking mashed potatoes. I didn't give a rat's ass what they put in front of me. I ate it.

You know what I hated, when we'd hit the racks, when they came and made us fucking present arms in bed. I hated it when they fucked with you like that. Right there, in the middle of your ten-minute sleep, there you were fumbling for your rifle. That didn't happen too much, though.

The thing is, you were always kept busy. My dad would have liked that philosophy. He used to get pissed off as hell when I sat around doing nothing. A man doesn't do nothing. A man works. Next to *freedom, work* was his favorite word.

We'd shower. Once I even heard a guy singing. I don't know why I remember that. Maybe I liked the song. Maybe I missed hearing people sing.

After basic, it was off to Infantry Training Regiment at Camp Pendleton.

That's where we got all our tactics training.

How to use a bazooka.

How to use flame throwers.

How to use our BARs.

How to throw grenades.

It was during those six weeks that I started writing a lot of letters. I think it was six weeks. Maybe it was more, maybe less. Those days sort of ran into one another. No one day stood out. Every day the same. Or at least, that's how I remember it.

I wrote my dad. I wrote my mom. I wrote my sisters. I even wrote my little brother. They all wrote back. I saved their letters. I don't know why I bothered. In the end, I lost them all.

I wish I still had them. To remind me who I was.

## charlie

Wednesday, September 20, 1967

Rosaries. Nothing more than a priest standing before the friends and relatives of the dead and leading them in the recitation of the rosary. Always, on the evening before the funeral, everyone gathered, dressed in their finest, sober clothes, rosary beads and novenas in hand. That was the tradition, though I have no idea where the tradition began. Most rosaries were held in small chapels of funeral homes that tried to approximate the idea of sacred calmness, imitations of real churches, and only the blind grief of survivors allowed the fiction of serenity to stay intact. I hated funeral chapels. I was happy when Monsignor La Pieta allowed my grandmother's rosary to be held at Holy Family Church. I always loved that church, loved the smell of it, the intimacy, the smallness of it, the way you could hear every creek in the floor of the choir loft.

"The dreaded *pinche* rosary," Gus said. *Pinche.* He loved that word. But he sure as hell didn't love all those rituals we grew up with. I think the idea of God was just another ritual for Gus. As useless as the rest.

"What's so bad about rosaries?"

"Look, even if there is a God, don't you think we're boring the crap out of him?"

"Well," I said. "It's okay, I think. I mean we should have a rosary. I mean, her name was Rosario after all. So I think it's okay. It's a good idea. She liked the rosary and she liked going to them. And I don't think God ever gets bored. Too many things going on."

Gustavo looked at me accusingly. Well, maybe *accusingly* isn't the right word. He just gave me that look that made me feel compromised, a look that said, "Don't you have any balls?" He loved to give people that look. He shook his head. "Okay. Right. We'll all do the rosary thing."

I thought maybe he was going to skip out on the funeral altogether. Mom and Dad had stopped trying to make him go to Mass.

"Don't you think Grandma Rosie would be happy that we're having her rosary in a real church?"

"The dead are above all that crap, Charlie."

"How do you know?"

"Because they're dead. Dead means dead. Dead means you're not alive anymore. It means you don't need to eat anymore. It means you don't need to sleep anymore. It means you don't get tired anymore. It means you don't have to believe in anything anymore."

He was annoyed. But also distracted. There was something in his voice. But I was persistent. I was nothing if not persistent. "What about resurrection, Gus?"

"Resurrection." Gus made that face of his. "Let's say there is such a thing. Let's just say there is. Does that mean we just keep doing everything we've been doing while we were alive? Why would anybody want to keep on feeling the same damn things they felt when they were alive? What's the point?"

"Maybe we just get to keep feeling the good things?"

"I would expect that from someone who likes the Monkees." He wasn't smiling—but I knew a part of him was.

"You're doing it again, Gus."

"Doing what again?"

"Being superior."

Then he laughed. There was something in his face. Something. "Look, Charlie—" he stopped. He was whispering. "I'll never be better than you. Not ever. You can put that in your pot and smoke it." And then he did something that he'd never done before. Not ever. He pulled me next to him and hugged me. I felt really small and it was strange because I felt, well, like I wished Gus were my father instead of my brother.

And then he let me go.

He just looked at me.

I looked back at him. I wanted to ask him what was wrong. Gus didn't go around hugging people for no reason. He wasn't like that. Something was really wrong. I had a feeling it had something to do with that letter. I had a feeling I knew what that letter was about. I wanted, I don't know, I don't know what I wanted—to speak, that was it. To speak. But something in his eyes told me not to ask, told me not to say anything. So I didn't.

We both started dressing for Grandma Rosie's rosary. We didn't say anything as we changed out of our everyday clothes. Gus was whistling something. I didn't recognize the tune. It was sad. Or maybe it wasn't. Maybe I just remember that it was sad. But even if it was sad, I liked listening. I admired that about him, that he could whistle entire songs. I couldn't even call a dog with my style of whistling.

I changed into my black pants and my white shirt to the tune of Gus's whistling. I took off my tennis shoes, put on a pair of black socks. As I fumbled with my shoelaces, Dad came in to check on us. He studied us, making sure we were dressed properly. He was holding two black ties in his hand, one for me and one for Gus. My father, he had a supply of black ties. He handed them to us. He stayed in the room until we put them on. Gus struggled with the tie more than I did. I liked the knots on ties, double Windsor, that's what they called it, the knot on the tie. I thought it was very cool. I thought of it as an art I had conquered. It made me feel like I was part of something. I wondered about the tradition of ties and the art of tying them, where that came from. England, probably. Ties, rosaries, whistling, silence—I was surrounded by traditions. Maybe that was part of Gus's problem—the traditions he hated followed him around.

Dad didn't say a word. It was as if he'd forgotten all the words he'd ever learned. And just then, at that moment, I noticed he was tired—tired because he was sad and being sad made you tired as hell. That was it, he was tired—or maybe—or, or, or. Gus always said that's what my name should be: Mr. Or.

On his way out the door, Dad shook his head at me and smiled. "Shine your shoes." His voice was hoarse and he barely spoke above a whisper. When he left the room, Gus looked at me and we both laughed. Then Gus bent down and took my shoes off. "I'll shine them," he said.

# a family

## Wednesday, September 20, 1967

The saccharine smell of affordable perfume. The faint but pungent odor of cigarette smoke on the black suits of the men clutching their rosaries without grace. The aging women in their black dresses, most of them wrapped in Mexican silk shawls to protect them from the chill of the over-air-conditioned church. The warm greetings in Spanish on everyone's lips: *comadre, hace años que no la veía y usted la misma, ni muestra los años . . .* The embraces, the warm glances, the tears running down the women's faces, the kind gestures, the soft lilts in the voices, the sympathy in the expressions—even from people whose affections were suspect.

They were all here. Everyone.

In the front pews, the grieving sons and daughters, all of them with their wives and husbands at their sides, each of them lost in some memory of Rosario, grandmother, mother, mother-in-law, godmother, aunt—beautiful—a spoiled and difficult woman who had cast her lot with a man who lost his land and fortune to a revolution. Rosario, a harsh, superior woman who had softened at the hands of a daughter-in-law who took her in, cared for her, nursed her, bathed her, read to her, prayed with her, loved her; Rosario, a woman who had learned, at last, to return the affections that had been given her, had learned the meaning of kindness, had learned to forgive, had let go the controlled, relentless veneer of the class she had been born into. A good life. That is what they were all thinking. A good life. And for once, what they were thinking was not a lie.

And sitting just behind: the next generation, half of them already adult and married with children of their own, completely and utterly American—Mexico already a dream, and a bad one at that. The youngest among them residing in that awful, liminal age, not yet adult, no longer boys and girls, no longer needing to be told to behave, but not knowing exactly what was expected of them. They, too, had become utterly, completely American, the Spanish on their tongues, more graceless than their ever-changing voices and bodies.

They were all there. Everyone.

Octavio and Lourdes stood at the entrance to the church, directing traffic, shaking every hand, receiving every embrace—face after familiar face. Sometimes, Octavio would glance over at his wife, and once, she caught his gaze. He hoped she knew what he was trying to say: I have never loved you more.

Then, the hour arriving, Octavio and Lourdes made their way through the crowd to the front of the church, the mourners making a path for them through the crowded aisle. The two of them knelt in front of Rosario's open casket, her body no more than a relic of another time and another country, an emblem of inheritance and disinheritance, a reminder of exile, a finger pointing at all of them. This is where the journey ends.

Octavio and Rosario took each other's hands, prayed, *To thee do we cry poor banished children of Eve, to thee do we send up our sighs, weeping and mourning in this veil of tears . . .*

Octavio didn't flinch as he softly, slowly, loosened the ring on his mother's finger and wordlessly pushed the ring into his wife's palm.

Lourdes looked at him with a question.

He leaned toward her and whispered, "She wanted you to have it."

"No."

"She made me promise."

"It's too much like stealing," she whispered—then shook her head.

"I promised her." Lourdes stared at the ring. Rosario had never taken it off—not ever. The last reminder of her lost fortune. It was too much like payment. The thought of that insulted her. "No," she whispered.

"She made me promise," a pleading in Octavio's whisper. "You can just put it away. It doesn't matter. She made me promise."

She was dead. This argument was futile. She would put it away, never wear it, never advertise this extravagant gift. She took the ring from her husband and clutched it in her fist. Octavio gently took her elbow. They took their place in the front pew.

The priest appeared at the front of the church, sprinkling holy water on Rosario's body. A lone voice sang the Ave Maria and the grieving congregation stood, crossing themselves. Monsignor La Pieta's voice boomed out into the church with a faith so complete it bordered on arrogance, *Pray for us Oh Holy Mother of God,* and the voices responded like a well-practiced choir, *That we may be made worthy of the promises of Christ. . . .*

Lourdes made no effort to stop the sobs. *I hate, I hate this hurt.*

• • •

"I hate this."

"Shhh."

"I'm whispering."

"Shhh." Xochil clutched at her rosary.

"Even if there is a God—"

Xochil reached over and whispered directly into Gustavo's ear. "Pray. You don't have to believe. Just pray."

He nodded. Yes. Make believe that you are like the rest of them. He felt his brother leaning into him—then felt his small body trembling. "Why," Charlie whispered, "why do we have to die?"

Gustavo reached over and placed his arm around him.

"Tell me, Gus, why?"

"Shhh." He held Charlie close, then closer.

"Why, Gus? Why?"

"Pray," he whispered. "Just pray."

The house was loud, crowded, friends and relatives eating, drinking, beer, coffee, food, cigars, cigarettes, a different conversation in every room. In the kitchen, his aunts consoling one of their friends, her son busted for using marijuana, *It will be all right, I have a cousin, Ricardo, a good lawyer;* in the living room, an argument about the war, Gustavo surprised that all of his uncles didn't think alike, one of the women breaking into their discussion, *Have some respect in the house of the dead;* in the backyard, yet another discussion about that bastard Francisco Madero and someone bragging that a relative had been one of Pancho Villa's assassins. Everyone eating, everyone drinking, everyone talking, everyone commenting on Lourdes's beautiful children, Lourdes, *bandito sea Dios, que hijos tan hermosos.* And her own sister interjecting, *Yes, such beautiful children—but so disrespectful. Where did your twins get their politics? And Gustavo, well, he's a man, and his hair! And I hear Xochil is passing out flyers against the war at the university!* Lourdes smiling at her sister's accusations, squeezing her arm a little too firmly. *Their politics? From their mother.* Her sister's expression turning to stone. And in the bedroom, three old women, the last of their generation, sitting quietly, inconsolable, pointing at all the pictures on Rosario's wall.

Nobody noticed when Xochil slipped out. Except for Gustavo. He followed her, had almost called out, but changed his mind as he saw her climb into Jack's car.

He watched as they drove away.

He lit a cigarette and walked down the block. A few minutes later, he found himself at the steps of Holy Family Catholic Church. He sat on the steps. He thought of his grandmother's body, lying inside. He hadn't said good-bye. But why did that matter? Why couldn't you just die? Why couldn't you just leave? Why did you have to embrace everyone around you with awkward hugs and say things you weren't sure you meant? Why did you have to go to hotel rooms and make love to someone?

Why couldn't you just dispense with the all the rituals?

That's what he would do. He would dispense with rituals. He would just leave.

He walked back home and stared at the house as if it were a person. He walked inside, smiled at his mother as she cleared some plates from the dining room. He walked into his room. He found his backpack in the back of his closet. He took out a few things from his drawer, some socks, underwear, some T-shirts. He took a few shirts from the closet, folded them, not neatly, then threw in a couple pairs of jeans. He fumbled through the bottom drawer and found some pictures—Xochil, Charlie, his mom and dad. He packed them in one of the pockets of his backpack. There wasn't much to take.

He had some money—a hundred and twenty dollars. It might be enough. For a while. Until he thought of a plan. He sat down on Charlie's bed. He thought of smoking a cigarette. *No smoking in the house.* "Yes, Mom," he whispered. "I promise. No smoking in the house."

*You are a young man.*

*But your world is gone. It has disappeared.*

*Your grandfather is gone.*

*Your grandmother is gone.*

*The dog you loved as a boy is gone.*

*You did not take the rifle your father gave you. And now your country offers you another. Your country offers you a manhood you do not want. And you think that perhaps Jack Evans is right. You are just a coward. You are just afraid. You are a young man who refuses to become a man. Coward. And you wonder what it is like to be Jack Evans. To think the things he thinks. To feel the things he feels. To believe the things he believes. You do not blame him. You want to make yourself like him, like Jack Evans. You do. Then you would know peace. Then you would be like all the other boys who accepted their inevitable manhood with grace.*

*But you were born to be another kind of man. You cannot change what is in your heart. And you hate, you hate that you have one, a heart. You hate, you hate your heart. But it is all you have. You must stand it. You must bear it.*

*You picture your grandmother's eyes. You picture her old, soft, wrinkled hands on your smooth face. You will never feel those hands again.*

*You know that more losses are coming. If you go to war, then you will have to learn to kill. They tell you it is for your country. They tell you it is to protect your way of life. They tell you it is for freedom. They tell you it is your duty. They tell you that this is the way the world is, and you are a part of that world, and the world knows more than you, is wiser than you, you, you who know nothing—but you know that you are not a part, have never been a part, will never be a part. Can you go? Will you go to that strange land?*

*And you know that you will not, cannot go. And you hate yourself. And you hate the country that gave you yourself—the self that you hate.*

*You will lose your father—though you know you lost him long ago.*

*You will lose your mother.*

*You will refuse to break.*

*You will lose your sister.*

*You will lose your brother.*

*Your mother, your sister, your brother, your mother, your sister, your brother.*

*Mother, sister, brother. They are everything.*

*You will refuse to break.*

*You hear your mother telling you that you are afraid of hurting the people you love.*

*You know what you have to do.*

*You will refuse to break.*

*You will bury your grandmother.*

*You will leave.*

*You will go to Mexico.*

*You will live in exile.*

*Exile will become the only freedom you know.*

*You will be alive.*

*But you will also be dead.*

He shook his head. He stared at his fists, clenched around the twenty-dollar bills he was clutching. He stuffed the money in one of the pockets of the jeans he'd packed. He hid the backpack under his bed, and made his way back into the living room. There were people there. In the living room.

# adam

## Da Nang, Vietnam, September 21, 1967

He couldn't sleep.

Smoking that shit never helped, made him feel funny, like people were looking at him. It was supposed to relax you, but that's not how it worked on him. Whit, hell, it made him feel like he was on top of the fucking Empire State Building. That's because the sonofabitch was one happy motherfucker.

But he wasn't Whit.

Never would be Whit.

You know, he thought about how he'd felt when he finished all his training. Man, that had felt real good. Better than being drunk. Better than pot, better than all that shit. Man, he'd felt like everything was gonna be just fine.

He'd remembered what he'd talked about with Whit as they sat on the beach. "You know maybe all this isn't such a good idea."

Whit just laughed. "What, shit, everyone smokes this shit."

"Not this, fuckwad. The war, the fucking war."

"Shit, too fucking late to be asking that question, asshole. We're in it, now, buddy, so let's just go to it, do our bit, and go fucking home."

"You think we'll win it?"

"I don't think about it."

"Why not?"

"It's not on me. Winning this war—that's just not on me, baby. You got that? You know, we got our piece of it. That's what we got. I don't think you should be fucking thinking shit like that, either. We do our job. If we do it just right, we won't get our fucking asses shot off. We do our tour, try to have as many good times as we fucking can, then get the fuck home. That's it, buddy."

"What about the big fucking picture, Whit? What about that?"

"You know what? I don't have that view from my window. You don't fucking either, motherfucker. We just don't live in the right house. Some people got a nice view of things. You and I, we don't. So just fuckin' relax. I got your back. You got mine. We're gonna do all right."

He wished he were like Whit. Everything would be all right with Whit. But him? Hell, he wasn't so sure anymore.

It didn't help, the news about Salvi.

Made it back home—then fucking offed himself.

He'd gotten a postcard. Whit too. "Guess I didn't fucking make it after all."

*Shit, Salvi, what the fuck did you do?*

## xochil

At the Desert Lodge Hotel on Montana, he parks his car right in front of the room. You have seen this place before as you passed it and wondered about it, and wondered even more when your uncle once remarked, "You can rent a room there by the hour." You remember that remark as he pulls his car up in the space in front of the room. He has made all the arrangements. He looks at you and smiles, then rubs his sweaty palms on the lap of his pants and you can see he is trembling. That makes you happy, that he is more nervous, more afraid, than you. You reach over and kiss him, and you think he tastes like a salty desert. You are lost in that kiss and you are happy to be lost and you are no longer scared.

You pull away from each other, and he gets out of the car and rushes to open the door for you, and he seems like a boy who is playing at being a man. You step out, he pulls you close, and you walk toward the door. You can feel the heat of the day on the concrete, almost as warm as a human body.

You laugh and he looks at you with a question in his eyes. So serious. That is what you say. "Such a serious soldier." His trembling hands cannot get the key into the door. So you laugh, take the keys from him, unlock the door for him, and push it open. "There," you say. And you look at him and he looks at you and you walk into the room, which has the faint smell of cigarettes and vomit.

You both laugh.

"It doesn't smell nice, does it?" he says. "I'll get another room."

You shake your head. "No," you say. "This one. I like this one." And you turn on the lamp and you feel something inside you, not a bad thing, not an ugly thing, but something else, something that resembles the morning light, something that resembles a star in the night, and it is a freedom to tell yourself, *I love him I love him I love him.* And the future does not matter. The future, what is that? The future is a kind of death you do not seek or want. You stand before each other, you and him, and you are as still as you have ever been as you watch him take off his shirt, and then you hear yourself speak. "Touch me."

# a family

"Mexico threw us out. And then, as we left, it spit on us. Isn't that what the old man said before he died?"

"He said that only once. And that was long before he died. He wasn't that bitter about the whole thing. Not in the end. Just wasn't in him to be bitter."

"Mom was bitter."

"She wasn't used to life without servants."

"That's a mean thing to say."

"Don't you remember? There was at least one servant for every member of the family—and that didn't include the men who worked the land."

"Strange—it doesn't feel real anymore—"

"We were just boys."

"Yes. If things had been different—"

"We'd still be rich."

"Maybe. Maybe not. We could have still lost everything."

"I would have liked the chance. You know, maybe I'm the one who's bitter."

"How old were you, when we left?"

"Eleven. I loved that place. I still dream it."

"I remember your horse."

"San Pedro. Black as night."

"That's right."

Gustavo watched his uncles, studied their faces as they talked. Tonight, they seemed sedate and pensive, and he liked them. He didn't always like them. They could be mean—all of them, none of them as gentle as his grandfather. They mostly felt foreign, his uncles and his father. Tonight they felt like home.

He listened to their voices—and then he remembered, Xochil! And a wave of panic, Xochil. *Shit Xochil. Dad would kill her—*

# charlie. gustavo.

Charlie? Charlie, are you out there?"

Charlie held his breath, made himself perfectly still.

"I know you're there. Charlie? I know you like to hide there."

Charlie refused to move.

"Charlie? I know you're there." His voice was closer. "Charlie?"

He looked up from where he was sitting and saw Gus standing over him.

"You can't hide from big brothers."

"Guess not. Especially big brothers who need favors."

"Guess that's true." Gustavo reached over and pulled Charlie up from the ground. "Listen, Charlie."

"What's wrong?"

"Nothing."

He looked at his brother, something about the look on his face in the dull light shining from the front porch. "You sure. It seems like—"

"I need a favor."

"Sure."

"You don't even know what it is yet."

"Doesn't matter what it is."

Gustavo smiled. "I need you to lie for me."

"Okay," he said quietly. "Tell me."

"If Mom and Dad ask where I am, tell them Xochil and I went for a walk."

"Xochil? Where is she?"

"Look, if Mom and Dad come looking for either one of us, just tell them that we went for a walk. It's important. They won't ask any questions. That's what we do."

Charlie nodded. "Everyone knows that."

"Exactly."

"But I don't understand, Gus."

"I'll explain it later. I promise. Please—"

"I promise."

"You're not a good liar, so don't say too much."

"I can lie as good as you can, Gus."

"Bullshit."

"I can."

"Sometimes we have to lie."

"I know."

"Do you?"

"Everyone knows that."

"It's important."

Charlie nodded. He didn't like that thing in his older brother's voice. Something new, that panic. But his face, it seemed calm. What was it? What was happening?

"Good. Just say we've gone for a walk."

"Yes," he said. "If they ask."

## gustavo

He could see everything from the porch of that empty house. No one could see him, across the street and two houses down. He could see people coming and going—mostly going now. He didn't know how long he'd been there—an hour, longer maybe. He'd smoked ten cigarettes, he knew that. He'd heard it took seven minutes to smoke a cigarette—so that was seventy minutes. That's how he figured it. And there had been some time between each cigarette—so he had been there for an hour and a half. And Xochil had left a good half hour before he had come out here—so she had been gone for two hours. Two hours. That was long enough. To do what they were going to do. He hated that, didn't want to think about it. His sister and Jack.

That sonofabitch.

*And Dad will kill you, Xochil, he'll—* He saw a car park a little up the street.

He knew it was them.

He heard his heart pounding.

For a moment, there was nothing but relief—and then he felt the anger.

# octavio. charlie. lourdes.

"Has he disappeared again?"

Lourdes handed her husband a plate full of *bizcochos*. "Your sister made these. Will you take them out for me?"

"You didn't answer my question. Where is he?"

"I don't know. I've been busy."

"Too busy for your children?"

"And you, Octavio?" Lourdes took a deep breath. "I'm tired. You're tired. I don't want to argue. I don't want to—"

"They took a walk."

Lourdes and Octavio stared at Charlie, who was sitting at the kitchen table, staring at a plate of food—but not eating anything.

"When?"

"About an hour ago. You know, like they always do. They went for a walk." He looked down at his plate and picked at his food with a fork. "Don't be mad, Dad," he whispered.

Lourdes nudged Octavio with her elbow.

"I'm not mad, Charlie. It's just that— Well, your brother worries me."

"They're just taking a walk," he said, his face glued to the plate of food.

"Charlie, look at me."

He nodded and looked up at his father, tears running down his face.

"I'm sorry. Look, son, I'm sorry."

Lourdes nodded to herself and squeezed her husband's hands. Apologies didn't come easy to him. She leaned into him and kissed his shoulder. Then she pushed him toward Charlie.

He sat next to Charlie at the table. "Son, don't cry."

"No, it's okay. I don't know why I'm crying. I've been doing it all day."

"Don't worry about it."

Charlie nodded.

"You're not eating."

"I'm hungry—but I'm not hungry. That doesn't make sense."

"Eat."

He had the sudden urge to ask his father if he loved Gus. He wanted to ask, but he was afraid of the answer. "Okay," he said, "I'll eat."

# gustavo. xochil.

They were looking into each other's faces. He was whispering something. She was listening. The door to his car was still open as they stood there on the sidewalk.

They didn't notice he was standing there.

He lit a cigarette, and they both looked toward him at the small sizzling sound of the match as he struck it on the matchbook. "Give me one good reason why I shouldn't tear you a new asshole." It was mean what he'd said—but somehow his words lacked conviction. More like he was upset. Hurt. He'd meant to sound angry. But the anger had left him, though he didn't know why.

"Don't be mad," Xochil whispered.

"Why'd you go? With him, Xochil? With him?"

"Because I had to."

"I hate his fucking guts."

"Gustavo, I love her."

"Who asked you, Jack?"

"I love her. I respect her."

"If you say another fucking word, I swear I'll go for you, you motherfucking bastard."

*"Gustavo, stop it. Just stop."*

"Are you coming?"

"I'm coming. Can you—can you give me one minute? Just one minute, Gustavo, that's all I'm asking."

"One minute, Xochil. You get one minute. After that, I'm gonna go mental on you. I swear I am." He walked up the block, far enough away so that he wouldn't have to listen to whatever they were saying to each other. He looked away, then tried to concentrate on his cigarette. He took in a deep drag—then let it out slowly—then did it again. He closed his eyes. He opened them again as he felt Xochil's hand on his shoulder. "Don't be mad. Please don't be mad."

"I don't know what to say," he whispered. "What if Mom and Dad had caught you? They could have caught you. They could have. They'd kill you."

"Mom wouldn't kill me."

"She wouldn't exactly be thrilled—her daughter going all the way with some warmongering gringo—"

"Don't talk like that."

"Which part didn't you like? The part about the daughter going all the way? Or the part about the warmongering gringo?"

He felt the slap, the sting, the burning, as if his face were a match being lit. He felt dizzy, numb, the strange pain but the pain was somewhere else, not in his cheek, but somewhere closer to the center of his body and he suddenly felt sick. He found himself sitting on the curb of the street and the strange tears falling and everything felt so far, even Xochil, who was sitting beside him, clinging to him and begging, *I'm sorry, I'm sorry, Gustavo, forgive me, forgive me.*

. . .

She sat and listened to his sobs. He wasn't that way, didn't cry, didn't like to show you his sorrows, which to him were always private. But the last few days, he was different. They were all different.

When his sobs subsided, she took his hand. "You have to say you forgive me."

He nodded.

"You have to say it."

He nodded. "I forgive you." He looked up, "And you?"

"Me what?"

"You forgive me?"

"Are you trying to make me cry too?"

"There's a lot of that going around at our house these days. I think it's a disease we're all catching."

She kissed his cheek. Where she'd slapped him.

"When I made love to him—"

"Don't, Xochil—"

"I have to say this."

"Okay."

"Making love to him. It was my way of saying good-bye."

"It's a very generous way of saying good-bye." He grinned— then laughed. And then they were both laughing, unable to stop, until they were almost crying again. He pulled her up. "Let's go home."

She nodded. "I love him."

"I know."

"But it's over. That's what I meant by saying good-bye. I mean, for him it meant hello. But for me it meant good-bye."

"Does he know that?"

"He doesn't want to know it. I think he thinks that he'll go off to war—then come back and marry me. And we'll have a house *full* of coyote kids."

"Why not?"

"You know why not."

"Tell me."

"Because I'm not Barbie."

"That's for fucking sure."

She smiled. "Do you think I'm a whore?"

"Course not."

"Really?"

"I swear."

"Good. Because you're not exactly a virgin."

"That's true. But I'm a guy."

"Which makes you a close relative to the dogs who roam the streets."

"Funny."

"Then laugh."

"Nope."

"*You are a close relative to the dogs who roam the streets.* You've slept with four girls."

"Who told you that?"

"I know things. And you only loved one of them."

"Who's counting?" He shrugged. "Two of the four I really liked. And I could've slept with a lot more but didn't. And, like you said, one of them I loved, I really loved."

"You're practically a saint."

"That's Charlie's area."

"Gustavo?"

"That's my name, don't—"

"Wear it out." She reached over and gave him rabbit ears. "Smile for the camera."

He grinned.

"I'm sorry I slapped you."

"It hurt."

"I made you cry."

"Don't get a big head."

"Gustavo?" She seemed to be searching for the right word—and then found it. "When?"

"Soon," he whispered.

"Soon?"

"Yes."

She nodded. "You'll tell me, won't you?"

"Of course."

"Don't say *of course*. Just say yes."

"*Yes.*"

"Give me a cigarette."

"I don't like it when you smoke."

"Just give me a cigarette and shut up." She reached into his shirt pocket and pulled out his cigarettes. "You have only two left."

"I smoked a bunch tonight. Waiting for you to come back. I even made an excuse for you—just in case."

"Just in case?"

"I didn't want you to catch hell."

"Even though I was with Jack?"

"It's not you I hate."

"I don't really think you hate Jack, either."

"I think I'd know."

"What was the excuse?"

"I told Charlie to tell them we went for a walk."

"Because that's what we do."

"Because that's what we've always done."

"Charlie can't lie worth a damn."

"Neither can you, Xochil."

"Yes I can."

"Only if you keep quiet. If you don't say anything—no one can tell what you're thinking. Except me. But Charlie, he's too sweet."

"I like him that way."

"Me too." He watched her smoke. Like a real pro.

"Are you scared?"

"Yes."

"You don't look scared."

"Good."

They stood in front of the house. It was late and the house was quiet, all the lights still on. Most everyone had left—except for his four uncles and their wives. They could hear the women cleaning up, the sound of plates clattering, the muffled sounds of conversation. Xochil squeezed her brother's hand. "Can't we stay like this forever?"

## gustavo

He could never come back. Not if he left. *Never.* The word hit him like a stone, striking him right in pit of his stomach. He heard their voices, his mom's, Xochil's, clear, pure, easy—like a song.

"How old were you, when you met him?"

"I was seventeen. I lived in one of the smallest houses in the neighborhood and your father used to walk in front of the house almost every day. Skinny, your father. Beautiful. He was graceful and awkward all the same time. One day he finally knocked at the front door. And he just stood there staring at me."

He heard Xochil laughing, then his mother laughing, and he wished he could laugh too. But there wasn't any laughter in him.

He looked at his mother as he put away the last of the dishes. He moved toward her and kissed her on the cheek.

She looked at him, studying him. Always studying him. "You must be tired."

"Tired?"

"You never kiss your mother anymore."

"Is that true? That's not true."

Xochil nodded. "Yes, that's true."

"I'm out of character. If you're not careful, I'll give you a kiss too. Today, no charge. Free." He felt the tears, right there where the stone was, in his stomach. He knew he had to leave the room, had to leave. Now. He felt Xochil's kiss. He felt himself smile at her. He felt himself whisper, "I'm going to bed."

When he found himself in his room, he took a breath, then another.

The tears did not come.

He lay there in the dark. He listened to Charlie's breathing. His breathing was like a clock that kept time. He thought he might want to listen to his brother's breathing forever.

When the house was dark and silent, he slowly, quietly, took out his backpack from under the bed. He tiptoed down the hall and out the back door. He walked across the yard and through the door to the garage. He reached for the flashlight that his father hung next to the door, then flipped it on. He looked for a hiding place for his backpack—then saw the perfect place. There, behind the big tin trashcan where his father kept leftover pieces of wood. No one would see it.

Tomorrow, he could just grab it and go out the garage door that opened onto the alley.

No one would see him.

And he would be gone.

I was a Marine.

Not a maggot, not a lady.

A Marine. I felt like I was walking down the street with the biggest, meanest fucking dog in the world. No one would fuck with me. That's just how I felt. It makes me smile to think about it now. And I'm not making fun of myself either.

I hardly remembered who or what I'd been.

I remembered seeing myself that first day at boot camp. A little on the skinny side. You know, I didn't feel like an ugly fuck anymore. I was bigger. I was in shape. I had confidence. I'd never had that before, not really, didn't know what it was like to feel good in my own fucking skin. Graceful, that's how I felt.

I wasn't a boy. Not anymore. I was focused. I had some discipline. I'd become what I'd always wanted to become. I was fucking proud. I felt like I could do anything. I can still see myself, young, ready, tough as hell. I thought I was bulletproof. Shit, I was bulletproof.

I had the guts. I was gonna be a badass. I was gonna make a fucking difference. I wasn't gonna sit on the sidelines. I wasn't gonna let other people fight my fight, fight my war.

Every generation gets a chance to make their mark. You're either gonna be a part of something or you're just gonna fucking stay behind and be nothing. Not me.

I went straight to the staging battalion at Camp Pendleton.

Six weeks later, I was on my way to Vietnam.

I remember we got on this chartered plane. A whole fucking plane full of Marines. You know, since I left the service, I've never been on another goddamned chartered plane. Hell, for fucking years, I didn't fly at all.

So there I was on a plane full of Marines. I don't remember being scared. I mean, hell, I know we were going to war, but, I don't know. I just don't think I was scared. Maybe I didn't know any better. Anyway, fear would come. It sure as fuck would. But the thing about being scared, it never kept me from doing my job.

Being scared is nothing. I never gave being scared the fucking time of day.

I sat on that plane, smoked, and just listened to guys talk. I just listened. Some guys were talking about their last lays. Some guys were spilling out their life stories. Some guys were telling the stupid fucking dirty jokes they'd perfected. Some guys were just like me. They just watched. Those of us who watched, we're the ones who made it.

But right then, it felt good, to sit there. I belonged to these guys. This is the way it was supposed to feel.

We flew from San Francisco to Anchorage to Japan to Da Nang.

The first thing I remember is that the guys who picked us up, hell, they all smelled like shit. I never smelled anything like it. And I'm thinking, *Don't these guys ever take showers?* I mean, they really smelled like shit. And then I learned real quick that everyone smelled like shit. *I mean, it turned out that it was shit.* Buffalo shit, to be precise. It's what the Vietnamese women used to dry our clothes off base—dried buffalo chips for the fire. We weren't allowed to go off base unless, of course, we were on patrol. Our clothes got sent out, and well, our uniforms came back smelling like Vietnamese buffalo shit. Hell, in the end, that smell didn't matter a damn. It was like having a dime in your pocket. A dime was nothing. It wasn't even worth keeping.

Monsoons. That was more than a fucking dime. I'd take the smell of buffalo shit any day over the fucking monsoons.

Rain. Day after day after day, week after week, month after fucking month.

Nothing the Marines taught you in basic training could prepare you for that kind of rain. When we'd go out on perimeter defense or on security patrols, you know, for convoys and shit like that, when we did that sort of ground patrol during the monsoons, it was my idea of hell.

It didn't help that I was from fucking El Paso, Texas. I was sort of addicted to the sun.

God, I was cold. Always, always cold. It was pretty temperate really, but when you were basically wet all the time, well, that could make a guy shiver. Even a guy like me.

We'd huddle together to sleep in our ponchos and, hell, if the enemy didn't kill us, the fucking rain would. I hated ground detail. I fucking got to hate it.

I remember these things called bouncing Betties. They were a kind of antipersonnel mine. They were loaded on a spring, and you could hear the spring and a click when you stepped on one, you know, like one of those toy guns you spring-loaded when you were a kid. They shot up about five feet then exploded. They could kill you easy—either that or slice you up pretty damned bad. And they always, always slowed us down.

When a Betty went off, that meant one of our guys was down. We'd move in, help him out if he wasn't dead, then we'd have to radio for help. So basically the damn things took two or three guys out of commission for a while. Really slowed us down.

Bouncing Betties. There's a fucking memory.

You know, when I was in Nam, all my dreams were of home. When I came home, all my dreams were of war.

# xochil

I woke up early that morning, the house still dark, the sun about to rise, the house creaking softly as if it were afraid to wake us with its quiet, chronic angers. I wasn't tired but I should have been. I could still smell Jack on my skin, even though I'd showered before going to bed.

I didn't mind his smell.

I felt sad and happy.

I could explain the sad. The sad was about knowing my grandmother was dead. The sad was about knowing that Gustavo was going to leave—though a part of me still hoped he'd find another way. But what other way was there? I'd thought about it—it was either jail or Canada or Mexico or Vietnam. Those were his choices. Either way he would be leaving. The house would never be the same.

But the happy, that part, that was harder to explain. I felt free somehow. Free of Jack. Because I wasn't carrying him around anymore. I know what they mean by baggage. I do. That's what Jack was. I'd been carrying him around and now it felt like I didn't need to do that anymore.

The first time, it was me who had made love to him.

The second time, it was he who had made love to me.

But we didn't make love to each other at the same time. It wasn't so bad, knowing that. It made me happy.

I sat on my bed and watched the sunlight as it floated into the room. Sometimes the light was like a knife. It sliced the room, almost shredding it. But that morning, the light seemed to float in. I sat there a long time, studying the harsh shadows in the room. I remembered that Gustavo had once told me that he lived in the dark places, in the parts of the room where the sun never reached. He said it was Charlie who lived in the light. He said I lived in between, half in the shadows, half in the light. I didn't want to think about all the things Gustavo ever said to me. I finally placed my feet on the cool wood floor.

The house was so serene, everyone still asleep, and when I walked into the kitchen, I was surprised to see my mother sitting there, perfect and soundless, already dressed for the funeral. She didn't say anything, almost as if she were afraid to break the silence. She poured me a cup of coffee and we sat there in the kitchen. She reached over and combed my hair with her fingers. And then she took my hand and led me into my grandmother's room. "Your aunts and cousins will all want something of hers. I'm giving you first choice." She was half whispering.

I looked around the room. "That picture," I said.

She nodded.

I reached for the photograph and took it off the wall. It was a picture of my grandmother holding me and Gustavo. We couldn't have been more than a week old. I looked up at the wall and smiled to myself. "Someone's already taken a photograph," I said.

My mother nodded. "I know which one."

"Me too," I said.

"It was Gustavo," my mother said.

"It was Gustavo," I repeated.

My mother sat on the bed, not in any hurry to leave the room. She was wearing a simple black dress and a string of pearls. My father had given her those pearls when she came home from the hospital with me and Gustavo. She hardly ever wore them. She wasn't much for jewelry, didn't need ornaments, but wearing those pearls in that particular slant of light, she looked as soft and lovely as anything I'd ever seen. I felt like a camera trying to capture her image. In that instant, she was all there was, this woman who was my mother, still young with hardly any wrinkles, and soft hazel eyes and a streak of white against her otherwise raven hair. "You're so beautiful," I whispered.

She laughed, such a soft and kind and fragile laugh. And then suddenly I knew where Charlie had gotten his kindness. I don't know why I'd never noticed that before. "Beauty isn't worth as much as people think it is. It won't keep me from dying."

"And it certainly doesn't keep you safe from men."

"That's an interesting thing to say."

"Aren't you glad—that your daughter says interesting things?"

She smiled at me. "I hope he loves you," she said.

"Who?" I asked. I was afraid she was referring to Jack.

"Whoever marries you—I hope he loves you enough to know who you are."

"Does Dad—does he love you enough?"

"He tries."

"Is it enough?"

She nodded.

I nodded too. I didn't know whether I believed her or not. It wasn't that she didn't love my father. And it wasn't that he didn't love her. But, well, I wasn't sure if my mother was happy. I wanted that for her. And I think that's what she wanted for me. The pursuit of happiness, baby. That's a joke Gustavo and I had. Only it wasn't a joke. I wanted that—happiness—wanted to be with someone I didn't have to fight for every inch of understanding. Understanding was not in my father's lexicon. It wasn't in Jack's lexicon either.

I watched my mother as she walked to the dresser and reached for my grandmother's favorite perfume. She dabbed a little on her finger and rubbed some of it on my wrists. "There," she said. She kept looking at me. As if she knew something about me. That almost scared me. "I hope you don't marry him," she said.

"Who?"

She shook her head. "Jack."

"I thought you liked him."

"No. Your father likes him. But not me."

"I'm not going to marry Jack Evans."

She looked at me. It was as if she could see right through me. "Mom, I—"

"Shhh."

Later that morning, after I'd gotten dressed, she put her pearls on me. "There," she said, "now you look perfect."

Before we left for church, we all posed for a picture in front of the house. On the steps of the front porch. My father looked less weathered, and the sun on his face made him look almost shiny. He was still fit and thin—and I could almost see the young man my mother had fallen in love with. But I could also see the old man he was turning into. Charlie looked like he was beginning to turn into a man, leaving that little boy behind. God, when I saw him on the steps, for a minute, I held my breath. He looked older, looked as if he'd learned how to carry his body with grace overnight. But when he smiled at me, the boy came back. And I could breathe again. And Gustavo, he seemed more handsome and dangerous in a black suit than in a pair of jeans. I think every man in our world envied him, his thick, untamable hair falling over his eyes, his poise, his ability to control his gaze. Of course, no one could appreciate the price he paid for that control—except those of us who loved him.

# gustavo. octavio.

I suppose it didn't occur to you to get a haircut—out of respect."

"Grandma Rosie loved my hair."

"She was just being kind."

"It's not something she passed on to me and you, is it?"

"No. Kindness isn't one of our great assets."

Gustavo nodded. "And she did love my hair."

"Well, I don't."

"I'll wear it short for your funeral, Dad. Out of respect." Gustavo turned away from his father and moved toward the front door.

"They'll take care of that when you get drafted."

Gustavo turned around and faced his father. *Right, Dad, they shave us before they put a fucking rifle in our hands.* He wanted to shove those words down his father's throat, but it didn't matter, not anymore. In a few hours he would be gone and his father's voice would disappear. A part of him wanted to smile. And then he remembered that rifle, the one his father had put in his hands when he was ten. He saw himself, standing in the middle of a pecan orchard, looking up at his father, who was waiting for a response. *Don't you think it's beautiful?* "No, I don't think it's beautiful."

"What did you say?"

He hadn't realized he'd said the words out loud. He felt exposed, embarrassed. "Nothing."

"What's not beautiful?"

"Nothing."

"Nothing?"

"Sometimes, I talk to myself."

"Well, you're better at talking to yourself than you are at talking to your father."

"Yes."

"I don't understand you."

"Look, Dad, let's not—" He looked down at his shoes, then looked back at his father. "I loved her. Grandma Rosie wouldn't like this." As soon as he spoke those words, he wanted to take them back. Not because he didn't mean what he said, but because he'd sounded so soft when he said it. He hated being soft around his father.

Octavio nodded. He felt the weight of Gustavo's words. He couldn't remember the last time he had heard his son admit that he loved anyone, confess it so openly. In the moment that he spoke the words, he looked so much like Charlie. "Will you run a comb through your hair? Or a brush? Or whatever you run through it? Can you do that?"

# charlie

Me sitting on the porch, trying to imagine myself in a coffin. Underground.

Gustavo and my dad trying not to argue.

Xochil wearing my mother's pearls.

Me sitting on the porch trying to decide if the breeze was going to turn into a wind. I hated the wind. When the wind came to El Paso, it always threatened to tear up the sky. My mother looking at me and nodding her approval and telling me for the millionth time that I was the most beautiful creature she'd ever seen. *Charlie, Charlie, Charlie.*

My father taking out his camera and photographing all of us standing on the steps to the front porch. My mother and I, in the center. Xochil on the right and Gustavo on the left. My father's orders that we shouldn't smile. "In Mexico, you don't smile for pictures."

My father reprimanding me for ruining the first two pictures by smiling.

The smell of Grandma Rosie's perfume on Xochil and my mother.

The fact that my father refused to ride in one of the limousines—even when they offered to pick us up at home.

The fact that I was disappointed that I would not be riding in a limousine. The fact that I felt mean and small and stupid and shallow for being disappointed.

Arriving at the church early, Monsignor La Pieta waiting for us at the door so we could say our private farewells to Grandma Rosie.

Me wondering why people said things about the dead, things like "Doesn't she look beautiful?"

Xochil weeping into Gustavo's shoulder when they shut the casket.

I think I know why I kept lists when I was young. They kept me from falling apart.

*Maria del Rosario Espejo Zaragosa's funeral was a sad and formal affair, the church so full that there were people standing in the entry to the church. Latecomers stood on the steps, all of them holding that look of stoic resignation on their faces. Every family from Sunset Heights whose presence in the neighborhood could be traced to the Mexican Revolution was represented. She was the last of the old dispensation.*

It was right in the middle of the monsignor's sermon that I first started trying to write about my grandmother's death—her death and everything else that happened to our family during those six awful days. Maybe it was a way of putting everything into a container that I could handle. I don't know. We're all writers of a sort in our family. All of us. In our family, we just couldn't leave anything alone. Everything had to be poisoned with words. That's how Xochil put it.

So right there, in the middle of my grandmother's funeral Mass, I started writing. I wrote and rewrote those first few lines until I committed them to memory. I kept repeating *old dispensation* to myself. It was a new phrase I'd borrowed from a poem I'd read. I kept wondering which dispensation I belonged to—the old one or the new one. I knew Xochil and Gus, they definitely belonged to the new dispensation. And even though I was younger, I think I was much more in love with everything that was so much older than me. I thought that maybe I would always belong to the old.

I always see myself as a boy sitting in front of his grandmother's piano—playing the songs, the old songs she'd taught me to play. When we got to the cemetery and I touched my grandmother's casket for the last time and placed my white rose on it, I didn't have any tears left inside me. I didn't. Something had changed since the Saturday that she died. I had changed, my family had changed.

I stared at my father, who seemed numb and far away. And I thought he was beginning to disappear.

# gustavo

I sat next to Charlie and my uncles in the front pew because we were selected as pallbearers. We sat in the middle of a sea of men dressed in black.

I saw the look on Xochil's face when my father announced that Charlie and I were among the pallbearers. As I sat there in the crowded church, all I could think of was my sister's hurt.

I was only half listening to the old monsignor's sermon, my mind wandering to memories of my sister and grandmother. I half remembered her being angry once—at my father. What had he done to make her angry? Because he was aloof? Unkind? Because he was impatient with his wife? Had he done something? I tried to think back, but the memory wouldn't come—just the image of my grandmother standing over my father as he sat in his chair, an angry look on her face—but the words, I couldn't remember them, oh, yes, but I remembered how my grandmother had grabbed the book he was reading from his hands and flung it across the room. Xochil and I had watched from the dining room and as the book flew across the room, Xochil grabbed my hand and whispered, "Wish I could do that." I smiled to myself and was suddenly self-conscious. What if one of my relatives caught me smiling at my own grandmother's funeral? Smirking. Smart-ass, cocky kid. That's what they would think. But what the shit did it matter?

When we were at the cemetery, I kept thinking that I should have asked her. I should have asked her what she thought—about the war, about what I should do. Why hadn't I asked her? She was the keeper of all secrets, my grandmother. Why hadn't I said anything to her?

If I went back to Mexico, if I went there, would I be blessed? Would it be a return? Would I be cursed?

Is it true that the dead look after the living?

## lourdes

There was a breeze in the air that was almost cold and certainly bitter. The sun was out, the sky was cloudless, but there wasn't any calmness or sweetness or beauty in the day.

The house was full of people after the burial.

The murmur, the laughter, the whispers of all the guests spilled out into the street. There were people in the front yard, on the porch, in the living room, in the dining room, in the kitchen, even in some of the bedrooms. Uncles, aunts, cousins, friends were eating and drinking and talking, an afternoon party, a discussion in the kitchen about a cousin's pregnancy—another Espejo in the world and wasn't it all too beautiful?

I decided not to direct traffic that afternoon. I'd had enough of that. Instead, I kept an eye out. Wherever Gustavo went, I followed close behind—but not close enough for him to notice.

I had a feeling.

I'd woken up with that feeling.

# gustavo

He changed into a pair of jeans, kept his white shirt on, tucked it in, took off his black tie and his black coat, replaced it with a sports coat. He went into the bathroom and looked himself over. He stared at his face. He didn't seem to look the same. He felt like he was someone else now. He could feel his heart beating. He saluted himself, pretended to be a soldier, shrugged, laughed—then castigated himself for the mean and stupid joke that had come out of him. He noticed he couldn't keep himself from trembling. He went into the front yard and looked around. He lit a cigarette. He saw Charlie talking to his cousins. His hands were flying through the air, making signs, and he knew he was describing something to them, telling them a story. He was good at telling stories, had inherited that gift from their grandfather.

He let himself be lost in the listening.

He finished his cigarette, looked at his watch. If he didn't leave soon, he would lose heart, stay, delay. He had to do it now. Fuck this limbo he'd been living in, fuck it, fuck it. He had to leave right fucking now.

He walked into the living room where his father and all his uncles were talking. He watched them just as he had watched them the night before. He kept his eyes on his father as he listened to them, noticed all his reactions.

" . . .the truth is, Papá came here with more than just a few pesos. You think we swam over?"

"Of course we didn't."

"He bribed his way into this country, and had enough left over to buy a house—"

"It wasn't a mansion."

"It wasn't a shack."

"Well, we weren't rich."

"We used to have standing."

"Standing?"

"Yes. And here, what do we have?"

"Mortgages and kids. Goddamned revolutions always getting in the way."

Suddenly the whole room was laughing.

Gustavo laughed with them—with his uncles and his father and all these addicts of familial history. He wondered what it was about them that clung to their exile. And yet they didn't love Mexico. They didn't. *Mexico.* He repeated the country to himself. First in English, then in Spanish.

"Well, in the end, the old man didn't give a damn. He said every country was the same. Every country would betray you. Put your faith in a good woman. That's what he said. And that's what he did. Happiest man I ever met."

"You know, Octavio, your Charlie, he's just like him."

The whole room nodded. Yes, Charlie, just like his grandfather. Too happy. Too forgiving. Not a real man. A real man knows how to hold a grudge. That's what Gustavo put in their thoughts.

He walked out of the living room and looked for Xochil. Xochil, who had always been everything. And damn it to hell, wouldn't this all be easier if he hadn't been born a twin, if he'd just been born by himself, alone, like most other people in the world. He found her sitting in her grandmother's bedroom, surrounded by five cousins and three aunts. She was giving them a tour of their grandmother's jewelry. He wondered if she had told them that the really good stuff was in a vault. He smiled as she put a bracelet on their aunt Sofia. "It's the first piece of jewelry she bought for herself in this country."

He smiled at her as he stood in the doorway.

"Is that true?" Sofia never believed anything anyone ever told her.

"It's absolutely true," Xochil said. "Let me show you something." She took out an old shoe box from under the bed, shuffled through it, then took out an envelope with a note on it. She handed her aunt Sofia the note. Sofia read it—then smiled. "She paid a hundred dollars for it in 1919."

Xochil smiled at her aunt. "I think you should have it, don't you?"

Sofia stared at the bracelet on her wrist and smiled. "What about your mother?"

"My mother doesn't like jewelry."

Sofia smiled. "Yes, that's right. She likes art and books."

"Yes." Xochil smiled.

He watched her for a moment longer as she took out another piece of jewelry and began to explain its history. She'd paid attention. She could tell all the women in the room the story of their grandmother through the jewelry she'd collected in her eighty-seven years of living.

He smiled at her as he left—as if he would be back, as if he would see her in a few minutes, as if it were just another day, just another moment. He served himself a plate of food in the dining room, the table overflowing with the abundance of their lives. He wondered why he'd never noticed how absolutely wealthy they were. He took the plate, stared at the food, then, when no one was looking, he opened the door to the garage and disappeared behind it. He shut the door and took a breath. And then another. He stared at the plate of food and placed it on his father's work table. He thought of Xochil and Charlie—then made himself stop. He closed his eyes, then opened them. He remembered his father embracing his mother just as they left the cemetery. He committed that scene to memory, his father hugging his mother. Such a beautiful thing. So much easier to remember that than to remember sad lines from books he'd read.

He saw that the garage door to the alley had been left open. That made it easier for him; he wouldn't have to make any noise, trying to lift the door up, wouldn't trip on anything in the darkness of the garage. He walked to the place where he'd put his backpack. He stared at it, his heart thumping in his chest. So this is how you left home. This is how your world ended. Quietly. Like a thief stealing himself away. Like a criminal running from his past. He picked up his backpack—but just as he was about to put it over his shoulder, he heard a noise.

He looked up and saw his mother staring at him.

He stared back at her, but said nothing. He could hear his heart. The thumping had become a pounding—and he felt himself trembling. He forced his body to be still, waited, motionless, for what seemed an eternity. He wanted to think of something to say, but what was there to say? He was running away from them—from her, from his house, from his family. But that wasn't true. That wasn't true at all. It didn't have anything to do with them. He was walking away from a war, he was walking away from his country. Yes, that's what he was doing, though putting it like that sounded so nice and neat and logical and everything seemed more scrambled than that, his thoughts, the world he lived in, and he wished he were Conrad because Conrad could put everything into words and construct logical, moral arguments and all he could do was stand there, as inarticulate and inanimate as a rock.

He took a deep breath and then another. "You said I had to do what I had to do."

"Yes, that's what I said."

He couldn't tell what she was feeling. "Mom," he whispered. But that was the only word that came out. Nothing more, not even a whole sentence, just "Mom." He tossed the backpack over his shoulder and whispered quietly, "Mom. Walk with me."

"I can't," she said.

"I wanted to tell you. I didn't know— I just— Mom, I don't— Mom—"

"You didn't know how to leave."

"I'm doing it all wrong. I'm doing it all wrong. All wrong, Mom— I—"

# lourdes

She hated this. This watching her son struggle with himself, this battle he was fighting, hated being a witness, watching and watching this son of hers who was taking his fists out and turning them on himself, couldn't stand it. She'd watched that look of self-doubt in every argument he'd had with her husband, in every disappointment he'd ever had, always blaming himself, always telling himself that he was all wrong, that he didn't fit, that there was something bad about him. This was it then, her last chance to make him see that he was grace in the world, that he was hope, that he was loved, that he was beauty itself. How could she tell him that? How could she tell him that he was suffering from an uncommon and delicate decency that was dazzling beyond words?

And to hell with a world that didn't understand what her son was doing. To hell with them all. This is where she stood. With him. With her son.

She could not let him leave without knowing what she saw

when she looked at him—what she was seeing at this very moment. Since that evening when she'd read that letter from the draft board she had imagined what it might mean. And yet she'd always known that it meant he had to leave. So it came to this: a boy with a backpack who looked very much like a man standing helpless in a garage leaving his country and his family. This boy who was leaving, going back to a country they had all abandoned. This boy standing alone.

"Listen to me." She was whispering, yet she knew her whispers sounded loud and desperate. "You are not doing this all wrong, *amor*. All your life, you have thought that. When you dropped your puppy and you slapped yourself, that is exactly what you said. 'I'm doing this all wrong.' All your life you have thought less of yourself and I have watched you. I have been too silent, *amor*. So now you listen to me. You listen to me. You are not doing this all wrong. You are doing this because you have a conscience, because you have a heart, because you have integrity."

"I don't."

"You do."

"I'm scared."

"Yes, *amor*, you're scared. We are all scared. All of us."

He nodded.

*"You are not doing this all wrong."*

He looked at her.

"Say, yes, *amor*. Say, yes. Say you believe me."

"I believe you," he whispered.

She walked toward him and placed his face between her hands. She looked at him for a long time, a camera taking a photograph. She took a breath, took his face in one last time, kissed him—then let him go. She combed his hair with her fingers. "Wait for your sister and your brother at the Sunset Grocery Store."

"What?"

"Go. Wait for them."

# gustavo. xochil. charlie.

He didn't know how long he waited, sitting at the curb of the Sunset Grocery Store, which was closed for the afternoon in honor of his grandmother's funeral. There was even a sign on the door. His mother must have known that the store would be closed and he wondered why he thought that. Why would that matter?

Three cigarettes. Twenty minutes. That's how long he waited. Then he saw them walking toward him. He waved and smiled.

They waved and smiled back.

When they reached him, they all stood there, silent, staring at one another.

He could see that Xochil was trembling. He reached for her hand and took it—then squeezed it. Then let it go, then squeezed it again. Then let it go. Then squeezed it again.

"What are you doing?"

"I'm trying to keep you from trembling."

"Is it working?"

He shrugged.

"You were going to leave without saying good-bye." He had never heard that tone in Charlie's voice.

"Yes."

"Why?"

"It hurts too much."

"That's not a very good reason."

"Don't be mad, Charlie."

"I don't know what to be, what to say. I don't, Gus."

"Me neither."

"Don't leave us."

Xochil shot Charlie a look.

"I shouldn't have said that."

Gustavo smiled. "Did Mom give you instructions?"

Charlie nodded. He looked at Xochil.

"You can't leave this way." She pulled her hand away from Gustavo.

"I have to leave the only way I know how."

"Not without saying good-bye, you bastard. *You bastard.*" She was crying now, and as she said the word *bastard,* the cruelty of the word lost its power in her sobs.

"Don't," he said.

He held her, and he didn't know if it was she who was trembling or if it was him. "Don't," he said again, "If you do this, I won't be able to go."

"Good."

"You want me drafted? Is that what you want?"

"No."

"You want me in prison?"

"No."

"You want me in a war? You want me pointing a gun at someone? You want someone pointing a gun at me?" He was being cruel—but no matter what he said or did, it would be cruel.

"No," she said. "Stop it! Stop it! Don't, don't. You bastard."

"I don't know what to do, Xochil. I don't, I don't, I don't."

"Stop it!" Charlie yelled. "Stop it! It can't be this way. It's not supposed to be this way."

Gustavo pushed back his hair from his face and reached for his sister. "I have to go," he whispered. "You know that." He looked at Charlie and combed his hair with his fingers. "You know that. You know I have to go. Just tell me you know that."

Charlie nodded. "I know."

"Don't hate me for this."

"I don't, Gus. I promise."

"You promise because Mom made you promise?"

"No, that's not why."

"We don't hate you." Xochil forced herself to smile.

"Okay," he said.

"Okay."

They made their way to the Santa Fe Bridge, no hurry in their legs or their feet. No hurry, no words.

Xochil handed Gustavo a large brown envelope. "It's from Mom. There's an address and a phone number for her cousin Juan Carlos. She said he'll be expecting you. She's going to get in touch with him. She said to take the bus to Mexico City, but that you had to get a visa at the bridge. She said to ask, they'll tell you where you need to go. She's put your birth certificate in the envelope. She said you'll probably need it. She said you could get a visitor's visa for six months, she said—never mind—it's all written down. And she sent some money."

"I don't want money. I can't take it. Here, let me—" He started to open the envelope.

Xochil placed her hand over his and stopped him. "She said

you'd say that. She said to tell you— What did she say?" She looked at Charlie.

"She said that whatever money you had, it wouldn't be enough." He looked at Xochil, as if to ask her something.

She nodded.

Gustavo laughed.

Xochil was glad, that he laughed.

"Did you rehearse everything? Am I in a goddamned play?"

"Yes. Your mother wrote the script and she's the director— and she made you the hero, so shut up."

Charlie took the ring out of his pocket and held it out to Gustavo. "She said for you to take this."

Gustavo stared at the ring. "That was Grandma's."

Charlie nodded. "It's worth a lot of money. Mom said you would need it one day."

"What would I need it for?"

"I don't know. But Mom said you'd know when the day came—"

"Mom doesn't know everything. I can't take it."

Charlie shoved it into Gustavo's hand. "Mom does know everything. You have to take it, Gus. We have to give Mom a full report."

He put the ring in his pocket. He bit the side of his mouth. "Any last instructions from Mom?"

"Whatever we forgot, she's written down. Will you write?"

"If it's safe."

"Safe?"

"They'll come looking for me."

"Let them come, Gus." His little brother's voice was changing. He wouldn't be a boy for very much longer. "Let them come, Gus, let them come looking for you. I'll tell them you're gone. I'll tell them to go fuck themselves. I will, I swear I will."

He saw the tears rolling down his sister's face.

"This is serious," he said. "Don't tell them anything." He looked at Xochil. "What will she tell Dad?"

"You think she can't handle it?"

"I just don't want him to hate her—because of me."

"Don't worry."

"Okay," he whispered.

"You're going to worry, aren't you?"

"Yes."

"I thought you weren't a worrier. I thought that was Charlie's job."

"Everybody worries."

They stood there, the three of them, on the sidewalk, people all around them.

"I have to go."

"Smoke a cigarette, Gus. Before you go."

Gustavo smiled. "Sure." He took a cigarette and lit it.

"Can I have one too?"

He looked at his little brother. "You know how?"

"I've been practicing."

"Practicing."

"I bought a pack at Rexall's after school."

"They sold them to you?"

"I buy Dad's cigarettes there all the time."

Xochil laughed. "I'll take one too."

They sat on the curb and smoked. When they finished their cigarettes, they put them out on the concrete and stepped on them.

They stood there, inches from the Santa Fe Bridge.

The world had ended.

There was only the three of them.

Three small names on the map of the world.

Xochil held Gustavo for a long time. She let him go when she was sure the tears had gone away. She looked into his eyes one last time. Eyes as black as a perfect night. "One day, there won't be any wars," she said, "and there won't be any countries."

"Sure," Gustavo said. "Sure."

Charlie leaned into his brother. He remembered the promise he'd made to his mother. *This is so hard for Gustavo,* amor. *Don't make it harder. Promise me.* He let his brother go. "The next time I see you, I'll be bigger than you."

Gustavo kissed them. *Adios. Adios.* He turned and disappeared into the crowd that was walking across the bridge.

Xochil and Charlie took each other by the hand. They stood there on the sidewalk, at the entrance to the bridge, but did not move.

"He won't be there when we go home."

"No, he won't be there, Charlie."

"Maybe he will be. Maybe we'll go home—and he'll be there."

"No, Charlie. He won't be there." She held her breath as she watched Charlie fall to his knees on the sidewalk. He hugged himself and shook as he howled out his grief to the deaf and dispassionate sky.

# adam

## Da Nang, Vietnam, September 21, 1967

Today, you wake.

You have a roof over your head. That expression has never meant so much.

You open your eyes, then shut them. You know you will run your dream over in your mind, a game you have begun to play to distract you from the rain.

Your eyes still closed, you listen for the sound. The rain. It is there like the beating of a distant drum. You open your eyes, shut them. Open them, shut them. And then you run your dream: Your mother is arguing with your father. You cannot hear what she is saying but you know she is angry. Your father is lying on the couch, smoking a cigarette, drinking a beer. He throws the beer can at her, the beer pouring out into the room, onto your mother's dress. You see the anger on her face, the sadness, the brokenness.

And then you walk into the room. Your father is gone. Your

mother smiles at you. You smile back. You walk out into the sunlight, and the El Paso sky is as blue and cloudless and beautiful as it has ever been. You watch yourself as you breathe in the dry desert air. You stare out into the desert mountains and then you find yourself at St. Patrick's Cathedral. You are in the confessional, telling the priest you are sorry for your sins. *I hated my father. I hated him.* The priest is kind and asks you if you are suffering. *Yes, Father, I am suffering. I have been suffering all my life.* And then you are standing in the communion line and the same priest gives you the body of Christ. Amen.

And then you see yourself walking through the streets of El Paso. Up ahead, you see a girl. You know that girl. The sun is shining through her black hair. Her hazel eyes turn green. She smiles at you and for a moment you are both bathed in light. You whisper her name: *Xochil.* She whispers yours: Adam. And then everything changes, and you are in the jungle, the rain pouring down on you and you hear the sound of a spring as you step and a bomb blows up in front of you and then you find yourself in a coffin underground. You light a cigarette and see that you are lying next to your father.

You open your eyes. You take a breath. You sit up on your rack. You reach for your cigarettes. *Yes, Father, I am suffering.*

You wait. For them. On the front steps. Wait. For Xochil and
Charlie. You have been sitting here for half an hour, perhaps longer, standing up to embrace your guests as they leave, thanking
them for their presence, for their kindness, for their thoughtful-
ness, for their flowers, for their food, for their prayers.

A few people remain inside the house and you are beginning
to get a knot in your stomach. You do not repent from sending
your children to see their brother to the border. They had always
belonged to one another more than they had ever belonged to
you.

You wonder what they said to one anther as they parted, the
words they used, these children of yours who could be so articu-
late and could be so silent. You try to picture them, all of them,
trying to be brave, these children of yours. One day you will ask
them how it was and what was said on the day their brother went
away. And they will be hungry to tell you the whole story. But

today, when they come back to you, you will not ask. And they will be too spent to speak.

You will take them in your arms and tell them they were brave.

You see that the sun is beginning to set and the knot in your stomach is beginning to tighten. You made them promise they would be back before dark.

They will come.

They will come.

You sip on your coffee, which is getting cold, and you listen to the voices in the house. And you think that the house will be different now without her, Rosario, and without your Gustavo. The house will be empty and hollow for a long time to come. Gustavo will come to you in your dreams. And he will come to Xochil and Charlie—and on those mornings, when they wake, his name on their lips, they will wear tired, haunted looks.

The house will grieve for those who have left, for those who will never return.

You begin to think of what you will tell your husband and you repeat over and over to yourself, "He is gone, *amor*. He is not coming back." You know he will be angry when you tell him the whole story. He will be angry for days. He will be angry for weeks, for months. He will want to know why you did not tell him. *Because you would have stopped him. Because you would have taken him bodily to report for duty had he opened his mouth*—no, you will not tell him that. Whatever you say, you will not accuse him of anything. He will be angry for months. Perhaps for years. You tell yourself that he will either keep his anger or let it go. But you will not take the blame—though you know he will blame you forever.

He will take that blame to the grave.

He will tell you that Gustavo has shamed his house and that you were an accomplice to that shame. You know he will say this.

And you will say: *Yes, I was an accomplice to this great shame.* And he will know that you are mocking him. You must not mock. He is sincere in his beliefs. But you are sincere in yours.

He does not understand you. It is too much work for him. But you, you understand him.

There is nothing to be done but live in the aftermath of Rosario's death and Gustavo's leaving.

And then you see them. Your Xochil, your Charlie.

You see them walking toward you, *Thank God, thank God.* You run to greet them. Charlie sobs into you, "Mom, Mom, Mom, our Gus is gone." And then he looks up into your eyes and confesses. "I howled like a coyote. I did, Mom. The whole world heard."

You place your hands on his face. "But look at you—you did not break."

He shakes his head. "I did. I broke."

"*No*, amor, *you did not break.*"

# xochil

That evening, in our house, the knowledge of Gustavo's absence was the largest presence I had ever felt.

Everything was strange and unsettled. I kept telling myself that all this was good. My brother would be alive. He was starting a new life in Mexico. That knowledge made everything bearable for me and for Charlie and for my mother. My mother had given us a large and lonely and devastating and lovely gift: she had made us a witness to Gustavo's self-imposed exile. She had allowed us to say our good-byes, and in the end we had said so very little. But we had parted with as much grace as we were capable of.

Charlie and I helped my mother pick up the house and bring some order to it after the guests had left. There was that word again, *order*. That harsh, impossible word.

There were paper plates and napkins and cups everywhere around the house and the yard and after filling up several bags of trash, Charlie began to carry the bags into the alley where we kept the garbage cans. I offered to help him.

"But you don't like alleys," he said.

"I don't think I mind them so much tonight." I think I did some kind of strange and illogical math in my head. In my figurings, if my brother could leave the country of his birth because he refused to believe that the war was noble, then the very least I cold do was step foot in an alley.

I helped Charlie throw out all the trash that night.

I thought of the time we missed the bus and how safe I felt sitting next to Gustavo on the bus. Gustavo. The other half of my heart. When he was Charlie's age, he told me about a theory he had. He said that twins had only one heart. He said that half of the heart we shared was made of stone—his half. My half, it was made of the same thing that clouds were made of. Rain. Gustavo loved the rain. *Gustavo, my brother, you never understood. You could never see that you were grace. You never could see that, could you?*

I remember Charlie putting his head on my shoulder in the kitchen as we finished cleaning up. "He's gone," he whispered. In grief, the vocabulary of our house was reduced to those two words.

# lourdes

Lourdes put the dishes away wordlessly. The whole world had lost its ability to speak. And what of that, anyway? What were words in the end?

The house felt tired and empty, as if the knowledge of Gustavo's absence had filled the atmosphere with a kind of poison. Not the kind of poison that killed, but the kind of poison you were forced to breathe in every day. The kind of poison that destroyed you slowly.

She dried her hands on her apron.

"How are you going to tell him?"

She looked at Xochil. "I'll find a way."

"He's going to be angry."

"I suppose he will be."

"What if he doesn't forgive us?"

"Forgive me, you mean?"

"No. I mean *us. I mean all of us.*"

"He doesn't have much of a choice, does he?" Even as she spoke the words, she heard the harshness in them, the lack of repentance. Well, what exactly did she have to be sorry for? Gustavo had elected not to tell him. That was his choice. He would have to live with that. She, too, had elected not to tell him. She, too, would have to live with that. She forced a smile. "That sounded mean, didn't it?"

"I want to be there when you tell him."

She shook her head.

"Mom, you're not God."

Charlie watched them. "Mom, we should be there—when you tell him."

"No. I don't want you in that room."

"So you just want us to go hide, is that it?"

"No. It will humiliate him, if you're there. Don't you see? And what do you mean, I'm not God?"

"You've been directing traffic in this house for a long time."

"That makes me more of a cop than a god."

"You can't control everything, Mom."

"That would be your father's sin."

"Yours too. It only plays out differently."

"I'm not playing God, Xochil. I've just tried to intervene when I thought—"

"When you thought what?"

"When I thought—"

"Oh, Mom, what would we do without your interventions?"

The sarcasm, the rage in her daughter's voice. It was so much like a slap. On another day in her life, she might have been hurt. She might have been angry. She might have lashed back, might have even cried. But she was too tired and too numb to analyze her daughter's anger. "Your brother left," she said. "Go to your room and grieve."

"I'm not a girl, anymore. A girl you can just dismiss and send to her room."

"I have never dismissed you, *amor*. Not ever. I just think you're in pain."

"Don't be so condescending, Lourdes."

"You want to watch? Is that what you want?" She shook her head, and walked into the living room. She had a few things to say to her husband.

He was sitting quietly on his chair, his head down.

Lourdes watched him for a moment. He looked up at her and nodded. "Would you like a drink?"

She nodded. "I'll get it."

"No," he said, getting up from his chair. "Let me. What would you like? Brandy?"

"Yes. A brandy's fine." She watched him pour. Gustavo had his hands, almost too big for their bodies. She took the drink from him.

"Gustavo?"

She took a sip of brandy, felt the burning in her stomach.

"Where is he?"

She was relieved it was he who asked. It made it easier.

"He's gone, *amor*."

"Gone? What do you mean he's gone?"

"I mean, *amor*, he's gone."

# epilogue

## SILENCE

Let the Gods forgive what I
have made
Let those I love try to forgive
what I have made.

—Ezra Pound

# charlie

Xochil always said my problem was that I was too sincere. I don't think she meant that comment as a compliment. The word *sincerity* went along with another word she always associated me with: *optimism*. Those words were a sure sign of my American identity.

I really was the most un-Mexican member of the family. Well, no, not really.

This was my family's theory: I was the youngest child. I was the optimist looking at the future. I was free to imagine all the beautiful possibilities while Xochil and Gus and Mom and Dad were condemned to contemplate all the ways in which the past had bound them to an ungiving, ungenerous earth. Their only legacy was the tragedy of Mexico. But my legacy was the beatific vision of America.

The thing is that optimism has never been the exclusive property of America. And the other thing is that, in 1967, everyone was too sincere. Sincerity wasn't the exclusive province of thirteen-year-old boys. In 1967, I wasn't the exception—I was the rule. Xochil and Gus? They thought they were intellectuals—ironic and cynical. But they weren't. They were the most sincere people in the world. Along with my mother and father. Along with Jack Evans. Along with Conrad García. Along with the all the soldiers and Marines who went to Vietnam.

It may be true, what Xochil said, that some guys just manipulated the system. I think that was probably true. *But I didn't know those people.* Among the people I knew, sincerity was the drug of choice. That was the world I knew in 1967. The music we listened to, the books we read, the movies we watched, the clothes we wore. Sincerity was everywhere—all the way around. You know, I don't want to fall into a mindless and pathetic state of nostalgia—but sincerity wasn't so bad.

Sometimes, sincerity beats the hell out of irony. Sometimes sincerity *is* irony.

I remember everything about those last few days. Those last few days Gustavo still lived here. At home.

When he disappeared over the bridge, something happened to me and I became like an animal with no use for human speech.

I howled. Like a wild animal with a broken heart. Like a coyote.

I thought I would never stop howling. Right there, on the street, hundreds of people walking over to Juárez, watching me. Xochil had to pick me up. And even then, she had to slap me. God, my sister knew how to slap.

And then she kissed me.

So these are some of the things I have on my list, the list in my head, the list from that afternoon:

*My mother pulling us into Xochil's bedroom in the middle of my grandmother's wake, giving us instructions, the look on her face (serious and sincere).*

*Me, trying to memorize every word she said (serious and sincere).*

*Gus sitting on the curb in front of the Sunset Grocery Store and waving at us.*

*The silence as we walked to the bridge. The three of us. The silence.*

*The last cigarette we had together (I never smoked again).*

*Xochil holding my hand as we walked home (in silence).*

*The silence. (There would be a lot of silence.)*

One Saturday morning, some time after Gus left, some men in military uniforms came asking about him. I answered the door. My father was working that morning like he often did. And I was glad he wasn't in the house. He and my mother were in the midst of a cold war.

I went to get my mother.

Xochil and I stood behind her as the men asked her some questions.

"He's gone," she said.

"Where did he go?"

"I don't know. He just left. One day he was just gone."

"Did you know he had been drafted?"

"No," she said. My mother, she was an excellent liar. I greatly admired her for that trait at that particular moment.

"Do you know anything about your son's attitude toward military service?"

"I can speak only for myself."

"He said nothing to you about that?"

"Nothing."

"You're sure?" His voice was hard, challenging, and it was obvious he did not believe her. It was also obvious that my mother was not intimated by the gentlemen in uniforms who were standing on her front porch.

"Would you like to come in?" she asked. "I have coffee."

"No," one of them said. "We didn't come here for a cup of coffee."

"You're more than welcome to come in," she said.

"We came to arrest your son. He failed to show up to serve his country."

"His country," my mother repeated. "If you find him, would you tell him his mother misses him?"

They looked at each other, shrugged, walked to their car, and drove away. My mother looked at Xochil and me, and I couldn't tell what that look on her face meant.

"You think they'll come back?"

She nodded.

"And then what?"

"I don't know."

"They didn't believe you. And they didn't like you." I don't know why Xochil said that.

My mother laughed. "Good. Why don't we go to a matinee? Wouldn't it be nice to go and see a movie?"

During the movie, all I could think of was Gus.

I would never know, not ever again, where his name was on a map.

# xochil

I was angry with my mother.

I blamed her for everything.

That first night, I slept in Gustavo's bed. It smelled like him.

Charlie said it wasn't good to keep everything inside. He wanted to know why I was mad at Mom.

"Because she thinks she can fix everything."

"She did her best." It was such a quintessential Charlie response.

"Let's not talk about Mom," I said

"Are you going to forgive her?"

"Yes."

"That doesn't sound like you mean it."

"Yes," I whispered. "I'm going to forgive her."

"Good," he said, "Because she didn't do anything wrong."

He was right, of course. I didn't admit it, then. But he was right.

Later, we spoke about that night, my mother and I. We weren't like Gustavo and my father. Things between us would never be broken.

That night, Charlie told me about his first memory of Gustavo. "I fell on the porch. I was about three years old, I think. Something like that. And I started to cry. I think I was crying more because I was embarrassed. And Gus, he picked me up and sat me on his lap. And he said: *Hey, hey, it's okay, little guy. Even Jesus fell. He fell three times, did you know that?*" Charlie talked and talked and talked all night. Most of the stories he was telling, I already knew.

I fell asleep listening to his voice.

The next day, I felt hollow and numb. It was a Friday. I didn't go to class. The house was completely and utterly silent when I woke.

I left a note for my mom and went for a walk.

I was gone for hours. I walked passed Benny's Body Shop on Texas. I wondered if I should tell Mr. Ortega that Gustavo would never be coming back to work. But it didn't seem the right thing to do. He would find out soon enough. I walked through the streets of downtown for a long time, sat on a bench at San Jacinto Plaza, and then finally decided to go back home.

Jack Evans was waiting for me on the front steps.

"Your mother said I could wait for you here."

I was glad he came. Everything could end all at once. That's what I said to myself. Let the world as we knew it come to an end.

He asked for Gustavo.

I didn't feel like lying. "He's left. He's gone."

"Where did he go?"

"He just left."

"Why?"

"I don't know."

"I think you do know."

"I think I'm not going to discuss my brother with you."

"Well, someday he's going to be my brother-in-law."

I almost laughed. "I don't think that's ever going to happen."

"Why not?"

"Because I'd have to be your wife. And I'm not going to be anybody's wife for a long time. Not for a very long time."

"I can wait."

"Don't waste your time."

"But I thought that we—"

"No."

"But—"

"Jack. Go and march into your life. Just go."

"I love you."

I was tired and numb and I didn't want to do any explaining. I just wanted him to leave. I didn't know what to say. Then I just said it: "I thought for a moment that I loved you too. Turns out I didn't."

"That's not fair."

"I guess it isn't."

"You love me. I know you love me."

"Go home, Jack."

"In a few days I'll be leaving. I'm going to boot camp."

"I know. You're going to be a Marine."

"You should be proud."

"I'm not."

He was sad. He was angry. He was confused. "We slept together," he said. "I thought—"

It was mean of me, I know, but all I could think was that it wasn't my job to turn Jack Evans into a man. That's what he said that day. Make me into a man. And then I knew why I'd gone with him to that hotel—to get rid of the residual smell of the man who'd raped me. I wanted to be with a man that I chose. I chose Jack. Not a bad choice, really. He was beautiful.

But as far as turning him into a man? The hell with it. He could become a man on his own. I looked at him. "You thought what, Jack?"

"I thought—"

"Go away."

I was mean—and more than that, I just didn't care.

A part of me wanted to run after him as he walked away. But what would I have told him? Later, I was to get a letter from him. He told me I broke his heart. It wouldn't be the last time I heard from Jack Evans.

We all make our choices. Gustavo made his. Jack Evans made his. Me too. I could make choices too. Not that our choices always mattered. I remember my mother telling me that countries were bigger than boys. If countries were bigger than boys, then countries were certainly bigger than girls.

I knew my father would never forgive Gustavo for what he did. It wouldn't have mattered if Gustavo had told my father or not. No difference at all. It would all have led to the same thing, to the same place. Nothing would have changed. There might have been a little more drama. Who needed that?

My father was a sad and disappointed man. I never really saw him for what he was until those final days before Gustavo left. For all his intelligence and discipline, for all of his other virtues, my father lacked imagination. He was just another man among the countless army of men who had come before him and had discovered that his life would end in nothingness. That sounds cruel *and maybe it is cruel*. He had once told Gustavo that only great and brilliant men made history. He was too blind or too sad or too jealous to see the brilliance of his own son.

There were times I loved him deeply, my father, times when I was overwhelmed by his boyish and arresting tenderness. There was a baffling and inexplicable innocence about him that was both moving and infuriating. I understood perfectly why my mother fell in love with him.

But there were just as many times that I hated him.

I suppose some of the times that I hated him, I hated him unfairly, hated him for who and what he wasn't, hated him for his limitations, hated him for the expressions he wore on his face, for the way he smelled, for the shirts he wore, for the way he combed his hair, for not wearing anything except black ties. I judged him not for what he was or what he did, but for failing to measure up to some vague standard I had in my head, an imprecise and impossibly idealized definition of father.

I was so hard on him, my father who seemed always such a foreigner everywhere he went, never quite at home anywhere in the world—not even in his own home. My mother told me once that a woman should reveal her love and conceal her hate. I don't know where she got that from, but when it came to my father, I more than took her advice.

I'm sorry now for the hardness of my heart.

I still catch myself listening to my mother's silence. She was never more alone than in the days and weeks and months that followed Gustavo's leaving.

As for my father, *I hated that man who fathered me that night,* that night when Gustavo came in, wet from the rain. My father failed him. In his blindness, my father failed to see what Gustavo was made of. How could he not see? I forgave my father all things. Except for the cruelty of that night. I did hate him for that.

I am always in the next room. I am always too far away to comfort him. All I can do is listen to his sobs. I'm listening. Even now.

Gustavo, who didn't believe in God, at least believed in the possibility of his own life. He wasn't content to march into nothingness. He was more ambitious than that. He was more than a leaf torn from a tree. He was more than a stone with which you built a road. He was more than a turned up onion in a field waiting to be picked. He was brave enough to throw himself into uncertainty, knowing that he would live in that uncertainty the rest of his life. He would die in that uncertainty.

There had been many deaths.

My mother and father did not speak to each other for what seemed an eternity. When we went to Mass, Charlie and I sat between them. I told Charlie we were like a DMZ. For a long time, I felt as if there were traps set around the house. We tread carefully.

One day, three months after Gustavo left, we were all eating dinner, and my father said, "The stew is very good." Matter of fact. An ordinary thing to say to your wife who'd cooked your dinner.

My mother nodded. "I'm glad you like it." Matter of fact. An ordinary response.

There was no real drama in the moment. But those were the first words they spoke to each other since that night.

We limped along, each of us licking our wounds.

It was Charlie who had it the worst—because he, of all of us, expected life to be something good and beautiful. He expected happiness to be a way of life. Gustavo and I had always joked about the pursuit of happiness. But for Charlie, that was no joke.

One Saturday morning, Charlie forced my mother to take him to the humane society, where he picked out a female puppy. Six weeks old. He named the dog Gussie, and when he brought her home, he took her into the bathroom and bathed her.

My mom and my dad and me—we all watched.

That was the first time in months that I'd seen my mother and my father smile.

Charlie needed to love. And he needed to be loved. That's why he wanted the dog. But the rest of us, we weren't any different than Charlie.

## adam

Killed in action, Da Nang, Vietnam, December 21, 1967.

His remains were buried in El Paso, Texas, Fort Bliss National Cemetery.

It rained the day he was buried.

# lourdes

I studied the look on his face closely as I spoke to him.

He paced the room as I talked, occasionally stopping to drink from his brandy. He poured himself three or four glasses that evening, and he kept shaking his head.

His anger didn't surprise me.

I *did* wonder who his anger was aimed at—me or Gustavo. It didn't take me long to discover that I would be the target of his rage. Gustavo was gone. It was hard to aim your anger at someone who was absent—someone who was never coming back.

At a certain point, when he began to process the news that Gustavo had left the country to avoid the draft, he began to ask questions. I'd seen him become an interrogator sometimes when he wanted more information from his children. He had rarely behaved that way toward me.

"How long have you known that he was planning this?"

"I found his draft notice the night your mother died—folded up in his shirt pocket."

"So his first response was to go out and get drunk."

I didn't respond to that remark.

"Why didn't you tell me?"

"I'll tell you what I told him—it wasn't my job. That was his responsibility."

"You're letting yourself off the hook that easily?"

"That easily?" I could get angry too.

"You help your son plan an escape, and you don't tell me, and you think you have no responsibility?"

"I helped him plan nothing. I watched. That's what I do. Isn't that what you're always accusing me of—watching my children too much? I watch. *I watch, I watch, and I watch.* I have kept watch over them all my life. When he was leaving, I caught him."

"Then why didn't you stop him?"

"It wasn't my job to stop him."

"Not your job? Not your job to tell your husband that your son had received his draft notice? Not your job to stop him when he was escaping from his duties to his country? You're his mother. You've helped him become a criminal."

*"My son is not a criminal."*

"He is a criminal. And a coward. He's shamed this house. My house."

"Your house?"

"Yes."

"Perhaps we're all guests in your house. It's a wonder Gustavo didn't leave sooner—since he was always so unwelcome."

"He was never unwelcome."

"You're not lying to me, *corazón.* You're lying to yourself. Why do you think your son didn't tell you he'd been drafted? Why do you think he didn't tell you it was against his conscience to fight in a war he didn't believe in? Why? You want to blame that on me?"

"I could never fix what was wrong between me and Gustavo."

I didn't say anything. What was there to say? He paced the room like a caged and angry cat. He asked questions. I answered them.

"You sent them—Xochil and Charlie, you sent them?"

"I did."

"Why?"

"They love him." That was my answer. He grew angrier by the minute. He was frightening. I had never been afraid of my husband until that moment. But I was determined to answer all his questions and I was not going to lie for the sake of the peace. I knew there would be no peace in our house for a long time to come.

"How will he live?"

"I gave him my cousin's address in Mexico City. Tomorrow, I will send a telegram and tell him Gustavo is coming."

"You will do that?" There was nothing but contempt in his voice.

"Yes. I will do that."

"I can stop you."

"No. You can't."

He stood in front of me for a long time, saying nothing—though I am sure his silence was only seconds long.

"And what will he do for money?"

I knew he would ask that question. And I knew my answer would enrage him even more.

"I gave him Rosario's ring."

"*What?*"

"I gave him Rosario's ring."

I had expected his rage. But even I had not anticipated the slap—the feel of the back of his hand against my jaw.

I fell backward.

Somehow, I did not stumble to the floor. He raised his hand

again. And I am sure the only thing that stopped him was the look on my face. I had always hid my own rage. But in that moment, I let him see it.

I let him see the side of me I had always kept hidden.

In that moment I did not know if I would leave or stay. Somehow, I was free. Octavio would always live in a prison. But not me.

He trembled. He started to say something but I stopped him. *It will be a long time before I forgive you for that.* I think that's what I started to say. But I didn't say that because I didn't need to say it. "Gustavo is free of you." That's what I said.

I slept in Rosario's bed that night.

I slept there for many months.

The slap of the back of his hand.

Somehow I did not stumble.

## abe

Sometimes I think it was all a fucking dream. Except I know it wasn't. There are days when I almost forget that I fought in that war. It was such a long time ago. I was young, so young, so fucking young. And all that's left of my youth is in my head. You know, the head, it's like a map. Not a map that gives you directions, but a map with names on it—names of guys who were killed in the war, names of the people you left behind, names of countries and villages and cities. Names. After all these years, that's all that's left. Names. But no directions. And no way to reach them, no way to get back what you lost.

I came back to the old neighborhood and lived there for a while. Sunset Heights didn't change all that much over the years. The houses got older. So did the people who lived in them.

I went back to school at the university. I didn't tell anyone I had been in Nam. I didn't go around shoving the fact that I'd fought for my country down anybody's throat. Of course, some

people knew I'd fought there. Most people didn't. I was just another fucking student. I even grew my hair long. I heard people
say things. I tried not to explode. They didn't know what the fuck
they were talking about. So fucking cool to be against the war.
What the fuck did they know? Look, I never joined in the discussions. Like I said, I was never a talker.

One day, a girl came up to me and handed me a flier. I wanted
to grab it, rip it, throw it in her face. Except when I looked at
her, I remembered. Gustavo's sister. She was even more beautiful
than I remembered. She had the kind of eyes that really looked
at you, the kind of eyes that made you want to believe the world
was a good place to live in, the kind of eyes that broke your fucking heart.

She smiled at me. "Do I know you?"

I could have said *I knew Jack Evans, the guy who had a thing
for you.* I could have said I was in your house once. I could have
said I hate your brother. "No," I said. "You don't." I took her flyer,
folded it, and put it in my pocket.

She was walking away, then she turned around. "You were
there, weren't you?"

"Yeah," I said.

She walked back toward me, took the folded flyer out of my
pocket, and just nodded. She didn't say a word. And me, I was as
wordless as ever.

My parents were tender with me when I got home. They didn't
know exactly what to do with me. They always had a look of
confusion on their faces. For a month or two, all I did was sleep.
Drink booze and sleep. And smoke. And sleep. They must have
overheard my nightmares. I had me some scary fucking dreams.
Once, I woke up as I was crawling down the hallway, my mother
and father looking down at me. I could see the terror in their
faces.

My little brother was standing behind them. I could see the frightened look on his face. It fucking killed me.

That night, my father and mother took me into the kitchen. My father poured us all a drink. We drank. Then we drank another. "Talk," my father said. "Talk."

"I can't," I said.

My father nodded. We cried. All of us. Maybe that was the only conversation we needed to have.

I don't know when it was, but one day, I ran into Conrad García. I tried to avoid him. But he came toward me when he saw me. Shit, of course he did. "Come up to me call me a baby killer," I said. It wasn't a question. Something about that guy always set me off. Made me talk shit.

He shook his head. "Why would I do that?" He smiled at me and offered me a cigarette. That Conrad, always offering everyone a smile and a fucking cigarette. I took it. We walked down the street like we'd done a lifetime ago. Walking down the street and smoking cigarettes. We were good at that.

"You made it back alive," he said.

"Yeah, I guess so."

"I'm glad. Thank God."

I wasn't gonna fucking cry in front of the sonofabitch. I wasn't. But why the hell did I feel like crying? "Yeah, thank God. But no fucking thanks to you."

He didn't say anything.

I looked at him. "Did you go to prison?"

"Prison?"

"For not going?"

"No."

"No?"

"Community service."

"Fucking community service?"

"The parole board didn't know what to do with me."

"It's cuz you're a fucking freak."

"Guess so," he said.

He had a look on his face.

I knew he'd been through his own hell. I didn't want to know anything about it. Just didn't. There are a lot of fucking things in this fucked up world that we don't want to know.

Then I just laughed. I laughed and fucking laughed.

And he laughed with me. So there we were laughing, me and Conrad García. When we finally fucking pulled ourselves together, hell, we had us another cigarette.

You think you have a family—a wife, a daughter, two sons. You think you have a home. The day you bought this house, you imagined your future, and for a long time you felt you'd stepped into the beauty of that dream. Once you had nothing. And then you had everything. The love of a virtuous woman. A son and a daughter. And then, later, another son.

There was nothing you did not have.

You gave up dreams, it's true—but in the end, you thought it did not matter. You are just a man. Like all men, you exchanged one dream for another.

One dream is as good as another.

You don't know how it happened. Or when. But the dream began to fade. To erase itself. And you began to understand that you had become a stranger to your family—a stranger to your wife, to your son and your daughter—even to your Charlie. Your

Charlie, who forgave all things, who seemed to understand *all things*. Even to him, you were a stranger.

Now, you ask yourself, what do you have? What is your life? What has become of it? You cannot make sense of anything. You stare at all the books on your shelf. They are all neatly arranged and ordered. That is what you wanted for your life. Why? Why?

You have lost your mother.

You have lost your son—but you lost him long before the day he left. You never knew how to go looking for him.

You have lost your wife.

You see yourself raising your hand. You see your hand as it lands on your wife's face.

You see the hate in her eyes.

You do not forgive yourself. You would do anything to take back that moment, to take back the slap.

In all things you have failed.

Now you are only a piece of furniture. No more than that.

Your heart is a stone. Cold. Dead. Inanimate.

You have lost your wife. No. *You cannot accept this.* You did not go looking for your son. But you will, *you will go looking for her, for Lourdes. You will.*

# gustavo

All this was many years ago.

You always knew that something was going to go wrong with your life. Icarus falling to earth. You see yourself saying, *Gustavo Espejo, you are going to have a beautiful American life. A beautiful American life.* It's strange now, strange, to think of yourself as a boy whispering optimistic things to yourself. Whistling in the dark. You've grown so accustomed to living a nomadic, complicated life. Since the day you left, you have lived your life one moment at a time. And it seems like nothing was ever simple.

You have a memory. You hate and curse that memory, but it is your only possession. And sometimes that memory comes to you unexpectedly—though the visit is always unwelcome. There was a time when you lived in a house with a mother and a father and a brother and a sister and it was a simpler time. You don't like to think about that time. It is a futile exercise in nostalgia.

You were always on the margins—that is the truth of your past. But you were deeply loved. Is that nostalgia? You detest nostalgia. There is nothing in your life that resembles the past. There is nothing in the past except for the ruins of the cities that broke your heart. That broke and broke and broke your heart.

You wonder why you still dream that Saturday afternoon. Even now. You see Charlie sitting on the porch, that sincere look on his face, that hurt in his eyes he could never hide as you say something careless that wounds him. And in the dream, it is as if all the light of the afternoon is coming from somewhere inside him. And then—you don't know why exactly—you turn away from him.

Then Xochil is there, walking up the steps. You can see she's been crying. And then you hate the dream, because all the beauty goes away and there is so little beauty left in your life, all that beauty. Gone. And all that is left is everything that frightens you, and your heart begins to beat, beat, beat, and you feel hollow, strange, lost, and you want desperately to ask Xochil what's wrong, but you can't speak because all the words you know are stuck in your throat and you can't push them out, you can't, you can't—and then all of a sudden they're gone, Xochil and Charlie and your mother's oleander.

Everything is gone.

Everything is quiet as death. The street is empty, as if something has startled all the residents back into their locked homes and there isn't anyone else in the whole world except you and Mr. Rede. He waves at you. He is carrying a letter. And you know what the letter says. He walks toward you—the letter in his hand—and Mr. Rede isn't Mr. Rede at all, he's Charon, with his skeletal hand out demanding his coin so he can carry you across the River Styx or the Rio Bravo. You can smell the stench of the dead on his black robe, and you can't move, you can't, you can't and you think this desperation will stop your heart. All you can do is sit and wait, your heart leaping out of your chest, the earth trembling beneath you, almost as if the earth was as frightened as you.

For years and years, you've had that dream. It never changes.

You wake. And then you cry. You don't fight the tears anymore. Fighting tears is a way of lying to yourself. You don't do that anymore. But you've taught yourself to cry silently, and you've learned that tears can be the most silent thing on this sad and fierce and pitiless earth.

You know that trying to piece the story together is futile, the story of your leaving them and your country, the story of returning to your father's homeland and entering an exile that has become another name for home. But the story does not belong only to you. The story belongs to Octavio and Lourdes, who gave you life. The story belongs to those who went to war, Jack Evans and all the other young men whose names you do not know. The story belongs to Conrad, who refused to go to war—and did not run. The story belongs to Charlie, who searched his globe for years trying to discover the exact location of an older brother who disserted him. The story belongs to Xochil, who hated the idea of war almost as deeply and purely as she loved you. The story belongs to America. So why should your story matter more than anybody else's?

What about the dead?

What about those who died more slowly?

The story is not about you. Did you think the world would stop—just for you? Grieve for you? The world is a stranger to tears. The world has a heart made of stone. It did not stop its spinning to grieve for the men who died in Vietnam. It did not stop and grieve for the inhabitants of that country. Did you think it would stop and grieve for you? You, who left your country, you who always lived on the margins of America? You, whose story is the smallest part of history?

This is your only consolation. You were never unloved. That is the one sliver of the story that belongs to you.

There are visions of heaven. And there are visions of hell. For you, those visions are the same: forever, you are blessed and condemned to see yourself, a boy of eighteen, walking over the Santa Fe Bridge. Forever, you see yourself turning around, and breaking into tears of laughter as you stare into the eyes of your sister and your brother, whose faces are eternal flames of hope.

You were never unloved.

You remember the poem your sister gave you. You are the wolf that chewed his leg off to free himself from the trap. You no longer have a notebook where you spill out all your confessions, but there are words floating around in your callused, callused heart:

*Gustavo time, is that it?*

*Gus! Gus!*

*The best thing that happened in 1967.*

You see yourself on a bus going to Mexico City. It is the middle of the night. You have left everything you have ever known. You are taking a journey that millions of immigrants have taken. Immigrants who leave behind their homelands for reasons that are known to them alone.

You are afraid. You hear your mother's voice: You are afraid to hurt the people you love. Then all the confusion leaves you. Because you know why you are on this bus. You refused. The war. You refused it.

You are on a crowded bus.

You are going to Mexico City.

The road is dark and silent.

# acknowledgments

No author writes a book alone. I am surrounded by generous people and their contributions are everywhere to be found throughout the pages of this novel. I am profoundly grateful to Dolph Quijano with whom I had many conversations about his experiences as a U.S. Marine fighting in Vietnam. Without his reflections, the Vietnam sections of this novel could not have been written. My conversations with him led me to reflect on the deep wounds that the Vietnam War inflicted on millions of people. His recollections and memories were far more moving than any work of fiction can ever hope to be. I cannot thank him enough for his candor, his high-mindedness, his sense of humor, and his honorable humility.

I owe a lifetime's debt of gratitude to Ruben García, a man I have known since I was sixteen years old. His intellectual honesty and his moral integrity has been a beacon to hundreds if not thousands of people. It is not possible to express what I have learned by listening to him, speaking to him, and observing him as he has followed a path few men have even attempted to travel. True men of peace are rare in this all-too violent world. I count myself lucky to be among his friends. I would not only be a poorer writer without his presence in my life but I would also be a much poorer human being.

The voices of the 1960's can be found on every single page of this novel. I remain forever grateful for having been shaped by a generation who not only questioned their own country and its political leaders but also who questioned themselves with equal tenacity and vigor.

As always, I am grateful to my agent, Patty Moosbrugger, who continually offers not only encouragement but also intelligent insights and good humored conversations. Her faith in my work never fails to move me.

I am the luckiest of writers to have Rene Alegria as my publisher and my editor. He has proven time and time again not only to be a fierce and thoughtful reader but also a warm, good-natured, generous friend. He is a good and decent man who has more than earned my gratitude and affection.

And finally, I thank my wife, Patricia, who resides in my head and in my heart. I stand in her presence, wordless and inarticulate. My gratitude for her presence in my life *is* beyond words.

## About the author

## About the book

## Read on

Insights,
Interviews
& More . . .

# Meet Benjamin Alire Sáenz

BENJAMIN ALIRE SÁENZ was born in 1954 in his grandmother's house in Old Picacho, a small farming village on the outskirts of Las Cruces, New Mexico. He was the fourth of seven children and was raised on a small farm near Mesilla.

He graduated from Las Cruces High School in 1972. That fall, he entered St. Thomas Seminary in Denver, Colorado, where he received a bachelor of arts degree in humanities and philosophy in 1977. He studied theology at the University of Louvain in Louvain, Belgium, from 1977 to 1981. Living in the Belgium rain made him desperate to return to the desert—but he also fell in love with Paris and Spain and Italy. During those years, he spent a summer working in a facility for the homeless in Kilburn (in what was, at that time, the Irish slum of North London). The home was operated by the Missionaries of Charity, the order founded by Mother Teresa. He also spent another summer living in Tanzania.

Arturo Enriquez at Vantage Point Visual Studios, Inc.

In 1985, he returned to school and studied English and creative writing at the University of Texas–El Paso, where he earned a master's degree in creative writing. He then spent a year at the University of Iowa as a doctorate student in American literature. A year later, he was awarded a Wallace E. Stegner Fellowship in poetry from Stanford University. While at Stanford, and under the guidance of Denise Levertov, he completed his first book of poems, *Calendar of Dust*, which won an American Book Award in 1992. After two years as a Stegner Fellow, he entered the doctorate program at Stanford and continued his studies for two more years. Before completing his doctorate, he moved back to the border and began teaching at the University of Texas–El Paso in the bilingual master of fine arts program. That same year, he published his first collection of short stories, *Flowers for the Broken*.

His first novel, *Carry Me Like Water*, was published in 1995. The novel was a saga that brought together the Victorian novel and the Latin American tradition of magic realism and received much critical attention. That same year, he published his second book of poems, *Dark and Perfect Angels*. Both *Carry Me Like Water* and *Dark and Perfect Angels* were awarded a Southwest Book Award by the Border Regional Library Association. In 1997, HarperCollins published his second novel, *The House of Forgetting*. Sáenz's third book of poems, *Elegies in Blue*, was published in the spring of 2002.

In addition to his poetry and prose, he has also authored two highly successful bilingual children's books, *A Gift from Papa Diego* and *Grandma Fina and Her Wonderful Umbrellas*, which was given the Best Children's Book of 1999 award by the Texas Institute of Letters. His third bilingual children's book, *A Perfect Season for Dreaming*, will be available in Spring 2008.

His first young adult novel, *Sammy and Juliana in Hollywood*, was published in 2004 and won numerous citations and awards, including the Americas Book Award, the Patterson Book Prize, the J. Hunt Award, and was named one of the top ten books of the year by the American Library Association.

His most recent novel, *In Perfect Light*, was published by HarperCollins, which also issued the Spanish edition, *En el tiempo de la Luz*.

His second young adult novel, *He Forgot to Say Goodbye*, will be available in June 2008.

Benjamin is married to Patricia Macias, and he continues to teach in the creative writing department at the University of Texas–El Paso. He lives, writes, and breathes on the U.S.-Mexico border. ∾

# Reflections
## Why I Wrote
## *Names on a Map*

### 1.

THE REASONS WHY I finally decided to sit
myself down to write this novel were not as
clear in my head when I began as they are now.
To begin with, I think I always wanted to write
a political novel. I have always been what people
call *political*. I have my father and the sixties
to blame for that—though I should be more
accurate and use the word *thank* instead of
*blame*. After all, I'm hardly passive about
my politics—they are not merely something
I have inherited.

I have embraced my politics. Actually,
I'd like to think I have earned my politics.

I admit that I am probably more political
than the average citizen, and probably more
political than most novelists and poets, which
partially explains why I have been more than
a little obsessed with the idea of war.

If war is anything, it is political. We can
cover the word war with flags and blankets
and the rhetoric of freedom. But war, finally,
is always about politics and ideologies.

### 2.

MY LAST BOOK OF POEMS, *Dreaming the End of
War*, was a reflection on war, killing, violence,
nationalism, and male identity. It included
reflections not only on our post-9/11 world
and the war in Iraq but on war in general. The
poems also included some meditations on the
war we are fighting on the U.S.-Mexico border.
Some people don't call that a war. I do.

I have come to believe that we have stopped
seeking an alternative to violence. We have
stopped trying to imagine political solutions
and have decided to rely on military solutions
instead. This is an old and tired paradigm.
What happens to the world when we refuse to

> I have always been what people call *political*. I have my father and the sixties to blame for that—though I should be more accurate and use the word *thank* instead of *blame*.

sit down and talk to our enemies? J. G. Ballard's *Empire of the Sun* reaches its climax at the end of WWII, but his novel ends by anticipating the next war. His novel is beautiful and terrifying, and I have never managed to keep the harsh truths in his novel out of my head. Somehow, even after my book of poems was published, I knew that I wasn't quite finished with the topic of war—or, more accurate, the topic of war wasn't quite finished with me.

3.

WHEN I FIRST STARTED to think about *Names on a Map*, I had just finished *In Perfect Light*, a novel that had left me emotionally exhausted. And yet, I felt compelled to begin yet another novel. As a writer, I am not always sane. I don't always do things that are good for me. I have instincts and those instincts have a logic all their own. I'm used to those instincts—they've taken me to some interesting (if dark) places. Those instincts took me directly to the writing of this novel.

When I start a new writing project, I never know quite how to begin. I get an idea. I turn that idea over and over in my head until it feels like it's something solid and formed. I think and think. That's how I start. And somehow the idea begins to feel familiar, not at all strange, and I start to feel at home in that world. That's when I start writing. I always begin with a scene— a scene that's not the beginning but belongs somewhere in the middle. I take the idea of in medias res quite literally. So I wrote a scene— two brothers on a front porch, their parents inside arguing, their mother sometimes looking out in awe and wonder at these two astonishing creatures that are her sons. The father lacks that sense of wonder when he watches other people. He lacks imagination. That is his curse— though, like most people who lack imagination, he doesn't know he is cursed. I gave each of the characters a name.

So now the members of my family had names. My novel began to take form. ▶

> " I have instincts and those instincts have a logic all their own. I'm used to those instincts—they've taken me to some interesting (if dark) places. Those instincts took me directly to the writing of this novel. "

## Reflections *(continued)*

**4.**

I WALKED AND THOUGHT and walked and thought and rewrote that scene. And really, I discovered that I had my entire novel in that one scene. All the ideas I wanted to examine were all there. I suddenly knew what the fates of my characters would be. And I also knew that this would be the darkest novel I would ever write. I didn't want to back off from that darkness. Because, you see, I live in the darkest of times I have ever lived in. Whatever you might say about the sixties, it was a time that held out great promise. The sixties, despite the violence and confusion, held out the idea of a great and just society, the idea that equality was an achievable goal, the idea that peace was a moral imperative.

**5.**

I CAME OF AGE LISTENING to arguments about the war in Vietnam. There were public debates between public figures, and there were more intimate (and perhaps more explosive) arguments in people's homes. I remember listening to President Johnson on the television. I remember listening to Martin Luther King, Jr., and Bobby Kennedy and Eugene McCarthy and George McGovern and Richard Nixon. I think I was the kind of kid that was trying to memorize their faces. I can almost hear their inflections as they articulated their positions.

Closer to home, I had an uncle who had very definite feelings about Vietnam. He called the peace sign the footprint of the "American Chicken." He was the kind of man who made fun of people he disagreed with. I never laughed at that old joke. I don't laugh now. My father was more restrained. He said very little about the war, but I knew in my heart of hearts that he did not approve of what was happening. My father knew a great deal about how racist the military could be. His knowledge was firsthand and he understood very clearly that not all soldiers were equal. Not in his day. My grandfather said

66 I also knew that this would be the darkest novel I would ever write. I didn't want to back off from that darkness. 99

nothing, and just shook his head as he followed Walter Cronkite's body count.

Arguments, debates, and discussions started exploding everywhere I turned. I listened to classmates as they argued back and forth. People always got angry and upset. People called each other names: *Coward! Baby killer! Communist! Un-American!* People are still calling each other names. People like Ann Coulter and Bill O'Reilly do it for a living. Imagine getting paid for calling people names.

6.

THERE WAS A STRONG SENSE of duty that I felt from the generation ahead of me. The army made a man out of you. Everyone said that. For all I know, everyone believed it. I don't know why I didn't.

The people around me were well versed in the language of patriotism. It was clear they loved America. But because so many of the adults around me were also Mexican Americans, they also understood that their country was mired in racism. The adults around me knew they were not equal—though many did not want to be reminded of that fact, and there was hell to pay for the bearer of that particular piece of bad news. Denial was a large part of my formative years.

No one said a word when we turned on the television and watched white authorities aim fire hoses at black people as if they were fires that needed to be snuffed out.

I was always vaguely dissatisfied by the bumper-sticker argument of the time: *America, Love it or Leave it.* Those who were against the war were blamed for the fact that we were beginning to lose the war. This made no sense to me. Dissent was essential to a democracy. Or did we just value dissent in the signers of the Declaration of Independence? Those same arguments (take out old Cold War rhetoric, insert anti-terrorist rhetoric) were resurrected ▶

> People are still calling each other names. People like Ann Coulter and Bill O'Reilly do it for a living. Imagine getting paid for calling people names.

**Reflections** *(continued)*

and applied to the war in Iraq. I wrote this novel to turn those arguments around in my head and on the page—especially the arguments in people's homes. Politics on the public side of things don't interest me nearly as much as the way politics affect the way we absorb those very politics in our homes.

I grew up in an age that made me think and challenged me. I learned to analyze people's politics. I tried to figure out why people believed the things they believed. I was always trying to get at the source of all those ideologies. You might say that I was learning how to think.

7.

ONE OF MY CIVICS TEACHERS in junior high school told us about SDS (Students for a Democratic Society) and "Pinkos" and "Marxists" and "Communists." I looked forward to her outbursts in class. I think I enjoyed adults who were out of control—though as I've grown older I enjoy them less and less. She had a hairdo like June Cleaver on *Leave it to Beaver* and talked about "Leftists" as if they were the devil. I didn't know what a "Leftist" was at that time in my life—though I decided then and there to try my hand at it. I wrote this novel to recapture the way that people thought about things in 1967. I'm not convinced we've evolved that much since then—which is another reason I was compelled to write this novel.

I listen to the way people mimic arguments, and I wonder if people actually believe the things that come out of their mouths. When the war in Iraq first began, I was teaching a class entitled Introduction to Literature. The students weren't English majors—one of the reasons I'd signed up to teach the class. When we read Kerouac's *On the Road*, one of the students began her reflection by saying: "He should get a job." I hardly knew how to respond. When we read *Johnny Got His Gun*, several students questioned my patriotism.

> 66 Politics on the public side of things don't interest me nearly as much as the way politics affect the way we absorb those very politics in our homes. 99

Let me be perfectly frank here, it is difficult for me to be respectful of young people's opinions when they themselves are so disrespectful toward those who disagree with them. In our class discussions, I wanted to focus on the origins of their strong reactions. They all readily admitted they were not "well read." They all readily admitted that they did not watch the news or read newspapers. They all readily admitted that they were not particularly interested in politics. They also readily admitted that they did not vote and were not interested in voting in the future.

One young woman, who was in the military, told me that I "owed" her. Essentially, her argument went something like this: *You get to stand up there and pick any anti-American book you want because of me. Because of my service in the military.* Really? All of this took my breath away.

There are reasons why I'm not convinced our thinking has evolved all that much since the sixties. Just because we've stopped saying "far out," "groovy," and "bitchin'" doesn't mean we're more sophisticated.

## 8.

THE FATHER OF ONE of my best friends used to sit us down and ask us questions about how we felt about Vietnam. I told him I was pretty suspicious of the things my government did and told him I didn't feel like dying. He said that the war wasn't about me and reminded me it was a man's duty to do what his country asked of him. I told him I didn't think I was a man yet, and he wholeheartedly agreed. This was the thing: if I really wasn't a man yet, why would he want to send me off to fight in a war?

I wrote this novel to meditate on the different ways we see the same world. I'm not convinced people share the same idea of what America is and should be. Who, after all, does America belong to? In the world of my novel, ▶

> 66 Let me be perfectly frank here, it is difficult for me to be respectful of young people's opinions when they themselves are so disrespectful toward those who disagree with them. 99

## Reflections *(continued)*

Jack believes that America belongs to him. He believes he is the rightful heir to the fruits that America has produced. Gustavo and Xochil Espejo are interlopers at best, traitors at worst. They are not America.

Who does America belong to? Do you think we all have the same answer to that question?

### 9.

THE AMERICA I GREW UP IN was extremely conservative—and in many ways inexplicably naive and innocent. Never mind that we had no right to be as naive and innocent as we were in 1960s America. But there it is. America in the sixties was just the kind of place that breeds a counterculture. A counterculture that would keep the nation from dying. I don't give a damn what anybody at the *National Review* says: The sixties saved America from its worst impulses, from the excesses of anti-Communist Cold War rhetoric, from the mediocre aesthetic of middle-American tract housing, and from the unexamined discourse of nationalism, male identity, duty, and homogeneity. I wrote this novel to remind myself of the journey this country has made since 1967.

### 10.

TO TELL YOU THE TRUTH, my cultural and political passions aside, I never had any intentions of writing a novel centered on the Vietnam War and how that war affected, crippled, and perhaps destroyed thousands of American families. Everything was Vietnam when I was growing up. Everything. Everyone was writing about it—poets, novelists, political pundits, and journalists. I wanted to read about something else, talk about something else, think about something else. I just wanted to run away from the whole damn thing.

History had other plans. Along came another president from Texas and a war in Iraq. The Vietnam years were shoved back down my

66 Who does America belong to? Do you think we all have the same answer to that question? 99

throat. Had we learned nothing? And there it was, that awful, haunting feeling: *We have learned nothing.* I wrote this novel because history keeps repeating itself, and writing a novel is the only tool I have to rebel against the repetition of history.

11.
AND SO, with the war in Iraq on my mind, and with a sober sadness, I went back in time and wrote this novel. As I wrote it, I became aware of this one fact: *war is inescapable.* In one way or another, all of us are caught in that large and terrible word. *Espejo* in Spanish means "mirror." A perfect name for my fictional family, a family caught up in one war or another, from the day they fled the Mexican Revolution to the day the oldest son, Gustavo, receives his draft notice on September 16, 1967.

12.
LIKE SO MANY NOVELISTS, I have a great desire to write about things that matter. The sad fact of war is harsh and ugly, and in order to examine that large and impossible word I had to do a great deal of soul-searching and exert a great deal of discipline. While fully aware that I was writing a political novel, I set out to map the lives of an entire family, to voice the pain and confusion of characters confronted in a very personal way with the overwhelming realities of war.

13.
I HAVE FRIENDS who fought in Vietnam. I have friends who *refused* to fight in Vietnam. Each of these friends fought with their own demons, did what they felt they had to do—and paid a price. I interviewed some of those friends during the writing of this novel, had conversations with them. I wrote this novel with profound respect for the different roads men of my generation chose to travel. ▶

> " I wrote this novel because history keeps repeating itself, and writing a novel is the only tool I have to rebel against the repetition of history. "

**Reflections** *(continued)*

14.

MY NOVEL IS AN INTIMATE TRAGEDY that mirrors the tragedy of a nation. In the face of this tragedy, thousands of people's actions were heroic. I wanted to capture that tragedy and those moments of anonymous, personal heroism. I think, in writing this novel, I explained my own country to myself. As Xochil, one of my characters, reflects:

> Whatever else that country was or is or meant—for me, it became a symbol that very nearly swallowed me whole. How many wars does that word *Vietnam* conjure? How many? In one war, there are a thousand wars within that war—each one private, singular, inaccessible, a fragment, a piece of a larger whole, parallel yet forever separate. And all we ever do in life is struggle with our impoverished efforts to put our war into words. I don't believe most of us ever succeed in our translations. It's an art most of us never conquer. That's why we argue with each other. We're like countries—each of us clinging to our separate histories. We're fighting each other about our translations, about what really happened. Which is another kind of war.

15.

I WROTE *Names on a Map* because I wanted to write about the private, singular, inaccessible wars that Vietnam conjures. I wrote *Names on a Map* to remind myself (and perhaps a few other readers) that we have to find a way to move beyond tragedy. I wrote *Names on a Map* because we have to remind ourselves that we are in charge of history. I wrote *Names on a Map* because we have to find a way to transcend that terrible word *war*. Along the way, I hope I have created a work of art that is worthy of my subject.

—from the U.S.-Mexico border
Benjamin Alire Sáenz ∿

66 My novel is an intimate tragedy that mirrors the tragedy of a nation. In the face of this tragedy, thousands of people's actions were heroic. I wanted to capture that tragedy and those moments of anonymous, personal heroism. 99

# Author's Picks
## The Literature of War

I OFFER A FEW BOOKS for further reading without commentary, except to say that they are all books which have influenced the way I think about war:

*Johnny Got His Gun* by Dalton Trumbo
*Empire of the Sun* by J. G. Ballard
*The Things They Carried* and *Going After Cacciato* by Tim O'Brien
*The Brothers K* by David James Duncan
*Chicanos in Vietnam* by Charley Trujillo
*Vietnam: A History* by Stanley Karnow
*The Great War and Modern Memory* and *The Bloody Game: An Anthology of Modern War* by Paul Fussell
*Slaughterhouse-Five* by Kurt Vonnegut
*Catch-22* by Joseph Heller
*Poems: 1960–1967* and *The Poet in the World* by Denise Levertov
*An Atlas of the Difficult World* by Adrienne Rich
*The Naked and the Dead* by Norman Mailer
*The Enormous Room* by E. E. Cummings
*The Red Badge of Courage* by Stephen Crane
*Days and Nights of Love and War* and *Open Veins of Latin America* by Eduardo Galeano
*A Hundred Years of Solitude* by Gabriel García Márquez
*Gravity's Rainbow* by Thomas Pynchon
*The Quiet American* by Graham Greene
*Night* by Elie Wiesel
*A Treasury of War Poetry: British and American Poems of the World War 1914–1917*, edited by George Herbert Clarke
*First Love and Other Poems* by Edwin Rolfe
*Collected Poems* by Federico García Lorca

# Have You Read?
## More by Benjamin Alire Sáenz

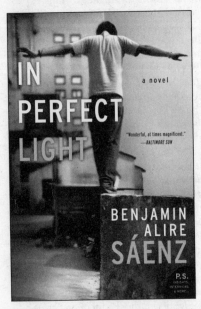

**IN PERFECT LIGHT**

From award-winning poet Benjamin Alire Sáenz comes *In Perfect Light*, a haunting novel depicting the cruelties of cultural displacement and the resilience of those left in its aftermath.

*In Perfect Light* is the story of two strong-willed people who are forever altered by a single tragedy. After Andrés Segovia's parents are killed in a car accident when he is still a young boy, his older brother decides to steal the family away to Juárez, Mexico. That decision, made with the best intentions, sets in motion the unraveling of an American family.

Years later, his family destroyed, Andrés is left to make sense of the chaos—but he is ill-equipped to make sense of his life. He begins a dark journey toward self-destruction, his talent and brilliance brought down by the weight of a burden too frightening and maddening to bear alone. The manifestation of this frustration is a singular rage that finds an outlet in a dark and seedy El Paso bar—leading him improbably to Grace Delgado.

Recently confronted with her own sense of isolation and mortality, Grace is an unlikely angel, a therapist who agrees to treat Andrés after he is arrested in the United States. The two are suspicious of each other, yet they slowly arrive at a tentative working relationship that allows each of them to examine their own fragile and damaged pasts. Andrés begins to confront what lies behind his own violence, and Grace begins to understand how she has contributed to her own self-exile and isolation. What begins as an intriguing favor to a friend becomes Grace's lifeline—even as secrets surrounding the death of Andrés's parents threaten to strain the connection irreparably.

With the urgent, unflinching vision of a true storyteller and the precise, arresting language of a poet, Sáenz's *In Perfect Light* bears witness to the cruelty of circumstance. Rather than offering escape, the novel offers the possibility of salvation.

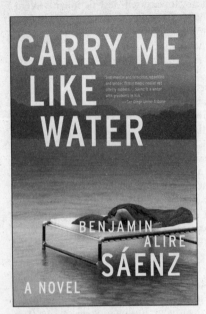

**CARRY ME LIKE WATER**

This immensely moving novel confronts divisions of race, gender, and class, fusing together the stories of people who come to recognize one another from former lives they didn't know existed—or that they tried to forget. Diego, a deaf-mute, is barely surviving on the border in El Paso, Texas. Diego's sister, Helen, who lives with her husband in the posh suburbs of San Francisco, long ago abandoned both her brother and her El Paso roots. Helen's best friend, Lizzie, a nurse in an AIDS ward, begins to uncover her own buried past after a mystical encounter with a patient.

With *Carry Me Like Water*, Benjamin Alire Sáenz unfolds a beautiful story about hope and forgiveness, unexpected reunions, expanded definitions of family, and, ultimately, what happens when the disparate worlds of pain and privilege collide.